SIRENS
&
MUSES

SIRENS & MUSES

A Novel

Antonia Angress

BALLANTINE BOOKS

NEW YORK

Copyright © 2022 by Antonia Angress

Published in the United States by Ballantine Books, an imprint of Random House,
a division of Penguin Random House LLC, New York.

BALLANTINE and the HOUSE colophon are registered trademarks
of Penguin Random House LLC.

Grateful acknowledgment is made to Princeton University Press for permission to reprint
"The First Step" from *C. P. Cavafy: Collected Poems, Revised Edition* by C. P. Cavafy, translated by
Edmund Keeley and Philip Sherrard, edited by George Savidis, translation copyright
© 1975, 1992 by Edmund Keeley and Philip Sherrard. Reprinted by permission of
Princeton University Press; permission conveyed through Copyright Clearance Center, Inc.

Library of Congress Cataloging-in-Publication Data
Names: Angress, Antonia, author.
Title: Sirens & muses: a novel / Antonia Angress.
Other titles: Sirens and muses
Description: First edition. | New York: Ballantine Books, [2022]
Identifiers: LCCN 2021037705 (print) | LCCN 2021037706 (ebook) |
ISBN 9780593496435 (hardcover; acid-free paper) | ISBN 9780593496442 (ebook)
Subjects: LCGFT: Novels.
Classification: LCC PS3601.N55449 S57 2022 (print) | LCC PS3601.N55449 (ebook) |
DDC 813/.6—dc23
LC record available at https://lccn.loc.gov/2021037705
LC ebook record available at https://lccn.loc.gov/2021037706

Printed in Canada on acid-free paper

randomhousebooks.com

2 4 6 8 9 7 5 3 1

First Edition

Book design by Caroline Cunningham

For Connor

For the story goes that the Sirens were persuaded by Hera to compete with the Muses in singing. The Muses won, plucked out the Sirens' feathers, and made crowns for themselves out of them.

—PAUSANIAS, *Description of Greece*

PART ONE

CHAPTER ONE

Louisa's first assignment at Wrynn College of Art was *paint home.* She'd left home twelve days ago, and now, as she looked out the classroom window, it startled her still to see hills and sullen, huddled townhouses, the New England sky close and cold, nothing like at home, where the sky overwhelmed the land, a drama of clouds and rain and strange shafts of tawny light.

She'd never been on her own before. Her year at South Louisiana Community College didn't count. She had slept in her old bedroom, borrowed her mother's car to get to class, worked the same shifts at Chez Jacqueline, eaten Sunday dinner at Grandma and Pepere's.

Louisa was homesick. It was normal, she told herself. Even at nineteen-almost-twenty, it was normal. And so, alone in her studio, she'd cried a little as she painted Lake Martin at dusk, bald cypresses echoed by their dark reflections in the water. It was a placid scene, but ominous, tinged with danger, curdled at the edges like a faded bruise. In the background, low, swollen clouds gleamed with uncanny clarity and a flutter of pintails took off over the marsh. In the foreground, an ibis waded in the shallows, its bow-shaped beak slicing through the water.

Its plumage was a soft, unglossed white, except for its black wingtips. Its pearly blue eye met the viewer's.

She'd chosen an ibis because Grandma had once told her that it symbolized resilience; it was the last animal to take shelter before a hurricane, and the first to reappear after the storm.

"No, not resilience," Mom had said, overhearing. "Regeneration. And wisdom."

Danger, Louisa thought. *Optimism.*

"Dinner," Pepere added. Hunting ibises was illegal, but he'd grown up shooting them for the table and occasionally still brought one home. The meat was orange and fishy.

Now, a thousand miles away from him, Louisa stood alone in an empty classroom. She'd arrived early to secure a spot on the southern wall, and she was pleased with how her painting looked there, bathed in that diffuse northern light, what Mom called painterly light. One window was cracked to let in a breeze, but the room still smelled sharply of oils and turpentine. Afternoon sun gilded the floorboards. As Louisa's classmates arrived and hung their work, she turned to the wall and ran her fingers over the thumbtack holes. The other sophomores all knew one another already, had spent Foundation Year together, and in their presence, Louisa felt furiously shy.

Maureen walked in, a manila folder under her arm. All professors went by their first names at Wrynn, which did nothing to make Maureen less formidable. Though her wardrobe consisted entirely of overlarge T-shirts and paint-stained cargo pants, the pockets full of jangly objects, she carried herself with the pugnacious confidence Louisa occasionally saw in certain older women who'd stopped caring what the world thought of them.

"Everyone ready?" said Maureen. She opened the folder. "We'll go alphabetically this time. Louisa Arceneaux, you're up." She pronounced it *Are-SEE-necks.*

"ARE-sin-no," Louisa corrected her softly. "It's French." She shifted so she was standing next to her painting with her back to the wall. She hugged her sketchbook to her chest as her classmates, all fifteen of them, gathered in a semicircle. Only Maureen brought a chair, its legs squeaking against the floor. She set it in front of Louisa's painting and sat down, crossing her arms.

There was a long silence, her classmates' faces unreadable. Maureen wore bifocals, and she had a habit of tipping up her chin when appraising a painting, as though she were looking down at it. Finally, Jack Culicchia, who wore a baseball cap embroidered with *eat the rich*, said: "My problem with your painting isn't that it's kitschy, exactly." He stood near the back, but he towered over everyone, his voice carrying clear across the room. He was known for his digital mashups of assassinated presidents and murdered rappers: The Notorious J.F.K., Tupac Lincoln, Freaky McKinley. "My problem with it is that it screams 'I'm from the South,' but it's, like, Southern Gothic Lite."

Louisa bristled. She wasn't just from the South. She was from Acadiana. Expelled by the British from Nova Scotia, her Acadian ancestors had settled in the swamps of southwestern Louisiana before it was even a part of the United States. Pepere, who as a child had been beaten for speaking Cajun French at school, had served as an interpreter for American troops in France during World War II. She wasn't Southern; she was *Cajun*.

Louisa flipped to a blank page in her sketchbook. She hunched over and wrote *southern gothic light*, slowly, in neat cursive.

"What do we think about the formal elements?" said Maureen.

Emma Ochoa, who made brooding canvases about being in a long-distance relationship, said something about the blue in the clouds picking up the color of the bird's eye and giving the painting nice movement. Demir Erdem, who was Turkish and movie-star handsome, smiled at Louisa and praised her use of red in the cypress bark.

Movement, Louisa wrote. *Cypress bark. Red.*

While making the painting—building the frame; stretching and gessoing and sanding the canvas; sketching out the composition, consulting her photos of Lake Martin, refining her lines with each iteration—Louisa had fallen in love with it. She'd seen what this painting might do, how it might make someone feel. She'd hoped to convey how intensely she experienced the landscape of her home, how heavily the air weighs, hinting at deluge and decay, how plants grow with such vigor that a cat's claw vine can crack a house's foundation.

"The brushwork is really accomplished," said Alejandro Díaz, who always wore the same pair of lace-up boots, which Louisa took to mean he was probably also on scholarship.

"Say more about that," said Maureen.

"Like, the texture of the paint on the surface of the canvas, the impasto. It's almost liquid, like stormy water. Sort of a form-follows-content kind of thing."

Impasto, Louisa wrote. *Frenzied.*

"Good technique," said Karina Piontek, Louisa's roommate.

Karina stood apart from the group, slouched against the wall. She had her long hair gathered up in both hands. She'd been braiding it as she listened to the crit. Now she dropped the braid, letting it unravel. "But I feel like I've seen this painting before."

Louisa wasn't sure how she'd ended up with Karina as a roommate. The other sophomores had singles, or else they roomed with friends. And Karina was wealthy—her parents were art collectors, and the other day Louisa had sat behind her in lecture and seen her order a pair of two-hundred-dollar sunglasses. Surely she could've had her pick of housing. Louisa had decorated her side of the room with family photos and a *Festival International 2009* poster from two years ago; Karina had hung only an oval mirror and a small canvas that evoked a squall at sea and seemed, in its perfection, less painted than conjured. Karina hadn't been mean to Louisa, but she hadn't been nice, either. Each morning she woke at seven and drew in bed for an hour, sketchbook propped against her knees. Her duvet was creamy white with thin threads of light blue, but she didn't seem to care about dirtying it. Louisa had admired this ritual and resolved to imitate it, but the other day when she'd pulled out her own sketchbook, Karina had looked over and lifted a single pale eyebrow. Wordlessly, Louisa got dressed and went to the common room, where, instead of drawing, she spent an hour playing Angry Birds on her phone and brooding over whether her roommate liked her. Which was stupid, because she wanted to be a great artist, and great artists didn't care about people liking them—they were too busy disappearing into their work.

Since that morning, Louisa had continued to wake at the same time as Karina, but instead of drawing in bed, she fixed a mug of instant coffee in Hope Hall's kitchenette before walking to Williams Park, the bluff that overlooked the town of Stonewater, where she drew the skyline until her first class at nine. She skipped breakfast to save dining room credits—her scholarship covered only the smallest meal plan—and put lots of milk and sugar in her coffee to compensate.

Maureen gave Karina a sharp look. "You've seen it before? Explain."

The truth was, Louisa would've liked to draw Karina. She wore elegant, billowy clothing, wide-legged trousers and floor-grazing skirts, patterned shawls and complicated wraps. Her face had an austere, graven quality, like an old statue, and she had the most magnificent hair Louisa had ever seen: thick and silky, a sort of icy blond. Once, Louisa dreamed she'd cut it all off with her X-Acto knife while Karina slept. Another night she dreamed about kissing her.

"It's the way I imagine an L.A. or New York artist might depict the South," said Karina. "It's just a landscape. It's just a bird. What's it trying to do? What's it trying to say?"

You weren't supposed to talk while being critted. *Just a bird,* Louisa wrote. She thought about how Karina knew what she looked like first thing in the morning or when she came back from her shift at the cafeteria, fingers pruned, smelling of dish soap. Crit was a different, more brutal kind of intimacy.

"If the painting's meaning could be expressed in words, why would she paint it?" said Ivy Morton. A foxtail always hung from her back pocket—real or fake, Louisa couldn't tell.

"It's an accomplished painting," said Karina. "I'm not saying it's *bad.* I'm just reminding Louisa that art has to *do* something."

In her sketchbook, Louisa wrote *Do something* and drew a quick little doodle of an egret. Every artist had something they drew for reassurance. For her it was birds. Mom was always doodling intricate little insects all over her grade books. She wondered what Maureen drew for comfort. What Karina drew.

"What about self-expression?" said Ivy.

"What about it?" said Karina.

"What if the painting reflects an experience of Louisa's that you're not aware of?"

"Just because something is meaningful personally doesn't make it meaningful as art. It's, like, just because something actually happened doesn't make it a good story."

Louisa wrote *meaningful?* under the egret.

"Enough," said Maureen. "You're veering too theoretical. I'd like you to go back to discussing Louisa's painting now."

Face burning, Louisa looked at her canvas for the first time since the crit had begun. She saw it now as Karina did. How was it possible to love something so much when you were alone with it only to hate it as soon as other people saw it?

Alejandro spoke: "I don't think the painting's about a bird. To me, it makes me really aware of time. I think it's about the moment before something terrible happens, the loneliness of being alone in that moment." Alejandro had delicate, almost pretty features and wore a gold chain that disappeared inside his shirt. Louisa wondered what hung on it. Something glib? A stranger's dog tags? Or something sincere, like a crucifix?

"Yes," said Maureen. "Maybe it's the contrast between the large, smooth areas in the sky and the active, textured water. It has this contradictory quality of both stillness and movement that Louisa executes well." She opened up the manila folder again. "All right, Jack Culicchia, you're up."

They shuffled to the opposite side of the classroom, where Jack had hung a piece titled *Still Life with Family,* a dark, blurry painting in shades of ochre and burnt umber, where the only distinguishable objects were a pair of ashtrays, a broken mirror, and several pink pills. A few conflicting interpretations were proposed. Jack seemed pleased. Louisa hovered near the back of the semicircle and kept quiet. Then they moved on to Alejandro's painting: a hazy rendering of a deserted city bus stop at sunset, telephone wires crisscrossing a sky of pink and gold and ocean-glow blue.

"I have this theory," said Maureen, "that every male artist goes through a telephone wire phase."

Louisa glanced at Alejandro in sympathy, but he betrayed no reaction.

Karina went last. Her painting was a large abstract piece that seemed to mute the paintings hanging alongside it. She was unafraid of bold colors, cursive loops of pink, pools of blue, slivers of black. To these glowing fields of color she'd added bits of cloth, frills of lace, even embroidery. The result was a painting so lively it seemed to leap off the wall. It teased the eye; it took up space; it was unapologetic. It seemed to say: *All those aesthetic dogmas you old men spent your lives squabbling over? Here they all are, in bed together!*

Jack Culicchia said something vaguely critical about the painting being self-consciously feminine, but it was largely admired. Karina absorbed the praise without expression, long arms folded over her chest. She didn't take notes.

After class let out, Karina paused at the top of the Painting building's steps to light a cigarette. As Louisa walked by, Karina called: "Hey! Heading back to our room?"

Louisa turned. "Yeah?"

"I'll walk with you," Karina said, coming down the steps.

"Okay," Louisa said warily.

They set off across the green. Students lounged in the grass with their sketchbooks and water bottles emblazoned with Wrynn's crest: an ornate *W* above the words *Pro Arte Utile*, Latin for "For Useful Abilities." This motto was the subject of many jokes, but Louisa, who'd read up on the school's history, thought it made sense. It had been founded in the 1800s by early feminists who wanted women to apply the principles of art to trade and manufacture to become economically self-sufficient. Now Wrynn was coed and its students seemed less interested in trade and manufacture than in curating their aesthetic identities. Your identity, inseparable from your work, was what you'd sell when you went out into the world.

"Do you have siblings?" Louisa asked Karina. She wasn't sure that she wanted to be friends with her roommate, but she'd been taught it was polite to ask people questions about themselves.

"No, it's just me."

"I'm an only child, too. I used to beg my mom for a sister."

They passed under one of the stone archways. It was a lovely school. Ivy, brick, a clock tower, paper-pale houses converted into classrooms. A spare, Puritan beauty—"quaint as fuck," people said—though one often blighted by rogue installation artists erecting sculptures on the quads in the middle of the night. They were made of things like Legos and packing pellets and old furniture, but the administration let them stay till they fell apart. Louisa had applied because famous artists had studied here, people whose work hung in museums, whose names appeared in her Art History readings. Sometimes she had to pinch herself: *I am here.*

"Did you have Maureen last year?" Louisa said. "For Painting?"

"No. First semester we had Ellen Hoang. And then we had Clark Strickland."

"How were they?"

"Ellen was fine. Clark was kind of a dick."

"How so?"

"Oh, he was just sexist. He'd encourage the girls to paint from life and the boys to do abstraction."

"Yikes," said Louisa, though what was wrong with painting from life?

"Old-school macho bullshit," said Karina, exhaling a cloud of smoke. "That was Clark's thing."

They fell silent as they crossed Valence Street. Casting about for something to say, Louisa asked Karina what she'd done over the summer.

"Um, I traveled a bit."

"Where'd you go?"

Karina tossed her cigarette into the street, then stopped in the middle of the sidewalk to light another. "A few different places." Her gaze snagged on something over Louisa's shoulder. Louisa turned to see what it was. They were standing in front of the Wrynn Museum, where a banner advertised a new exhibit by someone named Robert Berger.

"I know him," Karina said abruptly.

"Robert Berger?"

Karina nodded.

"Like *know* him know him?"

"Yeah."

"I've never heard of him. How did you meet?"

"Through my mother," said Karina, in a tone that invited no further questions.

The rest of the walk passed in silence. When they got back to Hope Hall, Karina went to take a shower. Louisa was debating what to do—it was early for dinner, but if she went to the cafeteria now there'd be fewer people to see her eating by herself—when she noticed Karina's sketchbook peeking out from her bag. She hesitated, then furtively crossed the room and slipped it out, flipped through it quickly. God, Karina was talented. There were studies for future abstract paintings, sketches from their figure-drawing class, some lustrous pastel work, and—Louisa made a little noise of shock in the back of her throat—a drawing of Louisa's own face. In the drawing, her eyes were downcast, half-closed, her lips slightly parted in an expression of bliss or stupefaction. She wasn't sure she'd ever made such a face in her life. It was a beautiful drawing, intimate and violating. Down the hall, she heard the shower stop. She closed the sketchbook, stuck it back in Karina's bag, and went off to a dinner she was no longer hungry for.

CHAPTER TWO

On her first afternoon off that semester, Karina went to the Wrynn Museum to see Robert Berger's retrospective. The museum was a silvery glass-and-steel cube surrounded by stately brick buildings. In the evening it glowed softly, like a child's nightlight. At the front desk, Karina flashed her student ID and took a map from the attendant, though she didn't really need it. She'd been here many times before, the first when she was fifteen for the opening reception of *The Harry & Fiona Piontek Collection: Fifty Works for A New Age.* In his toast, the curator had called the loan "an extraordinary act of philanthropy," which was another way of saying "tax write-off." She'd felt ill at ease at the reception, disgusted by *people*—their chatter, their picture taking, the way they fawned over her parents. When Harry and Fiona threw parties at home, she was free to hide in her room.

Karina unfolded the map to double-check what floor Robert's retrospective was on and noticed a new private collection on loan. She always liked to browse other families' collections, if only to assure herself that hers was superior. Karina didn't know anyone who was rich *and* happy, and though she'd never felt resentful or ashamed of her family's wealth, she recognized the limits of what money could do for a person.

The one thing it *could* do was surround you with the kind of beauty that to most people was unimaginable.

She took the elevator up to *Selections from the Jeffrey & Abigail Rahman Collection.* The gallery was empty save for the security guard in the corner. There was a game Karina liked to play in museums. It was called "We Have One of Those." In less than a minute, she'd scored her first point:

Katsushika Hokusai
The Paddies of Ono, Suruga Province
Polychrome woodblock print, ca. 1833

We have one of his. The Pionteks' Hokusai hung outside the door to Harry's study: a mountain range etched with threadlike paths. To Karina, it evoked the vast unknowable. Her parents' tastes tended toward modern artists, though as Harry always said, "Dead is better. Limits the supply." The Hokusai was an exception, an investment piece they'd all grown fond of. Harry had bought it shortly after the 2008 crash, when prices for Classical Japanese art were moribund.

In the next room Karina found an Agnes Martin, an oil on canvas from the sixties. *We have one of hers.* It presided over the dining room table. Karina had grown up tracing and retracing its serene, fine-lined grid at every meal, tuning out her parents' arguing. As Karina took in the painting—it described the bleak loveliness of loneliness, she decided, the lush austerity of the isolated mind—she realized she wasn't alone.

"Shhh!" someone hissed. "She's right there."

Karina turned and saw Emma Ochoa and Ivy Morton—in her head she always called them Long-Distance Relationship and Foxtail— sitting on a bench opposite a Jasper Johns flag (*we have one of his*).

"Hey," said Foxtail.

Karina had slept with Foxtail's boyfriend last spring, a mussed, handsome boy who talked too much about himself. Sometimes her femaleness vexed her—even now, in 2011, women's art was ignored and undervalued—but not when it came to sex. Apart from art, sex was the force majeure of her life. Even when she was a virgin, she'd felt it thrumming inside her: her desire and the desire she aroused in others. It had made her feel powerful to fuck Foxtail's boyfriend, but Foxtail had found out. Wrynn wasn't very big, about a hundred people per class, and Karina soon found herself friendless. And then, after what had happened in studio last semester—well, Foxtail had been there. Doubtless she'd helped spread the rumors.

"How was your summer?" said Long-Distance.

"Fine." Karina smiled her iciest smile.

"Glad to see you're feeling better," said Foxtail.

The guard walked by, his walkie-talkie crackling.

"Thanks?" said Karina. "See you around."

Long-Distance and Foxtail wore identical thin-lipped smirks as they said goodbye. Karina tried not to care. She continued playing her game.

> *Yves Klein*
> *Untitled Blue Sponge Sculpture*
> *Dry pigment and synthetic resin on natural sponge, ca. 1960*

We have one of his. A winged statue in the downstairs bathroom, a twist of sky against the white tile. After Harry and Fiona bought it, they'd flown to Rome to renew their vows. Each time they went to auction and bought a new piece, they became, if only for a short time, utterly besotted with each other. Like clockwork, the fighting always resumed a few weeks later. "Your father and I have the exact same taste," Fiona had once told Karina in one of her rare voluble moods. That was why they'd fallen in love, she explained. Their affinity was all the more remarkable given that, unlike Harry, Fiona had grown up poor. She was from Lawrence, Kansas, and had been eighteen the first time she set foot in a museum.

Karina's phone vibrated in her pocket, jolting her from her trance. A text from Louisa: *I'm washing my towels, want me to throw yours in, too? It's no trouble.*

Karina tensed. She didn't know what to do about Louisa. Penelope Mandelbaum, her freshman roommate, had refused to live with her again, so she'd entered the housing lottery and pulled a terrible number and ended up on the summer waitlist. She'd promised herself she'd stop asking Harry and Fiona for help—which was how in August she was assigned to a double with a transfer student. *Louisa Marie Arceneaux,* the email said. *Breaux Bridge, Louisiana.*

The first thing Karina did was look her up online. But the Internet held little trace of Louisa. No Facebook page, only one brief mention of her name in a local newspaper, something about a high school track meet.

Karina expected to disdain Louisa, as she did most people, but when she met her in person a few weeks later, she felt a hollow, falling sensation in her stomach. Louisa was small and birdlike, dark-haired with neat features and large, hooded eyes. It wasn't till late that night as Karina lay sleepless in her narrow bed, Louisa's deep, steady breathing marking the seconds, that it came to her: Louisa reminded her of Wally. It was something in the eyes, in the mouth. A certain way she held herself.

Karina had slept with girls before, but Louisa unnerved her. It wasn't just her attractiveness, it was the directness of her gaze, the clarity of her sight. You could see it in her art. In crit, Karina had had what her old therapist, Dr. Ellis, called a "defensive lashout," which was another way of saying that her innate capacity for cruelty had sensed an ingress, a cleft, and had swollen to fill it.

Ruthlessness, Karina reminded herself. She replied to Louisa's text: *no.*

It wasn't until the very last room in the gallery that she saw it:

Egon Schiele
Woman in Black Stockings
Ink and watercolor on paper, 1913

I have one of those. I have her. Karina's heart sped up in recognition. The woman in black stockings was Wally. A painting of the same model hung in Karina's childhood bedroom. In Karina's painting, the woman sat topless, her hands thrust inside the pockets of her blue skirt. Sinuous lines traced her spine, her muscular arms, her sharp little breasts. She was milky pale, a wash of blush on her cheeks, her skin dabbed blue in places, echoing the color of her skirt and of her wide, clear eyes. Her face was turned toward the viewer, her rust-red hair gathered up, a sin-

gle escaped curl dangling at her temple. The corners of her mouth—
coral, like her nipples—were turned slightly upward, and her gaze was
intent and penetrating, or perhaps teasing, as though daring the artist
to put down his brush and touch her instead. As a child, Karina had
pictured her living a hundred different lives. She'd often conducted
long, one-sided conversations with her, particularly on sleepless nights
when Harry and Fiona were downstairs screaming at each other, but
she hadn't learned the woman's identity until she was thirteen, when
one of her parents' artist friends, a pretty young photographer named
Ines, had wandered upstairs during a party and poked her head inside
Karina's half-open door.

"Heya," Ines had said, and Karina, who'd been sprawled across her
bed reading a Tamora Pierce novel, startled.

Ines was new to Harry and Fiona's circle. Young, a few years out of
grad school. Up-and-coming artists often came to Harry and Fiona's
parties, hoping to place a work in their collection.

"Just surveying the holdings," Ines said with a grin. She looked
around with interest, her eyes, dark with mascara, widening as they
flicked from the fireplace to the en suite, where Karina was mortified to
see a pair of her panties balled up next to the toilet.

"Wow," Ines said. She wore a red dress and high-heeled sandals. In
one hand she held a sweating flute of champagne. Her fingers were
strong and broad, the nails trimmed short, the nail beds bitten, wor-
ried-at. "What are you reading?"

Karina showed her the cover of *The Woman Who Rides Like a Man*. Ines
smiled knowingly. "I loved those books when I was your age. So much
gender-bending, right? So much sex." And Karina didn't know what it
was—the curl of Ines's lips, or maybe it was how the neckline of her
dress bit into the soft flesh above her breasts—but she felt a gut-wrench
in her stomach, like the drop on a roller coaster. Heat rose under her
skin, but Ines wasn't looking at her anymore; she'd seen the drawing of
the red-haired woman. She drew close, examining it.

"That's not a *Schiele*, is it?"

"Yeah."

"It is? Like, an original?"

Karina told her yes, it was.

"In their kid's bedroom," Ines muttered to herself. Turning to Karina, she said: "Do you know who this woman is?"

Karina shook her head. The red-haired girl had always seemed real in the same way characters in books seemed real. But that the girl was someone who'd *actually* lived and breathed and cried and eaten and menstruated—this possibility hadn't occurred to Karina.

"This is Wally Neuzil. She was Egon Schiele's muse. She's in lots of his other work." She sipped her champagne, considering the drawing. "She's beautiful, isn't she?"

Karina's pulse jackrabbited. "Yeah. She is."

Ines smiled at her. "How old are you?"

"Thirteen."

"Wally was sixteen when she met Egon." Ines glanced back at the drawing. "He loved her. Can't you tell, from the way he drew her?"

Karina said she could. Ines came and sat down on the bed next to her. "Wally didn't just pose for Egon, she handled his whole life, all the paperwork, his rent checks, all the administrative stuff. He would've been nothing without her." Karina thought of her own mother, how she was the one who kept the house running, who made Harry's travel arrangements even though he had a secretary, who planned all the parties, hand-lettering the invitations in her little study on the third floor. How Harry was always saying to her, "What would I do without you?"

Karina couldn't meet Ines's gaze, but she also couldn't tear her eyes away from her legs, the way her thighs spread across the floral pattern of the duvet. "Wally and Egon were married?" Karina ventured.

"No. She was too low-class to be his wife. He dumped her and married someone rich. And before *that* he got accused of molesting little girls. Sorry, I probably shouldn't say that. Tender ears and all."

"No, it's okay," Karina said quickly. "I know about . . ."

But Ines stood to leave then, smoothing her dress over her hips. "There's your history lesson for tonight. You're a lucky girl to have Wally on your wall."

Karina never saw Ines again after that night. The next time she heard Ines's name, her father was complaining about her on the phone—she'd published an open letter condemning the Pionteks' lack of support for women and artists of color. Karina later found it online: it was cogently argued, psychologically shrewd—particularly the parts concerning Harry's behavior—and it bespoke both formidable intelligence and profound bitterness.

The guard's walkie-talkie spat out a cloud of static. Seeing Wally on this sterile white wall, Karina felt not homesick exactly, but unmoored. Harry had repeatedly refused to allow her to bring her Wally drawing to school. Not even the events of last semester or her desolation over the summer had softened him. "You want to stick a priceless work of art in a dorm?" he'd said the last time she'd asked. "Are you insane?" Which, after everything she'd been through, had felt especially cruel, even coming from him. He'd been in a foul, dangerous mood for years now, it seemed, since the financial crisis. It was always a relief to get away from him, from his anger and contempt, and from Fiona, too, from her weakness, her helplessness, the infuriating way she cowed to Harry. But Karina still missed that sense of groundedness that she felt when she was alone in her bedroom with Wally.

Karina could hear Foxtail's and Long-Distance's voices approaching again. She located the staircase and escaped to the third floor, where she found Robert's exhibit. *Robert Berger: Thirty Years of Sound & Fury.*

She skimmed the wall text: *scathing political satirist . . . the overlapping realms of culture and politics . . . challenging assumptions about the role of art in the public sphere . . .*

The funny thing was that Karina had never thought of Robert as one of her parents' artists. He was the soft-spoken man who doodled cartoons on napkins and helped her persuade Fiona to let her order a second Shirley Temple when the three of them had lunch together. That whole year, Fiona had been different—light and sunny. Happy. It was the only time Karina could ever recall her mother seeming truly happy. In retrospect, of course, it was obvious that she and Robert had been having an affair.

Karina hadn't seen Robert on campus yet, but he was doing a Q&A next week that she planned to attend. She hoped he'd recognize her. It'd be nice to have a friendly face at Wrynn.

She wandered through the exhibit. Among the works on display were blank 1040 forms on which Robert had inked silhouettes of U.S. troops and fighter jets (*Death & Taxes*), an oil painting of Ronald Reagan rimming Margaret Thatcher (*Our Two Great Nations*), a dark, tumultuous canvas teeming with disembodied hands and feet (the wall text explained that they represented the Latin American victims of military juntas), and an ACT UP poster.

The work was a little disappointing. Robert's paintings seemed to want to spoon-feed their audience. And even though they were meant to be provocative and politically charged, there was something sort of pandering about them.

She made one more loop, then went back downstairs to the lobby. Night was falling as she left the museum. Clusters of students migrated toward the dining hall. She followed them, out of habit more than hunger, feeling unaccountably sad.

CHAPTER THREE

W hen Robert Berger was young, he'd earnestly believed that art could make things happen, but all art made for him now were the piles of administrative paperwork accumulating with alarming speed on his desk. He'd been given the biggest office on the floor. He'd heard from the Painting Department's secretary, Alberta, that the three adjuncts who'd previously occupied it had been ejected with no prior warning. Alberta told Robert that they were pissed about having to hold office hours in the lobby. Robert felt guilty about this, but not too much. He doubted the adjuncts' office hours were well-attended. Hardly anyone came to his.

Ping! went Robert's computer, warning him that his Visiting Artist Q&A started in an hour. He took one of the Xanax his new shrink had prescribed, then got his one-hitter from his desk and had a nice little smoke, blowing the evidence out the window and spraying air freshener when he was done. He was almost positive that he wasn't the only one who indulged at work—this was Wrynn, not Princeton—but that Alberta couldn't keep her mouth shut. She told anyone who would listen that she, too, had graduated from the Painting program. Her presence at the front desk couldn't be good publicity for the department's job placement rate. Also, she had some kind of symbol tattooed just below her jaw that, from a distance, looked like an insect crawling up her neck.

The walk across campus to the auditorium was enjoyable in a way that had become as familiar to Robert as the smell of paint. After so many years at so many schools, the scenery had blurred to a generically pleasant haze of fall foliage, shitty student installations, and stray Frisbees. It never ceased to amaze him that it had taken only two solo shows—the first when he was twenty-nine, the second sixteen years later when he was forty-five—to yield such a steady stream of visiting professorships and lectureships and fellowships and residencies. Wrynn was Robert's fourth school in nine years. He hadn't lived in his Crown Heights apartment since George W. Bush's first administration. In his absence, the neighborhood had changed beyond all recognition. Recently, he'd leased the apartment out to an advertising executive, his yoga teacher wife, and their three-year-old son, Striker, which was apparently now an acceptable name.

The auditorium, designed by a famous architect, bore a distinct resemblance to Darth Vader's helmet. Inside, Maureen Bolton was waiting, perched in one of the two armchairs onstage.

"Oh good," Maureen said. "Glad you're early."

She didn't look glad. The Painting Department's vice chair, Maureen was a steely-eyed, sturdy woman around Robert's age who made angry paintings about the female experience that struck him as decidedly masculine in their execution—thickly layered canvases stabbed with nails and shards of glass. Maureen had made it clear that she thought Robert and his work were overrated. Robert tried not to let it bother him. He'd experienced his own share of professional jealousy.

"So," said Robert, taking a seat. "What's the plan? Will you be interviewing me, or . . . ?"

"Yeah," said Maureen. "I'll introduce you, ask some questions, and then we'll open it up to the audience."

There was a broken fluorescent light somewhere. Its dull buzz filled Robert's head. He was getting those spots in his vision. Fuck. He'd smoked too much. *Fuck.* He got up and found a water fountain.

People began trickling into the auditorium, settling themselves into the furthermost rows, filling the air with chatter. When the seats were no more than a quarter full, Maureen approached the lectern, notecard in hand.

"Good afternoon," she read. "Today we welcome to Wrynn the painter Robert Berger, who will be the Painting Department's artist-in-residence for the next two years. Berger is best known for his Reagan-era satirico-political paintings. His work straddles the line between satire and criticism, poetry and politics. He is the recipient of an NEA grant, among other honors. His retrospective at our very own Wrynn Museum has just opened. Please give him a warm welcome."

There was a smattering of applause. Maureen peppered Robert with the usual questions to which he'd long ago perfected answers. Yes, political art is more relevant and necessary than ever. Yes, even in the age of Obama. Then Maureen threw out a question he hadn't heard before: "Do you think political art can be moving? Can it teach us how to feel?"

Robert thought of *Dying Man,* the painting that had catapulted him to success, the one that became the fulcrum of his career, spinning him out from its center. He hadn't set out to make a political painting. He'd sketched the preliminary studies for it in pastels at the ICU in Beekman Downtown Hospital, where his childhood friend, Vince Russo, lay dying. Having something to do with his hands, he'd found, kept his grief at bay, kept it, at least, from swallowing him whole. It was near the end by that point, and Vince spent his days drifting in and out of consciousness. When he was awake and lucid, his demeanor was sweet and funny, almost childlike. Other times he sank into delirium, mumbling nonsense. At one point, during one of his more lucid moments, he said, "I hear you drawing. What are you drawing, Robbie?" Vince had gone blind by then, and he hadn't called him Robbie in years, not since they were boys.

"The sky outside your window."

"Is it beautiful?"

"It is."

After Vince died, Robert used his sketches as the basis for a deathbed portrait. It was a flawed, youthful painting—the brushstrokes hurried and incautious, as though he were hurtling toward some finish line he couldn't yet see, as though time itself had been doused in accelerant—

but it had a kind of spectacular urgency, a *right-fucking-now-ness* that was absent from his later work. After Robert's first solo show, the Whitney acquired *Dying Man,* though Vince's mother begged him not to allow it to be displayed. The painting generated some controversy when it first went up, but it was generally well-received: a critic called it "a modern Christ on the cross." But later, in the mid-2000s, when it appeared on the cover of the *Art, AIDS & Activism* catalog, a prominent blogger Robert had never heard of called him a "straight opportunist," accusing him of "appropriating the AIDS crisis." There'd been protests at the museum, people holding signs reading QUEER DEATH SPECTACLE. Death threats, too, though not as many as when Robert's Nancy Reagan painting had made headlines.

"I think," said Robert, "that politics versus beauty and emotion—it's a false dichotomy."

"Explain what you mean," said Maureen.

Robert scratched his head. The truth, he was beginning to realize now that he was solidly in his late middle age, was that he'd become a political painter only because he'd made a personal painting that other people had politicized. His former gallerist, Brian Parrish, told him that he had the makings of a great political satirist, that that was his brand. And at the time, it made sense. For as long as Robert had known him, Vince had been an activist. As teenagers, they'd attended anti-war demonstrations together, and later, when Vince was in law school at Brooklyn College, he'd helmed the campus anti-apartheid movement. It *made sense* that Robert would try to continue Vince's work through his own. He spent years riding that wave, trying to tap into the zeitgeist, trying to anticipate the Next Big Issue. The trouble with the zeitgeist, though, was that it was always changing. It was always proving yesterday's all-consuming shitstorm to have been a blip in the indifferent march of time. And somewhere along the way his work lost the element that had made *Dying Man* such an affecting painting. He lost the thread that led back to Vince's hospital room and whatever it was that he'd touched in there—purity, maybe the word was, or authenticity. At that point, Brian Parrish—and most other people, for that matter—lost interest in him.

"Oh," said Robert vaguely, "just that the aesthetic and the political have always been intertwined. Politics are rooted in emotion, especially in this country." He squinted into the shadowy depths of the auditorium. "I think I see some hands. Do we want to start taking questions?"

More questions. Questions about his process. Questions about his current projects. Questions that were thinly veiled excuses to name-drop other, more successful artists. Robert expatiated, obfuscated, exaggerated, counter-name-dropped, and lied.

One girl asked, "What kind of relationship do you have with your collectors?"

"None, really," he said. That one was true, at least. It'd been years since he'd had rich friends.

A blond, muscular boy with close-cropped hair, sitting by himself up in the front row, raised his hand. Robert recognized him: his name was Preston Utley, and he was a senior in Robert's Persuasive Art seminar. Last week, his students had turned in their first projects. Preston's had been memorable only insofar as it involved a paint-daubed, vacuum-sealed raw rib eye steak and Whole Foods receipt, plus an artist statement so lengthy and oblique Robert lost interest halfway through and gave it a B. He gathered from comments other faculty had made that the boy was a troublemaker.

"Go ahead, Preston," Robert said.

"To be blunt," said Preston. "Why aren't you using the Internet? If you want to spread ideas—and you want to spread them fast and to the largest audience possible—then you need to use the Internet."

Robert gazed at Preston, attempting to rearrange his face into benign curiosity. "Well, I do have a website. Not one I built myself"—he laughed self-deprecatingly—"but still."

"But think of what, say, Occupy Wall Street is doing," said Preston. "The way they're using social media."

Preston had hit a nerve. Robert was enthralled by Occupy Wall Street. The movement was barely a week old, but already there was something new and exciting about it, something *authentic*. Maybe it was that sense of collective fury, the gasoline stench of the world on the cusp of revolt. As soon as Robert had heard about it, he'd reached out to an organizer and was now in talks to create an original piece of protest art for the movement. At no point had the organizer said that the piece *shouldn't* be a painting.

"My theory," Preston went on, "is that you guys—the elites, the gatekeepers—are afraid of the Internet."

"Excuse me," said Robert in his best no-nonsense voice, rankled at the implication that he was part of the elite. Him? The son of Jewish refugees? Abandoned by his father, raised by a seamstress? The kid who never would've gone to college, let alone art school, if Cooper Union hadn't offered him a full ride? "What you're talking about has nothing to do with the topic of political art."

"Sure it does," Preston said. "The Internet has democratized the distribution of information for the first time in human history. So the way to disseminate ideas—the way to be seen, to be heard, to reach the largest audience you possibly can—is to produce frenetically *online,* not to put stuff in galleries or, you know, do performance pieces in museum lobbies. The art world wants to believe it's at the cultural vanguard, but it's not. It's designed to only pedestalize ideas that it thinks are money-makers."

Was this the culmination of Robert's life's work? Arguing with an artsy frat boy in a mostly empty multimillion-dollar auditorium? He worried, of course, about his own relevance. He worried that he was sleepwalking through life, going through the motions, finding less and less meaning in his work. Was this what it was like, getting old? His mother had died three years ago. He'd moved in with her for the last month, slept in his childhood bed, getting up in the middle of the night to bring her ice water. Like Vince, she'd become sweet and childlike near the end. "I love you," she'd said, over and over. "Let's love each other till the end of time."

"So . . . speed?" Robert said. "And mass production? That's the kind of disruption you're proposing?"

"Not just that. Artists should bypass museums and galleries and put work directly out into the world. Tap into the attention economy. Stop letting money dirty the water. The next Rembrandt won't be a painter. He'll be a hacker."

Robert worked hard to swallow his irritation. Preston was wearing Nike athleisure, and his wristwatch was the heavy Swiss kind you saw in ads in glossy men's magazines. More than likely he was from a well-off family. Most of the kids here were; this place cost sixty grand a year.

How could someone like him, someone who hadn't grown up eating noodles and margarine and scrounging between couch cushions for loose change, possibly understand what it felt like to receive a check for *something you'd made with your own two hands*? How could he understand that that feeling was the thing that kept you going, even when being an artist felt like devoting yourself to being lost?

He was getting one of those dull, pounding pot headaches. His eyes felt like glazed donuts. The most effective cure for this was to smoke more pot. He shot Maureen a meaningful look. She nodded. "I think it's time to wrap this up," she said. "Thanks for your questions."

Maureen directed the audience to help themselves to wine and food in the lobby. Robert would've liked to escape through a side door, but instead, after splashing water on his face in the men's room, he made his way to the refreshment table and poured himself some lukewarm pinot grigio. Soon he got roped into a tedious conversation with the assistant curator at the Wrynn Museum. No sooner had he managed to extricate himself than Maureen beckoned him over and introduced him to Clark Strickland, a short, stocky painter whose bald head looked like a speckled egg, a condition for which his body seemed to have compensated by growing hair everywhere else. His eyebrows looked like salt-and-pepper caterpillars clinging to the smooth plane of his forehead.

"Great talk!" said Clark. "Terrific to have you here!"

"Clark lobbied very hard for you to be granted one of the residencies," said Maureen.

Robert glanced at her, but her expression was unreadable. Clark grinned, leaning forward conspiratorially. Close up, the eyebrows had a crude, pubic quality. "Between you and me, the artists we've invited in the past few years have been overly conceptual for my taste. A little 'let's smash everything with a sledgehammer and throw the pieces in a bonfire.' It's good to have someone old-school."

Robert smiled weakly. "I'm very glad to be here," he said. "Excuse me, I'm going to get some food."

So Clark had *lobbied very hard*, had he? What the hell was that supposed to mean? Was there a whole contingent of Maureens at this school resenting him and his hetero-whatever work? Angrily, he ate an olive.

"She is *huge* in Berlin," he heard someone say.

He felt a tap on his shoulder and turned around. Preston Utley. He had a big fistful of orange cheddar cubes, which he was popping into his mouth one after another like Tic Tacs. "Hey, Robert," he said, mid-chew. "I hope you didn't feel like I was attacking you or anything."

Robert disliked this students-calling-professors-by-their-first-name thing. He liked to cultivate an air of aloofness, which was hard to maintain when the kids were allowed to pretend to be friends with you. "Of course not." He forced a smile. "Vigorous debate is why we're here. Bedrock of higher learning."

"Cool, cool," said Preston. He rubbed his hands together, dusting off cheese crumbs. "Just wanted to make sure no hard feelings. See you in class, man."

As soon as seemed socially acceptable, Robert told Maureen he was heading out.

"Everything okay?" She tipped her chin up at him. Robert's ex-wife, Diane, used to give him the same look.

"To tell you the truth," he lied, "I feel a migraine coming on."

As he made his way toward a side door, a girl approached, the one who'd asked the question about his relationship with collectors. "Excuse me," she said. "Robert?" She was pretty, tall and very fair but with dark eyes, an unusual combination, and under normal circumstances he would've chatted with her. "I'll be right with you," he said. "I'm just going to the bathroom." He found a different side door and slipped out, the one-hitter in his office at the forefront of his mind.

CHAPTER FOUR

Even now, almost a week later, Robert's snub still stung more than Karina wanted to admit. As she stood in her studio, surveying her half-finished canvas, her mind flashed to the way he'd looked at the Q&A: his curly hair grayed, the skin around his neck a little looser. But he was still gangling and boyish, and he still made those funny little flapping gestures with his hands when he spoke.

He hadn't recognized her. On the one hand she couldn't blame him—she'd been, what, eleven or twelve the last time she saw him?—but she'd been told all her life that she was her mother's spitting image, so what did his failure to see his ex-lover's face in hers say about how much Fiona had mattered to him? And that whole year he'd spent with Fiona, that year when it seemed as though he were auditioning for the role of Karina's father—a kinder, gentler father than Harry—hadn't it meant anything?

Karina tied her hair back, tugged on a smock, and forced herself back to her work-in-progress. For most of the summer, she'd been unable to paint, but in recent weeks she'd felt her old intuition returning to her. Now she was more reckless, aggressive in her gestures. Like riding a bike with no hands and no helmet. The canvas erupted with deep purples, dusty reds, and brownish yellows, like a field of dying flowers. It was smeary and messy and edible-looking.

As she worked, she slipped into fantasies of painting like Joan Mitchell, drawing like Egon Schiele, manipulating motifs and materials like Sigmar Polke. Inhabiting greatness. She moved in and out of herself, jumping from one influence to the next, weaving a web of associations, appropriations, commentary. Unlike some of her classmates, Karina had never felt weighed down by the past. The past was a template, a map.

Karina had been told she was a prodigy often enough that most of the time she believed it. Still, her work rarely satisfied her. Every time she applied herself to a canvas, she was trying to make a new world, to show herself something she hadn't seen before, but the result was always somehow naggingly familiar. Since childhood, she'd harbored the secret belief that her best work—her *masterpiece*—was suspended out there somewhere, waiting to channel itself through her. She searched for it with increasing impatience.

But there was another, wilier part of her that was always assessing her own work with a sharp monetary instinct. She knew that reds and blues sold better than browns. Sunny landscapes cost more than dark ones, calm seas more than rough ones. A female nude was more valuable than a male one (the biggest-spending collectors were men). This knowledge didn't embarrass her. She was proud of it. It was no accident that she'd won Best Painting at Winter Exhibition last year. Most women didn't know their own worth, didn't know how to make themselves more valuable. Or if they did, they downplayed their worth in service of some ridiculous false modesty. But Karina knew that it wasn't enough to be excellent—you had to maintain that excellence over time, you had to make sure no one forgot about it, and most of all, you had to make it appear effortless.

These were thoughts she'd never spoken aloud, not at home and not at school. Money was taboo at Wrynn. The outside world, its auctions and galleries and collectors, might as well not exist. Sometimes Karina wondered what her classmates would think if they knew the extent to which she thought about the cash value of her work.

She painted for a couple more hours, then cleaned up and started back across the softly lit campus. As she passed the glass-blowing studio, her phone buzzed with a call from her mother. Since everything last summer, Fiona had called at least once a week. Her voice tight with worry, she'd ask if Karina was doing okay. Was she taking her meds? Did she need anything? Her mother's anxiety was grating, but it also made Karina feel cared for. In a way she welcomed it.

"Karina? Can you talk?" Something was off. Fiona sounded breathless. "Has your father called you?"

Karina stopped under one of the red elms and kicked at a pile of dead leaves. "I talked to him maybe two weeks ago, but—"

"So he hasn't told you then?"

"Told me what?" Karina picked up a handful of leaves and crumbled them.

Gently, Fiona told Karina that her father had asked for a divorce. Karina stood frozen. She'd always taken a certain perverse comfort in the solidity of her parents' marriage, had always felt secure in the knowledge that their lives couldn't be untangled, that they were each the other's parasite. True, they often fought, and it was no secret that they'd both been unfaithful, and Karina had long ago sworn to herself that she'd never let a man treat her the way her father treated her mother, but they also shared a baroque bond that Karina would've found nearly impossible to explain, had anyone thought to ask. They'd met young, freshman year at Yale. They had in common an obsession with aesthetics and a certain way of presenting themselves to the world, a sort of social performance—watching them make the rounds at parties, Karina was reminded of a pair of figure skaters, perfectly synchronized and in tune with each other. Their arguments were the same: calculated, almost choreographed, and they seemed to emerge from them somehow energized, inflated by a sense of noble suffering. Karina's childhood had been colored by the knowledge that she would never be as interesting to her parents as they were to each other. They would never know her as well as they knew each other.

"What happened?" Karina demanded.

Fiona cleared her throat. "It's nothing you need to worry about—"

"But why *now*?"

Hadn't the time to divorce been three years ago, when Harry's drinking had gotten out of control, or six years before that, when Fiona had brazenly brought Karina to lunches with Robert Berger? But no, Fiona wasn't capable of leaving the marriage. Karina had once overheard her telling a friend: "It's not just him I'm married to. It's the lifestyle. When you grow up like I did, you can't just let go of something like that."

"Your dad is moving out," Fiona was saying now, on the phone. "And I need you to know we might sell the New York house, so when you're home for Thanksgiving I'll ask you to sort through your things—"

"Did he leave you for someone else?"

The blue light on the emergency phone at the corner of Prospect and Meeting kept blinking on and off.

"Mom? Did he?"

Despite the way Harry treated Fiona, Karina had always thought her mother wielded a certain subtle power over her father. Even when it looked like she was firmly under his thumb, she'd found ways of bending him to her will. There was a push and pull between them; there always had been.

"We'll likely sell the Florida place, too," her mother was saying now.

"He did leave you for someone else, didn't he? Who is it?"

"And the art collection."

Karina opened her fist, sprinkling her clothes with bits of crumbled leaf. "What?"

"I said we're selling the Florida place and the collection."

"Why?"

"We hardly ever used the Florida house—"

"No, why are you selling the art?" Karina had a wound-up feeling in her chest.

Fiona sighed. "It's complicated."

"Can I at least keep the Schiele that's in my room?" Karina tried not to sound too desperate. "The drawing of the red-haired girl?"

"No."

"Why not?"

Fiona sighed again. Wearily, she explained that her lawyer and Harry's had fought for months over what the collection was worth; they'd even hired separate experts who'd arrived at wildly different valuations. "In the end the judge decided that if we couldn't come to an agreement, then the only real way to determine the value is to sell the collection and split the proceeds down the middle. So I can't just give you a piece of it. Your dad's lawyer would accuse me of hiding assets."

"Wait—hold on. What judge? How long has this been going on?"

"Since July."

Karina had been in a fog all summer. Of course it had been easy for her parents to hide this.

"Don't be angry with me," Fiona said plaintively. "If I want my fair half, this is what needs to happen. The last thing I want is another court battle." She took a shaky breath. "None of this is my fault. I need you on my side. I need my daughter."

Until then Karina hadn't been angry, but now she felt rage flare up inside her, sudden and strong. It was the first time she could recall her mother saying such a thing to her—that she *needed* her. It was unimaginable, Fiona needing her. "Why are you just giving him what he wants?" Karina heard herself say. "You're so weak and selfish!"

She hung up and surprised herself by bursting into tears. She felt it like a pain in her chest: her miserable family, her poisoned childhood. Her parents' art had been her first teacher. And now Harry and Fiona were going to dismantle it, piece by piece, literally sell it to the highest bidder. They were going to sell Wally. The girl she'd shared her childhood with, gone.

Karina often thought about the night Ines had first told her Wally's name. It was the night she'd brought herself to orgasm for the first time, holding in her mind visions of Ines and Wally. As the waves of euphoria crested and receded, Karina had lain shaking, a strange metallic taste in the back of her throat, warm and coppery like blood, but sweeter. Gradually, her heartbeat slowed. She looked at Wally. She understood then that she wanted girls just as much as—maybe even more than—boys. It unnerved her how much Ines's presence had disarmed her, how vulnerable her desire for Ines's body had made her feel. And Ines had seen straight through her, she was sure of it. Now, years later, Karina felt that same vulnerability around Louisa, and she worried that Louisa, too, could read it on her face.

Her dorm room was unlocked. Inside, Louisa was sitting barefoot on the floor, elbow-deep in a cardboard box. Louisa's name and school address were scrawled across the side in slanting, untidy cursive, alongside a lopsided smiley face drawn in Sharpie. Louisa looked up as Karina came into the room. "My mom sent me a care package."

"Cool." Karina's eyes went to Louisa's calloused heels, the fish-belly-pale arches of her feet. Her stomach twisted.

"Do you want some pralines?"

"Um, no thanks."

Louisa took out a bag of chips and tossed it onto her bed. "You know what I found out today?" she said in a determinedly friendly voice. "You probably already know this."

"What?"

"You know Ivy Morton? The girl who always wears a foxtail?"

"I call her Foxtail," Karina said, surprised at her impulse to reveal this. "In my head."

"Ha," said Louisa. "That's funny. So apparently she buys chicken feet at the Chinese market downtown and desiccates them in salt. And then she puts them in her sculptures. I can't decide if it's gross or brilliant."

Under different circumstances, Karina might've taken this as an invitation to gossip about Foxtail, but now she felt her mouth clamp shut. If she stayed in Louisa's presence any longer, she'd dissolve into tears again and tell her everything. "Yeah, so . . . I'm going out," she said. "See you." She dropped her school bag on her bed and headed back down the stairs, but not before catching a glimpse of Louisa's disappointment.

Karina wandered around campus in the snapping air. Everyone said fall was New England's loveliest season, but under the gloom of the rust-colored treetops Karina saw only death. She needed a drink, badly, and she'd left her flask in her room. She passed Sayles Hall all lit up and remembered the Bob Ross paint-along party she'd seen advertised on posters in Hope. *Hot apple cider!* Someone would've spiked it. Someone always did.

Inside, one of the lecture rooms had been cleared of desks, the floor covered with plastic sheeting to protect the hardwood. The Bob Ross YouTube channel was queued up on the projector. People milled about, sitting on the floor with their paintbrushes and canvas boards, half-jokingly following along as Bob Ross painted a mountain vista.

"Look what we have," said Bob Ross. "Look around. Beauty is every-where."

"*God*," Karina heard someone say. "His voice is like Xanax."

She poured some cider, drank it—spiked, indeed—and refilled her cup.

"All you need to paint," said Bob Ross, "is a few tools, a little instruction, and a little imagination."

"Did you know Bob Ross was kind of a douche?" came a loud voice. Karina turned to see a tall, muscular boy with golden hair and golden skin, the kind that would turn to leather in middle age. He had bright blue eyes and wore an athletic jacket with shiny reflective stripes the color of traffic cones.

She recognized him: Preston Utley, the guy who'd humiliated Robert Berger at that lecture last week. Karina had had little sympathy for Berger after he'd snubbed her at the reception, but Preston she'd found funny and sharp, if a little full of himself. He was a controversial figure on campus, both admired and reviled, which Karina could relate to. Last year he'd gotten into trouble for leading prospective students and their parents on fake campus tours that grew progressively more outrageous as they went on. He'd also replaced the museum's guided audio tour with a recording of someone reading *Das Kapital*. The administration hadn't caught wind of it until admissions season rolled around and applications dipped by nearly fifteen percent. Preston was also behind that vaporwave Tumblr whose images, at first glance, appeared to be jokes. Upon closer inspection, however, they were uncanny in a way that was hard to classify. A round, bubblegum-pink slice of bologna nestled inside a Discman. A bottle of kombucha displayed on a white plinth. A Tampax box full of corn dogs. It was unclear whether any of it was supposed to mean anything.

"Now then," said Bob Ross. "Let's come right down in here and put some nice big strong arms on these trees. Tree needs an arm, too. It'll hold up the weight of the forest."

"The dude was a total tyrant," said Preston. "That whole Mr. Zen thing? Fake as fuck."

Around him, people were laughing like he was doing a stand-up comedy routine. Which maybe he was. Karina chugged a third ladleful of boozy cider. She'd heard that Preston was a total asshole in crit, relentlessly disparaging of his classmates' work. She'd heard that he railed against galleries and auctions and collectors—people like her parents. That he'd joined the new campus Occupy group just so he could lobby for defacing buildings and hacking into Wrynn's computer system.

"Little bird has to have a place to sit there," said Bob Ross. "There he goes . . ."

"And those paintings aren't as spontaneous as they look," said Preston. "He made one beforehand and kept it off-camera as a reference while he painted."

Karina watched him. Preston had power over people; you could see it in the way they looked at him, the way they listened to him. And his blog, too: crude as it was, it commanded attention. He noticed Karina looking at him then; when their gazes met, a grin spread slowly across his face, his eyes fastening on her in a way she'd seen a hundred times before. Already she knew the kind of sway she—her body—would hold over him. Karina had been fifteen when she'd begun finding herself in the darkened bedrooms of acquaintances, fucking boys she barely knew—blithe, lacrosse-toned sons of CEOs and bankers and neurosurgeons, so sure of their place in the world that they always let her be on top, always let her hold the reins, sit on their faces. She'd close her eyes and think of Wally and come with such abandon that the boys would smirk in self-congratulation, as though their golden cocks had anything at all to do with it.

Karina had slept with women twice before. Both encounters had been one-night stands, but they'd felt strangely, almost overwhelmingly intimate, much more so than the sex she'd had with men. Afterward, she'd felt tender and raw, like the soft pink skin under a peeling sunburn. The encounters had left her unable to paint for days.

Karina walked over to Preston. "You know you might as well be dunking on Mr. Rogers," she said. "Or Alex Trebek."

If Harry and Fiona ever met him, they'd hate him.

Preston's apartment had an open floor plan, the kitchen sharing space with the living room, and a big window overlooking a courtyard. The couch was beige and looked like it came from IKEA. A can of Lysol was perched on a rowing machine, which stood, in lieu of a coffee table, in the middle of the living room. Karina had expected some sort of decoration, posters at least, but the walls were bare. When Preston opened the fridge to get them each a beer, she saw that the whole top shelf was crammed with energy drinks. She opened her beer and took a tiny sip. She still had a buzz from the cider.

"What are you studying?" Preston said.

"Painting."

He made a face, and she laughed. "Don't tell me you're one of those 'painting is dead' types."

"No," he said. "I'm one of those '*objects* are dead' types."

Karina draped her coat over a chair. "If we're using 'dead' as a synonym for 'inanimate,' then yes, you're technically correct."

Preston smiled. "'The world is full of objects, more or less interesting; I do not wish to add any more.'"

"Douglas Huebler."

Preston raised his chin at her. "I'm impressed you know that."

"I'm a painter, not an idiot. Personally, I've always thought that when people become conceptual artists, it's so they can have an excuse for not being able to draw."

Preston laughed. "I can draw. I drew that damn bike, same as you."

Wrynn was famous for requiring applicants to submit a pencil drawing of a bicycle. In September, the Wrynn Museum displayed the incoming first-years' bike drawings in the lobby.

Karina held the beer can to her cheek, feeling the cold seep into her molars. "I heard that once, someone just wrote the word 'bike' on a sheet of paper."

"And?"

"They got in. Supposedly."

Preston set his beer down on the kitchen table with a dull *clack*. He stepped forward, slid his hand around Karina's waist. His breath was warm and yeasty. His lips, when he kissed her, were surprisingly soft. As her arms snaked around his neck, she remembered the hard pleasure of a man's body. A simple pleasure, like butter on warm bread.

Preston's bed was made with military precision. His sheets were the color of asphalt. His body was deft and quick-moving. He kept his condoms in a pickle jar on his nightstand. She closed her eyes as she rose and fell above his golden chest, but when she came it wasn't Wally she pictured, but Louisa.

When Preston fell asleep, Karina got dressed and left. She googled his name as she walked back to campus. Hundreds of hits. She clicked through them and began to piece together the story of him. It was all there, written in plain language, scrawled across the open face of the Internet.

CHAPTER FIVE

Preston's father had always been against Preston going to art school, so it came as a surprise when he offered to cover senior year's tuition, plus the cost of an off-campus apartment, under two conditions: (1) Preston would refrain from further run-ins with Wrynn's disciplinary board, and (2) Preston would decline the all-expenses-paid residency he'd been offered at the Budapest Art Factory and, instead, spend the summer before senior year doing an internship with his father at the Pentagon, the unspoken purpose of which was to keep Preston under parental supervision.

He thanked his father and said it was a very generous offer. Then he called his older half brother Andrew and relayed what his father had said. After the residency was over, Preston had planned to take the train to Frankfurt to visit Andrew. It would be the first time in nearly eight years that they'd see each other in person, and Preston would finally meet his sister-in-law and nephews.

"Okay," Andrew said after Preston explained the situation. "Let's think."

Up until then, Preston had been paying his tuition and living expenses out of the small trust their mother had left each of them when she died, but now that money was mostly gone. It should've lasted Preston all through college, but he'd been profligate his first two years, and by the time he forced himself to stick to a budget, it was too late. Now what remained in the account would only cover him for six months, and even then, he'd have to be careful.

"Do you think there's any way you'd qualify for financial aid?" Andrew said.

"Not with my dad's income, no."

Andrew was quiet. In the background, Preston could hear the kids nattering, Andrew's wife speaking to them in German. The clatter of forks and knives. Preston had interrupted their dinner.

"Is there any way . . . ?" Preston began, "that, uh—that you'd be willing to call my dad and talk to him?"

There was a long silence. "I can't," Andrew said finally. "I—I just can't. I'm sorry."

As far as Preston knew, the last time his father and Andrew had spoken—yelled, more like—was at their mother's funeral. Preston had just turned fourteen; Andrew had been twenty-four. Their mother had been dead less than a month when Andrew accepted a job at Siemens and moved to Germany. Preston hadn't seen his half brother since, though they exchanged frequent emails and the occasional phone call.

"It's just one year," Andrew said. "You just have to make it till graduation. After that you'll get a job or start selling your art or something and you'll never have to deal with your dad again."

"Yeah," Preston managed. "You're right."

What he didn't want to have to explain to Andrew—they just didn't have that kind of relationship—was that he was opposed to selling art and horrified by the idea of participating in the capitalist hellscape. So he said goodbye and tried not to feel like a fourteen-year-old who'd just been abandoned by both his mother and brother, which was how he'd felt, off and on, for the last eight years.

Preston turned down the residency in Budapest and took the Pentagon internship, even though the daily reminders of his father's disappointment and anger made his stomach churn. At the end of the summer, he flew back to Stonewater and moved into a one-bedroom on

Pitman Street six blocks from campus. And, he had to admit, it was nice having his own place. It was nice to put on Fugazi and hop on his rowing machine at seven A.M. without having to worry about waking his roommates.

And despite everything, his senior year was off to a great start, thanks to Karina. It wasn't like Preston hadn't noticed her before: she was pretty, rich, and, he'd heard, crazy. What he hadn't expected when he took her home was that she'd also be a formidable intellectual opponent. He'd never given the rumors that she was a prodigy much credence—what did it even mean to be a prodigy of a dying art form?—but it was only a matter of days before he found himself besotted with her, body and mind. It was a bit of a shell shock. He'd never felt this way about anyone.

After that first night at his apartment, they'd quickly established a routine: in the evenings after dinner, Karina came over to his place and they fucked, usually more than once. Then they lounged around, drinking and talking. Their conversations felt like the best kind of tennis match: two equally balanced players volleying the ball over the net, intent on keeping it—and each other—moving for as long as possible. They veered from topic to topic so quickly Preston had to exert himself keeping up: the Wall Street bailout, artists they each admired, the Arab Spring, Internet memes, swine flu. Because what she believed was almost always the opposite of what he believed, they never ran out of things to argue about. She was totally unflappable, which could be both infuriating and deeply arousing. And she was unbelievable in bed, savage and inventive. He was always sorry when she got dressed and left to go to her studio. She said she did her best work between ten P.M. and two A.M.

On a Friday morning in early October, Preston woke up in a good mood. Karina was coming over for dinner and, for the first time, had agreed to spend the night.

Preston worked out on his rowing machine, then made himself a protein shake. He knew what people said about him—that the jock thing was just his shtick, a gimmick, or else that he was a bro who'd only gone to art school because the male-to-female ratio worked in his favor, neither of which was true. Other students were junkies; Preston was an athlete. His peers spent their time engaged in dark-age toil, but Preston was a twenty-first-century specimen whose digital efficiency freed him up to work out, keeping his brain tip-top. Too much introspection was destructive. Before he got serious about art, he'd been a nationally ranked tennis player, and there was a part of him that still identified as the overdog and wanted nothing more than to dominate. When he was a freshman at Wrynn, he'd discovered that the feeling he got from throwing down in a debate was the same as beating someone in a tennis match. In crit, he always imagined himself hustling his opponent back and forth along the baseline, drop-shooting them before moving in for the kill. Sometimes these fantasies were so vivid that Preston could almost hear his old coach screaming at him from the sidelines. He could smell the rubber and feel the court under his feet. He'd had that feeling last month at Robert Berger's Q&A. By the end of it, Preston could tell from Berger's expression that he knew, even if only on a lizard brain level, that he'd been owned.

Preston scrubbed out the blender and brushed his teeth, gargling twice with Listerine. Then he ran downstairs to check his mailbox. Nothing yet. The package was supposed to arrive last week; he was getting antsy.

Back in his apartment, Preston opened his laptop and clicked on the folder labeled RAW_Z, containing thousands of images that he'd culled, over the years, from the Internet, an eclectic mix, everything from toothpaste ads to cat pictures to memes to celebrity glamour shots to screen grabs from online message boards to porn. Today, he selected a photograph of a tall, busty blonde wearing nothing but gold stilettos. She pouted at the camera, glassy-eyed. Preston opened the file in Photoshop and played around with different filters for a while, but nothing satisfied him—all the effects softened the image, or else made it too straightforwardly artistic. Eventually he settled on swapping out the woman's pubes and nipples with brand logos. He tried Nike swooshes and Target bull's-eyes before deciding that Puma's leaping cougar was a better fit, conceptually. Once he'd desaturated everything but the gold stilettos, he uploaded the image to The Wart. *Pussy, 2011.*

Preston took a quick shower and went to class, slipping into the auditorium a few minutes late. In addition to thesis credits and Berger's Persuasive Art seminar, Preston was also taking a lecture course on Post-Conceptual Art. There was a guest speaker today.

"When feminist theory refers to the woman being situated as 'other' within patriarchal society," said the lecturer, who wore a dung-colored skirt that grazed the floor as she paced behind the lectern, "what it's really talking about is the idea that, throughout history, women's bodies have been reduced to aesthetic objects produced and reproduced for male consumption."

Preston found this neither interesting nor revelatory. On his laptop, he minimized his notes and pulled up The Wart. In the time since he'd posted *Pussy*, just under an hour ago, it had accrued nearly two hundred likes. He checked on yesterday's post, a Marlboro box full of e-cigarettes, their tips glowing electric blue. One thousand three hundred and nineteen likes and four hundred reblogs. Not bad. And The Wart had fifty-three new followers since he'd checked the stats last night.

His highest-performing post of all time remained *Phone Bath*, a picture of an iPhone submerged in a punch bowl full of cherry Kool-Aid. It had topped out at nearly ten thousand likes and sparked online debates about whether the image was real or Photoshopped. Back in high school, when he'd started posting his Photoshop experiments on Tumblr, he hadn't expected them to be a hit. But within a couple of years, The Wart had blown up. A midlist hip-hop artist had even used an image from it as the cover for one of his albums. The Wart, more than anything, was what had saved him during those dark years following his mother's death. It was indescribable, the rush he got from watching the page views mount, the likes accrue. Attention was the most valuable resource in the world, more powerful than any drug.

Keeping an eye on the clock, Preston scrolled idly through last week's posts:

> —a shampoo ad supermodel washing her hair with green
>   paint (*Our Most Potent Formula Yet!*)
> —a barnacle-crusted soda fountain machine (*Naturally Filtered*)

—Christ the Redeemer standing in a McDonald's PlayPlace
   ball pit (*McMass*)
—five iPod Shuffles floating in a bowl of clear broth and noodles (*Soup of the Day*)
—a jar of Vicks VapoRub labeled "Chakra Formula: Soothes &
   Relieves Minor Spiritual Aches & Pains!" (*Alternative Medicine*)
—a pair of crash test dummies locked in an embrace (*Love
   Story of Our Time*)
—the blue Powerpuff Girl, hugely pregnant (*Dad Is a Pedo*)

At 11:28 Preston closed his laptop and slipped it into his backpack.
At 11:30 the auditorium filled suddenly with rustling and chatter as
three quarters of the students rose at once and began streaming out the
door. The guest lecturer looked up from her notes in confusion.

Preston walked out of the building and onto the green, where a hundred or so students had joined the walkout. Some sat chatting in the
grass; others held signs: *Master of Debt*; *We Want a University for the 99%*;
Education Is a Right; *You Raise Fees, We Raise Hell*. In the middle of the
crowd stood Sammy Nakamura, megaphone in hand. Preston headed
toward him.

"Hey," Sammy said. "Did everyone in your class join?"

"Most," said Preston. "We had a guest lecturer. I don't think anybody
told her about the walkout."

Sammy raised the megaphone to his lips and said, "Tell me what democracy looks like!"

There was a squeal of feedback, and Preston winced, but an obedient
cry rose from the crowd: "This is what democracy looks like!"

"Tell me what democracy looks like!"

"This is what democracy looks like!"

Preston felt his mood turn sour. Skipping class wasn't exactly a radical political act. Why not hack into the bursar's website? Why not barricade President Fowler inside his house? But at the meeting he'd been
overruled, Sammy going on about *in my experience as an organizer,* as
though getting your private high school to fly a gay pride flag counted
as activism.

Still, Preston tried to stay on friendly terms with Sammy. There weren't that many other people at Wrynn engaging in Post-Object Art. Not that Sammy's work—performances where he invited people over for Thanksgiving dinners that he served without utensils while projecting a video montage of people chewing with their mouths open, which he called "Experimental Gastroaesthetics"—was very interesting.

At the base of one of the red elms, Honey Windrow, Ryan Merrick, Daniel Reyes, and a girl Preston didn't know well, Rowena something, were setting up tents. Preston went over to help them. Sammy handed the megaphone off to Nina Gabriel, who took it and said, "Why doesn't Wrynn pay property taxes? Stonewater is an impoverished community, people!"

Preston unfurled a set of tent poles and threaded one into the flap.

"Need a hand?"

Preston squinted up at Sammy, who'd followed him over to the encampment. "Sure."

Together they raised and straightened the tent before staking it to the ground.

"You sleeping here tonight?" said Sammy.

The plan was for people to take turns sleeping in the encampment, a prospect Preston didn't especially relish. "No, I have a date. You?"

Sammy shook his head. "I need to work on my portfolio."

"Huh."

"Yeah, this gallerist saw some of my stuff online. He's interested in maybe repping me."

Preston forced a smile. "Cool. Good for you." In theory, he believed the gallery/museum industrial complex was corrupt and outdated, but it still rankled when someone he considered his artistic inferior received institutional recognition.

"Yeah, he represents some super edgy artists," Sammy said. "So I'm pretty stoked."

"Cool," Preston repeated. Sammy's gloating pissed him off for a very simple reason: Preston had no idea what he was doing after graduation. Some people talked about applying for jobs as curatorial assistants or in advertising or marketing; those keen to wait out the recession's dismal job market had started putting together applications for MFA programs; everyone, regardless of their postgraduation plans, was vying for gallery representation. None of this appealed to Preston. The trouble was, what had seemed totally plausible when he was eighteen—forging a life for himself outside the capitalist economy—looked more tenuous from his vantage point now. The trouble was money. Always money. It was really very difficult to circumvent the problem of not having any money.

Preston wasn't an idiot. He understood that his ambition to live outside capitalism was contingent upon the accident of his birth—his father's position, his mother's modest family wealth. He didn't like the word *privilege*—there was something accusatory about it, as though he were somehow responsible for being born himself—but it did have a certain ring of truth. He'd long treated it like a nasty wound under a bandage: he knew it was there, but as long as he never lifted the gauze, he didn't have to think too hard about it. He consoled himself with the knowledge that he was hardly alone in having a background that clashed with his political leanings. Basquiat was from a nice middle-class family. So was every member of Rage Against the Machine. Even Trotsky's parents had been landowners.

"You got lunch plans?" Sammy asked Preston.

He didn't. "Yeah, sorry."

Pleading homework, Preston said goodbye and jogged back to his apartment building. In the vestibule, he unlocked his mailbox and pulled out an electric bill, the newest issue of *Men's Health*—the articles were idiotic, but he liked the workouts—and a plain brown parcel bearing a New Jersey return address, no sender's name.

"*Yes.*"

Once inside his apartment, he dead-bolted the door, yanked down the shades, and slit open the parcel with a steak knife. He pulled out a little baggie of cocaine, a blotter of acid, and a blister pack of MDMA. He'd been aware of Blind Tiger since the website's launch earlier that year but had only gotten up the nerve to buy from it recently. To ensure his anonymity, Preston had placed the orders from a computer at the Stonewater Public Library on which he'd installed Tor, funneling the Bitcoin transaction through an account he'd set up under a fake name.

For lunch, Preston heated up some leftover lo mein, then spent the rest of the afternoon trawling online for his RAW_Z file and messing around on Photoshop. When it started getting dark, he did a half hour of cardio, showered, and ordered a pizza. As he waited for Karina and the food to show up, he typed her name into Google. He googled Karina incessantly, even though there wasn't much online about her. What he did find was plenty of information about her parents. Today, an intriguing headline popped up: *Harry and Fiona Piontek Announce Plans to Sell Collection, Valued at $70 Million.* He skimmed the article, which included a photo of Karina in a high-necked red dress standing between a woman who looked exactly like her and a balding, tuxedoed man. The caption: *Trustee Harry Piontek with his wife, Fiona, and their daughter Karina at the Frick Collection Young Fellows Ball.*

Karina arrived soon after the pizza, but they skipped dinner and went straight to sex. Afterward, he said, "You know, I really hate people like your parents."

Karina was sprawled on the couch, where he'd had her pinned just moments before. Her face was flushed and damp. She laughed. "I'm sorry, what?" She sat up and gave him a curious look. "When did you meet my parents?"

Preston put his boxers back on. "I don't hate them *personally,* but I hate what they stand for."

"You mean you hate the rich. Which is another way of saying you hate yourself."

"No, I'm saying that if you're someone who thinks, for example, that Rothko belongs to the cultural patrimony—and if you're a collector, presumably you do—I don't see how keeping *your* Rothko where only your rich friends and, like, the maid ever get to see it isn't morally reprehensible. Don't you think?"

She gave him a level look. "You're asking me if it's bad for valuable things to be valuable." She shimmied back into her dress, a stretchy black number that clung to her hips. "If Rothkos didn't have commercial value, nobody would have any incentive to preserve them. Do you think museums are morally reprehensible?"

"I mean, I think they're elitist, but at least they're a little more democratic."

Karina let out a *pffft* of laughter. "Oh my god, do you hear yourself? You think they're elitist but also democratic." She shook her head with amusement, her bright hair catching the lamplight. He wanted to seize a handful of it in his fist, pull her head back to expose her throat. But she moved away from him, bending to gather the rest of her clothing off the floor. "Okay, Preston. That might be the most ridiculous thing you've ever said to me."

He grinned at her. He liked the way she took control, the way she called him on his bullshit.

"But about my parents . . . I kind of agree with you. They're fucked-up people. We're not close."

He'd become so used to the way she kept herself secret. During sex—even when she came—she seemed to be having an experience wholly detached from his. It was strange to hear her so forthright. She was bent over now, fiddling with her phone; he couldn't see her expression. "Are you close to yours?" she asked, her face still hidden.

Reflexively, Preston replied, "No. I hate my dad."

His father had visited two weeks ago. In uniform, the jackass. They'd had lunch at a burger place in downtown Stonewater and he hadn't cracked a smile the entire time. While they waited for the check, he said, "It's coming up."

"I know." As though Preston could forget.

"Are you coming home?"

"Of course."

Every year since Preston had left for college, he'd flown home on October 22. He'd spend the night in his old bedroom and the next day he and his father would go to his mother's memorial mass. In the afternoon, Preston would go sit at Evelyn's grave for a half hour. The next day, Preston would fly back to school and call Andrew to tell him how the grave had looked and what kind of flowers he'd left there.

Karina put her phone down and looked up at him. "Why do you hate him?"

"Because he's an asshole."

"What about your mother?"

"She's dead," he replied flatly. *Feel sorry for me*, he might as well have said. "But after she died, for a long time I was mad at her." He wanted

Karina to ask why. He wanted to tell someone the whole story, the empty garage, the uncanny horror of police sirens on a sunlit afternoon. But she didn't ask. She suggested they reheat the pizza.

As they ate, she said, "Why'd you bring up my parents? Were you google-stalking me?"

He smiled guiltily, though he didn't feel especially guilty. "I hear they're selling their collection."

Karina dabbed the grease off her slice with a paper towel. "I used to go with them to the auctions. I watched them bid on half the pieces we own."

"Was it a meat market?"

"No, it was thrilling. Like watching history being made."

They fell silent. The radiator hummed. Preston's upstairs neighbor was running her hair dryer for the millionth time.

"Do you have a lot of work this weekend?" said Preston.

"Not a ton. You?"

"Some. I have a project coming up for Robert Berger's class."

"How *is* that?"

Preston smirked, helping himself to another slice. "Mediocre."

"Really?" She looked surprised.

"I mean, he's just kind of deflated and toothless. A total sad sack, you know?" Worse, he was arrogant and completely uninterested in his students, not seeming to appreciate that he was at one of the best art schools in the country and therefore statistically likely to be in the presence of genius. The vacuum-sealed rib eye thing had gone completely over his head. It had only been half a joke: Preston was interested in making consumer goods, especially ones with cultural cachet, unconsumable, but Berger didn't get it. It hadn't taken very long for Preston to begin to feel the urge to *troll* him.

"I also have some reading for my Post-Conceptual Art class," said Preston. "And The Wart, obviously."

"You put a lot of work into that, huh?"

He met her gaze. He couldn't tell if she was mocking him. "I didn't use to, but since it's gotten bigger, it's become more time-intensive."

"How'd it start?"

Preston rose to throw his crusts in the trash. "It was just kind of a photography blog at first."

That whole first year after his mom died and Andrew left, Preston's stomach hurt anytime he was alone with his father. When Preston wasn't in school, he spent hours biking around Arlington, headphones on, his mom's camera swinging from his neck. From the get-go, his eye gravitated toward uncanny, often disturbing imagery. Some of his early efforts included the carcass of a rotisserie chicken moldering in a dumpster, the remains of someone's cat smeared across the intersection at 6th and Norwood, and the charred skeleton of a Christmas tree poking out of a torn black garbage bag.

But eventually, Preston realized that the world was full of images. Every advertisement ever printed, every photo, every piece of art, every billboard, every security camera still—all of it was up for grabs. And now, in the age of the Internet, everything that had ever been created was freely available to be spliced and diced and remixed and recontextualized. So he stopped being a photographer and instead became a Photoshopper.

"Want to watch Netflix or something?" Preston said.

Karina agreed, though she pulled out her sketchbook and drew while they watched *Twin Peaks*. When she got up to pee, he snuck a look at it. She was drawing some girl's face.

CHAPTER SIX

I t was October before Louisa decided to speak to Maureen privately. For the past few weeks, she'd been mostly silent in class. She kept her head down and did her work, turned in her color wheels and her value exercises and her single-light still lifes, said little during crits. She was also taking Sculpture, Drawing, and Art History. Three days a week, she rose at four A.M. to work the breakfast shift in the dining hall, scrubbing dishes and flipping French toast alongside a handful of financial aid kids and the Cape Verdean kitchen workers, who spoke to one another in rapid Portuguese. She was always scrambling, always treading water; one little slip, one missed deadline or bout of the flu and she'd fall irrevocably behind. She pinned her hopes on Winter Exhibition at the end of the semester—if she managed to win one of the cash prizes, she'd be able to cut down on her work-study hours in the spring.

When Louisa hung back after class and asked Maureen if she had a minute to talk, Maureen peered at her over her glasses as though surprised that Louisa possessed the power of speech. "That depends," she said. "Is it an honest-to-God sixty-second minute, or a half-hour minute? I have a department meeting at five-thirty."

"Ten minutes?" Louisa's voice came out small and hard, as though there were something lodged in her throat.

Maureen seemed to soften. "Ten minutes I can do, sure, if you don't mind tagging along while I pick up a coffee."

"Thank you, ma'am."

Maureen smiled in amusement. "You don't have to call me ma'am."

As soon as they were outside, Maureen produced a pack of cigarettes from her shirt pocket and tipped it toward Louisa. "Smoke?"

Was she joking? She didn't appear to be, and Louisa didn't smoke, but she accepted anyway, cupping her hands around the cigarette as Maureen sparked it for her, trying not to cough. Maureen led the way across the green. The treetops were aflame; every time Louisa went outside she wanted to paint them. On the main quad, the Occupy Wrynn encampment was a hive of activity. It had been up for nearly three weeks now, but the administration seemed to view it as just another student installation that would eventually fall apart. In the center of the encampment, a boy in a bright yellow hoodie juggled oranges while a girl spoke into a megaphone: "We are angry about the amount of debt we must go into to attend this school and the appalling lack of employment opportunities!"

Louisa felt a twinge of sympathy. She tried not to think too hard about the money she'd borrowed to come here. Maureen gestured at the protesters. "I'm with them," she said, the cigarette dangling from the corner of her lips, bobbing as she spoke. "But if what you wanted was a job, you shouldn't have gone to art school. Anyway . . . what's up?"

"I wanted to talk to you about my work. I want to get better. I mean, obviously that's why we're all here, but I was wondering if you had any more advice, or . . ."

Louisa's last two canvases, landscapes inspired by photos she'd taken back home, had received similar receptions to her ibis painting. During the crits, she'd found herself hyperfixated on Karina, but both times her roommate had remained silent. Louisa hadn't looked in Karina's sketchbook since the evening of her first crit, though she'd wanted to. She'd felt this way about other girls before—brief, confusing infatuations that vacillated between attraction and jealousy, between wanting to touch the girl and wanting to *be* the girl, to slip inside her skin—but never this intensely. She'd never told anyone about these feelings, never acted on them. Her crushes on boys had always felt straightforward in comparison. Easier.

In the doorway of Beanie's Coffee, Maureen tossed her cigarette butt onto the curb. Louisa did the same, feeling guilty for littering. Inside, jazz was playing and there were unappetizing vegan pastries on display. Maureen ordered a latte and jerked her chin at Louisa. "What are you having?"

"Just a tea."

"What kind?" said the barista, a gaunt girl with a pierced lip and a tattoo of a pineapple on her biceps.

"Uh, green. Thank you."

Sullenly, the barista began banging around with the espresso machine.

"Look," said Maureen, handing the cashier her credit card. "I'm going to tell you what I tell everyone: at this stage in your education, at least half of what you make is going to be trash."

"Okay."

"So my advice to you is this: at the end of every year, take half the work you made and destroy it."

"*Destroy* it?"

"Yes. Take a knife to it. Or paint over it. Your work isn't precious. You have to be able to reinvent yourself. It's *hard,* what you're trying to do here. You're chasing something that will constantly evade you. It's like trying to catch water in your fist."

"Okay . . . But is there something *specific* about the work that I should address, or . . . ?"

Maureen looked at her with sympathy. "My dear, kill the Southern Gothic. Stop trying to perfect what you're already good at. You're here to take risks. To fail. Paint something completely different. Spend a month focusing on a single color. Or experiment with a new medium. Or paint rhinoceri, or ham and cheese sandwiches, or, I don't know, vitiligo."

"What's that?"

"A skin condition," Maureen said, accepting her latte from the barista. "Very striking to look at."

"Vitiligo," Louisa repeated, struggling to hide the doubtfulness she knew her expression betrayed.

Maureen blew on her coffee and took a sip. "I'm sorry, I've got to go. Come to my office hours if you want to talk more."

When Maureen was gone, the barista handed Louisa her tea. "I had a class with her," she confided. "Sophomore year. Painting II."

"That's the class I'm in now," said Louisa.

"She's brutally honest."

"Yeah," said Louisa. "I'm learning that."

"One time she went on this rant about how impossible it is to make it as an artist if you're a woman. She said you get passed over in favor of lesser talents, you get groped and harassed, and dealers make comments about your body. She said this one famous artist—she wouldn't tell us who—once asked her her bra size. We all felt pretty dejected by the end of it. The girls in the class, at least."

"Damn," said Louisa. "Are you a painter?"

The barista shrugged. "Yeah."

"Is that your major?

"It was. I graduated in 2007. Enjoy your tea."

Dusk was falling as Louisa stepped back outside, a moody indigo creeping across the sky. She stood under the Beanie's awning and debated what to do. She could go to the dining hall for dinner, but she wasn't really hungry, so that'd be a waste of a meal credit. She could go back to Hope and see what people were up to in the common room, but she didn't trust herself to be convincingly sociable in her current state, especially if drinking was involved. Or she could go to her studio and start a new piece. Maureen had assigned a grayscale painting, which pleased Louisa. She loved gray. It wasn't really a color—it was a vast expanse just beneath the surface of color. If you mixed red and green and a little bit of white, you'd get a neutral gray, because red and green were on opposite ends of the color wheel. But if you bent that geometry just a little and swapped out the green for something yellower, you'd end up with a warm, sandy gray.

When Louisa was eight or nine, Mom had explained color theory to her, placing different paint swatches side by side against a sheet of white printer paper. Louisa would never forget how her perception shifted as her mother cycled through color combinations: a green that appeared green on its own became bluer or yellower or even slightly red when contrasted with the right color. It was like witchcraft. Later, Louisa had made magic with her paints: phthalo blue, the color of a deep, clear lake on a cloudless day, became a fathomless black when mixed with burnt umber. And cadmium orange and cyan made not the brown that she'd expected, but a plush green, like algae in a spring.

If Louisa was quick, she could get to the hardware store downtown—cheaper than the campus supply shop—before it closed. Invigorated, she hurried through campus, schoolbag bouncing against her hip—past the Ceramics building where sculptors emerged all smudged with clay, past the glass-blowing studio that smelled of beeswax and burning newspaper—and down the hill to downtown Stonewater. At the hardware store, she spent twenty dollars on two eight-foot one-by-fours and some quarter-round molding. She went straight to the campus wood shop, where she glued the quarter-rounds to the one-bys. Out of the corner of her eye, she saw one of the furniture majors, a lanky boy in a plaid shirt and oil-stained jeans, staring at her. When she went to use the miter saw, he approached and offered help.

Louisa smiled politely. "I'm all set, thanks."

"You need to go to a training before you can use the power tools."

She began measuring the wood, marking it with a pencil. "Are you the shop monitor?"

"No." The boy had had sawdust in his hair and a cigarette tucked behind his ear. Louisa had overheard Emma Ochoa saying that furniture majors were practically the only straight males on campus. "Architects, too, I guess," she'd added. "And filmmakers."

Louisa lowered the blade to the wood to check her alignment. "I went to the training," she lied.

Pepere had taught her to use his power tools when she was twelve. She loved his wood shop. It smelled dusty and sweet, and it had a big window overlooking the river, sluggish and brown and beaded with light. When Louisa was in high school, he'd given her a key to the shop, presenting it with a gruff nonchalance that belied the significance of the gesture. No one else, not Grandma, nor Mom, who'd lived in the little sand-colored bungalow at the back of the family property since before Louisa was born, nor her uncle Rick, who helped run Pepere's plumbing business and was always around, had a key. The thought of Pepere filled Louisa with warmth and gratitude. He was the one who'd convinced Mom to let her come to Wrynn.

Louisa pulled on safety goggles and switched on the saw; if the boy said anything else, she didn't hear it. When the snarl and rattle ceased, he'd gone. She secured the corners of the stretcher and put it into clamps to dry. While she waited, she wandered around the wood shop, watching the furniture majors at work. The air was warm, full of sawdust and exertion. Furniture makers weren't guarded like painters; they didn't seem to mind being watched. Cutting wood, bending metal—these things made you feel powerful, whereas nothing elicited more vulnerability and anxiety than a blank canvas. In Pepere's wood shop, Louisa was the master of her domain, but at the easel she was a pilgrim.

When the carpenter's glue was dry, she put on her jacket and shouldered her stretcher. Outside, the boy who wasn't the shop monitor sat smoking on a bench. He looked up as Louisa shut the door. "Hey," he said. He'd tucked a fresh cigarette behind his ear, which he removed and offered to Louisa. Once more, she found herself accepting without quite knowing why.

"What've you got there?" the boy said.

"Um, a stretcher? For canvas?"

"You're a painter."

"Yes."

The boy exhaled through his nostrils, narrowing his eyes against the smoke. "I used to be a painter."

No, Louisa thought. She wasn't going to let him ruin her night. "Cool," she said. "Have a good one. Thanks for the cigarette."

She went off. It was good to be outside in the bracing air, under the treetops. She took one last drag off the cigarette and threw the rest away. The nicotine had gone to her head; her fingertips buzzed pleasantly.

I am here.

I am the girl walking across the green alone.

At the Painting building she took the freight elevator to the top floor. As soon as the doors opened she smelled the studios, an acrid mix of oil paints and solvents and mineral spirits. The top floor consisted of a single cavernous loft with angled skylights and two huge balconies overlooking downtown Stonewater. Individual studios, about twice the size of a disabled bathroom stall, were delineated by three-sided plywood partitions. The whole floor was a dense maze of self-contained artist spaces. Some people wrote and drew and painted directly on the whitewashed partitions, or taped up photos or Pantone chips or swatches of fabric or printouts from that weird blog that everyone here followed. Some studios were stuffed full of clothes, books, half-empty jugs of resin and varnish, bits of wood, hotplates, electric kettles. One had a paint-spattered fainting couch with plum-colored cushions. Louisa passed Demir Erdem mixing inks in an egg carton and talking on the phone in Turkish—he raised his hand in greeting, flashing his megawatt smile—and Alejandro Díaz, who was standing very close to his canvas, dabbing at it with a fine-tipped brush. She thought of saying hi. He was wearing headphones, lost in his work. She left him alone.

The walls of Louisa's studio were blank. She liked exuberance and color, but not in her workspace. Too distracting. She dropped her bag on the floor and went to cut a rectangle of canvas, which was stored by the sink in huge seven-foot-tall bolts, like giant paper towel rolls. Back in her studio, she tacked the canvas to the frame, pulling it taut and stapling it to the wood. Then she opened her tub of gesso and got out her old flat brush, which was starting to fray. It would work fine for gessoing, but she'd need to replace it soon. Already she'd spent nearly half of what she'd earned last summer waitressing, and it was only October. At this rate, she'd need to request more hours at the dining hall. Or start putting expenses on that credit card Mom had helped her apply for, the one that was only for emergencies. Whatever happened, Louisa promised herself, she wouldn't ask her family for more money.

She painted her canvas with a light wash of gesso. While she waited for it to dry, she thought of Karina, who bought her canvases prestretched and was always ordering new paints and brushes online, the Utrecht boxes accumulating in teetering stacks in their room. Would

Karina even notice if that new sable-hair brush or a tube of those but-
tery oils went missing?

The gesso dry, Louisa sanded the canvas with a sheet of fine-grit
sandpaper. Then two more layers of gesso, its chalky scent filling her
nose, followed by another pass with the sandpaper till the canvas had a
nice eggshell texture and was drum-tight. This was tedious, time-
consuming work, but it served a purpose. It was a kind of consecration;
it rendered the canvas precious, inviolable. The last thing you wanted to
do was fuck it up.

Louisa set the canvas aside and opened her sketchbook. This was the
moment she'd been dreading.

When she was young, Louisa had discovered that there was a certain
state of mind that could be achieved through making art. The first time
it happened she'd been sprawled on the living room floor, drawing her
mother, who sat reading on the sofa in a puddle of lamplight. *See what's
in front of you,* Mom was always telling her, *not what you think you see or want
to see.* That evening, as Louisa looked up from her sketchbook, there
ceased to be a difference between her eyes and her hands—roving,
roving—and all at once she *saw,* so clearly:

    —the velvety texture of the shadows under her mother's eyes
    —the arc of her foot curled against the sofa
    —the weights and levers of her mother's arm as she turned
        the page, its balances and counterbalances

And that was it. That was all she needed—just those three details—to
breathe light and movement and beating heart into the page. And she
tipped headfirst into the feeling: it was the sensation of teetering on the
precipice of something momentous, of reaching her hand out into the
dark and grazing a strange, exciting shape that had been waiting—just
for her—all her life. She'd felt such joy, such curiosity. She'd felt free.

But now, staring at her sketchbook in the chill emptiness of her studio, Louisa couldn't slip into that feeling. As a warm-up, she drew a bird
from memory—one of those egrets that stalked the lawn back home,
moving like ghosts through the early morning mist.

Just a bird.

She clenched her teeth, erased what she'd just drawn, sweeping the rubbings onto the floor. She was too self-conscious, too eager to prove herself, too full of desire. Maybe that was the problem.

Mom liked listening to Alan Watts recordings while she worked, and Louisa had once overheard a lecture of his about a Zen monastery that tested any would-be monk's resolve by repeatedly turning him away at the door. "There's no room for you here," the temple roshi would say again and again, dissuading all but the most determined. Any man who stuck around waited outside the gates for days or weeks, begging for admittance until finally the roshi deigned to receive him. The novice monk then began his training, the single goal of which was to give up desire, because desire was the root of suffering, its renunciation the door to enlightenment.

Now, recalling this story, Louisa wondered how you could desire to be free of desire. It was as mind-bending as an Escher drawing. It was a problem that fell into itself again and again. How could you make something pure and unself-conscious if there was a preconceived idea in your mind of what would be perceived as pure and unself-conscious? How could you paint something new if you'd never painted it before?

Maureen had talked about taking risks, about destroying your work. Louisa flipped through her drawing pad until she landed on a sketch she'd made several days ago in her figure-drawing class. The model was a middle-aged woman with sharp, nervous features and very short gray hair clinging sleekly to her skull. Louisa had captured her from behind, cross-legged on the dais, her head turned in profile. The Drawing teacher had tacked the sketch up and pointed out the flow and rhythm of the lines, their confidence, how this action line expressed the forward cant of the model's posture, how a subtle increase in line weight captured the heaviness of her arm. Louisa had swelled with pride, even though she knew that the ability to draw accurately from life didn't make you special here.

Push it further. Her pencil hovered over the page. *So what if you ruin it? It's not precious.*

As she hesitated, her thoughts drifted to a photo Mom had emailed earlier that day: a pelican covered in thick black sludge. It had been a year since the BP spill, but they were still finding slicks in the Gulf and tarred, dying animals in the marshes. *Little bird,* Mom wrote, *I cried when I saw this, and I wished you were here.* She'd cried when the spill happened, too, then volunteered for the cleanup, building cages and nets for the wildlife rescuers.

Louisa lowered her pencil and lightly traced the shape of two wings over the woman's back. No, too cheesy. Too much like angel's wings. She took out her phone and pulled up the photo from the email. She tried again, softening her lines, layering them, making the wings ponderous and clumsy like the pelican's. Switching between soft and hard graphite, she blocked in different shades of gray, then pressed the pencil hard for a sleek and unctuous black. She finished by carving out slivers of light with her kneaded eraser.

She set the sketch pad on her easel and examined it from a few steps back. There was something unexpectedly eerie about the image, something dreamlike and disturbing that she hadn't intended. Did she like it? Maybe.

Fatigue was catching up to her. She ought to sleep. She was on a path, maybe the right one—tomorrow, she could keep venturing down it, see what lay around the bend.

She returned to her room expecting to find it dark and warm with sleep, but all the lights were on and Karina was sitting up in bed, staring into her laptop screen.

"Insomnia?" said Louisa. She was glad, but also not glad, that Karina was still awake. She never felt entirely relaxed around her roommate, but there was also something *physically* compelling about Karina— being around her was like eating in a restaurant with a TV above the bar: no matter how tasty the food or engaging the conversation, your eyes kept drifting toward the screen. And Louisa had begun to suspect that this interest was not one-sided. Several times in the past few weeks she'd locked eyes with her roommate; whenever this happened Karina would quickly look away, her expression flattening into blankness. Still, Louisa didn't put too much stock in this: Karina had recently started dating a senior named Preston Utley, a cocky, handsome boy built like a football player whom she often saw hanging around the Occupy Wrynn encampment.

"Some nights," Karina said, "I just can't unscrew my head."

"What are you doing?"

Karina rubbed her eyes. "I've wasted the last two hours of my life on Chatroulette."

"Video-chatting with strangers?"

"One in five is just some guy jerking off," said Karina. "But there are some gems."

"Can I see?"

"Sure."

Louisa dropped her schoolbag on the floor and perched on the edge of her roommate's bed. Karina had supplemented the mattress with a featherbed topper; Louisa felt it slope under her weight as she peered at the screen. The browser showed a simple white window with two boxes. One of them enclosed Karina's face, a slice of Louisa's cheek peeking in on the side of the frame; the other displayed a grainy feed of two college-age girls dancing in a pink-carpeted bedroom.

"They've been at it for two minutes straight," said Karina. She smiled, shaking her head with apparent delight. One of the dancing girls attempted a handstand. Karina laughed. Her face opened, unfurling like a sail. Louisa had never seen her so unguarded.

"Watch this." Karina typed *do the worm!* into the message box and hit enter. After a moment, the two girls dropped to their stomachs and began flopping. The sound was muted, but Louisa could see that both were in hysterics.

"So to chat with someone else you just click next?" Louisa said.

"Yeah." Karina tapped the mousepad, and the dancing girls were replaced with a close-up of an eyeball. *Click.* A man in oversized sunglasses flipping the bird. *Click.* A woman lying motionless on her side. *Click.* A masturbating stranger, webcam pointed at the folds of his crotch. Louisa made a noise of surprise and disgust, but Karina just wrinkled her nose and clicked next again. A teenage boy stared into the camera, expressionless. After a moment, he reached for the keyboard and his box went dark.

Karina closed her laptop. Louisa slid off the mattress and hovered by the bed, touching her fingertips to Karina's nightstand, where there was a jar of Clinique moisturizer, a pot of lip balm, a crushed pack of cigarettes, and their Art History course packet.

"Why do you think it's so addictive?" Louisa said.

Karina did that remote one-shouldered shrug of hers. "I don't know." Her face was closed again.

Bitch. The thought came unbidden. Louisa turned back toward her side of the room, and as she did Karina said, "I didn't know you smoked."

Louisa looked at her in surprise. "I don't."

"You smell like cigarettes." Her tone had softened; it was more curious than accusatory.

"I did smoke a little today, but it's not, like, habitual. People keep offering me cigarettes and for some reason I keep saying yes?"

Karina half smiled. "Well. I was just about to say that I'm going to have one. If you'd like to join."

Louisa hesitated. The other times, she wasn't sure why she'd said yes, but now if she accepted it would be for a reason she was all too aware of.

"Sure, why not."

She thought they'd go outside, but Karina lifted open the window by her bed, scooting over to make room for Louisa. Karina took a lighter and a glass ashtray from her bedside drawer, placing them on the sill. She tapped the cigarette pack against her palm and glanced at the smoke detector. "If we get caught you can blame me. I'll tell them you couldn't resist my siren song."

Snick went the lighter. Louisa inhaled. This time the smoke went down smooth. The tobacco's buzz blunted her fatigue. "Isn't it funny," she said, "how everyone here bends over backward to distinguish themselves, but also everyone smokes?"

Karina let out a low-pitched laugh. "Stereotypes die hard, I guess."

They sat cross-legged on the bed, their knees an inch apart. Both of them faced the window, and when they exhaled at the same time a density of smoke hung before them for a moment before dissipating. The ginkgo in the courtyard had gone saffron. Every time Karina took a drag, a tiny crinkle appeared on the bridge of her nose. Louisa felt the hairs on her arms rise up.

"To answer your question," Karina said, flicking ash off her cigarette.

"My question?"

"Why Chatroulette is so addictive."

"Right."

"I think it's because it represents this promise that there's someone out there who will understand you perfectly."

Louisa pictured an ocean full of lonely people placing their hopes in the engine of randomness.

"Were you in studio just now?" said Karina.

"Yeah. Working on something new."

"How's it going?"

"Okay. I tend to go down rabbit holes with my work. It can be stagnating. But this one's different, I hope."

Karina inclined her head. "I have the opposite problem."

"I think it's because my mom always treated everything I made as incredibly significant. It was like she was using my paintings as windows. Like she was trying to look inside my head." Louisa sucked on her cigarette, smoothing Karina's duvet under her palm. Down the hall, a toilet flushed.

"She didn't want me to come here," Louisa went on, exhaustion and nicotine loosening her tongue. "She thought it was too far away and too much—" She stopped herself. She didn't want to get into the intricacies of her scholarship and loans and FAFSA and Expected Family Contribution, not with Karina. Ash from her cigarette fell onto the duvet. She licked her thumb and rubbed at the fabric, but a gray smear remained.

"Leave it, it's fine," said Karina. Swiveling her long neck, she regarded Louisa intently. "Too much what?"

"Too much . . . risk."

Karina looked confused. "Stonewater's not that dangerous. It used to be, but not anymore."

"Not that kind of risk. For my mom it was more, like, existential."

"Existential."

"Yeah."

Karina smiled. "No, sorry, I was just repeating the way you say that word."

"How do I say it?"

"You replace the second *e* with an *i*. Like, exist*i*ntial."

"I do?"

"Yeah. It's cute. Sorry, you were saying about your mom?"

Cute. "She tried to be an artist and it didn't work out for her, for a lot of reasons."

"Your mom's an artist?"

"Yeah. She teaches high school art. Everyone always says she's really talented, she could've been big, but I've always thought, I don't know . . ."

"What?"

Louisa hesitated. "That she lacks discipline. A certain seriousness. Like, she was the first person in my family to go to college, but she ended up dropping out to have me. She's just sort of a flighty person."

"But you love her," Karina said.

"Of course I love her. She's my mother."

"It's not always a given." Karina put out her cigarette. "I think I'll make an attempt at sleep."

"Yeah, I should, too. Thanks for the smoke."

Louisa brushed her teeth, then sank into bed dizzy from hunger and nicotine and having sat so close to Karina she could see the peach fuzz on her upper lip.

That was the night the bird woman first appeared in Louisa's dreams: she had glossy white wings sprouting from bloodied shoulder blades, and the fierce, elegant head of a scarlet ibis, and when Louisa awoke the next morning she knew she had to paint her.

CHAPTER SEVEN

Robert's Persuasive Art seminar was going surprisingly well. By and large, his students were smart and creative. Joanna Schwartz had designed some interesting pro-choice posters, Tyrone Richard painted a moving elegy to New Orleans's Ninth Ward, and Colin Moretti did some incisive cartoons criticizing the Catholic Church. A few students' attempts were decidedly more muddled: Sammy Nakamura filmed himself consuming an entire stick of butter for some reason, and then there was Preston Utley's incomprehensible vacuum-packed steak, which he followed with a large slab of wild-caught salmon covered in rainbow sprinkles.

On a Tuesday afternoon in mid-October, Robert arrived at Adler 306 for the seminar's weekly meeting to find that all the chairs had been pushed up against the wall. In the middle of the room was a long table draped in a dingy white cloth, laden with several varieties of hummus, a bowl of baby carrots, and a half-used roll of paper towel. Two small black portable speakers stood sentinel on each end of the table.

It *was* Tuesday, wasn't it? Did he have the wrong room?

"Hi, Robert," said a thin voice. He turned to see elfin Leila Fayad standing in the doorway. She'd dyed her short curly hair flamingo pink since he'd last seen her. In her hand was a shrink-wrapped stack of paper plates.

"I hope you don't mind, I got here a little early to set up. Alberta unlocked the room for me."

Right. Leila's thing was today. He hadn't expected her to make such a production out of it. (Food? Really?) She'd asked if she could do an "installation slash performance piece" in lieu of a painting or sculpture or drawing, and he'd said sure, why not.

"I'm going to ask you to wait outside," Leila told Robert. She ripped the shrink wrap off the plates. "If that's all right with you."

Robert went out into the hallway. Leila taped up a sign—*Wait here*—and went back in, the door clicking shut behind her. Robert slouched against the wall, letting his mind go blank as he thumbed his phone. Soon the rest of his students arrived: it was a small class, just thirteen kids, but clustered in the narrow hallway they were as loud as a group three times their size. They mostly ignored Robert and talked among themselves, rehashing their weekends. This didn't bother him. When he was in school, he'd had teachers who were always surrounded by groups of fawning students, who partied with their advisees and told long, meandering stories about their ayahuasca trips. Robert had always thought there was something self-indulgent about these men (they were always men), about their decision to remain in the insular world of academia, basking in the adoration of their young devotees instead of venturing out into the real world, where they might be panned, or worse, ignored.

"... and I was, like, can we *not* ..."

"... should've seen your face ..."

"... finale of *Breaking Bad* ..."

"... only three shots, but I'm a lightweight ..."

On his phone, Preston Utley was showing Nick Nguyen, he of the wooden ear gauges and Marxist psychobabble, an image from his blog. The Boil? The Wart? The Wart. It had been popular for some time now. Robert had looked it up once, out of curiosity, but he'd failed to see the appeal.

Several times now, Robert had seen Preston at the student-run Occupy Wrynn encampment on the main quad and experienced a strange, discomfiting mixture of resentment and grudging admiration. Robert looked back down at his phone and refreshed his inbox. Still waiting on an email from that Occupy Wall Street organizer.

The classroom door swung open, and Leila's shaggy pink head poked out. "What's up, guys? You can come in now."

Everyone filed into the room. Leila gestured at the snacks. "Help yourselves."

Sammy Nakamura dipped a carrot into a tub of red pepper hummus. The sound of screaming children erupted from the speakers.

"The fuck?" Sammy yanked his hand away. The noise stopped. Tentatively, he touched the carrot to the dip again; more screaming. A grin of understanding spread slowly across his face.

Leila smiled thinly. "Go ahead and eat."

Joanna Schwartz swirled a chip through the sun-dried tomato hummus, jumping as she set off the *rat-a-tat* of machine guns.

Leila glanced at Robert, pointing her chin at the table. "Go ahead, Robert, please enjoy."

He took a chip and ate it dry, then sat down and began taking notes. Giggling, the kids swarmed the table, sampling all the flavors. Caramelized onion triggered the blast of exploding shells. Roasted garlic was ululating women; olive tapenade, wailing sirens. With everyone eating at once, it sounded like a war zone. Only Katie Rasmussen, a dour, round-faced girl who said little in class, hung back. She sat near Robert and determinedly examined her fingernails.

After about ten minutes, Robert told the students to drag their chairs into a circle for crit. "Leila, before we begin our discussion, is there anything you'd like to share with the class about your performance?"

Leila pressed her lips together and shoved them out. "I guess I thought it would be self-explanatory, but the fact that it's not kind of proves my point."

Robert made his face smooth and placid. "Uh-huh. Could you say more?" He hadn't the faintest idea what her performance had been about, but he wasn't about to let on.

Leila jiggled her foot. "So, Sabra Hummus is co-owned by PepsiCo and the Strauss Group, which is an Israeli company that provides food to the Golani Brigade, which is a division of the Israel Defense Forces with a documented history of human rights abuses. There's actually a group of us that's been lobbying the administration to stop stocking Sabra products in the snack carts. Dining Services has been uncooperative, but I won't get into it. Anyway, I wanted to do a piece that forces participants to confront their complicity in the suffering of the Palestinian people through something as seemingly innocuous as their snack food." She paused and looked around. "Judging by the laughter, I'm not sure I succeeded."

A guilty silence. "Okay," Robert said, "so maybe one takeaway is that your intentions didn't align with the audience's reaction. Which, remember, isn't always something you can control, but maybe something you can weave into future iterations with an addition as simple as, say, a prefatory artist statement. We can talk about possibilities for that when we get to the fourth part of the crit."

Preston said, "I'm curious about the mechanics of the performance, like how you rigged the whole thing up."

His question seemed to appease Leila. "Right, so I cut a little hole in the bottom of each hummus container and threaded a wire into it. And then I ran the wires under the tablecloth and connected them to the speakers. Hummus is actually a conductive substance, so."

"Okay," said Robert. "Why don't we start by going around and just describing the performance. In just purely objective terms to start. Remember Step One. Statements of meaning."

"It was like the food table at a gallery opening," said Sammy Nakamura, "except there was no art."

"Leila kept telling us to eat, but she didn't eat any of it herself," said Joanna. "I see why now. But it still felt like a trap."

"I was actually super impressed," said Preston. "It's refreshing to see someone swinging for the fences in this class. Although if I could offer one critique, I think the piece would've been more powerful if you'd used real video footage of what's been happening on the West Bank. I have a few suggestions—"

"Preston," interrupted Robert, trying not to let his irritation show (he'd gone over his preferred crit structure so many times! Suggestions for improvement was Step Four—it was *on* the fucking syllabus). "Why don't we—"

"Oh, sorry, Robert, I'll be quick," said Preston. He turned back to Leila. "I noticed you didn't have anyone filming. You might want to think about that for next time. You might even consider livestreaming."

"I'd liked to steer this conversation back to our critical response," said Robert testily. "We're still on Step One. What was interesting and evocative about this piece? What was striking in the work Leila's shared with us?"

Katie Rasmussen's chin wobbled, and she began to cry. Robert felt himself stiffen with the urge to flee. It wasn't uncommon for students to become emotional in crit, but he had this reaction anytime he was in the presence of female tears; at this point, it was probably Pavlovian. All his life, when a woman cried it was usually because of something he'd said or done—beginning with his mother, then on to his college girl-friend and ex-wife Diane and even easygoing Fiona Piontek, whom he gladly would've married if only she'd been willing to even entertain the possibility of leaving her psychopath of a husband. With the tears came the expectation that he be the soother, the comforter, the make-it-all-better-er.

Some of the students made sympathetic noises at Katie; others averted their eyes.

"I'm sorry you found the piece upsetting," said Robert. He reached out and awkwardly patted her shoulder. "Do you need to step out and get a drink of water?"

Katie shook her head and accepted a tissue from Colin Moretti.

"I think this speaks to the power of your performance," Robert said to Leila.

"Why wasn't there a trigger warning?" Katie's voice was tiny.

"Because," said Leila, "then it would've given away the surprise."

"You know," said Nick, "studies have shown that trigger warnings ac-tually *increase* people's self-reported anxiety."

This made Katie's eyes well over with fresh tears, and Robert felt a bone-deep wish to disappear.

"Can I say why I object to a trigger warning in this instance?" said Leila.

"Go ahead," said Robert wearily.

"My feeling is that Palestinians don't get to opt out of the occupation of their homeland, so why should anyone else?"

"Uh-huh," said Robert. Shaky logic there, but okay. "I'd be interested to hear you all situate this discussion in the context of the history of political art, where audience discomfort is often not just a by-product but the aim of the work."

Robert noticed, then, that Preston was behaving strangely. He had his phone out, but he wasn't cradling it surreptitiously in his lap the way Sammy had been for the past half hour. Instead, he was holding it against his knee, perched at a ninety-degree angle. Was he *filming* this?

Panic rose in Robert's throat. He had to nip this in the bud. He raked his fingers through his hair, clearing his throat. "Put your phones away. Everyone. Right now. If you were filming this, you need to delete it."

Preston tapped his screen twice before sliding it into his pocket. "Okay," Robert said, taking Katie gently by the elbow. "Why don't we step outside for a minute." He ushered her out into the hallway, where she appeared to calm down a little.

"You seem really distraught," said Robert. "Is there anything I can do?"

Katie shook her head. She leaned against the wall and took a long, shuddering breath.

"It's just that—" Katie bit her lip. "My brother. He's in the army. He's in Iraq right now and, I just, I just—" She dissolved into fresh tears.

"That—that sounds really difficult. I'm sorry. I see now why Leila's piece upset you."

Katie wiped her nose on her sleeve.

"Why don't you, ah, take the rest of the day off?" Robert saw Alberta coming down the hall, holding a sheaf of paper. "Alberta?" he said. "Will you come here for a second?"

"Oh, sweetie," Alberta said when she caught sight of Katie's tear-streaked face. "What's wrong?"

"Could you take Katie here up to the break room and make her some tea? And make sure she gets back to her dorm okay? I need to get back in there." He jerked his thumb at the classroom door.

Alberta put her arm around Katie. "Of course."

As the two women began walking away, Robert blurted something he'd never said before in his life: "Tell your brother thank you for his service."

He slipped back into the classroom, where the kids were still discussing Leila's piece.

"My question," said Joanna Schwartz, "is do you think Israel has a right to exist?"

"Do *I* think Israel has a right to exist?" said Leila.

"Yes, obviously you."

"I think that's a meaningless question, to be honest."

"Okay!" Robert interrupted. "I think it's time for our break."

By the time he returned to his musty apartment two hours later, Robert felt wretched, completely exhausted. He should check in with Alberta and email the dean of students about Katie. Something something student mental health. But first, a drink.

He sat on the couch nursing a Scotch and trying to pinpoint when his students had become such a mystery to him. In some ways they were older than he'd been at their age, but in other ways they seemed so fragile. So frightened, anxious, and intemperate. They masked it with irony and self-righteousness. Maybe he shouldn't be so hard on them. What did they have to look forward to but mountains of student debt, a nine percent unemployment rate, a planet on the verge of environmental collapse, and an art market that would ignore the vast majority of them while lavishing millions of dollars on a favored, seemingly randomly selected few?

He checked his email again. And there it was, finally:

From: garrett.wynter.platz@gmail.com
  To: rberger@wrynn.edu
  Subject: Possible OWS collaboration

Hi Robert,
  Glad to hear you're still interested in Occupy! Personally, I'd like us
to be an aesthetically conscious movement, following the legacy of,

for example, Emory Douglas's work as the minister of culture for the
Black Panthers, as well as your and the art collective Gran Fury's
graphic activism during the AIDS crisis. The right-wing media has
made us out to be gutter punks and homeless grifters. I'd like to show
the world that we're not just hippies sleeping in the park. Many of us
here admire the work you did in the 80s and 90s, and we're hoping
you can bring some of that same sensibility to bear on OWS. A great
first step would be for you to come camp out at the park and see the
movement for yourself.

Evidently, Garrett was unaware that Gran Fury had taken issue with
Dying Man, condemning Robert's depiction of Vince Russo as a victim.
That aside, the email seemed promising, but the bit about camping out
in the park made Robert uneasy. Still, out came the credit card. He
bought round-trip Amtrak tickets to New York for the Friday after next.
And then, because his shrink had been talking a lot about *self-care* recently, he also booked a room at the Wall Street Holiday Inn, because if
clean sheets and indoor plumbing weren't self-care, he didn't know
what was. His spirits considerably lifted, he poured another Scotch.
There was something else, though, at the back of his mind, nagging
him.

Ah. Right. Preston Utley.

Robert booted up his computer again and pulled up The Wart. It was
as he'd feared. Preston had filmed that day's disastrous discussion and
posted it on his blog, titling the video *Snowflakes/Old Dog, 2011.* Robert
steeled himself before clicking play. The footage was a bit shaky, and
Preston had done something to everyone's voices. They were squeaky
and high-pitched, like cartoon chipmunks. Poor Katie Rasmussen
looked like she'd been pulled, midbreakdown, off some trashy reality
TV show. With shame and rage blooming in his chest, Robert watched
himself: his expression of punch-drunk stupefaction; his mouth hanging open as if he'd been doped up or shot with a stun gun. Only toward
the end did he compose himself. Robert could see his jaw clamping
shut, his gaze snapping into focus. The lighting was bad. He looked sal-
low, a sheen of sweat on his forehead. When the video ended, Robert
scrolled down the page and read the first few comments:

lulz
the chick w/pink hair is hot 19⁄10 wld bone
XD
hahaha
love how the old dog's eyes bug out

Robert thought of what Dr. Sullivan would say, which was that he was feeding his self-destructive tendencies. He closed the browser and poured himself another Scotch, then another. He was solidly drunk by the time he pulled up a Word document and started to type. He'd always found that inebriation made him more eloquent, both in speech and in writing—he often said or wrote things while drunk that shocked him later. He wrote until he had four single-spaced pages, then sent the document off to his old friend Dean Blanchard, a critic and editor who'd recently landed a job at *Artforum*. Over the years, Dean had been a reliable source of side income, occasionally commissioning Robert to write short reviews and columns.

Robert slept for fourteen hours that night, waking around noon to a churning in his gut and a hangover of soul-crushing magnitude. Seized with regret, he rushed at once to his computer.

To: dblanchard@artforum.net
  From: rberger@wrynn.edu
  Subject: Never mind

Hey Dean—
  Please disregard my last email. I'd like to withdraw the essay. I wrote it impulsively, Fit of rage, you know how it is. My best to Linda and the kids.

Two hours later:

From: dblanchard@artforum.net
  To: rberger@wrynn.edu
  Subject: RE: Never mind

Are you kidding? We love it. Please reconsider??

Robert let the email sit unanswered for a few hours, weighing the trouble the essay might cause versus the instant clout a byline in *Artforum* would afford him, not to mention the sincere pleasure of speaking his mind. He pictured himself as a boy catching a bully off-guard and finally, after weeks of scheming, pantsing him in front of the whole school. At last he wrote back:

OK. I'll have a revised version back to you by next week.

He should probably tone it down, shouldn't he?

CHAPTER EIGHT

The first few weeks of the semester had passed slowly for Karina: solitary lunches on the green, long days in studio, the snide, averted gazes of her classmates, evenings in Preston's bed, walks with her flask and a cigarette. She was so lonely sometimes she thought it might turn her feral, the way it had last semester. But if her work was suffering, nobody seemed to be able to tell. Her teachers offered pointed praise; her peers' crits were tinged with barely concealed jealousy. *You are brilliant,* she reminded herself. *You shouldn't expect to be happy, too.*

But then one night in early October Karina had opened up to Louisa—cigarettes and Chatroulette, who would've thought?—and she'd felt deliriously happy. The sensation was so unfamiliar that it almost felt like fear. It felt like losing control.

The following night, Karina waited up for Louisa again, offered her another cigarette. Louisa accepted. They sat by the window and talked about their classes and about the hideous new carpeting in the common room, and it was almost as though they were normal roommates. Friends, even. Two nights later, they did it again. And again three nights after that. Louisa showed Karina photos of her family dressed in fringed, patchworked costumes for Cajun Mardi Gras, and told her about her cat, Napoleon, and the teacher she'd once had who called his students *learned dogs* when they displeased him. ("I think I'd like him," Karina said, laughing, and Louisa smiled cryptically and replied, "You would.") Karina told Louisa about her parents' parties, how she used to sneak downstairs to steal joint roaches and cigarette butts from the ashtrays, then smoke them out her bathroom window. ("So *that's* how you became such a tobacco fiend," Louisa said. "Did your parents ever catch you?" She seemed surprised when Karina said no.) Their conversations had none of the dynamism of her conversations with Preston, none of their verve and zing, but with Louisa, Karina never felt like she was performing.

"Can I ask you a question?" Karina said one night.

"Sure."

"You seem really connected to where you're from."

Louisa laughed. "That's not a question." They were sitting on Karina's bed again, and Louisa reached across Karina's lap for the pack of Dunhills. She'd stopped asking if she could bum cigarettes; now she helped herself with a kind of familiarity that made Karina giddy.

"I just mean, like, your work," said Karina. "It's always imagery from where you're from."

"I've been trying for a different direction lately." Louisa spoke lightly, but there was a defensive edge to her voice. She lit her cigarette, then tossed the lighter at Karina's nightstand. It missed and fell to the floor.

"But do you consider yourself a regional artist?" said Karina.

Louisa shrugged. "Yeah. I guess so, yeah."

"So why are you here, then? You're a Southern painter—why did you come to an art school in New England?"

Louisa seemed amused. "Well, I mean, it's prestigious."

Karina scooted over slightly, and their knees touched. "You don't really seem like someone who cares about prestige."

Louisa snorted. "Anyone who says they don't care about prestige is either lying or kidding themselves."

"No, I just mean—you seem like someone who puts a lot of value in the silence and solitude of creating alone."

Louisa shifted; now their knees were pressed firmly together, Louisa's stubbly like sandpaper, and Karina felt a great wave of happiness rise up inside her.

"I thought I needed to get away from home in order to see it clearly," Louisa said. "You know J.M.W. Turner?"

"Yeah," said Karina. "All those sky and ocean paintings. Romantic era, right?"

"Right. But he didn't live in any of the places he painted. He was a Londoner his whole life. I just think . . . he must've been starved for sky, living in a city, you know? And then occasionally he'd travel to the seaside and make these amazing paintings of the clouds and the water."

"So you're starving yourself of home so you can paint it better?"

Louisa smiled. "When you put it that way it sounds a little crazy."

The next morning, when Karina opened her eyes and looked up at the horseshoe-shaped crack in the ceiling, it took her a moment to remember who she was, and where, and why she was here. She'd experienced these dissociative spells since childhood, but lately they were becoming more and more frequent. In a way they felt strangely liberating, even though they made her doubt her cohesion as a human being.

She sat up. She'd drenched the sheets in sweat last night, a side effect of her new meds. Since her breakdown last spring she'd been on several different combinations of mood stabilizers and SSRIs. The most recent cocktail appeared to be working, night sweats aside. Her panic attacks came less often. She could think again, breathe again, despite the loneliness. The psychiatrist she'd seen over the summer had expressed concern over her "lack of emotional support network at school." He'd said, "For some people, it can be really helpful to involve friends in watching for warning signs of an episode."

The dorm room stank of cigarettes, and Karina thought of how Louisa had looked last night, hazed in smoke and exhaustion and something else she couldn't put her finger on. She made a quick sketch of Louisa's face, as she had nearly every morning since the day she'd met her. Her drawing hand knew the shape of Louisa's jaw, the slope of her nose. A muscle memory. When Karina flipped back through her sketchbook she could see the ways Louisa's face had changed over time. In recent drawings her resemblance to Wally became more pronounced, and it occurred to Karina that when she'd left home she'd replaced the Wally on her wall with a living, breathing girl who slept three feet away from her.

She climbed out of bed and opened a window to air out the room. She got dressed and smoked her first cigarette of the day on her way to her Art History section. All over the green and gold campus, everyone else was walking to their first class, having their first cigarette of the day. In the Occupy Wrynn encampment, two students were arguing with a campus security guard over the smoldering remains of a campfire that the guard, who was holding an empty water bottle, appeared to have just put out. Preston—who'd mentioned with some displeasure that he was supposed to take a turn sleeping in the encampment this week—was nowhere in sight.

In Art History, Karina sat in the back of the classroom, behind a boy with oily hair and Foxtail, who ignored her. The TA talked about the Pre-Raphaelites, the projector whirring as he changed the slide from *Proserpine* to *Ophelia* to *The Death of King Arthur*. Dust motes spun in the gloom.

After Art History was lunch—turkey sandwich, black coffee, her second cigarette—and then Painting.

Louisa was already there when Karina arrived, hanging up her gray-scale painting. It depicted a woman with a long face and thin, wispy hair that Karina recognized as the figure-drawing model from a couple of weeks ago. But in translating it to canvas, Louisa had elevated her drawing's quiet mundanity into a kind of monstrous beauty. The woman in her painting had enormous, misshapen wings dripping with something unctuous and black, and the expression on her face was hungry and fierce.

"Wow," Karina said.

Louisa turned and looked at her. "Yeah, it's different for sure," she said, with the same defensiveness as last night.

"No, no, I like it."

Louisa half smiled. She looked surprised. "You do?"

"Yeah, it's . . . chimerical."

At this, Louisa blushed, and a wave of want passed through Karina.

"That means a lot, coming from you," Louisa said quietly, almost as if to herself. "Where's yours?"

"Over there." Karina pointed. "I came in yesterday and hung it."

Maureen walked in then with her manila folder. "Good afternoon, everyone, let's get started."

They went in reverse alphabetical order this time, which meant that Karina was second. Her painting was a vast sort of grid. Close up it looked like a pixelated cloud, but from afar it transformed into something reminiscent of a water-stained map. Her classmates called it *dizzying* and *prismatic*, but in their tone and affect there was unmistakable hostility.

Karina zoned out for the rest of the class, snapping to attention only when Maureen said, "Arceneaux, Louisa, take us out."

The class's response to her painting was largely positive.

"It's *surreal*," said Jack Culicchia. "I mean that in the best possible way."

"The image is so layered," said Alejandro Díaz. "Like, formally but also conceptually. There are so many different ways of reading it."

Maureen called the painting haunting. "I like this direction," she told Louisa. "Keep pushing."

Karina cleared her throat. "It's like a mythological creature that Louisa invented." She paused. "I love it."

She felt the eyes of the entire class on her and realized dimly that this was the first time she'd publicly praised someone's work. For the past year she'd opened her mouth in crit only to find fault.

"Any last comments?" said Maureen. Nobody said anything. "Okay then, see you all next week."

As the students gathered their belongings, Karina tried to catch Louisa's eye, but she was deep in conversation with Alejandro Díaz. Karina had noticed the two of them hanging out recently, and though she'd never had any feelings about Alejandro one way or the other, she found herself suddenly wishing he'd disappear. But he didn't: he took Louisa's arm and walked out of the classroom with her. Karina followed them out of the building, then stood on the steps and watched them cross the quad and disappear around the corner.

She lit a cigarette and headed toward Preston's apartment. On the walk over, she reminded herself why she liked him: he was fun. Fun to fuck and fun to be around. She'd never met anyone quite like him. It was endlessly entertaining to watch him thumb his nose at everything and everyone. To watch him create chaos and then walk away without a backward glance. Preston Utley was someone who'd go out into the world and attract not only attention but powerful people. Not the kind of power her parents had—Karina could access that anytime she wanted—but the kind of power that wasn't tied to money or status or who you knew but to that ineffable *something* that made people want to pay attention to you. She'd known other boys with that kind of swagger and bluster, but what made Preston different was his raffishness, his unconcern with traditional power structures. He didn't want to run a hedge fund or become president or win a Pulitzer. He didn't even pretend to want those things. And if he was a hypocrite, a wannabe-Marxist with a dad who paid his rent? There were worse things.

Most of all, she liked the way Preston adored her. Because even though she found him intelligent and attractive, she didn't adore him. And that, she knew, was the most important thing: to care less than the other person did.

CHAPTER NINE

The end of October was normally a bad time for Preston. He spent the week or so before his mother's memorial mass in a deep funk. Today, however, Preston was in decent spirits, even though he'd just spent a near-sleepless night in a borrowed sleeping bag at the Occupy Wrynn encampment and was scheduled to fly to Arlington the next morning. There were two reasons for this: (1) Preston's childhood friend Slade Carney would be in town during his visit, and (2) Karina had agreed to spend the night again.

Since it was a Thursday evening, they both had work to do. Karina was sprawled on the couch studying for an Art History test while Preston sat at his kitchen table typing up a paper for his Post-Conceptual Art class. He was poking around on *Artforum*, looking for articles to cite, when his gaze caught a link in the sidebar: "When Business Masquerades as Art" by Robert Berger. Preston clicked on it:

A new generation of artists, rightfully jaded by the corporatization of the art world, has turned to the Internet as an inexpensive, efficient means of distributing work and reaching a wider audience. The web is full of talented and innovative Internet artists, none of whom are the subject of this essay. In recent months, I've become interested in the proliferation of blogs that function as meme factories for pseudo art, websites like K-Hole, The Jogging, and The Wart.

These blogs churn out daily content with the obvious (though never explicitly stated) goal of making their images go viral. They are uniformly anti-establishment—The Wart presents itself as explicitly anti-capitalist—but for all their posturing, they function chiefly as ambassadors for their creators' personal brands. What at first blush looks like art—or at least like an aesthetic—is in reality closer to an elaborate marketing campaign. What appears to be a critique of capitalism is actually a capitalist ploy.

It went on. Without ever naming Preston outright, Berger accused him of hypocrisy and careerism. He claimed that Preston and artists like him weren't anarchist renegades—they were conformists. *To the average web surfer, The Wart and other blogs like it may seem fresh and cool,* Berger wrote, *but that's only because they are corporate strategy cleverly masquerading as art—and no one has caught on yet.*

A muffled buzzing filled Preston's ears. He got a beer from the fridge, slamming the door shut. Karina looked up from her laptop. "What?" she said.

"Nothing."

Her brow furrowed, though the look she wore wasn't exactly of concern. "Preston."

"What."

"You're clearly upset about something."

He took a breath. "One of my professors just published a takedown of my blog." In a smaller voice he added, "There's gotta be some school rule against that, right?"

Karina set aside her sketchbook. "I don't know." She came and looked over his shoulder. "Wait, Robert Berger?"

Preston curled his fingers against the table. "Fucking hack."

"He's the one who wrote this?"

"Do I take this to the dean or something?"

Karina put a hand on the back of his neck. "You could write your own piece. A rebuttal. Or something about his retrospective at the museum here. I saw it; it's pretty flawed."

Preston rubbed his eyes till he saw starbursts. "Yeah. Maybe. I could post it on The Wart. Or maybe the school newspaper would publish it."

"You don't think you should aim a little higher than the *Daily Herald*?"

"Like where?"

Karina fixed him with one of her level looks. "Preston, if you write a rebuttal and email it to *Artforum*, as long as it's cogent and well-argued, they'll publish it."

"Why? Our audiences aren't exactly the same demographic."

She sighed patiently and ran a hand through his hair. "Because it's juicy. Everyone loves drama. Even *Artforum*."

He considered this. "Yeah. Maybe I will."

She went back to her studying, but Preston couldn't focus and soon gave up on his paper in favor of mindless web scrolling. When he tired of that, he rolled a joint with some Purple Kush he'd ordered off Blind Tiger, and they smoked it together on the couch. Later they had sex and went to bed, but in spite of his exhaustion, Preston couldn't sleep. He'd thought Karina's presence would soothe him, but she tossed and turned and sweated so profusely that eventually he went to sleep on the couch. When he woke up the next morning, she was gone. He waited for a text from her, but by the time the flight attendant was instructing passengers to turn off their electronic devices, he still hadn't heard from her.

Preston arrived in Arlington in the late afternoon, but having lied and told his father that his flight didn't get in till the evening, he killed a few hours in the airport lounge, drinking Jamba Juice smoothies and browsing the Internet on his phone. He finally took a cab home around eight and found his father waiting in the big wingback chair, watching Fox News. He didn't smile when Preston greeted him, but then again he rarely did. His father's public persona was charismatic and gregarious; in private, however, he ruled his family with grim coldness. Preston's mother had been the same: lively and charming in public, reserved and wary at home. "She wasn't that way before, you know," Andrew had once told Preston. "After she married your dad, she became a different person. God forbid she give us any affection that could've gone to him."

"Good to see you," said his father. Preston was struck anew by his agelessness. He had a ruddy complexion, but his face was unlined. His eyes were deep-set and flinty, his sandy hair thick and full. Had Preston not known better, he might've suspected him of indulging in Rogaine and Botox. Or maybe the Pentagon fed its generals some kind of ultra-classified elixir of life. Or maybe it was just genetics, in which case the future boded well for Preston. In his latest Facebook photos, Andrew was starting to look a little paunchy, a little saggy in the jowls.

"Good to see you, too," Preston lied. He glanced around the living room. It all looked the same. There were framed pictures of his mother everywhere, including one of her on her wedding day, standing between Preston's father and a nine-year-old Andrew. The sight of it made his throat close up. His father's performative mourning had always struck Preston as the obscenest part of Evelyn's death: his insistence on the annual memorial mass, his long yet oddly cold social media posts full of old photos and randomly capitalized words. As though he were a normal widower. As though he hadn't driven his wife to suicide.

"How are you?" said his father.

"All right. Pretty tired."

"Of course. You should go to bed." He waved Preston upstairs. "Catalina made up your room for you."

It wasn't really his room anymore; all the stuff on the walls was gone and everything had been painted the color of hummus. Preston closed the door and tossed his suitcase on the bed. He was hungry, but to go downstairs and raid the fridge was to invite another conversation with his father. He lay on the bed with his shoes on. After some time, he heard his father switch off the TV and come upstairs. Preston waited until the master bedroom's door clicked shut before texting Slade.

I'm here. Save meeeee.

Slade had dropped out of MIT last year and moved to New York after selling his micro-investing startup, but he still came back to Arlington regularly to see his parents and sister.

Preston's phone vibrated: *be there in 30*

Slade picked him up not in his mom's minivan but a silver Porsche.

"Holy shit," said Preston, sliding into the passenger seat. "Spoils of the tech boom?"

Slade had been a genius at making money long before he sold his startup. In high school, he'd earned a tidy income hacking into St. Martin's computer system to alter the grades of anyone willing to pay. He'd collected his fee in the form of drugs, cash, or—during the holiday season—gift cards.

"Spoils of Bitcoin, actually." Slade revved the engine—a little showily, Preston thought—and pulled away from the curb. He'd grown a goatee since Preston had last seen him, and he was way more jacked, his biceps straining at the fabric of his hoodie.

"You're into crypto now?"

"Of course," said Slade, as though it were the most obvious thing in the world. "A year ago one Bitcoin was trading for fifty cents. Now it's ten dollars."

"Seriously?"

"Yeah. You should get in on it."

"That's nuts," said Preston. "I've only been using it to buy shit off the dark web." He felt, as he sometimes did around Slade, slightly stupid.

Slade turned onto George Mason Drive and headed north, past the hospital.

"Wait, we're not going to the golf course?" said Preston. When they were both in town at the same time, they usually went to the Army Navy golf course to get high.

Slade shook his head. "Blythe's on some student government retreat and my parents are in L.A. visiting my grandma. I'm picking them up at the airport tomorrow after your mom's thing."

Preston looked at him. "You're coming to the mass?"

Without taking his eyes off the road, Slade replied, "Yeah, man."

Preston thought then about how often his jealousy of Slade—the Carneys were the kind of family that took ironic Christmas photos together and joked about diarrhea at the dinner table—was mingled with gratitude.

Slade's bedroom looked just like it always had—same *Sopranos* poster curling at the corners, same blue bedspread—with the exception of the desk piled with thousands of dollars' worth of brand-new electronic equipment.

"Got myself an early birthday present," said Slade, noticing Preston's glance.

They raided Mr. Carney's liquor cabinet, and Slade packed a fat bowl, and soon Preston felt himself relaxing into the shag carpet.

"So how are you?" said Slade, passing him the pipe.

Preston took a hit. "Doing okay."

"And school?"

"It's okay."

"I see the blog is going strong still."

Preston shrugged. "Yeah, chugging along."

Slade looked at the ceiling and made a noise halfway between a laugh and a cough.

"What?" said Preston.

"Nothing. I mean, you're just kind of a sad panda."

Robert Berger's face flashed in Preston's mind, and he felt his hackles rise. He hunched over, worrying at a hole in his sock.

"Are you depressed? Is that it? It's fine if you are, you can tell me."

"I'm not depressed." He didn't know how to explain that in his head, everything felt connected—The Wart and Robert and Karina and Occupy Wrynn (the encampment, as Preston had predicted, had accomplished nothing so far) and his whole fucking future. He hesitated. There was an idea he'd been mulling over for some time, but he knew that as soon as he said it out loud he'd feel like the biggest hypocrite in the world.

"Hey, Slade?"

"Yeah?"

"Do you think there'd be a way to monetize my blog?" He needed to find a way to free himself from his father's money. And if he could take The Wart to the next level, then maybe his career would take off, and Karina would respect him, and he wouldn't have to worry about finding a job six months from now, and—

He was aware, even as he was having these thoughts, that he was contemplating doing exactly what Berger had accused him of in *Art-*

forum. Corporate strategy masquerading as art. The irony didn't escape him, but for now he resolved to just deal with the cognitive dissonance.

"Oh sure, lots of ways," said Slade. Preston's question seemed to perk him up. In his own weird way, Slade liked helping people. In high school, he'd always refused Preston's money. *This one's on me,* all gruff and big-brotherly. And then he'd hop on his computer and pound away at the keyboard and—ta da!—magic Preston's Spanish grade from a C to a B+. When Preston was younger, there'd been a part of him that doubted Slade's motives, an ugly vein of thought: that Slade was just being charitable to the poor kid whose mom had died so shockingly and suddenly. But now Preston understood that it wasn't altruism that drove Slade but a kind of Mafia-like pragmatism: he considered it useful for his friends to feel indebted to him.

"The easiest thing would be selling ad space." Slade swigged Bacardi straight from the bottle.

Preston shook his head. "Not on board with that."

"There's also affiliate links and sponsorships. More discreet, if that's what you're worried about."

Preston made a face. "That could end up undermining The Wart's vibe, you know? I feel like the money needs to come directly from the users themselves."

Slade tapped the ash out of the bowl and repacked it. "I'm thinking something along the lines of the Kickstarter model, then."

"Like having users contribute money toward a specific project?" Preston could find a way to be okay with that.

"Exactly," said Slade. He held the lighter to the pipe and took a puff. "But if I were you, I'd start off by trying to get The Wart on the map in some huge way, you know what I mean? How many daily users would you say you get right now?"

"On a good day? It fluctuates, but maybe a thousand?"

Slade passed him the pipe. "Not bad, but honestly I think you should be aiming for higher user engagement before you try to monetize. Like, think of what your fundraising potential would be if you had, say, a hundred thousand unique visitors per day. Aim for virality, you know."

"Yeah," said Preston, "that makes sense."

They fell silent. A car came down the street, headlights slicing through the curtains.

"What would you think," said Slade, turning to Preston with a grin, "about you and me playing some pranks right now? I've been feeling really pranky."

"I thought we outgrew that phase."

When they were in sixth grade, they used to go over to Preston's after school and make prank calls. Once, they called the Starbucks on Clarendon and ordered forty venti mocha Frappuccinos with extra whipped cream; another time they found their gym teacher's number in the school directory and, in high-pitched voices, let him know that the black lace bra and matching thong he'd ordered from Victoria's Secret was going to be late on account of the Christmas rush. The game came to an abrupt halt when Preston's father discovered an angry voicemail from a local Air Force recruitment office (Preston and Slade had called to say, "Hello, would you like to help us reestablish Communism?") and thrashed Preston with his belt while Evelyn sat on the staircase shielding her eyes and crying mutely. Andrew had been off at college by then, and when Preston told him what happened, he'd sighed and said, "What did you expect?"

"I'm of the firm belief that you never really outgrow pranks," Slade said.

"What did you have in mind?"

"We could hack someone's Facebook. There's this guy at my CrossFit who's a total asshole. We could fill his profile up with nudes. Or pictures of Teletubbies. Remember Teletubbies? My sister used to be obsessed with them."

"Mmmm." Preston checked his phone. It was nearing midnight and he was getting sleepy. He should wake up early tomorrow, get a long run in before his mom's mass. Physical exhaustion tended to blunt him emotionally. It was only after Evelyn's death that he'd become a serious athlete.

A smile touched Slade's lips. "Or what if we did prank emails? Dude! I could email all the D.C. mayor's staff being like, 'Hi everyone, we'll be filming our holiday video early this year, so on Monday please wear red and green and any holiday apparel you own. Santa Claus outfits encour-aged!'"

Preston curled into the fetal position and nestled into the shag rug. "They'd know it was fake right away."

"Not if it came from the chief of staff's email."

Preston squinted up at Slade. "You can do that?"

"I can try. Or what if . . ."

Preston tuned him out, thinking about tomorrow, knowing he should call a cab but finding the prospect of getting up and putting on his shoes semi-insurmountable. He closed his eyes. When he opened them again it was daylight and his head was throbbing. He sat up. Slade was in bed, snoring softly. The Bacardi bottle lay empty on its side. Preston's phone vibrated.

Where are you?

It was a little past eleven A.M.

"Hey, Slade?"

Nothing. Preston got up and nudged him. "Dude, let's go. My mom's thing's in less than an hour."

Slade groaned, rolling over onto his stomach.

"Fuck you," Preston muttered. He called a cab, gave the driver the last of his cash, and was home by 11:40.

As soon as he walked through the door, his father was on him.

"Where the hell have you been?"

"Sorry. I went over to Slade's last night after you went to bed. I guess I fell asleep." He could hear Catalina in the kitchen.

His father stood in the entrance hall with his arms crossed, blocking Preston's way. "You're hungover."

"I'm just tired, sir."

Preston could see the struggle taking place inside him.

"We need to leave in five minutes. Go get dressed."

He went upstairs, feeling strangely grateful for his father's willing-ness to let this one go. That was what men like him did, Preston thought as he buttoned his shirt: they took and they took and they took so that when they finally did give, you were left feeling thankful even though all you got was scraps.

CHAPTER TEN

The days began breaking leaden and frigid. Even so, every morning Louisa rose at seven and went to Williams Park with her coffee and her sketchbook. She watched the sun rise over Stonewater and drew the supple bowl of light and dark. It had become a necessary ritual. Happiness slunk over her sometimes, so stealthily that she was unaware of it until it hit her: *I am here. I am happy.*

Her paintings were improving, everyone said so. And she was starting to make friends. She'd never been good at approaching people—in high school, her only close friend had been Nolan Guidry, and she'd known him since kindergarten. But now she found that once they got to know her, most people—even Karina, it seemed—liked her. Alejandro Díaz had been the first to befriend her. It had happened back in late September, the day she got Mom's care package in the mail. She'd offered Karina some pralines, and Karina had refused and then abruptly stormed out of their room, and Louisa had been sitting there feeling sorry for herself when Alejandro poked his head in the half-open door.

"Hey," he'd said.

"Oh, hey."

"Just letting you know people are downstairs playing the Hope drinking game if you want to join."

"What's the Hope drinking game?"

"It's when you watch one of Obama's speeches and take a drink every time he says the word *hope*. . . . You okay?"

Louisa shrugged. "Having a hard day."

"Oh no!" he said, and he seemed genuinely sympathetic. "What's going on?"

It all came spilling out: how lost and homesick she felt, how she thought things had been getting better with Karina, but now she was sure her roommate hated her, and she didn't know what she'd done to deserve—

"Don't," said Alejandro. "Don't even try to wrap your head around that girl. She's crazy."

"Crazy?"

"That's my impression." Alejandro perched himself on her bed. He took a bag of Voodoo Zapp's from the box and examined it with interest.

"Help yourself," she said.

Alejandro tore open the bag. "Last semester she had some kind of breakdown." He popped a chip into his mouth. "These are good!"

"What happened?"

"Shit went down in studio during finals. I wasn't there, but I heard she started crying about how everybody hated her and threatened to jump off the balcony."

Louisa tried to picture this. She felt her understanding of her roommate shift, and her heart clenched in irrational sympathy.

"Someone told me," Alejandro went on, "that she was hospitalized over the summer."

"Oh wow."

"And what's wack is that generally when something like that happens the school makes you take like a year off. They call it a medical leave of absence, but what it really means is they want to make sure they're not gonna get sued because you killed yourself on school property. It happened to this girl I knew last year. One visit to Psych Services 'cause she was having a bad week, and that was it. She's not allowed back on campus till next fall."

Louisa broke off a piece of praline. "And that didn't happen to Karina?"

"No."

"Why?"

Alejandro shot her a sidelong glance. "Why do you think?"

"She's rich?"

"Uh, yeah. Bet you her parents have donated." He popped a chip into his mouth and chewed thoughtfully. "And she's kind of a prodigy, too. The school is probably weighing the odds, you know? If they can put their stamp on this person who's definitely going to have a career because she's got the connections and the talent, they might as well get her out the door as soon as possible."

"Hm."

Alejandro wiped his fingers off on his jeans. "She'll be dead by the time she's forty."

Louisa looked at him in shock. "What makes you say that?"

"She's an unhappy, mentally unstable prodigy. Like, I know you're not supposed to romanticize madness and art or whatever, but Karina Piontek's a walking cliché."

Louisa wanted to ask him more, but that was when he invited her downstairs again for the Obama drinking game, and afterward she tagged along with him to a protest at the Occupy Wrynn encampment and screamed herself hoarse about ballooning student debt and out-of-control tuition, righteous outrage swelling pleasurably inside her. Then she went out for more drinking with Alejandro and some of his friends. The next morning Karina wasn't in her bed when Louisa woke up, hungover, and later when she went to the dining hall for lunch Alejandro waved her over and told her to pull up a chair and ate a fry off her plate as though they'd known each other forever.

"Hey, how y'all doing?" she said to people sitting with him, Emma Ochoa and Ivy Morton, the girl with the foxtail, and a sculptor named Neel Kulkarni.

They smiled and asked how she was, too, and when she said, "the most hungover I've ever been in my life," everyone laughed.

Since then, she'd started hanging out with them. She could tell that they didn't really consider her part of their group, not yet, anyway, but they were friendly and invited her to things, and for that she was grateful. Still, there were some uncomfortable moments, like the time she was walking with Emma and Ivy and Neel across the green and they passed the Occupy Wrynn encampment and Ivy said something snide about *virtue-signaling crust punks,* and Emma and Neel laughed, and Louisa got the strange feeling that Ivy wouldn't have said it had Alejandro been there. None of them were on financial aid. Neel's parents were both doctors, Emma's dad was a Spanish fashion designer, and Ivy's family owned a chain of supermarkets in Florida. The three of them were removed and ironic and determinedly apolitical in a way that chafed at Louisa—not that she, herself, was particularly political, but she didn't see why sincerity and fervor were so laughable.

In October, Emma and Ivy and Neel made plans to go to New York for the weekend for the opening of the debut solo show of a Wrynn alum. They asked Louisa if she wanted to come.

"We're going to see *The Book of Mormon,* too," Ivy said. "The three of us were going to split a hotel room, but if you and Alejandro come, too, then we could get two rooms, or like a suite or something."

"Are you taking the bus, or . . . ?" said Louisa.

"Yeah, it's only three hours away. There's a Greyhound station downtown."

"Greyhounds are so gross, though," said Neel. "Like, Amtrak's *worth* it."

Louisa imagined the cost of a bus-maybe-train ticket plus food plus Broadway tickets plus some variable fraction of a hotel room. "I don't know," she said. "I have a lot of work this weekend."

Alejandro was blunter: "Can't afford that, sorry."

There was a moment of awkward silence before Alejandro made a joking comment about the cum-like texture of the gravy in the cafeteria's version of biscuits and gravy, and everyone moved on, but for the rest of dinner he seemed quieter than usual.

The other thing they did that bothered Louisa was gossip about Karina.

"She'll fuck anything with a pulse," Ivy said. "Freshman year she fucked the guy I was dating."

Neel said, "As soon as she got here you could just tell she thought she was better than everyone else. And there's something just kinda *off* about her, you know?"

"It sucks that you have to live with her," Emma added. "I'd be scared she'd stab me in my sleep."

It didn't surprise Louisa to hear people talk shit about Karina. She'd seen how cruel and impatient Karina could be, how aloof. But since that night Karina had offered her a cigarette, Louisa had found herself drawn into a strange intimacy with her roommate, one that seemed to exist only between the hours of midnight and three A.M. Through their late-night talks, Louisa felt that she had come to know Karina—or *a* Karina, in any case—and this Karina could be prickly, yes, but she was also intelligent and disarmingly honest and sometimes even vulnerable. Whether these qualities were incompatible with craziness remained an open question.

Louisa wondered what Emma and Ivy and Neel would think if they knew about the strange pull she felt toward her roommate. Alejandro was the only one she considered telling. The feeling she had when she was with Karina was akin to what she felt when a drawing was coursing through her—the feeling of being on the precipice of something momentous, of reaching her hand out in the dark and grazing a familiar shape—and she thought that maybe Alejandro would understand because she was pretty sure he was gay, but saying it out loud would make it real, and she wasn't ready for it to be real.

But she could talk to Alejandro about other things, like their byzantine FAFSA paperwork (he was, as she'd suspected, also on financial aid, though his package was entirely grants, unlike her largely loan-based one) and how weird it felt to skip mass and sleep in on Sunday morning for the first time in her life (he'd grown up Catholic, too; that gold chain she'd noticed around his neck turned out to be a Saint Christopher medallion) and where to buy cheap flights home (he was from a Texas suburb about a four-hour drive from Louisa's hometown) and the feeling she sometimes had of being invisible ("I don't think that ever goes away," he told her).

Her friendship with Alejandro brought her happiness. And then there were the bird woman dreams, visions that woke Louisa nearly every night, different every time. One night the woman was nude, glossy white wings sprouting from her bloodied shoulder blades. Another night, she reappeared slumped over, her back stippled with lacerations; a pair of herons flanked her, gazing cannily at their handiwork. The next night the woman's body had split in half, and the two halves held each other, their embrace a tender, anguished confusion of overlapping flesh and feathers. When one of these dreams woke her, Louisa climbed silently from her bed and slipped out into the hallway to put her visions down on paper. She learned to subsist on a Russian roulette sleep schedule—six hours one night, three the next, sometimes none.

The bird woman clamored to be painted, but Louisa wanted to do it right. She needed a model to sit for her. *Will you pose for me?* she imagined asking her classmates. People posed for each other all the time at Wrynn. Sometimes when Louisa was out and about on campus, she recognized a model from a painting or drawing she'd seen in class, and the sight was always a little jolt, like glimpsing a celebrity. But to pose for someone was a kind of public contract; it announced that you were not merely friends but aesthetic collaborators.

On Halloween there was an event called Artist Ball that you had to buy tickets for ahead of time. "A costume party?" Louisa asked Alejandro.

"Yeah, but almost everyone makes their outfit by hand, so some people get pretty intense about it. And there's a costume contest and stuff. It's like . . . like a group show meets Fashion Week meets that masked ball scene in *Eyes Wide Shut*."

"Oh!"

"Minus the orgy," he clarified.

"Right. Of course."

"Maybe I'm exaggerating. But it's fun!"

This sounded like an experience she was unlikely to have after she left Wrynn, so even though tickets cost eight dollars and she'd had to start putting expenses on her credit card, she reserved one and went thrifting at the Salvation Army, where, for an additional ten dollars she bought a sequined mini-dress and a silver wig. If someone asked what she was, she figured she'd say a disco ball.

Artist Ball took place inside a cavernous hall used for job fairs and formal dinners. Alejandro wore a suit and tie with the word *SORRY* written on it in black Sharpie. ("I'm a formal apology, get it?") Ivy was a character from a TV show Louisa hadn't seen, and Emma was a zombie Audrey Hepburn complete with a tiara, silicone gore, and a long cigarette holder. Neel had dyed his hair, eyebrows, and beard red, painted his face, and tied a cloth around his head: Van Gogh post–ear amputation. Louisa also saw a Marie Antoinette in a foot-high white wig, corset, and pink ruffled ball gown, an Edward Scissorhands who kept pretending to stab his friends, and a No Face from *Spirited Away*.

Emma, Neel, and Ivy headed straight to the dance floor. Alejandro tugged at Louisa's hand, but she shook her head. "I'm not drunk enough yet." She felt surprised and a little displeased by her own reticence. She'd grown up dancing—partner dancing, even—at zydeco nights in town. Everyone in Breaux Bridge had. But now she felt a creeping sense of embarrassment at the fact of her own body. She watched Alejandro as he joined the group. He was a buoyant, joyful dancer, more enthusiastic than skillful.

After a minute she turned away and wandered over to the food table, where a Black Swan in a stiff tutu and dramatic eye makeup was picking through the trail mix. Louisa poured herself a cup of punch. It was cloying and fruity with a rubbing alcohol aftertaste; someone had spiked it. She was starting in on her second cup when she saw Karina from across the crowd. She wore a sleeveless frock gridded with black lines and squares of red, yellow, and blue—a Mondrian dress. Her hair was loose around her shoulders. In the bright strobes, she was electrically beautiful. She was dancing with Preston Utley, who wore a purple velour tracksuit. She had her arms around his neck; his arms circled her waist, his face buried in her neck. Watching them together, Louisa felt a rocking sensation in her chest.

A sweaty Alejandro appeared beside Louisa. He popped a can of Sprite. "It's fucking hot in here."

"Yeah," said Louisa. She was still looking at Karina and Preston.

Alejandro followed her gaze. "Oh my god, she's hooking up with *him* now?" He sipped his soda. "That figures."

"Why?" Louisa's mouth was suddenly dry. She chugged some punch.

"Because Preston Utley's aggressively mediocre and has a pathological need to attach himself to talented, insecure women."

"Yikes."

"Yikes is right."

"Yikes," Louisa repeated softly. She was maybe a little buzzed. Karina and Preston had disappeared from view, swallowed by the crowd. Louisa drained her cup of punch and poured herself another. Alejandro took a battered plastic flask from his back pocket and had a long pull before tipping it toward Louisa. She started to tell him her drink was already spiked, then changed her mind and took a swig. Whatever it was, it burned all the way down but warmed her stomach once it settled.

"You should come dance," Alejandro said. "Don't let all those sparkles go to waste."

"Okay." She took his hand. That buzz was spreading from her head to her limbs. Alejandro was right—she needed to move. She needed to shake loose this feeling, this uneasiness Karina had lodged in her. They danced to the soul sister song and the one about finding love in a hopeless place and the Lady Gaga song "Alejandro."

"It's about me!" Alejandro cried, passing Louisa the flask, and together they screamed the chorus: *Don't call my name, don't call my name, Alejandro!*

The DJ announced the results of the costume contest: a group costume had won, four girls who'd dressed up as a group of grotesque, glowing anglerfish. Second place was a boy who'd 3D-printed a mask of his face and then coated his own face with fake blood to simulate having peeled his skin clean off.

Then there was more dancing and more punch, and by the time Louisa decided it was time to go home and put herself to bed, her head was spinning and she kept succumbing to fits of uncontrollable laughter.

"Bye!" she told Alejandro, who was soaked in sweat but gave no signs of wanting to stop. "Remember to hydrate!"

Outside, the cold air sobered her up. Her classmates bellyached about the approaching winter, but Louisa was mesmerized by this season that she'd seen only on screens. Snow, in particular, was a novelty she was sure she'd never tire of. It had snowed very early that year, to Louisa's delight and everybody else's dismay. For the past two days snow had fallen relentlessly, but the clouds had dissipated sometime during the dance and now a ripe moon hung low in the sky. The campus was silent, blanketed in white. The elms lining the streets were leafless and skeletal, their branches plucking at the sky, and she looked at them and imagined they were the neurons in her brain bristling against one another.

I am here.

I am the painter walking through the snow alone.

Hope was empty; everyone was still at the dance. She unlocked her door. Karina was bent over Louisa's desk, looking at Louisa's sketchbook, the leather-bound one Mom had given her before she left home. She didn't use it for class assignments; she saved it for her own private projects. It was the sketchbook she took to Williams Park every morning, the one where she made her bird woman drawings. Watching Karina page through it was like seeing someone read her diary. She felt the blood drain from her face.

"What are you doing?"

Karina startled and took a step backward. She was still wearing her Mondrian dress. Her eyeliner was smeared. She opened her mouth, but no sound emerged. It was then that Louisa realized something: it was *her*—Karina was the woman she'd been dreaming about. Karina was the bird woman.

"I'm sorry," Karina said. She closed the sketchbook and stepped away from the desk. "I was just really curious."

Remembering the time she'd also been curious and had indulged her curiosity exactly as Karina had, Louisa flushed. Beneath her shock and discomfort she felt a stirring of excitement.

"I like the ones you did of the woman with bird wings," Karina said quietly, almost tonelessly. "They're very . . . striking."

Louisa thrilled. Was Karina as drunk as she was? "Thanks."

Karina sat down on her bed. Louisa mirrored her. From across the room they faced each other without quite meeting each other's eyes.

"How did you come up with her?" Karina said.

Louisa's heart was pounding. "The bird woman? She came to me in a dream."

She thought she saw on Karina's face a flash of something ugly, but then it disappeared and Karina half smiled and gave an odd little laugh. "How romantic."

"Or cheesy. I don't know. I'd like to do a series of paintings based on those drawings, though."

"Like the one you turned in for class the other week?"

"Yeah, but better. I want to push it further."

"That could be interesting."

"But I need a model." Louisa found herself speaking with deliberation. "I want to do these right. The one I made for class . . . I didn't have anyone to sit for me, and it didn't turn out the way I wanted."

Karina looked straight at her. "Yeah, it's definitely better to work off a model."

Louisa held her gaze. "You wouldn't be interested, would you?"

"Me?" Karina tapped her chest.

"Yeah."

"You want me to pose nude." It wasn't a question.

Louisa's face grew hot, but she didn't look away. "You can see the body's articulations so much better on a nude figure. And the compositions I'm planning . . . they'd look wrong with a clothed subject."

Karina brought her hand to her mouth and chewed her thumbnail. "Yeah, I can do it. I'm busy for the next couple of weeks, but yeah. Maybe after Thanksgiving break?"

"Whenever," said Louisa. She thought her heart might burst from her rib cage.

"Okay then. It's a plan."

CHAPTER ELEVEN

When it came time for his trip to Occupy Wall Street in early November, Robert was relieved to get out of town for the weekend. His *Artforum* essay had caused only a small kerfuffle—he'd gotten a few raised eyebrows from colleagues and a reprimand from the dean, and Preston Utley had skipped two classes in a row before showing up again, sullen and taciturn—but campus was starting to feel suffocating.

Robert arranged to meet the OWS organizer, Garrett Wynter-Platz, in Zuccotti Park under the red di Suvero sculpture. Garrett turned out to be not a grizzled, middle-aged anarchist, as Robert had expected, but a pale, bespectacled redhead in his early twenties. He wore an NYU sweatshirt under his peacoat.

"Thanks for coming," said Garrett. "Did you bring a sleeping bag?" He eyed Robert's canvas tote, containing only his sketchbook and drawing supplies. Robert had dropped his duffel at the Holiday Inn before heading to the park.

"Uh . . ."

"That's okay," said Garrett. "We'll find you one later. Should we start with a tour maybe?"

The park's encampment was almost village-like, and it all seemed very well organized. The walkways between the tarps were clearly delineated, and there was a makeshift kitchen area serving wraps and sandwiches, a small lending library, and a rudimentary medical center. Robert would've guessed there were maybe three or four hundred people in the park: college-age kids strumming guitars; older men, clearly homeless, smoking hand-rolled cigarettes; people in suits who looked like they'd come straight from work; punks with dogs on leashes; silver-haired hippies handing out foil-wrapped burritos. Cops were stationed around the park's perimeter.

As Garrett led his tour—"recycling's here; those stationary bikes are actually powering the encampment, people take turns pedaling them; that area over there with the drum circle we call the ghetto, those guys are kind of a pain in the ass, to be honest"—it quickly became apparent that Robert had gravely misjudged his host's position in the Occupy Wall Street hierarchy.

"We're a horizontal revolution," Garrett explained. "Leaderless. Democratic."

Robert's face must've betrayed his dismay, because Garrett quickly added, "But I'm one of the facilitators spearheading the Arts and Culture Committee." He explained that he'd taken it upon himself to reach out to a handful of political artists to request commissions. "Pro bono, of course."

"Things are really getting rolling," said Garrett. "The Smithsonian is collecting art from the movement to put in the National Museum of American History."

"Is that right?" said Robert, his interest piqued.

Garrett nodded vigorously. "Listen, I don't believe in God. I don't believe in capitalism. But I believe in art. I really do. I think it's a tool for meaningful social change."

Robert didn't talk much about his time with ACT UP—the topic veered too close to Vince, and he didn't, as a rule, talk about Vince—but now that he was here, so close to the Stock Exchange, the memories came flooding back: March 1987, Vince with less than six months to live but not yet bedridden. Walking together to the busy intersection of Wall Street and Broadway. SILENCE = DEATH signs—the pink triangle not yet iconic, not yet art. An effigy of FDA head Frank Young hanging from the façade of Trinity Church. The die-in: lying in the sun-warmed street next to Vince. Blaring horns, snarled traffic. *Release those drugs! Release those drugs! Release those drugs!* All of them united in anger. How thrilled and alive he'd felt, even with death all around him. Sirens and shouts as cops lifted protesters off the street by their arms and legs, placed them on stretchers like corpses.

It had worked, though: shortly after, the FDA announced that it would shorten its drug approval process by two years.

And a year later, March 1988: same place, another die-in. Robert hadn't gone, but he'd seen pictures in the papers. Signs everywhere: WITH 42,000 DEAD, ART IS NOT ENOUGH.

Garrett started to tell Robert something else, but he was interrupted by a crowd of people gathered nearby who began chanting in unison.

"Mic check!" a man yelled.

"MIC CHECK!" the crowd repeated.

"We amplify each other's voices!"

"WE AMPLIFY EACH OTHER'S VOICES!"

"No matter what's said!"

"NO MATTER WHAT'S SAID!"

"That's the human microphone," explained Garrett. "Megaphones aren't allowed in the park, so that's how we get messages to each other. It's totally democratic. Anyone who has something to say can yell 'mic check' and get their message broadcast."

Somewhere in the back of Robert's mind his mother's reedy voice inquired, *If you want to say something, why not write a book?* Ida Berger would've liked him to become a lawyer or a doctor or some kind of scholar. He'd disappointed her by taking after his father. Ida had met him in a National Refugee Service English class when she was nineteen and "still delighted to find myself alive." Wolf was neither a reader nor a worker, but he was an excellent drinker and an even better draftsman—though he never, in Robert's memory, called himself an artist. Despite the drinking, his mind was precise and mathematical. In Robert's first year of art school, when his drawing professor quoted Cézanne—"Treat nature by means of the cylinder, the sphere, the cone"—his first thought was of his father. By then, he hadn't seen him since he was thirteen.

When Garrett excused himself to check on a food drive at a nearby church, Robert was relieved to be alone. He sank onto a bench and opened his sketchbook. There'd been a time in his life when blank surfaces transformed him, when the work ran through him like water through a river. He never paused to question it, never second-guessed himself. Now he dreaded this blank moment every time—stalling in the dust of his own dry riverbed—but he forced himself to pick up the pencil and began sketching some of the protesters and their hand-lettered signs: Middle Class and Sinking Fast; I'm So Angry I Made a Sign; Honk If U R in Debt; Wall $treet = Out of Control Greed; Bring Back Crystal Pepsi!

"You're not tryna sell that, are you?"

Robert glanced up. One of the homeless-looking men hovered nearby. He wore a faded windbreaker and was drinking out of a Big Gulp cup.

"Pardon?" said Robert.

"Are you gonna sell that?" The man took a step closer.

"I wasn't planning on it. It's, uh, pro bono."

The man tongued his straw and took a long pull. "The other day a guy was here tryna sell cartoons. Twenty bucks a pop."

"That's cheaper than what you'll get in Central Park."

"Yeah, but this ain't Central Park, that's what I told him. You ask me, though, half these people here are tourists."

Robert nodded blankly. The man sat down next to him. "'We're all homeless,' they say, but they're not, you know. So it doesn't actually mean anything."

"How long have you been here?" Robert asked.

"Since day one. Came as soon as I heard. This is my shit. I was in Tompkins Square Park, too. Fucking cops broke my nose."

Robert had vivid memories of Tompkins Square Park. Hardly a year after that first ACT UP protest, but by then he'd had his debut solo show and the portrait of Vince had sold, and he had enough money to leave his East Village walkup and move into a newly renovated loft in Christodora House on Avenue B. The night of the riot, protesters had rammed a police barricade through the building's glass doors and invaded the lobby, yelling, "Die, yuppie scum!" The whole time, Robert kept picturing Vince down there. As soon as his lease was up, he moved out.

"I'm Kenny," said the man.

"Robert."

They shook hands; Kenny's was gnarled like a knot of wood. Robert spotted Garrett hurrying toward them. "Is this man bothering you?" he said breathlessly.

"No," said Robert and Kenny at the same time. "Fuck you," added Kenny.

"No need for that," said Garrett.

Kenny fixed Garrett with a glare. "You having fun?"

"Excuse me?"

"Having fun pretending to be a big scary anarchist?"

Garrett rolled his eyes.

"It's fun to take a break from college and play the homeless game, isn't it?"

Robert thought of the welcome mint he'd eaten in the hotel elevator. The twinge of guilt in his stomach felt like an empty gesture.

"Robert," said Garrett. "There's someone else I'd like you to meet and she just texted to say she's waiting at the statue."

Robert gave Kenny an apologetic shrug. As soon as they were out of his earshot, Garrett said, "I'm so sorry about that. I should've warned you we get a lot of crazies."

"He didn't seem crazy to me," said Robert. "More like a gadfly." He smiled to himself. "The gadfly of Zuccotti Park."

Garrett made no comment. They came to the red sculpture again, and a woman with a silver stud in her nose, long, thin dreadlocks, and a T-shirt that commanded UNFUCK THE WORLD walked up to them and introduced herself as Vanessa Campbell. "I can't wait to see the work that results from your immersion in our movement," she said, shaking Robert's hand. She was older than Garrett, late thirties maybe, with soft laugh lines around her warm brown eyes, and Robert liked her immediately.

"Vanessa is one of the organizers with Occupy Museums," said Garrett.

Vanessa handed him a flyer. "Let me know if you're interested in getting involved."

ENOUGH IS ENOUGH. Cultural institutions have been hijacked by Wall Street, operating via the same corrupt system of entrenched inequality, exploitation, and enrichment of the elite at the expense of the 99%. Art is for everyone. It should not be a luxury. Museums for the people, by the people NOW!

Preston Utley could've written it.

"Our demands," Vanessa said, "are for more art jobs, better funding for art education, and for museums to return looted artifacts and reflect the desires and interests of the public."

"That sounds great," said Robert. "But I don't agree with that last part."

Vanessa tipped her head at him. "Why not?"

"Not the looted artifacts thing," said Robert. "The thing about the desires and interests of the public. I don't think people know what they want. And I don't think it's my job to give them what they think they want."

Vanessa gave him a searching look. "You don't think that's elitist?"

"If the general public got to decide what goes in museums, the Met would be full of kitsch."

"But if people want kitsch, why not let them have it?" Her tone wasn't angry or confrontational; it was musing, curious—it had that friendly yet probing quality Vince's voice used to take on when he was arguing with someone he disagreed with. "You don't think *kitsch* is just a word that elites use to shame the rest of us into liking what the one percent stands to make money off of?"

Robert smiled. "You remind me of a friend of mine."

"A good one, I hope. Well, hey, listen, if you change your mind and want to get involved, there's an email address on that flyer."

"Thanks. I guess I should—" Robert fumbled for his wallet and handed Vanessa a bent business card. She took it and turned to Garrett. "Can I borrow you for a minute? I have a question about tomorrow."

As Robert was folding up the flyer, Kenny reappeared at his elbow and thrust a faded sleeping bag at him. "Noticed you didn't have one." His haggard face was mild and meek, emptied of the scorn he'd shown earlier.

"Thanks," said Robert. "Don't you need it, though?"

"Nah, I been doing this a long time. Got a whole stash of shit. You need anything, you come see me."

Robert rummaged around for some spare cash to give him but found only the joint he'd planned on smoking in his hotel bathroom with the fan on and a towel stuffed under the door. Kenny brightened at the sight of it but grabbed Robert's wrist as he sparked the lighter.

"Not *here*. There's a cop right over there. You blind?"

Kenny led Robert through the maze of tarps to a nest of blankets and pillowy black garbage bags. Once they'd settled in and started passing the joint back and forth, Robert could almost pretend it was cozy.

Kenny started recounting some story about his old weed dealer, which turned into a story about a dog he'd once had. Robert wedged the sleeping bag behind him and leaned back. A few more hits off the joint and he felt himself go all floaty.

"How long you here for?" Kenny asked.

Robert blinked Kenny's face into focus. "Just today and tomorrow. I have to get back to Stonewater to teach my seminar."

"You're a teacher?"

"I'm an artist who teaches. I'm supposed to be making a piece for all . . . this." He waved his hand vaguely.

"How's that gonna help?"

Robert coughed on a hit. "Spreading awareness, and um, you know, galvanizing people."

"People are aware. This shit's all over the Internet."

Robert was high. He was so high. His body was fusing with the asphalt. If Vince were here, he wouldn't be getting high with Kenny. He'd be holding one of those signs, or more likely organizing something. Handing out flyers. Writing letters. The reason they'd become friends in the first place was because Vince had written a letter that got him death threats.

They'd both been thirteen at the time, though they'd known each other their whole lives. For as long as Robert could remember, Vince, his mother, and a rat-like schnauzer named Myra had lived in the apartment directly above him. The building's tenants regarded Vince as an object of pity—his father had been killed in Korea before his birth, his mother took in laundry to scrape by, and there was something angelic and forlorn about his thin white face and shock of black hair that re-fused to lie flat no matter how much Mrs. Russo slicked it down with a dab of spit.

Robert's father had left shortly after the end of eighth grade, and he spent that whole summer before the beginning of high school on the building's rooftop making meticulous, hyperrealist drawings of the New York skyline from across the Newark Bay. After finishing each drawing, Robert embellished it with flames, Godzillas, falling corpses, and giant spiders. In mid-June, Vince began appearing on the rooftop each morning with a stack of Kurt Vonnegut novels and a towel to spread over the hot tar. Vince didn't speak to Robert, didn't acknowl-edge him aside from nodding hello, but Robert, whose capacity for anger had swollen a hundredfold since his father's departure, fumed at the intrusion. He endured Vince's presence for several days before it burst out of him: "Why are you here all the time?"

Vince looked up from *Player Piano*. "I'm under house arrest."

"What?"

Vince set the book down. He wore sunglasses and swim trunks. His long legs had straw-colored scabs on both knees. "I'm not allowed to leave the building."

"Says who?"

"My mom."

"Oh."

"The rooftop is technically the building, though. If I spend one more day cooped up with that yappy little dog, I'm gonna throw her out the window." Sunlight glinted off the silver cap on his front tooth.

"Are you grounded?" said Robert.

"Not exactly. I got some death threats and my mom overreacted."

Intrigued, Robert put down his pencil. "Why'd you get death threats?"

Vince told him about the letter he'd written to the *Jersey Journal* de-fending Muhammad Ali's refusal to be drafted. "I always keep the clip-ping on me," Vince said, scooting over to make room for Robert on the towel and pulling a square of newspaper from his pocket. "So if I'm found dead the police will know the motive. And then my death will have stood for something."

Robert couldn't tell if he was joking.

I am writing to give you my view on John Richardson's letter which said that Muhammad Ali was refusing to enter the army because he wanted publicity. This is the most ridiculous statement I have ever heard. He does not want to fight because:

HE IS A MINISTER, and should be deferred.

HIS RELIGION is opposed to the war.

HE DOES NOT WISH to participate in an illegal, dirty war that defies the Geneva Conference.

Why should a person participate in an illegal war when we burn the huts and possessions of innocent persons, torture captives, burn away people's skin, kill children, kill women, not to mention the hundreds of soldiers we kill each week?

Call it preventing Communist aggression. Call it preserving freedom. Call it whatever you want. I call it murder. No one ever declared war on us.

Some people are proud to be Americans. I'm ashamed to be one.

VINCENT S. RUSSO, JR., 13, Ezra Nolan Junior High

Robert shot him a darting glance, his annoyance giving way to grudging admiration. Vince pointed his chin at his sketchbook. "What are you drawing?"

Robert showed him the sketch he was working on. In it, a gigantic mushroom cloud bloomed over the skyline. Whenever Robert showed Ida his art, she grimaced and said, "How horrible, Robbie. Can't you draw something nicer?" But Vince seemed fascinated.

"Damn," he said. He ran a finger over the page, smudging the cross-hatching. "Oh, sorry."

"It's okay."

Vince flipped through the sketchbook. "You're really good. These are amazing."

"Thanks."

"What're they about?"

"I dunno."

"They're so angry. Are they about how the whole world is going to shit?"

Robert shrugged. "I guess."

That skinny boy with silver in his mouth was the greatest champion Robert ever had, and that day on the rooftop was the moment when his life really began, though he wouldn't realize either of these things until decades later.

The drum circle started up again. Robert felt it in his body like an extra heartbeat. He wanted to curl up and go to sleep. How could anybody sleep in this park?

"Do you have another joint?" Kenny asked.

"I do, but it's back at my hotel."

"I thought you were sleeping here."

"I—" His thoughts were moving at half speed. What was he doing? He was supposed to be making art. "Can I draw you?" he said.

Kenny made a face like Robert had asked permission to take a shit in his mouth. "No," he said. "Fuck no."

Robert recoiled. "Right," he said. "Never mind. I'm sorry." He clambered to his feet and waved a halfhearted goodbye, a spastic flick of his hand, and hurried down the sidewalk. As he shuffled past the tarps, he couldn't help hoping there'd be a fresh welcome mint on his pillow when he got back to the hotel.

CHAPTER TWELVE

In the three weeks between Halloween and Thanksgiving, the way that Louisa interacted with Karina didn't change much. When they saw each other in class or in the dining hall, they nodded and said hello, and if there was a strange anticipatory electricity when their eyes met, nobody but Louisa seemed to notice. It was only at night, when Louisa returned from the studio to find Karina sitting up in bed, already palming a pack of cigarettes, that the fragile barrier between them dissolved. Something inside Karina seemed to want to make itself known. Louisa pictured it like the windows in her heart opening up one by one. For the first time, Karina spoke of loneliness, of despair. She alluded to what had happened last year. "I felt unmoored," she said. "Like something in my mind had become unhitched."

"And now?" Louisa said.

Karina looked away. "I don't know." That was as much as she'd say. The night before Thanksgiving break started, she asked Louisa, "Are you excited to go home?"

Louisa hadn't originally planned to fly back to Breaux Bridge for the holiday—it was an absurd amount of money for a four-day trip, enough to keep her in art supplies for a month—and she'd been almost looking forward to having the empty campus to herself. But then, two weeks before break, Mom had called announcing that she'd bought Louisa a round-trip flight, leaving Wednesday and returning Sunday. "It's a stretch, but I miss you," Mom said when Louisa protested.

"I am excited, yeah," Louisa replied. She was finishing her packing, a cigarette dangling from the corner of her mouth (the first time Karina had seen her doing that, she'd laughed and said, "Oh no, I've made you an addict").

"So are you going to come back with some amazing sky and water paintings?" said Karina. She was sitting cross-legged on her bed, wearing only a tank top and shorts even though the window was open and it was snowing outside.

"I probably won't have time to paint," said Louisa. "I'll just be seeing my family."

"Do you miss them?"

"Yeah, but not, like, terribly. It'll be nice to see them." Louisa zipped up her bag and perched herself next to Karina on the bed. "I really miss *home,* though. Like the place itself. Do you ever miss New York like that?"

"Not really. What do you miss?"

"Where my family lives, out in the country, it gets so dark at night that you can see the Milky Way. You can pretend it's a thousand years ago." Louisa glanced at Karina. "I know what you're thinking."

Karina looked amused. "What am I thinking?"

"That I'm idealizing a place that most people here think of as backward and racist."

"I never said that."

"It's not the people I'm interested in."

Karina ground her cigarette into the ashtray. "What are you interested in, then?"

"Like I said, the landscape there. The animals, the plants, the quality of the light. It's all so fragile. The oil industry is destroying the wetlands. The land is literally sinking into the ocean." She sighed. "But right now the weather is perfect. It's the one time of year you can go outside without worrying about mosquitoes."

She saw her mother in the arrivals lounge before her mother saw her. Mom was perusing a rack of *Vogues* and *Elles*, though Louisa had never known her to read fashion magazines. She had her long thumbs hooked through the belt loops in her jeans.

"Mom?"

Her mother turned, her face breaking into a smile. Her lipstick was new, the color of crushed berries. "Hi, little bird."

They hugged, and she smelled just as Louisa remembered, like grass and lemon hand lotion. They were the same height, and for a moment Louisa was overcome by the sensation of holding in her arms an older version of herself. The fungibility of their bodies struck her—that her mother had carried Louisa's body inside her, that she'd molded it and guided it—*hold the pencil like this, move your arm like that, see what's in front of you, not what you think you see or want to see*. Did that fungibility grant Mom authorship? Did it make anything of Louisa's a little bit her mother's?

"Did they tell you which carousel number?"

She had an accent. Louisa had never noticed it before.

"I didn't check a bag. They charge now. Like thirty bucks, it's ridiculous."

In the Volvo the air between them seemed to contract, Louisa remembering the last time they'd ridden in a car together. Late August. The hour-long drive from Breaux Bridge to the Baton Rouge airport. Mom asking if Wrynn offered pre-professional classes like advertising or art education, and Louisa saying she didn't think so.

"Hm," Mom had said.

"What now?" They'd fought all spring, right up to the deadline for Louisa to accept Wrynn's offer of admission and financial aid package. Afterward, she couldn't help feeling that she'd pulled one over on her mother, that she'd gotten away with something she shouldn't have.

"I just think," Mom had said, "that it'd be good to start thinking about what kind of job you want after you graduate."

Louisa allowed a flat "Okay."

Mom sucked in her lips, sweat beading in the little scoop of flesh above her chin. The Volvo's AC was finicky. "Lulu," she said. "You know how incredible I think you are. But I just want you to remember that you can work real hard and do everything right, but there's never any guarantee—"

"I *know*." Louisa let a long silence elapse before adding, "You don't think you'll ever see my art in a museum?" She knew it was a childish question even before she asked it. There was another long silence, during which Louisa wanted to disappear. Then Mom said, in a quiet voice, "I don't know."

Now, as she steered through rush hour traffic, Mom asked, "How's school?"

"Good. A lot of work, but good."

They got on the highway and headed west toward Breaux Bridge, Baton Rouge giving way to bruised clouds above and wetlands below.

"Discipline was always your forte," said Mom.

Louisa looked at her long fingers gripping the steering wheel, the hook of her half smile. "Were you disciplined when you were my age?"

The half smile stretched into a grin. "God, not at all. Your uncle Rick never told you? Mama was always threatening to send me to juvie if I didn't behave. I'd draw naked men—not anyone I knew, just men I made up in my head—and I'd leave the drawings around the house, but Rick would always find them first and rip them up. I was furious, but he said he'd be lonely if I got sent away."

Louisa laughed. Mom glanced at her. "I was always a little in awe of you."

"You were?"

"I couldn't believe I'd given birth to such a serious little girl. Even when you were very little, you always knew exactly what you wanted."

Louisa was pretty sure she hadn't inherited this quality from her father, a guy named Aaron that Mom had briefly dated at LSU. She'd asked to meet him once, out of curiosity, when she was ten or so, and Mom had acquiesced, but Louisa had found him so bland and uninteresting that she'd never again felt any desire to interact with him. She thought back to Mom's art class, the one she'd taken her freshman year of high school. It was an advanced course full of seniors, a tight-knit clique of artsy potheads who'd known Mom since their freshman year.

She'd been envious of their ease with her, the way they joked with her, confided in her, competed for her attention. Later, at community college, Louisa had been in a class with one of them, a girl named Annie Gauthier, who'd said in reverent tones, "Caroline Arceneaux changed my life. Your mom is so awesome. You're lucky."

Louisa had only nodded and smiled. After that semester with Mom, she'd only signed up for classes with Lafayette High's other art teacher, elderly Mr. Doucet who was losing his hearing and blasted opera in class.

"So listen," Mom said. "Before we get home, I just want to let you know that a couple of weeks ago Pepere had a stroke."

"*What?* Oh my god, Mom—"

"It was minor," she cut in. "And he's fine, but I didn't want to tell you over the phone because you seemed so stressed. This is why I wanted you to come home."

Louisa put a hand over her mouth.

"He's fine," Mom repeated. "He's been going to physical therapy and he's doing great. But he's going to need to take it easy, so he's retiring— finally, for real this time—and Rick is taking over the business."

"Okay. That's good."

"But Lulu, here's the thing." Mom licked her lips. "Rick took a look at the books, and . . . it's a little dicey. People just don't hire plumbers as much during a recession. Rick thinks Pepere and Grandma need to start being more careful with their finances. That money they were paying toward your tuition—and they would never admit this, but it's what Rick thinks, and I agree with him—that money, they need to be saving it."

"But it's not a ton, right? I thought it was only like a few hundred dollars per semester?"

Her mother looked at her in disbelief. "Louisa, they've been paying the entire family contribution or whatever it's called. Did you think *I* was the one writing those checks? On my salary?"

A tremulous silence spun out between them. So when Pepere had intervened on her behalf, that afternoon last spring when he'd found her crying in the wood shop, when he'd said, "Let me talk to your mama, chère," he hadn't actually convinced Mom of anything. He'd just offered to shoulder the cost. The entire cost. Louisa's throat was on fire. "So you're saying I have to drop out?"

"There are other options. There are loans, there's financial aid . . ."

Louisa worked hard to keep her voice steady. "I'm already on financial aid. And I already *have* loans."

"We'll do some research, okay? Maybe you can take out another loan."

Louisa shook her head. "I'd have to borrow too much. For an art degree. It'd be insane. And I have credit card debt on top of that."

"*Already?* I told you to be careful, Louisa."

"I know, I know." Louisa felt a hot wrench behind her eyeballs. She swallowed, held the tears at bay. "I can't really add more hours at my campus job because my workload is already so heavy. And the materials are *really* expensive. And we go through them so fast. It's not like at SLCC."

Mom sucked in her lips again, her gaze fixed resolutely on the road ahead. "You thought of transferring back? You were doing so well last year."

Louisa shook her head.

"Nothing else you can apply for?"

"Well . . ." Louisa thought of the Winter Exhibition prizes. They'd been endowed by some rich alum a long time ago, so they were worth serious money: five thousand dollars for Best Painting, Best Sculpture, and Best Mixed Media. Seven thousand dollars for Best in Show. She relayed this to her mother, whose eyes widened.

"That is . . . insane. You should try for one of those."

"Great advice," Louisa said sarcastically. The prizes were decided by outside critics, and they tended to favor work that resembled whatever happened to be trendy at the moment. It was widely acknowledged that winning a Winter Exhibition prize basically guaranteed you gallery representation after you graduated. According to Alejandro, Karina had won Best Painting at Winter Exhibition last year and probably would've won again at Spring Exhibition if she hadn't left campus after her breakdown.

The rest of the car trip passed in silence. It was getting dark when they arrived. The main house, a squat, sprawling ranch home where Grandma and Pepere lived, had recently been repainted; the porch railing gleamed bone-white. Louisa followed her mother through the un-

kempt grass toward the back of the property. From the treetops, lush
and leafy even in winter, came the soft thrum of cicadas, and in the
distance a great blue heron squawked, a deep, rumbling sound like a
barking dog, *roh roh roh*. Their bungalow stood a few yards from the
wood shop, overlooking the river, low and listless this time of year, and
beyond that the jagged stalks of burned and harvested sugarcane. The
bungalow had originally been a shed, but in the years before Louisa's
birth Pepere had added on to it for his own amusement. Now it was
about nine hundred square feet, with a front porch and a sunroom. In
another time and place, he might've been an artist, too.

Inside, the potted succulents cast sawtoothed shadows on the walls.
The rug was in need of a vacuuming, the sofa fuzzed with cat hair. "Put up
your stuff and then we'll go say hi to Grandma and Pepere," Mom said.

Louisa gave Napoleon a chin scratch before going into her room, shutting the door, and allowing herself, finally, to cry. She'd been so close, so
close. The shape in the dark was just beginning to reveal itself to her.
When she'd calmed down, she washed her face and changed her shirt.

"Mom?" she called. "I'm ready."

No answer. Her mother wasn't in the living room or in the kitchen.
Louisa checked her bedroom, then peeked into the sunroom, which
Mom used as her studio. "Hello?" She flipped on the light. The studio
had always been cluttered, but now it was so densely packed with canvases and supply bins that there was hardly any room to walk. The only
evidence that the room was still being used as a workspace was a patch
of empty floor where Mom had left a dirty coffee mug and a half-
finished painting on the easel. Louisa picked her way through the clutter and examined it. The canvas was divided in half down the middle.
On one side was an aerial view of what she recognized as the sinking
wetlands that she'd mentioned to Karina last night. The other side depicted a melting glacier. The two halves echoed each other, visually and
thematically. It was some of the best work Louisa had ever seen of her
mother's.

Mom had never sold anything, as far as Louisa knew. Someday soon
she'd run out of room in her studio and her work would spill into the
rest of the house. Someday she'd die and leave it behind. Nobody would
ever see it.

+ — +

On Thanksgiving Day, Louisa helped Mom and Grandma in the kitchen. She chopped the onions and stirred the gravy, occasionally slipping off to bring Pepere some water or a snack. Mom had minimized the severity of his stroke, Louisa was sure of it. He walked with a cane. When he spoke, he often slurred and lost his train of thought. Sometimes he slipped into Cajun French. His eyes were hazy and unfocused, and his hand shook when he drank the iced tea she'd brought him. He'd been so happy to see her last night that she'd nearly cried, pressing her face into his chest to hide her guilt. Here was her grandfather, old and sick and full of love, and here *she* was, wishing that this break could end already so she could fly away from him, from all of them, so she could start figuring out what the hell she was doing with the rest of her life.

Thanksgiving dinner was just Mom, Grandma, Pepere, and Rick, a perpetual bachelor. After they said grace, Rick reached past Louisa for the mashed potatoes and said, "Mais, no green hair? No piercings? Sure you've been at art school this whole time?"

Louisa smiled tolerantly.

"C'mon, stick out your tongue. Show me your tongue piercing. I won't tell your mama."

Mom snorted as Louisa set down her fork and gamely stuck out her tongue.

"Damn, well, there's still time. Dating any girls yet?"

Louisa stiffened. Did Rick sense the change in her? Did any of them?

"Hush, ça va," said Grandma.

"What?" said Rick. "What'd I say?" and at the same time, Mom said, "Lulu, for the record, *I* don't care if you pierce your tongue or date girls. Your uncle's the one who'd be scandalized."

Louisa didn't doubt it. When she was twelve she'd idly referred to him as Ricky Martin, amused that he shared a first name with a razzle-dazzle pop star. He'd reddened and barked at her to cut it out.

"I think Lulu looks perfect the way she is," said Grandma. "Pale pale, though."

Pepere said something lengthy in Cajun French. He was gnawing on a turkey wing and had grease all over his chin.

"English, Dad," said Rick.

Silently, Mom handed Pepere a napkin.

"I guess I'm just disappointed," said Rick. He rested his forearm on Louisa's shoulders. "Not even a lesbo haircut." Louisa looked at his handsome, meaningless face and felt a surge of hatred for him. The force of it astonished her a little. But Pepere was chuckling at Rick's remark, and Louisa was reminded of the time he'd called a client of his a "goddamn fruitcake."

"You found a church up there at school, chère?" said Grandma.

"Um . . ." Louisa met her mother's eyes before quickly looking away. Growing up, she and Mom had accompanied Grandma and Pepere to mass every Sunday, with the understanding that this was meant purely as a conciliatory gesture to the older generation. "There's a chapel on campus." This was true, though it was mostly used for lectures.

"Catholic?"

"I think it's nondenominational."

Pepere pointed a finger at Louisa. "When did you and me meet?"

Mom set her knife down. "Daddy . . ."

"When did you and me meet?" Pepere repeated, still pointing at Louisa.

"Would've been when I was born," Louisa said. Nobody laughed.

"Jacques," said Grandma sharply. "That's Louisa. That's your granddaughter."

"I know," Pepere said indignantly.

"I'mma grab another beer," Rick said, his voice a little too loud. "Y'all need anything?"

Pepere pushed his plate toward Louisa. "Want some?" he said. He pointed at the gray lump next to his greens. After a second, she registered what it was: chewed-up boudin.

"No—no, thank you."

"Daddy, she has food already," Mom said gently. She lifted his plate and set it back down in front of him.

Pepere was still looking at Louisa. He wore an expression of dispassionate curiosity, as though she were an interesting animal at the zoo. There was a very real possibility that she was going to start crying right here at the table. She excused herself and went to the bathroom, sat on the toilet, and stared at the floral-patterned wallpaper until she'd pulled herself together.

By the time she returned, the conversation had moved on to other things: people from church, a new restaurant in town, a city council race. Pepere didn't participate except to repeatedly ask what was for dessert. Louisa felt strangely detached from it all, as though the scene were unfolding in front of her like a TV show someone had put on for background noise. When dinner was over, she went straight to bed and slept for twelve hours.

The next morning, Louisa borrowed Mom's car and Rick's little pirogue, strapping it to the roof, and drove to Lake Martin. She paddled out into the middle of the water. The sky was winter blue, the clouds tall and dense. For several hours, she floated among the bald cypresses and swamp tupelos, photographing all the birds she saw: snowy egrets, great blue herons, an anhinga, white ibises, a flock of roseate spoon-bills. The birds didn't notice her. They didn't care. When she had enough shots she went home and uploaded the photos to her laptop. All day long she'd expected to start feeling weepy and fragile, but instead, from the moment she woke up, she'd felt resolute. In two days, she'd fly back to Wrynn. She'd use these photos in her bird woman series. She'd work hard, harder than she'd ever worked in her life. She'd try to win one of those prizes.

The following day, Louisa got a text from her friend Nolan Guidry: *u in town?* Nolan had stayed in-state for college—he studied history and folklore at the University of Louisiana at Lafayette—and last year, when Louisa was at SLCC, she'd hung out with him often. She'd promised to keep in touch when she left for Wrynn, but now she realized with a guilty pang that she hadn't texted him all semester.

Ya, she replied. *Wanna come over tonight? My fam wld luv to see u.* They were all fond of Nolan, particularly Grandma, who'd often hinted that Louisa should date him. In high school, she and Nolan had occasionally hooked up—mostly when they were both drunk and bored—but they'd stopped after Nolan met his girlfriend Theresa in freshman English at UL.

Nolan texted back: *Sounds good!*

He arrived around eight in his rusty Toyota pickup. He'd grown his hair down to his shoulders; it kept falling in his face, and he kept tucking it behind his ears in a gesture that was touchingly guileless. She hadn't thought about him at all while she was at Wrynn, but now his handsomeness struck her anew.

Nolan hugged her and said, "You look tired. Was Thanksgiving that bad?"

Louisa laughed weakly. She didn't feel like explaining about Pepere. Nolan would find out soon enough. "Let's go inside."

In the main house's living room, Grandma was waiting with two chilled bottles of sweet moscato. Mom poured the wine while Nolan sat on the sofa, answering Grandma's questions about the classes he was taking that semester. He was so charming, so at ease. Louisa was reminded suddenly of Alejandro. She took a giant gulp of wine.

"Horse people give you trouble?" Pepere interjected. He held a glass of the iced tea Mom had served him instead of wine, and some of it had dribbled down his chin and onto his collar.

"Pardon, sir?" said Nolan.

A terrible sadness reared up inside Louisa.

"Horse people. They give you trouble?"

Nolan shook his head, smiling quizzically.

"He had a stroke," Mom said quietly. "Did Louisa tell you?"

Nolan glanced quickly at Louisa. "No."

She had the same heavy on-the-verge feeling she'd had at Thanksgiving dinner, and she wondered if she ought to go sit in the bathroom again and compose herself, but then it passed. They all chatted for a little while longer, but something in the air had shifted. Mom's smile was strained, and Grandma sounded overly cheerful, and Nolan kept fidgeting, rubbing his palm against his thigh, and Pepere just sat there, sipping his iced tea and staring off into space. Finally, Grandma announced it was her and Pepere's bedtime, and Mom said she was getting tired, too. Grandma pressed the remaining bottle of moscato into Nolan's hands, and Louisa walked him to his car. He took out his keys, then turned to her and said, "Actually, wanna go for a walk?"

"Sure." It was a mild, cloudless night, the moon nearly full. They headed toward the river, and Nolan opened the wine—the bottle was the kind with a screw top instead of a cork—took a swig, and handed it to Louisa. She drank deeply, though she was already tipsy from earlier. They came to the water and ambled down the riverbank, their shoes making soft sucking noises in the wet sand.

"Sorry about your grandfather," said Nolan.

"Thanks. How's Theresa?"

"We broke up."

"Oh, shit. I'm sorry."

"Don't be." He took the bottle from Louisa and drank some more.

A little past the property line, they came to the neighbor's boat dock. They took off their shoes and socks and dangled their feet in the river. The water was soft and cold and alive. Nolan dug into his pocket and pulled out a pack of Marlboros.

"Can I bum one of those?" said Louisa.

Nolan handed her a cigarette and lighter. "Since when do you smoke?"

"I don't." She held the flame to the tip.

Nolan regarded her shrewdly.

"I don't buy my own cigarettes," she said. "Just mooch off other people."

"That makes it okay?"

"Never said it makes it okay. I'm saying it makes me not a smoker." Louisa kicked her feet in the water, splashing him a little. "I'm really sorry about Theresa."

Nolan peered at her. "You're drunk."

She laughed. "No, I'm not."

"You fixate when you're drunk."

"What am I fixated on?"

"Theresa."

"Not true," Louisa protested.

Nolan took a long drag. "You dating anyone?"

"No."

"Anyone you like?"

Louisa would see Karina tomorrow. She needed to check with her about when she was available to pose. At the thought of painting her, Louisa felt a mixture of nerves and dread and excitement. "Kind of," she said.

"What's his name?"

"Umm . . ." She tossed her cigarette butt in the water. "It's actually a she."

There was a slight pause before Nolan said, "Oh. Okay. That's not *not* unexpected, I guess."

"What's that supposed to mean?"

"Ha, yeah, I guess that might sound strange coming from me. Given, you know . . ."

"That we've boned?" she finished for him, surprising herself.

"Whoa." He laughed, holding up both palms. "You *have* changed, haven't you? I like bisexual Louisa. You're bi, right? You haven't sworn off guys?"

She felt her face heat up and was glad for the darkness. "Not at the moment, no."

Nolan leaned over and kissed her. She was surprised and also not surprised. His mouth was warm and familiar, his hands cupping her face were hands she knew. "Want to come back to my place?" he said. "My roommate's out of town still."

She hesitated before saying no. Nolan kissed her again, which she knew was his way of trying to convince her. She tasted the faint tang of wine in his mouth. The next time they came up for air, Louisa said, "I might be coming back."

"Here?"

"Yeah."

"Really?" His face broke into a smile.

"Maybe. I don't really know what I'm doing. Might have to drop out of school 'cause of money stuff, so, yeah."

His smile faded. "Oh. Shit, Lu, I'm sorry to hear that."

She shook her head. "It's fine. I should probably get back, though. My flight's tomorrow morning and I haven't finished packing."

They polished off the rest of the wine, leaving the bottle on the dock for the neighbor to find, then walked back toward Nolan's parked car.

"You okay to drive?" she said.

"I'm fine." He kissed her once more before climbing into the driver's seat. "I hope you do come back. Selfishly."

"Thanks, Nolan. Be safe."

She watched his taillights disappear down the long, snaking dirt driveway. As she turned toward the bungalow, she heard a *pssst*.

"Lulu, that you?" came Pepere's voice. He was sitting on the porch in his pajamas, his face bathed in shadow. Had he seen her kissing Nolan?

"Does Grandma know you're out here?" Surely not.

"Come see."

She crept up the steps as quietly as she could and crouched next to his chair. "Does Grandma know you're out here?" she repeated.

"Do you remember when that Sunday school teacher caught you drawing in the Bible?"

"Yeah, Andy Miller's mom. She was *mad*."

"It was a pretty drawin. I still remember it. That teacher, she came up after mass and shook the Bible in my face. All fachée, she was. Nothin crazy, just the back of someone's head, whoever was sittin in front of you, but I remember it was pretty pretty. I remember thinkin God gave you a gift."

For the first time since Louisa had come home, Pepere sounded like his old self. For a moment she wanted to yell, wake up Mom and Grandma, tell them to come look. Instead she said, "I was probably just bored."

"No," Pepere insisted. "There was something about it. God was showin off your gift. Lache pas la patate, Lulu."

Don't drop the potato. Don't give up. His earnestness made her stomach twist with shame. A great wave of anguished love rose up inside her. She reached out and squeezed his hand. "You should see the wood shop they have at my school," she said, and as she spoke she realized she hadn't set foot in Pepere's wood shop all break. Now it was too late.

"Got a feeling your eyes are getting smaller," Pepere said. And just like that, he was gone again. He'd been himself, briefly, and now he was someone else.

Louisa stood and held out her hand. "Come on," she said. "Let's get you back to bed."

CHAPTER THIRTEEN

I t wasn't that Karina had actually been too busy to pose for Louisa until after Thanksgiving—she'd just been stalling for time. She needed to prepare somehow, to steel herself. Why had she agreed? She couldn't fully explain it. Sometimes she chalked it up to her own weakness, or else her talent for self-destruction. Other times she wondered whether she just wanted someone—someone clear-sighted and free of delusion—to look at her, to understand her and render what they saw so that she, in turn, might look and understand, too.

And Louisa's bird women intrigued her, as did the fact that they'd come to Louisa in a dream. Karina had sometimes wondered whether her own masterpiece would arrive in dream form. Part of her was jealous—she hardly ever remembered her dreams.

For some time now, Karina had been letting her parents' calls go to voicemail. Even so, she decided to go home for Thanksgiving. In an email to which Karina didn't reply, Fiona had mentioned that, for now, the art would remain in the townhouse until the court appointed a receiver to work out a plan for selling the collection. *I understand you're upset,* Fiona wrote, *but I hope you'll consider spending the holiday with us. It may be the last time the three of us will be together under one roof in the house you grew up in.*

On the Wednesday before Thanksgiving, Karina caught the evening train from Stonewater. It was late when she arrived at Penn Station and took a cab to the house on East Eighty-first. In the foyer, the alarm key-pad glowed UFO green. Karina punched in the code and wheeled her suitcase into the living room.

"Hello?"

Footsteps upstairs. The house smelled strange, musty and close.

"Who's there?" came Fiona's voice. Karina's eyes traveled upward. Her mother leaned over the handrail on the second-floor landing, eyes narrowed against the gloom.

"It's just me."

"God, I can hardly see you."

Karina fumbled for the light switch. Fiona screwed her eyes shut in the sudden brightness. "What are you doing here?"

Karina dragged her suitcase up the stairs before answering. "Didn't you say you wanted me home?"

Fiona was wearing her green kimono over yoga pants; she looked like she'd been woken up. "I did, but Jesus, Karina, you've got to let me know. You never answered my email. I thought you weren't coming." She sighed, then stepped forward and kissed Karina on the forehead. Her lips were cool and chapped, like the skin of a date.

"I'd better find a caterer," Fiona murmured. "And text your dad. Hopefully he's able to change his plans."

"Where is he?"

"He moved out," Fiona said matter-of-factly. "He's got an apartment somewhere in Midtown."

"You were going to spend Thanksgiving alone?" Karina felt a pang of remorse for ignoring her mother's calls.

Fiona swept her hair behind her shoulders. "Go unpack, love. I'll call a caterer."

Karina heaved her suitcase onto the bed and washed her face in her bathroom sink. Around the edges, the medicine cabinet mirror was tacky with residue from old stickers.

Downstairs, she found Fiona poking around the fridge. "Fallier's said they can squeeze us in tomorrow. Are you hungry?"

"I'm okay. Why don't you just cook?"

Fiona laughed. "I assume that's a rhetorical question." Smiling slightly, she took a pint of strawberries from the crisper and rinsed them in the sink. "I texted your dad. He says he can join us after."

After what? But Fiona didn't say. She thumbed a speck of dirt off a strawberry, lips thinned in concentration. "So we'll eat late," she finished, emptying the fruit into a ceramic bowl. Karina popped one in her mouth. Sour, flavorless. Why did her mother insist on buying summer fruit in November? She hopped up on the kitchen counter, banging her legs against the cabinets. "Hey, Mom?"

"Mm?"

"Do you remember Robert Berger?"

Fiona glanced at her in naked surprise. "Why?"

"He's teaching at Wrynn. He has a retrospective up at the museum." Karina ate another strawberry. Fiona's cheeks had gone pink.

"Is he your teacher?"

"No."

"Does he know you're a student there?"

Karina thought of how he'd looked at her after the Q&A: with no recognition whatsoever, his smile evasive and remote and shatteringly polite. "We saw each other once, but I don't think he recognized me."

Fiona nodded, her eyes downcast.

"I did go see his retrospective, though."

Her mother's eyes flicked toward her. "Did you?"

"I don't think it's very good, his work. It's kind of strident."

"Your dad always thought the same thing." Fiona wiped her hands on a dish towel.

"Did *you* like his work?"

"I did. It was one of those rare times when we disagreed." She bit into a strawberry. "We never bought anything, though." For a moment she looked pained. "I liked him a lot. It's too bad we lost touch."

"You should have left Dad for him." Karina hadn't planned to say it; it just slipped out.

There was a stunned silence. Fiona's mouth dropped open; she looked at Karina with frank astonishment. "If I'd left him," she said at last, choosing her words with care, "I would've left you, too."

Karina didn't know what to say to this. She wasn't even sure how it ought to make her feel. Fiona placed the bowl of strawberries back inside the fridge. "I'm very tired, love," she said. "I'll see you in the morning, okay?"

After Fiona had gone to bed, Karina wandered around the house, checking on her favorite pieces: the Hokusai, the Agnes Martin, the Yves Klein sculpture. Though it had been drilled into her since she was small that she mustn't touch the art, now she allowed herself to brush her fingertips against each piece, feeling the texture of the paints, the smooth and the rough and the gritty. She pictured leaving behind traces of her DNA. She wondered, for the first time, who had owned this art before her parents bought it, who else had touched it, looked at it with love or hate or indifference. *Goodbye,* she thought. *Goodbye, goodbye, goodbye.*

Thanksgiving dinner began late, as her mother had warned. By the time Harry arrived, it was nearly nine and Fiona had consumed half a bottle of wine.

Karina was the one who answered the doorbell.

"Hey, kiddo," her father said, pulling her in for a stiff hug. Despite his tailored coat, he looked shabby somehow, rumpled. What remained of his hair was sticking up in the back.

Dinner started off pleasant—Harry joked and teased Karina, and she was reminded how charming he could be when he was in the mood— but gradually grew more tense. Harry and Fiona sat at opposite ends of the table, with Karina between them. Harry ate very little; it was obvious he'd already had his Thanksgiving somewhere else. He and Fiona hardly spoke to each other, addressing themselves mostly to Karina. How strange, after a lifetime of feeling alone and ignored, to find herself the center of her parents' attention. A few drinks in, it became almost funny.

"Do you have a boyfriend?" Harry wanted to know.

"I do." Karina smiled sweetly. "You'd hate him."

"I'd *hate* him?" said Harry, laughing. "Strong words."

"Probably."

"I'm not sure I like the sound of that." His face was flushed, his forehead damp.

Karina was just tipsy enough to consider rattling off a list of all the things her father had done that *she* hadn't liked: the way he'd been so doting when she was a child but lost interest in her the moment she ceased being an adorable little girl; the way that, after Dalton's guidance counselor called with concerns about Karina's "antisocial demeanor" and rumors of her supposed promiscuity, he'd forced her into therapy with Dr. Ellis, a willowy young woman whose office Karina had to sit in every Wednesday afternoon, staring at the nubbly beige walls and sun-starved spider plant; the time Karina came home from school to find Dr. Ellis in the kitchen with Harry drinking coffee and sharing a cigarette, passing it back and forth like a joint, and how at their next appointment Dr. Ellis said, "Your dad and I are friends, but there's no reason for that to interfere with our work here"; the time Karina heard gossip that Stella McNamara, a senior who moonlighted as a Ralph Lauren model, had fucked Harry on someone's yacht, both of them coked out of their minds, and the jealousy that rose like bile in her throat because she, too, had once wanted Stella. These were the things she was tempted to say but didn't. She sipped her wine and asked if the caterer had brought any pumpkin pie.

"I think so," Fiona said. She rose, grabbing a stack of plates, but as she turned to bring them to the kitchen, her heel twisted on the carpet. She stumbled and fell. Two of the plates shattered, spilling food scraps on the floor. After a moment she got on her hands and knees and swayed, breathing hard through her nose.

"Goddammit, Fiona," said Harry. When he was angry his voice grew high and tight and quavering. If you didn't know him well, you might think he was holding back tears. He pushed his chair back but made no move to get up.

Karina helped her mother to her feet. She put her arm around Fiona's waist and steered her to the downstairs powder room, where she threw up in the toilet. "Let's get you to bed," Karina said.

"Wait."

"What?"

"I have to tell you something."

"What?"

Fiona closed her eyes.

"Is it about Robert?" Karina whispered.

Fiona's head lolled to the side. Karina swallowed hard. She wrapped her arm more firmly around her mother's waist and half dragged her to the foot of the stairs. "Dad, I could use a hand over here."

Harry appeared from the dining room, his eyes bloodshot. In grim silence they hauled Fiona up to bed. "She'll be fine," said Harry. "I'd better get home."

"Who are you going home to?" Karina said.

Without meeting her eyes, he replied, "You don't know her."

That's a first, she was tempted to say. She followed him back downstairs. As he was putting his coat on, it burst out of her: "Why are you doing this?"

"Be more specific, please."

"Why are you making her sell everything?"

He blinked. "Because the judge told us to."

"Come on. You could've just let her have half of it."

He gave a half smile and a quick jerk of his head. "We both wanted the same pieces. How do you think that would've worked?"

Karina stood mute in the foyer.

"She's going to walk away with plenty of money," he said.

"It's not about the money, Dad. You know that."

Harry took another step toward the door. "Do you think this isn't hard for me, too? With our family history?"

Whenever he and Fiona went to auctions, Harry would put on the silver cuff links that had once belonged to his grandfather. "For luck," he'd say, winking at Karina. His grandfather had also been a collector, but he'd lost everything to the Nazis. Once in a while, on a visit to a museum, Harry would come across a piece that had been in his family's collection, and a shadow would fall over his face. Those were the only times Karina felt sorry for him.

"It doesn't look to me like you're having a hard time," Karina said. "Looks like you're having a *great* time." It dawned on her that her capacity for cruelty, her desire to manipulate—the impulse that had propelled her to pit Preston and Robert Berger against each other—she'd inherited it from her father. Fiona had had no part in it.

Harry shook his head. "Go to bed, Karina. You're almost as drunk as she is."

"Fuck you," she said.

Then her father did something he'd never done before, not to her at least. He slapped her across the face.

"You will never speak to me that way again," he said, his voice tight with rage.

She wasn't looking at him; she'd covered her face with both hands and was trying not to cry. She heard the door open, then slam shut.

In a blind fury, Karina went up to her bedroom and heaved her suitcase onto the bed. She unzipped it and removed the top layer of clothing. Carefully, she took Wally off the wall. The frame was about the size of a textbook, easy enough to wrap in a towel and hide in her suitcase. She unearthed an old Tegan and Sara poster from her closet, unrolling it and tacking it up in the spot where Wally had hung.

She rebooked her Amtrak ticket on her phone and set an alarm for six A.M. Then she took a shower, scrubbing herself numbly under the scalding water, and went to bed.

The next morning, she slipped into her mother's room and placed a glass of water and two aspirin on her nightstand. She took a cab to Penn Station, where she boarded the train and immediately fell asleep, stirring only to show the conductor her ticket. She woke just as they were pulling in to Stonewater.

As she walked up the hill to campus, she wondered how long it would take her parents to notice Wally was gone.

Two days later, on the last afternoon of Thanksgiving break, Karina was soaking in Preston's bathtub—he'd given her a key to his apartment after she'd shared with him her fondness for bubble baths—when she got a text from Louisa: *Hey, my flight just landed. Any chance u could meet me at my studio in like 2 hrs? It's #27. I want to get started on the paintings asap so I can have at least 1 ready for winter exhibition.*

Karina sat up, heart racing. She texted back: *OK.*

Preston was still at home in Virginia, so she had the apartment to herself. She dried off and got dressed, then watched two episodes of *Game of Thrones* on her laptop without registering any of the story. When the credits rolled, she put on her coat and walked in the sinking light toward the sophomore studios. The building was unlocked but deserted; most people wouldn't be back on campus until later tonight. Karina had never been in Louisa's studio before, and she was surprised to see that its walls were completely blank and that, save for a space heater, a few basic materials, and a stack of blank, gessoed canvases, it was nearly empty. A monk's cell. Karina treated her own studio as an extension of her living space. She'd outfitted it with a hotplate, a cof-feemaker, and a mini-fridge, and she always kept a stack of blankets and a change of clothes close at hand.

Louisa was kneeling by her locker, sorting through a bundle of paint-brushes. She wore a baggy smock over jeans and a long-sleeved T-shirt. "Hi," she said, glancing up. "Thanks for coming."

"How was your break?" said Karina.

Louisa shrugged. "Okay. Yours?"

"Oh, you know. It was fine." Karina took off her coat and scarf, fold-ing them over her arm. She stood there, shifting her weight from one foot to the other, watching as Louisa sharpened a pencil and set a blank canvas on the easel.

"So . . . how would you like me to pose?" said Karina.

"Cross-legged on the floor like this," said Louisa, demonstrating. "And a little bit slumped forward, but with your head lifted and kind of turned this way?" She stood, dusting herself off. "I'm going to paint you from the side but sort of at an angle from over here." She went to stand next to her easel. "I want to be able to see part of your back as well as your profile."

"Okay. Should I undress now?"

"That'd be great. Here, I brought this for your clothes." Louisa handed her a balled-up grocery bag. In the empty studio, the crinkling plastic seemed thunderous, almost rude.

Karina was wearing a loose, shin-length dress that was easy to slip in and out of, but first she unlaced her boots. After lining them up neatly against the studio wall, she peeled off her tights and lifted her dress over her head. Shivering in her underwear, she stuffed her clothes into the plastic bag.

Meanwhile, Louisa was stretching a floral bedsheet across the studio's open side, pinning the edges of the fabric to the plywood partition. "Oh, and I brought this for you to sit on." Out of her backpack she tugged a squashed pillow. The pillowcase's pattern matched the sheet's. Karina recognized both from Louisa's bed.

Karina pushed down her panties and unclasped her bra. Her nipples immediately puckered in the chill air. She reached down and switched on the space heater. Settled onto the pillow. Weird to think that later tonight Louisa would lay her head here. "Like this?"

"Turn your head toward me a little more? And lift your chin? Yeah, that's perfect."

Louisa switched on the floor lamp and adjusted the light's angle. Karina had never heard her speak so assertively. And she didn't avert her eyes from Karina's body the way she did when Karina undressed in their dorm room. The opposite: she looked at her straight on, with bold, electrifying frankness. She perched herself on the stool and pulled the easel toward her. She lifted her eyes and took Karina in. Then, without preamble, she began to draw.

The brisk flick-flick-flick of Louisa's gaze made the hair rise on Karina's arms, though she wasn't cold anymore. The space heater purred at her side. With her eyes closed, she could almost pretend it was sunlight on her skin. At first her body rebelled, twitching and trembling, and she had to force her muscles into submission, but eventually she settled into stillness. After about an hour, Louisa's voice broke through the silence, asking if Karina needed a break.

"Yeah, thanks." Her voice was hoarse. She stood stiffly, tugging her dress over her head, and padded to the bathroom. The three stall doors were covered in graffiti. Above the paper towel dispenser, someone had written: *Art is the only salvation from the horror of existence.* Underneath, scratched out in ballpoint: *Speak for yourself.* Karina peed, turned on the faucet, waited for the water to warm up. She examined herself in the mirror. Her cheeks were flushed, her pupils dilated, the irises dark and liquid. Her hands shook as she washed them.

When she returned, Louisa was mixing a batch of paints on a metal tray, filling the studio with their heady chemical scent. Karina slipped out of her dress and settled back onto the pillow. "Was this how I was sitting before?"

"Lean forward a little more." Louisa hopped off her stool and guided Karina's body into place. Karina's skin burned where she'd touched her. Louisa snapped on a pair of latex gloves and began to paint. She worked vigorously, applying the oils in bold brushstrokes with an easy, fluid confidence Karina had never seen in her before, a feverish intensity of purpose. Periodically, she took several steps back and looked at the canvas from afar, frowning slightly. And the longer Karina sat in the beam of her gaze, the more she sensed Louisa's inwardness, the hermetic quality of her mind, the elusive way she glided through the world. Karina watched her—the shifting landscape of her face, the pinched skin between her eyebrows, her mouth tightened in concentration, the thin, strong shoulders, the quick hands. And Karina wanted Louisa to touch her the same way she was touching that painting, gentle one moment and rough the next, smearing the paint with her fingers, working herself into the canvas.

An hour. They paused again so Karina could stretch and pee and get a drink of water. Another hour. Finally, Louisa set down her brush. She peeled off her gloves and let out a contented little sigh, an unconscious, involuntary sound, one she might've made in her sleep.

"I think I have all I need for tonight," she said.

While Louisa shuttled back and forth between her studio and the sink, cleaning up, Karina got dressed.

"Can I see it?" Karina said.

"Not yet. Not till it's done."

As they walked through the mantle of snow back to their dorm, they chatted about the final for Drawing class, but Karina couldn't shake the feeling that they were having an entirely different conversation beneath it. Back in their room, Karina changed into pajamas and climbed into bed. She lay there with her eyes half-closed, not sleeping, listening as Louisa took the pillow and sheet out of her backpack and remade her bed. She wondered how Louisa had painted her. Had she been kind, or had she been honest, homing in on Karina's little roll of belly fat, the pimple scab on her chin, her appendectomy scar? Louisa puttered around for a while longer before slipping out into the hallway with her shower caddy. She came back ten minutes later, turned off her lamp, and got into bed.

Just as Karina was drifting off, Louisa said, "Do you have time to pose for me again tomorrow night?"

"Sure." Karina smiled into the dark.

The next evening after dinner, Karina went to her own studio, where she worked for a while on a new painting. This one was an experiment in texture—she'd mixed her oils with cold wax, whipping it into paste, which she slathered onto the canvas like frosting before carving through the different-colored layers with a palette knife. Less than a week ago, the archaeological surface of the painting had absorbed her completely, but tonight she couldn't focus, kept fumbling with her scraper. *What am I doing?* She'd known this would happen. She'd known that if she became entangled with someone like Louisa—someone who fascinated her, who made her feel both molten with want and emotionally defenseless—her art would suffer. In agreeing to pose for Louisa, she'd set in motion something she couldn't stop. She felt vaguely disappointed with herself, embarrassed by the nakedness, the sentimentality of her desire.

At ten P.M., Karina cleaned up her workstation and made her way through the maze of studios to #27. Louisa had already tacked up the flowered sheet and was sitting at her easel mixing paints. When Karina pushed aside the curtain and walked in, Louisa looked up and smiled. "Hi," she said, and Karina felt a kind of swooning in her gut and was sorry she'd ever been cruel to her.

The pillow waited for her on the floor, in the same spot as yesterday. Karina undressed quickly and settled into her pose. By now it felt like a muscle memory. Louisa began to paint, and for a half hour or so they were both quiet. Then Louisa said, "I think I'm going to finish this tonight."

"What do you want to do with it? In your wildest dreams?"

"What do you mean?"

"Like, if you could wave a magic wand and choose your ideal—" Karina stopped herself. She'd almost said *buyer*. "If you could choose the museum this painting would be in, what would it be?"

Louisa laughed. "I've never thought about it."

"Really?" said Karina. She assumed everyone thought about it, even if they didn't admit it. She realized then how little she knew about Louisa, despite having shared a room with her for three months.

"Actually, no," Louisa admitted. "I have thought about it. I once asked my mom if she ever thought she'd see my art in a museum, and she said she didn't know." Her voice was casual, but Karina could tell the memory still caused her pain.

"If it makes you feel better, my mother's never said a single nice thing to me about my work," Karina said.

Louisa looked surprised. "But you're so—" She stopped herself, giving a slight shake of her head.

I'm so what? Karina wanted to ask. Instead she said, "What do you want to do after we graduate?"

Louisa laughed again. She had an easy laugh. "I want to be an artist. Just like everybody else."

"But what kind of career do you want to have? Are you going to New York after Wrynn? Or the West Coast? Or are you going to be, like, one of those American expats in Berlin? Or one of those outsider artists who disappear from society and live in the desert?"

Louisa looked worried, for some reason. "I'll probably go to New York for a few years, to establish myself. That's what you're supposed to do, right? But then maybe, down the line, I don't know . . . I'd like to live in Louisiana at least part of the time."

"So you want to be like Turner, essentially."

"Like Turner?"

"You want to live in a city where you'll be starved for the sky," said

Karina. "And then periodically leave and gorge yourself on air and water."

She'd meant this as a joke, but Louisa didn't smile. She set down her brush. "Do you need another break?"

"Um, sure." Karina wrapped herself in her coat and went to the bathroom. She felt overheated, as though all the lights had come on inside her, but when she looked in the mirror she saw only her regular self. Back at the studio, she sat down and said, "Do you ever think about immortality?"

If Louisa thought this was an odd question, she didn't say so. She selected a new brush, a thin filbert, and dipped it in red paint. "No, but I think about death sometimes. Do *you* think about immortality?" She dabbed at the canvas.

"I think about how I'm preserving myself in my paintings. Different versions of myself."

Louisa considered this. "I like that. I've never thought about it that way."

"I think of it like keeping a diary," Karina said. "But when I'm dead, instead of people knowing what I thought, they'll know what I saw."

All at once Karina wanted to tell Louisa about her secret childhood conviction that her best work, her masterpiece, was somewhere out there, waiting to channel itself through her. She wanted to ask, *Do you believe that, too? Do you think this is it, what you're doing now, painting me? Do you think this is the beginning of your best work?*

Louisa set her brush down. "I think it's finished."

"Really?"

"I think so." She peeled off her gloves. Almost shyly, she said, "Want to see?"

Karina got to her feet. Still naked, she walked around to face the easel and looked at the canvas. Louisa had painted her dark and secretive, more shadow than light. And, flanking her, she'd painted two haughty, long-legged birds, beaks dripping with bright blood. Deep wounds scored Karina's back. Louisa's thumbprints were visible in the wet paint. It was a strange, discomfiting, moody painting, like peering through a window into a dream Karina had once had a long time ago, one that had slipped unnoticed into the void of her memory. It was as though Louisa had flattened the secret room of her, laying it out in oil and linen for the whole world to see.

"It's really good," Karina said.

"I might need to adjust the—"

Without stopping to think, Karina took a step forward and closed the distance between them, hip bones and breasts colliding, and kissed her. Louisa made a little noise of surprise in the back of her throat. After a moment she curled her hand around the nape of Karina's neck, sinking her fingers into her hair. Louisa's teeth were small and slick. She tasted like Diet Coke and chewing gum. She was so much littler than Karina; her body felt so delicate under Karina's hands. The newness of it seemed to multiply time, stretching it out, so that by the time Karina fully registered the warmth of Louisa's tongue inside her mouth she couldn't say for sure how long they'd been kissing, and then together they fell back against the studio wall, clinging to each other, and Louisa's knee slid between her thighs, and Karina slipped her hands inside Louisa's shirt, pushed up her bra and cupped her breasts, rolling her nipples between thumb and forefinger. Louisa gasped, a smoky sound like a fire crackling to life.

They broke apart, and Karina looked at Louisa, and Louisa looked back at her, and it was a gaze charged with the thrill of mutual recognition.

"I—" Louisa began. Her face flamed with color. "Aren't you dating someone?"

"Sort of." Karina didn't want to talk about Preston. She didn't want to think about him.

Then they were kissing again, and Karina was tugging at Louisa's clothes, and then they were both naked, pressed together so closely that Karina pictured them slipping inside each other's skin. Louisa had a birthmark on her left breast, and as Karina bent her head to kiss it, she felt Louisa's pulse drumming under her ribs. They were still standing, leaning against the wall, and Karina jerked her chin at the pillow. "Over there?" she whispered. Louisa nodded. Karina spread her coat on the floor and lay down on it, jamming the pillow under her head. And it didn't matter that the floor was cold and hard, because now Louisa was on top of her, her small wet mouth like an electric shock. And now Louisa was kneeling between her legs, and Karina was crying out, sticking her fist in her mouth to muffle herself, it felt so good it was almost more than she could bear, and when she came there was no need to think of Louisa because Louisa was there, Louisa was right there, Louisa's fingers were inside her. As soon as she'd caught her breath, she grabbed Louisa round the waist and flipped her over and split her thighs and lapped at her over and over. Louisa came quickly, with a soft whimper, and afterward she propped herself up on her elbows and looked at Karina, the corners of her mouth turned up in a way that reminded Karina sharply of Wally. And in that moment she felt the way she sometimes had with Wally, a sense of total privacy, of being sealed off from the world, protected from it. She wanted it to be like that with Louisa. She wanted to keep this pure and good, like a very old painting preserved forever behind glass.

It was Louisa who finally broke the silence. "Karina?" she said.

"Mm?"

"My bird woman paintings are a series."

"I know. You mentioned that."

"I have to finish the series."

Karina smiled. "I know. You'll need a model."

CHAPTER FOURTEEN

Back in early November, when Robert had first returned from New York, he had started working on mockups for Occupy Wall Street. He had shut himself in the studio that Wrynn had provided, sat down with his sketchbook and a pencil, not allowing himself to move until the end of the hour, at which point he would reward himself with some whiskey or a quick hit off a joint. At first he'd worked at a halting pace, but gradually he'd become less self-conscious of his own rustiness.

The first designs he came up with were portraits of the Koch brothers and Bernie Madoff in the same grotesque style as his portraits of the Reagans and Margaret Thatcher. He also produced an image of a bear feasting on the carcass of the Wall Street bull in the tradition of an old-school political poster. When he was satisfied with his sketches, he reproduced them on canvas in oils. Then, on a whim, he incorporated some collage. He glued nickels onto the Koch brothers' eyes, layered the Wall Street bull's carcass with incendiary newspaper headlines, and spackled Madoff's face with pencil shavings to make him look scaly.

When Robert was done, he photographed the canvases and sent the jpgs off to Garrett Wynter-Platz. For a few days, he heard nothing back. Then, on the morning of November 16, Garrett wrote him to say that protestors had been "violently evicted" from Zuccotti Park the night before, a move Garrett characterized as "a desecration of our First Amendment rights."

For the time being, the Arts and Culture Committee is disbanding in order to focus on the more pressing matter of reoccupying the geographic heart of our movement.

Robert checked the news online. He watched a couple of cellphone videos of policemen forcibly clearing people out of the park and skimmed Mayor Bloomberg's statement—something about how the First Amendment didn't protect the use of tents and sleeping bags in a public space—before shutting off his laptop.

For the next week, Robert felt almost as terrible as he had following his divorce. At his next appointment with Dr. Sullivan, he asked her to increase his Zoloft dosage. She looked at him with the weirdly flattering intensity of therapy. "I'm sorry to hear you're feeling depressed. Are you practicing self-care?"

He told her yes, he was, though he didn't mention that his version of self-care consisted of Chinese takeout, Scotch, and weed. Dr. Sullivan wrote him a new prescription and told him to exercise more. By the time their next appointment rolled around, he wasn't feeling any better. He broke down and told Dr. Sullivan about what had happened, about how high his hopes had been for the project, how brokenhearted he was that it was over.

"Why do you say it's over?" she asked.

"They cleared out the park," he repeated dumbly.

"Yes, but it's a global movement at this point, isn't it? Just because there's one park where people aren't allowed to protest anymore doesn't mean it's over."

Robert looked at his hands.

"I don't think you should let this stop you from continuing to work on this project," Dr. Sullivan said. "I think you should keep going. Even if nothing comes of it, you'll still have been working to rebuild your creative practice. And remember, that was one of your goals coming in, trying to get your art practice back to where it was."

Robert spent Thanksgiving alone in his apartment, getting high, watching Netflix, and picking at a rotisserie chicken and grainy mashed potatoes. When the break ended and students descended on campus again, he was almost relieved to see them. The Occupy Wrynn encampment was still up on the main quad, though the students' enthusiasm for sleeping in the tents and hanging around with their guitars and megaphones and signs was waning as the weather grew colder.

He didn't teach on Monday, but he did have office hours from 3 to 4:30. After a sad lunch of leftover chicken he decided to head over to the Painting department a couple of hours early. He needed to get out of his apartment.

Robert's office was on the third floor, but on the second floor there was a small faculty lounge with a microwave, a fridge, and a coffeepot. Not infrequently, someone left a Tupperware container of baked goods on the table with a note reading *Help yourself!* He decided to stop by and see if anyone had dropped off leftover pie.

As he came down the hall, he heard Maureen Bolton's scratchy voice drifting from behind the closed door.

"—he was just saying what we were all thinking but no one can say to his face. The museum wouldn't have given him a retrospective if he weren't teaching here."

Robert froze.

"And it was well-written, too," said a voice he recognized as Alberta's. "I didn't expect that from him."

"Oh no, Preston's very smart." This from Maureen again. "He's just an asshole."

"Still, I wonder how much editing *Artforum* did before they published it."

Robert felt his legs moving beneath him, carrying him away from Maureen and Alberta's voices, up the stairs and to his office. He fumbled with the key and unlocked the door, went straight to his computer, and pulled up *Artforum*'s website.

"Robert Berger's Retrospective Is a Tale Told by an Idiot, Full of Sound and Fury," by Preston Utley.

Robert's eyes skipped down the page:

The height of self-indulgence . . . Deluded by a belief in his own historical significance . . . Berger's life's work adds up to little more than a decades-long ego trip . . . Those looking for intellectual rigor will be disappointed. Berger's images are laughably simplistic, catering to the lowest common denominator. Though the exhibit spans decades, it has nothing coherent to say about progress, social change, or how to make the world a better place.

Robert closed his eyes as waves of rage and humiliation roared over him. It was true, the retrospective at the museum could hardly be called a retrospective, but that was because it was missing all his best work. His portrait of Vince, for instance—why hadn't they included it? And for god's sake, where was the Nancy Reagan painting?

So this was what everyone here thought of him. A horrible fear rose in him: What if they were right? What if it was all true? He considered calling Dr. Sullivan and scheduling an emergency appointment, but the thought of having to show her Utley's article was unbearable.

He sat motionless at his desk, staring out the window at the naked elms. This wasn't the first bad review he'd gotten in his career, but to have it appear in *Artforum*? And for it to be penned by a twenty-two-year-old blogger who also happened to be his student? If his career hadn't been toast before, it was now. There was no way he'd ever come back from this.

Grimly, Robert popped two Xanax and leaned back in his chair with his eyes closed. When the knock came, he'd almost managed to drift off.

"Come in," he croaked.

The door opened, and there stood Preston Utley. "Hey, Robert!"

Robert stared at him. "What are you doing here?"

Preston glanced at the wall clock. "Are you not having office hours?"

"I am," said Robert slowly.

Preston took a seat. He was holding a folded piece of paper. "Got my project proposal for you."

Of course. Faculty were required to meet individually with students to discuss final projects and sign off on any works that would be publicly shown at Winter Exhibition. This was to ensure that all art abided by the rules outlined in the student handbook:

The following are prohibited: setting off fireworks, displaying or using weapons, the exchange of money or goods for sexual acts, the use of blood, urine, feces, or

other hazardous materials, and the possession or use of illegal drugs. Students are
also reminded that graffiti art on public or private property constitutes vandalism,
and that animals are to be treated in a humane manner when used in/as art.

From the circumspect, legalistic tone of the meeting where this new
policy had been announced, Robert gathered that it had something to
do with a recent lawsuit.

"Oh, more than one," Alberta (that bitch!) had confirmed. "A few
years ago, a girl sold her virginity on eBay and used the money to pay
her tuition bill. It was an art project; she documented the whole thing
for class. By the time the school realized where the money had come
from, the bursar had already processed the payment, and then it came
out that the *transaction* happened on school property, in one of the
dorms. Then there was this other girl—supposedly she inseminated
herself once a month and then self-induced an abortion and collected
the blood and painted with it. That was a project for class, too. People
will do anything as long as it's never been done before."

"Jesus," Robert said.

"Yeah, the school took a hell of a beating for that one, from both
sides. The Catholic Church *and* NARAL. Even though it turned out to be
a hoax. It was just regular period blood. I thought the paintings were
pretty good, actually."

Now, in his office, Robert glared at Preston. Preston gazed back at
him, placid as a cow, and handed him the sheet of paper. Robert
skimmed the proposal. It was very short and stated that Preston would
project images from The Wart onto a wall.

"This is it?"

Preston smiled blandly. "Yep."

The sight of him, the slippery hook of his grin, the way he sat with
his knees spread wide apart, shiny athletic fabric hammocking his
crotch, filled Robert with fury. He thought of the cartoons he'd watched
as a kid, how whenever a character was angry his shoulders would
scrunch up and steam would come whistling out of his ears.

"This is—this is incredibly lazy work." Robert handed back the proposal. "I'm gonna give something like this a C at best. You do realize
that, don't you? It's not even—how does it even fulfill—it's not persuasive art."

"Difference of opinion there," said Preston calmly.

"You do understand, don't you, that I'm—*I'm* the one who'll be writing you letters of recommendation? You grasp that?"

Preston suppressed a smile. "With all respect, I'm not going to be asking you for a recommendation."

"Nor would I give you one!" Robert cried, sending flying a drop of spit that landed on Preston's chin.

There was a pause during which Preston wiped the spit off, covering his hand with his sleeve. "So are you going to sign it, or . . . ?"

Robert snatched the proposal back and scrawled his signature under the boilerplate stating that Preston's project abided by the rules set forth in the student handbook.

"Get the hell out of my office."

As he stood to leave, Preston said, "You did start this, you know."

CHAPTER FIFTEEN

Night after night, Karina met Louisa in her studio. Night after night, she took off her clothes and sat statue-still while Louisa painted her. Painted her with scaly, jade-green skin, an inky riot of feathers erupting from her mouth. Painted her covered in dragonflies. As a feathered corpse with black oil oozing from her mouth, nose, and eyes. Karina's face was the most difficult part of her to render. Its particularities were muted, cloud-hidden.

It all felt precarious somehow, as though Karina might fly away should Louisa make any sudden movements. It was a bit like having a lucid dream—the thrilling awareness of the possibilities at hand coupled with the vertiginous knowledge that at any moment it all might fall apart. Perhaps, Louisa thought, this was what it felt like to make great art.

Because she *knew* that these paintings were great. For the first time in her life, she did not doubt herself, not even a little. And for the first time since she'd arrived at Wrynn she began to believe that she might actually win a prize at Winter Exhibition. Every night she changed her mind about which painting to submit; each new bird woman seemed to her more powerful than the last.

Every night when Louisa was finished with her work, Karina would come around to face the easel and for a moment they'd look at the painting together in silence. Then Louisa would ask, "Did I get it? Is it you?"

And each time Karina would reply, "Yeah, it's me," and Louisa would feel a thrill, even though it wasn't Karina, not really; it was the bird woman. But before Louisa could ever give this much thought Karina would turn to her and slip her long arms around her waist and kiss her, her hair falling over Louisa's face.

I am here, Louisa sometimes thought in the middle of it, breathless, jelly-kneed.

I am—

At first they only hooked up in Louisa's studio, late at night when the building was empty and silent, but after a few days they began having sex in their room, as well. It was surreal, Louisa thought sometimes: there were her posters on the wall, and there was her green plastic shower caddy, and there was her towel on its hook, and here was Karina's pale pink nipple in her mouth, and here were Karina's fingers moving inside her, and here was Karina's tongue on her neck, and here—

In the daytime, when Louisa returned to her studio alone, she stared at the paintings and marveled at what she was suddenly capable of. When she encountered Karina in public—in class, at the cafeteria—neither of them acknowledged what was happening. They made polite small talk; once, Karina plucked a piece of lint from Louisa's sweater and let her hand linger at her collarbone for an extra second.

Louisa wasn't sure how it had been decided that they'd keep it secret. Karina seemed to want it that way. She still had brief, odd moments of furtiveness around Louisa, times when her face went blank and cold, and Louisa would feel a hollow kick of something like shame. She consoled herself with the fact that she wanted it secret, too. It wasn't just that this was the first time she'd done anything remotely intimate with a girl, and that she still wasn't sure what it meant—it was also that she didn't want other people to know. She didn't want Emma Ochoa and Ivy Morton and all those people gossiping about her.

And it was beginning to nag at Louisa, what they said about Karina. There was an unmistakable whiff of truth to it. The stuff about Karina's promiscuity, for example: Karina hadn't broken up with Preston Utley—

on several recent occasions Louisa had seen them together at a coffee shop or walking across campus, huddled together against the wind. Each time, she'd felt a burning in her chest and hurried away before they caught sight of her. It wasn't shame, she insisted to herself. It was that she didn't fully trust Karina.

Yet she couldn't seem to stop herself from pushing forward with whatever it was they were doing together. Louisa had always secretly believed herself a more serious artist than anyone she knew, but here was someone just as dedicated as she, in an entirely different way. Karina painted because she believed that art was power.

"It can make people feel the way you want them to feel," Karina had said to Louisa one night. "Art is the ultimate seduction."

They were lying in Karina's bed. Because of its featherbed mattress topper, hers was the one they usually fooled around in.

"Clearly," said Louisa, smirking.

"Yeah, see? It worked really well for me."

Louisa raised her eyebrows. "Don't you mean it worked really well for me?"

Karina grinned and waved her hand dismissively. "Any painter can seduce their model. History is full of artists banging their muses."

Louisa shifted so that she was lying on her side. She draped her arm over Karina's torso. "But those were all men seducing women."

"So?"

"So there's a difference," said Louisa. "Don't you think? The male gaze versus the female gaze and all that."

"You mean this is more equal?"

"Yeah," said Louisa, though she wasn't sure that this was true at all, not in their case.

"I was thinking . . ." Karina began.

"What?"

"Oh, just that you could push your bird women further. Like, your backgrounds, for example. They're always blank, either light or dark, right? But what if you actually *did* something with that field? Like layer other imagery into the background, or even have the figure of the bird woman sort of bleed into that imagery. Get rid of the discrete borders, you know. Get messier, less controlled. What do you think?"

Louisa kissed Karina's earlobe. "I like my backgrounds the way they are. I like the simplicity. I want to keep the focus on the figure."

She loved these late-night conversations in Karina's bed. She loved Karina's dry little jokes, loved her arch comments about their classmates. And Louisa loved telling her about herself, about what life was like back home and how different and alien Wrynn was. She loved the rapt, almost envious look Karina got when Louisa talked about her childhood, the afternoons spent in her uncle's pirogue, the fais do-dos. But Louisa hadn't told Karina about Pepere's stroke; she hadn't told her that, barring a win at Winter Exhibition, she'd be leaving Wrynn at the semester's end.

The only person she'd told was Alejandro. She'd also finally confided in him about what was happening between her and Karina. "But you have to swear you won't say a word," she'd said.

"About what? You dropping out of school or the fact that you're hooking up with the mad heiress? I think people would be more interested in the latter."

She looked away, annoyed at his flippancy. Why were people at this school so averse to sincerity? Why did everything have to be coated in ten layers of irony?

"I'm sorry," he said after a moment. "I get how hard this is." It was finals period; classes were canceled and they'd taken advantage of the rare afternoon off to visit the greenhouse, which had been donated by a rich alumnus in the seventies to celebrate Wrynn's centennial. A futuristic dome made of hexagonal glass panels, it looked absurdly out of place among the staid brick buildings. Inside, the air was warm and thick like a summer rainstorm. Blades of weak winter light sliced through the canopy.

"How hard what is?"

Alejandro gave her a candid look. "You don't strike me as someone who's entirely comfortable with your sexuality just yet."

Louisa reached out to touch the long, serrated limbs of an aloe plant.

"And correct me if I'm wrong," he added, "but it sounds like Karina is maybe the first girl you've ever slept with?"

Louisa nodded. The turtle that lived in the greenhouse pond surfaced, blinked, and sank back into the murky water.

"And it sounds like your family's kind of conservative?"

She thought of her mother—Mom, who'd always had a soft spot for misfits, being one herself. Mom wouldn't care. The rest of them might, though. Pepere—she didn't know what Pepere would say.

"Yeah," said Louisa. "They are."

"So is mine." He sighed. "It's exciting and scary and fraught even under the best of circumstances. And right now this doesn't seem like the best of circumstances."

"Yeah."

Alejandro bent over a small fernlike bush with leafy fronds and fuzzy, pale pink flowers. "Look," he said, brushing the frond lightly with his fingertip. Immediately the leaflets folded themselves inward, like a baby's fingers curling shut. A moment later they eased open again. "I never get tired of that."

"*Mimosa pudica*," Louisa read. "Bashful plant. We have those back home."

He glanced up at her. "For what it's worth, I do think you have a shot at winning one of those prizes."

"Thanks. I just—I'm trying not to count on it."

"What's your plan if you don't? Will you move back home?"

She had a not-quite-maxed-out credit card and a little bit in savings and a plane ticket home for December 23, the day the dorms closed for winter break. She'd booked the flight months ago. "I was thinking I might stay," she said.

"Here? No, dude, you don't want to live in Stonewater. Can you imagine how depressing?"

"No, I was thinking New York." It was the first time she'd voiced this idea out loud, though she'd been mulling it over since Thanksgiving.

"Oh," said Alejandro. "That's actually a great idea."

"It is?" she said with some surprise.

"Yeah, that's where everyone goes after graduation anyway, you'd just be a couple of years early."

For the first time in days, Louisa felt her dread begin to lift. "That's what I was thinking, too. It just seems so soon, though."

Alejandro waved this off. "You can apply to stay in the dorms over winter break if you need time to figure stuff out. Dude, this is great! It's only three hours away. I'll come visit you! And you can come back and visit, too."

Louisa allowed herself to imagine what that life might look like: talking to Karina on the phone at night, taking the bus to see her on the weekends, or Karina coming down to see *her*, introducing her to her parents. But no. It was unimaginable. She couldn't picture *it*—the affair, the hookup, she didn't know what to call it, certainly not a *relationship*—existing outside of her studio and their dorm room. And what about Preston? Where did he fit into this fantasy?

"I'll need a job," said Louisa.

"Talk to the profs. They all know people, they can hook you up."

"I don't know, I'd feel weird asking. I haven't even been here a full semester."

Alejandro made a face. "Don't be silly. The networking opportunities are like half the reason people come here. Everyone should be taking advantage of them, especially people like us."

"People like us?"

He smiled wryly. "The gifted and underserved. The meritorious riff-raff."

"Right," Louisa said, but she felt guilty including herself in this category. Alejandro was on a full scholarship, which meant that his family was genuinely *low-income*, that the admissions committee had seen enough promise in his work to grant him a full ride. Whereas Louisa wasn't *poor* poor, not really—she just had a sick grandfather, twenty thousand dollars in student loans, a handful of community college credits, and fucked-up priorities in life.

Alejandro's gaze broke upward. "Is it snowing again?"

It was. Snowflakes fell on the dome and melted, sliding down the glass in rivulets. Louisa watched the snow fall and felt the warm, damp air and smelled its loaminess, and these sensations were so incongruous they made her skin prickle.

The next day, Louisa sought out Maureen for the second time that semester. She found her in her office on the top floor of the Painting building, a small room cluttered with filing cabinets.

Maureen looked up from her computer in surprise. "Louisa. What can I do for you?"

"I, um, I had a question."

"Why don't you have a seat?"

Louisa did, but this put her at eye level with Maureen, and she felt suddenly cotton-mouthed, ashamed at what she was about to ask for.

"What can I do for you?" Maureen repeated.

Louisa felt a mounting pressure behind her eyes. "I was wondering—" She blinked several times and swallowed hard, but it was too late: she was crying, ugly-crying, her nose loosing a stream of snot. Maureen looked startled, then concerned. She pushed a box of tissues toward Louisa before getting up to close the door.

"Give us a little privacy . . . that's better. Deep breaths now. Can you tell me what's going on?"

Louisa wiped her nose and told Maureen everything: Pepere's stroke, her family's financial situation, her desire to move to New York if and when she left Wrynn, the fact that she had no idea what came next.

"I just started looking at sublets last night," she finished miserably. "Hopefully I find something before the dorms close."

At this, Maureen looked alarmed. "Oh, honey, no. It's really hard to find a sublet in New York."

Louisa had never heard Maureen call someone *honey.* "Oh," she said.

"You don't have anyone you could stay with? A friend or a relative?"

Louisa shook her head. She was afraid she might start crying again.

"Okay, hold on." Maureen typed something into her computer, then turned it around so Louisa could see the screen. "Do you think you could copy these?"

Louisa recognized the images immediately, though she couldn't say for sure where she'd seen them. They were poppy and psychedelic, bold cartoonish graphics and candy-colored anime.

"Is that—"

"Akito Kobayashi, yes. You've heard of him?"

"I have."

"Do you think you could paint these if someone asked you?"

"I think so?"

"I think you can, too," Maureen said. "You're very technically skilled. But I want to make sure before I email Craig."

"Who?"

"The head of Kobayashi's New York studio. Old colleague of mine." She pointed at the image on the screen. "Do you like it?"

"Kobayashi's work?"

Maureen gazed at her evenly. "Yes, his work. Do you like it?"

Louisa hesitated. "Um, to be completely honest, not really."

"That's good," Maureen said. "If you don't like what you're making you won't get too comfortable. I don't want you to become one of those artists who get so wrapped up in being an assistant to someone big that they never paint again."

Louisa twisted her hands behind her back. "I don't want that either."

"Good," said Maureen briskly. "I'll email Craig, but I can't promise anything. They may not be hiring right now, or they may want someone with a degree. I don't know. But it doesn't hurt to ask, right?"

Louisa nodded.

"And I'll put out some feelers about housing," Maureen added. "I'll let you know if I hear anything."

Louisa thanked her. On her way out of the building, she checked the time on her phone. She was supposed to meet Karina in two hours for their nightly painting session. When was the right time to tell her that she might be leaving? Soon, the semester would be over. Several times in recent days the truth had been on the tip of her tongue, but she'd held back. Any conversation about Louisa leaving was sure to lead to a conversation about the future—about *their* future—and Louisa wasn't sure she knew how to handle that. Until she heard back from Maureen, she decided, she'd keep all this to herself.

CHAPTER SIXTEEN

Over Thanksgiving break, something in Karina had changed. She seemed elated. Sometimes Preston looked at her when she thought no one was watching, and the expression she wore was one of pure joy. But it always disappeared as soon as she became aware of his gaze. And she was spending a lot less time with him. She was busy with finals, she said; didn't he remember how much the workload ramped up after Foundation Year? The thought that they had so little time left together before winter break gnawed at him, and he began toying with the idea of asking her to stay on campus for Christmas, to come live with him in his apartment. His father would be furious if he didn't come home, but he'd cross that bridge when he came to it.

Preston tried to push these worries aside and stay busy prepping for Winter Exhibition. Originally, he'd planned on showing a slide projection of images from The Wart, but when he'd mentioned the idea to Karina, she'd said, "Really? That seems a little blah." So he'd panicked and stayed up all night brainstorming, and by morning he had a new plan: he'd order more stuff from Blind Tiger—including shit he'd never consider consuming, like heroin—photograph each item, and display the picture alongside a wax cast of the item, ensuring that he wouldn't be in violation of the student handbook's rules. He'd be kind of cheating on his anti-object stance, but he figured that since all the items in the installation were illegal and had come from the black market, he had some wiggle room in terms of adhering to his own artistic ethos.

The biggest issue with this new plan wasn't that he hadn't gotten it approved—it'd been easy enough to forge Berger's signature on the updated proposal—but rather its cost. The Blind Tiger products aside, the supplies he'd need were outrageously expensive. Twenty bucks for a measly pound of artist-grade carving wax? *Three hundred dollars* for a gallon of silicone putty? He ended up nearly draining his checking account, which made him itchy with panic but was one more thing he resolved not to think about for now.

One afternoon in early December, Preston was crouched on his living room floor, molding silicone putty around a glassine baggie of heroin when he heard the key turn in the door. For a moment his heart stopped; then he remembered he'd given Karina a key before break. She walked in, dropping her purse on the counter, and gave him a puzzled look. "What are you doing?"

He hadn't told her about his new plans for the installation. He'd wanted to surprise her at Winter Exhibition. Oh well. "Making molds of these so I can cast them in wax."

Karina glanced at the small pile of glassine baggies waiting to be coated in putty. "Uh, why?"

He explained his thinking behind the installation: it explored the nature of illegality by showcasing reproductions of illegal objects but not the objects themselves. "Another thing I noticed is how some of these products are, like, *branded*. It's like this weird corporatization of the black market." He plucked another baggie from the pile on the floor and wrapped a wad of putty around it.

"So that's *heroin*?" Karina said.

"Yup. I haven't used any if that's what you're asking. Not really my thing." Needles freaked him out.

"And you're making silicone casts of *all* of this?"

"Not of everything. Some of the stuff I bought isn't explicitly banned in the handbook, so I figure I should be safe displaying it." For instance: an illustrated tutorial on hacking into ATMs, a contract for a "killer for

hire," a polished black briefcase packed with neat stacks of counterfeit
cash, fake IDs from every state plus Guam and the U.S. Virgin Islands,
reams and reams of stolen credit card numbers printed on smudged fax
paper, a guide to synthesizing MDMA, and an extremely convincing-
looking Harvard diploma and transcript bearing Preston's own name.

"I was talking about the baggies," said Karina. "Are you making individual molds from all of them?"

"Yeah." He looked up, scanning her face for a reaction. "Why?"

There was a faintly perceptible shift in Karina's expression, a shadow
of a smirk, and he felt his chest swell with rage and impotence. Before,
her mocking had never seemed serious; it was always in the spirit of
their intellectual jousting. But now he caught a flash of true contempt.
He bit down on his bottom lip, stunned by the hurt flooding his body.
Soon, though, it turned into anger—at himself or at Karina, he wasn't
certain. In his head, the project had seemed smart, conceptually rigor-
ous despite the haste with which he'd thrown it together, but now, as
Karina looked down at him, a seed of doubt took root.

"If the labels are what you're interested in," added Karina, "why not
just display the empty baggies?"

"Yeah, maybe," Preston muttered. That was actually a great idea.
Why hadn't he thought of it?

"Preston," Karina said, "can we talk?"

The bottom dropped out of his stomach. This was it. She was going
to dump him. He drew in a long breath, tried to keep his voice steady:
"I'm really busy right now. Can it wait till after I'm done?"

She tilted her head, doubt playing over her face.

"How about this?" he said, speaking past the panic thickening his
throat. "I'll take you out for dinner after Winter Exhibition. I'll be all ears
then. I'm just . . . in a crunch right now. This is my last Winter Exhibition. Gotta make it count."

She looked at him as though he were very far away. "Okay." She
picked her purse back up and slung it over her shoulder.

He rose to his feet and kissed her deeply, and after what seemed like
a moment of hesitation, she kissed him back. After she'd left, he soothed
himself with a little coke from his stash and some mindless web surfing.
He'd just started scrolling through his Reddit feed when he saw the

news item: *After Hoax Email, D.C. Mayor's Staff Members Arrive at Work in Christmas Attire.*

"No fucking way," he said to the empty apartment. As he read through the article, he dissolved into helpless laughter. He texted Slade the link: *Was this u?*

Slade replied: *maybe;)*

But it was only a couple of hours later, as he was in the middle of his evening workout, that the idea occurred to him. How had he not thought of it before? If he pulled this off, the rest of the Occupy Wrynn organizers—even Sammy Nakamura, who was still martyring himself sleeping in the encampment almost every night—would be forced to admit that he'd been right all along. He hopped off the treadmill and called Slade, who picked up after two rings.

"What's going on?" said Slade.

Preston explained what he had in mind. "Is that possible?"

"For sure," said Slade. "Totally doable. When would you like it to happen?"

CHAPTER SEVENTEEN

By mid-December Louisa had finished five bird woman paintings and was almost done with a sixth.

"Have you picked one for Winter Exhibition yet?" Karina asked one night. "I just submitted a painting yesterday." She was posing for Louisa in a chair, legs slightly parted, one arm slung over her head in a posture of easy languor.

"Not yet," Louisa said. The deadline to submit work to the sophomore show—each class competed internally for prizes—was in two days. It was the first time the topic of Winter Exhibition had come up between them, and Louisa felt the specter of competition, and her own anxiety about the future, arise alongside it. There had been several evenings now when, on her way to studio, she'd promised herself, *I'll tell her tonight.* But each time she faltered at the sight of Karina's unclothed body, just as she faltered whenever she tried to select a piece for Winter Exhibition. Telling Karina, choosing a painting—both were a kind of foreclosing, a doing that could not be undone. And what if she said the wrong words? What if she chose wrong?

"You're cutting it close there," Karina said. "Have you narrowed down your options at all?"

Louisa pointed at a canvas drying on the far side of her studio. It depicted Karina with the head of a scarlet ibis. "Maybe that one."

"Oh." Karina went quiet, all the warmth draining from her expression.

Louisa set down her brush. "Is something wrong?"

Flatly, Karina said, "That's the only one that doesn't show my face."

"Yeah . . ."

Of course that was why she'd chosen it. Maybe not consciously, but now that Karina had called her out, there was no denying it. *I'm scared,* she realized. Scared of the possibility that Karina had participated in the creation of these paintings just as much as she had. The possibility that she couldn't do it alone.

"Do you not want people to know that I posed for you?" Karina spoke in the same flat tone. She broke her pose, bringing her knees up and hugging them to her chest. Another silence elapsed. Finally, Louisa said, "I thought you didn't want people to know either," and at the same time Karina said, "I just think it's shitty of you, that's all."

"What is?"

Karina gave her a level look. "I've put so much time into this project of yours and now you're basically saying that you don't want people to know about it."

Louisa felt a stirring of anger. "Karina, you *wanted* to pose for me. Don't act like I coerced you."

"You're dodging my point."

"What?"

"I'm not going to pretend like I don't know what people say about me." Agitation had crept into Karina's voice. "I just thought you were above caring what those idiots think."

Louisa spoke slowly. "You're acting like what they say has no basis in reality."

Karina went very pale except for two spots of color high on her cheeks. "What do you mean?"

"You *are* still seeing that guy. Preston."

Karina looked away.

"I saw y'all," Louisa went on. "Yesterday on Washington Street." They'd been walking down the sidewalk, Preston with his arm around

Karina's shoulders, a gut-punch of a sight. Louisa had dipped into the burger place to avoid them.

Karina rose and began pulling on her clothes. "We—we never agreed to anything. You and I, we never agreed to anything."

"Yeah, but have you considered how this feels from *my* perspective? Like, to me it feels like the thing you have with Preston is your real relationship and I'm just this . . . side piece."

Karina was tugging on her tights. She still wouldn't look at Louisa.

"You've been shitty to me, too," said Louisa. "You've made me feel—" She'd been about to say *unspecial.* "I don't understand what your deal is."

Karina was bent over, lacing up her boots. Now she jerked her head up and said, "My deal is that I think you're a coward."

Softly, Louisa said, "That's really unfair."

"You play it safe, Louisa. In your life and in your art. I give you a suggestion to make your work more interesting and you don't even pretend to consider it."

"It's *my* work. It's mine, and *I* get to decide—"

"Yeah, you *do* get to decide. You decided not to take a risk. You call your art regional, but it's not. It's provincial. You're a provincial artist."

Until now Louisa hadn't been in danger of crying, but now that on-the-verge feeling began to clog her throat. "So are you," she managed.

Karina scoffed.

"You think that because you're from New York you're exempt from provincialism?" Louisa said, her voice rising. "You make trendy shit for rich people. You make paintings that snobbish urban assholes can feel smart for liking."

For a moment, Karina just stared at Louisa, expressionless. Then she said, icily, "I'm going to go now."

For a while, she wasn't sure how long, Louisa sat in front of her unfinished painting. Finally, she cleaned up and went back to her dorm room. Karina wasn't there. She curled up and went to sleep without changing out of her clothes or brushing her teeth.

The next morning, she woke up to an email from Maureen: *I have news for you. Stop by during my office hours today and we'll chat.*

Louisa's spirits lifted momentarily. She hesitated before tapping out a text message to Karina: *I'm sorry.*

For the rest of the day, Louisa kept one eye out for her roommate and the other on her phone, but she didn't see Karina anywhere on campus. By midafternoon, when Louisa went to meet with Maureen, she still hadn't replied to her text.

"Good news," Maureen said. "Craig wants to set up an interview."

"He does?!"

"Yep. Said anytime after New Year's is good." Maureen reached for a sticky note. "I'll give you his contact info."

"Oh my god. *Thank* you."

"Oh! And on the housing front—you allergic to cats?"

"No. I have a cat back home, Napoleon."

"Good name. An old student of mine is looking for someone to cat-sit while she's at a residency in Italy. She can't pay you, but it'd be eight weeks' free housing in Washington Heights. You interested?"

"Definitely."

Maureen peeled off another sticky note. "Perfect. I'll give you her email. Her name's Ines Fidalgo. I think she said she'll be gone from early January through the end of February."

Louisa looked out the window. It had started snowing again; the red elms looked blurred. "Thank you," she said.

She went straight from Maureen's office to her studio. She still hadn't picked a painting for Winter Exhibition, and tomorrow was the last day to submit.

She surveyed her five finished bird woman canvases. For a long time, she stood there, paralyzed with indecision. At last, she stepped forward and lifted one up. *Please,* she thought. *Please let this be the right one.*

For the next week, Louisa didn't see Karina. Not in their room, nor in the studios, nor in the dining hall. She'd never replied to that text message.

Louisa received permission to remain in the dorms for the first half of winter break. She was informed that in order to save on heating costs, she'd be moved to a single in a different building where students wintering on campus were consolidated. She began packing her belongings. Slowly, her side of the room grew emptier; Karina's stayed the same.

On the evening of Winter Exhibition, Louisa called her mother to tell her she wasn't coming home when the semester ended.

"You're kidding, right?" said Mom.

"No. Unless I win one of these Winter Exhibition prizes, I'm moving to New York."

There was a lengthy pause. "What about money?"

"I have an interview lined up for a job as an artist's assistant."

"Okay. Do you have a place to live?"

"Yes."

Mom let out a bark of laughter. "Lulu, you know this is insane, right?"

"It's not insane."

"Why don't you come home for a little bit? Just till you get your bearings?"

"I can't. I've made plans, everything's arranged."

There was another pause. "I just want to make sure you're doing this for the right reasons."

"What are the right reasons?"

"I don't want you to move to an expensive place where you don't know anyone because you think that's what you're supposed to do."

Louisa was silent. There was some truth to this, she knew.

"It's not like your only two options are come home and move to New York," Mom went on. "It's not a binary. There are other things you can do. But from where I'm sitting . . ."

"What?"

"Well, chère, when I look at your paintings, I think to myself, 'This is something only a Cajun girl could've made.' I just wonder why you'd want to go all the way to New York to make Cajun art."

Louisa didn't know what to say. She didn't know how to explain that she wanted to amount to more than her mother had, that she was *hungry*, hungrier than Mom had ever been. That home wasn't enough anymore, that she feared it would snuff out the small flame she'd managed to stoke inside herself. That what she craved wasn't the well-worn love of her family, but the flinty indifference of the unknown, that it was a kind of inspiration, that it had fueled the best work of her life so far. That she wanted to see what it had to offer her now.

She didn't know how to explain it, so instead she said, "I'll call you tomorrow, okay? I promise." Then she put on her nicest dress, a dark purple sheath she'd bought for her high school graduation, and went to the museum.

She found her painting on the second floor with the rest of the sophomore work—the first-years hung on the first floor, the juniors on the third, and so on. She searched the walls for prize announcements but didn't see any.

The galleries were freezing, so Louisa kept her coat on. President Fowler, a balding man with the long, sorrowful face of a hound— she'd seen him only once before, at the convocation ceremony in September—was making the rounds, apologizing for the museum's finicky heating system and urging people to help themselves to coffee and tea from steaming silver urns. Flocks of visitors drifted through the white corridors, their footsteps echoing on the polished floor. You could tell the parents from the visiting dealers and critics by their clothes. The former were dressed as though for a graduation—fathers in suits and ties, mothers in heels and pearls—while the latter wore kimonos, floaty silks, jumpsuits and complicated wraps, chunky jewelry and cowboy boots.

Louisa wove her way through the sophomore show. Right away, she noticed her classmates giving her some weird looks.

"Nice painting," Ivy said. She wasn't wearing her foxtail, but she had on a white fur stole splashed—ironically, Louisa figured—with red paint.

"Oh, thanks," Louisa said. "Your piece is cool, too." It was a silicone sculpture that looked like ropes of slick, pale flesh draped over a sort of metal truss. Actually, Louisa found it weird and creepy, but maybe that was the point.

"You're funny, you know," said Ivy with a crooked smile.

"What? Why?"

"I just didn't take you for a dark horse, that's all."

Louisa couldn't think straight. "Isn't that, like, the definition of a dark horse?" Before Ivy could reply, she added, "Actually—I was on my way to the bathroom, sorry." As she walked away, Emma came up to Ivy and said, in a perfectly audible voice, "Dude, have you *seen* Louisa's painting?"

But Louisa was too anxious, too hopeful to care. Where was Karina? Once she showed up, once she saw the painting Louisa had chosen, everything would be all right.

Because in the end, she had submitted the first painting she'd made of Karina, the one that depicted her hunched over, her back covered in wounds. It was the painting that had made Karina kiss her, the one that had precipitated everything between them. Choosing it had been Louisa's way of apologizing. And of showing Karina that she was wrong, that Louisa wasn't a coward. That she was capable of doing something that scared her and not regretting it.

A tall man with a gleaming shaved head and tortoiseshell glasses strode past, and Louisa heard him say to his companion, "Nice to see the youth are keeping figuration alive." Her pulse sped up. She was one of the few painters in the sophomore class who made figurative art, and that man looked like a dealer or a critic, not a parent. Louisa walked faster now, scanning the gallery for Karina—for her painted self and her physical self—and nearly collided with Jack Culicchia. He gave her a genuine smile and said, "Well done, Louisa." Impossible now not to let herself swell with hope.

As she passed Neel's submission, a soccer-ball-sized snow globe filled with eerie leafless trees and tiny, headless figures, he stepped out from behind a column and touched her shoulder. "Hey," he said. "I just want to say, I think you were robbed."

"What?"

Neel pointed to the wall across from them, where Louisa saw a painting that she immediately recognized as Karina's. It was an abstract piece with swaths of bright orange and teal drop-shadowed over a background of jumbled, illegible text. Beside it, two ribbons, one red, one blue: *Best Painting* and *Best in Show.*

Louisa felt a cold wave of jealousy, a bitter surge that rose up in her and made it hard to breathe. She turned to Neel. "Have you seen her?"

"Who?" he said, though it was obvious he knew who she was talking about. She wanted to punch him.

"Karina."

"I don't think so, but Alejandro was looking for you. He went up-stairs to check out the junior show."

"Oh," Louisa said. "Sorry, um . . . see you in a bit?" She continued down the corridor, then looped back around and returned to her own painting. A few yards away, the elevator doors slid open and let out a group of chattering students:

"—pretty baller—"

"—d'you think Jo's is open—"

"—if my flight gets delayed or—"

"—Preston Utley's installation—"

Louisa shivered, coiling her scarf more tightly around her neck. Was Karina upstairs at the senior show, with *him*? She must be. Where else would she have been this past week? The thought of them together made something inside Louisa wobble.

President Fowler came hurrying down the corridor just then, hissing into his cellphone, his face the color of ham. What now? Had the HVAC system caught fire? Louisa pulled out her phone and checked to see if Ines had replied to her last email. They'd been exchanging messages for the past few days, coordinating logistics. Ines had also sent pictures of her cats: one was a calico, the other an orange tabby. Two unread emails sat in her inbox. The first was from her grandfather:

HI HONEY YOUR MAMA SAYS YOURE MAKING A GO FOR IT IN THE BIG APPLE. TELL ME YOUR ADDRESS ID LIKE TO SEND YOU A LITTLE SOMETHING TO GET YOU ON YOUR FEET BUT DONT TELL YOUR MAMA. ALL MY LOVE PEPERE.

Shame washed over her. Louisa glanced at the second message:

From: fowler@wrynn.edu
  To: allschool@wrynn.edu
  Subject: The future of Wrynn

Dear Wrynn Community,
    In recognition of the ongoing financial crisis, the College's board of trustees has voted to liquidate approximately fifty percent of the

Wrynn Museum's art collection. The proceeds, valued at around
$30 million, will make Wrynn tuition-free for all students from families
earning less than $120,000 per year.

She stopped reading as she felt happiness sneak up and overcome her. "Oh god," she said under her breath. "Oh god oh god oh god." She forwarded the email to her mother, adding a row of exclamation points. Then, too impatient now to keep searching for Karina, she called her. As the phone rang, she thought about what she'd say: *I'm sorry. I was wrong. I care about you so much.* But Karina didn't pick up. Never mind. She'd go looking for her later, apologize in person, lay her whole self out before her. Now that she was definitely staying at Wrynn, there would be plenty of time for them to talk, for Louisa to explain. For now, exhausted as she was from the night's emotional whiplash, she'd go upstairs and find Alejandro, celebrate with him.

Chapter Eighteen

Hurrying away from Louisa's studio that awful night, Karina's body hummed with distress. She crossed the quad and turned onto Washington Street, breathing raggedly. She went to Preston's apartment because she still had a key and couldn't think of anywhere else to go. She found him pounding away on the treadmill, shirtless, the light from the street glancing off his sweaty chest. There was heavy metal playing at a volume that struck her, in the back of her mind, as too loud for the hour.

"Are you okay?" He hopped off the treadmill and tapped his phone screen. The music stopped.

Karina wrapped her arms around his neck and kissed him. It was so strange. Just the other day she'd been on the verge of breaking up with him, and now she thought she might go insane if they didn't fuck.

Preston peered down at her, his brow furrowed with concern. "What happened?"

"Nothing."

"Why are you crying?"

"I'm not. It's cold out," she said. She stood on tiptoes and kissed him again, buried her face in his neck, pushed him toward the bedroom.

"Wow," he said. "Wow. Okay."

The next morning, she couldn't get out of bed. Her body felt leaden with dread. "I don't feel good," she mumbled, pulling the blanket up over her head to block out the sunlight. Her own warm, dark little cave, stale breath gathering inside it.

Gently, Preston pulled back the blanket and felt her forehead with the back of his hand, the way Fiona used to when Karina was small. "Are you sick, d'you think?"

"Maybe."

"Want me to bring you some ginger ale or something?"

She shook her head into the pillow.

"You should probably just chill here and rest, then."

Karina closed her eyes. When she opened them again the pattern of sunlight and shadows on the wall was different and Preston was standing in the doorway.

"Hey," he said. "How are you feeling? I picked up some dinner."

Had she really slept all day? She wasn't hungry, but she knew she ought to eat something. She forced down half a bowl of pork ramen from the place around the corner—it tasted like salt and heat, nothing more—before crawling back into bed.

"Karina? Should you see a doctor?"

"I'm fine. I just need to sleep."

The next time she regained consciousness Preston was sitting next to her, stroking her hair. She squinted up at him.

"Hi," he said. His eyes were gentle. "You've been asleep a really long time. I think maybe you should see a doctor."

With some effort, she rolled over so her back was to him. "I'm fine."

"Do you want me to call your parents?" Preston said.

"No."

It was like last semester all over again. Karina felt at once miserable and numb. There was a part of her that wanted to scream and cry and claw at things, and another, heavier part of her that was keeping her pinned to the bed. She was overwhelmed by a deep disgust toward herself, by the certainty that she was worthless, that no one loved or valued her. The last time this had happened because everyone, including her freshman roommate, Penelope, had stopped speaking to her, and after a few weeks she'd begun to feel as though she no longer existed. One night in studio she'd looked at the balcony and thought, *What if I jumped?* She hadn't, of course, because she was a coward. She'd cried, very messily and publicly, before going back to her room and crawling into bed and sleeping and sleeping and sleeping. Eventually, Penelope had called Psych Services, who'd alerted Harry and Fiona, who'd taken her to the lovely place upstate with a fountain in the courtyard and the grounds that she wasn't allowed to leave. She'd never finished last semester's coursework, but her parents must've pulled some strings, because when she returned to Wrynn in the fall she was in good academic standing. She'd read about the supposed link between creativity and mental illness, but in her opinion it was bullshit. If she made brilliant paintings, it was in spite of these episodes, not because of them.

"Are you sure you don't want me to—" Preston began.

"I'm fine. Please don't call my parents."

On the night of Winter Exhibition, Preston told Karina, "Your color's coming back." He'd been so sweet and solicitous, bringing her snacks and cold drinks, asking her how she was feeling, touching her delicately, as though she might break if he weren't careful. She looked at him, at his face alert with sympathy, and she felt a sudden rush of tenderness toward him, an ache under her breastbone.

"You should probably get ready," he said. "Doors open at seven. Do you have an outfit picked out?"

She was in her panties, socks, and a sleeveless shirt of Preston's. Her hair was piled on top of her head. "I think I'm gonna skip it," she said in an offhand voice. "I'm still feeling a little bit under the weather."

She hadn't crossed paths with Louisa since that night in studio a week ago, and the thought of seeing her—or the scarlet ibis painting that showed Karina's body but not her face—made her want to curl up inside herself and go to sleep again. Louisa had texted her once, but Karina had deleted the message without reading it. Then she'd erased Louisa's number from her phone.

Preston studied her, deep lines in his forehead. "Still? I really think . . . Karina, I really think you should see someone. If not a doctor, then a counselor maybe?"

She looked down and shook her head. "I'm fine. I think I'm out of the woods, but I just want to take it easy."

She lifted her gaze and saw that he was still studying her. Those pale, worried eyes. "Are you sure?"

"Yes," she said. "I'm sure I don't want to see anyone and I'm sure I don't want to go to Winter Exhibition. It's just going to be a bunch of people getting drunk and taking selfies and *not* looking at the art and eating canapés and talking out of their asses."

"But you know there will be critics there, right? And art dealers?"

"Since when do you care about that?"

"I don't," he said calmly. "But I thought you did."

He left soon after. Karina smoked some of his weed and went to bed.

She woke up some time later to Preston shaking her. "Hey," he said. "You up?"

She peered at him through slitted eyes.

"I have good news and bad news," he said.

Blearily, Karina sat up. "Yeah?"

"I just got expelled."

But he was grinning. Why did he look so happy?

"What's the good news?"

"I got an offer of representation. From Axiom Art. The creative director wants to set me up with a show."

Karina ground her fists into her eyes. She'd heard of Axiom, of course. She yawned. "So you're a capitalist now. Cool."

Preston's smile dimmed. "Sometimes you have to work *within* the system in order to dismantle it."

Karina blinked at him. She was pretty sure she was still stoned. "Keep telling yourself that."

"What?"

"I said, 'Keep telling yourself that.'"

He wasn't smiling anymore. "I need to make a living. I'm not gonna be waiting tables."

"That's fair," she said flatly. "Just don't be a hypocrite about it."

He leaned toward her, as though to physically push past the tension, and took her hand. "Come with me."

"What?"

"I already showed Brian your work—the painting you had up at the exhibition and also some pictures on my phone—and he says he'll take you on, too. He thinks you're incredibly versatile. Oh, and you won Best Painting at the sophomore show. And Best in Show. I think Brian might've been judging, actually."

"What—who's Brian?"

"Brian Parrish! The art dealer! I told him we were a package deal, and he said he'd represent both of us. He's even going to give us each a monthly stipend so we won't have to get day jobs while we wait for our shows to go up."

Karina's first thought was: *This is what you've always wanted.* Her second: *Not like this.* Not like it was some trinket Preston had picked up for her on his way home. Then she thought of Louisa, of the pained, twisted look on her face the last time Karina had seen her. With Preston she'd always be in control. He adored her. Nothing would change that. And besides, wouldn't it feel glorious to leave Wrynn in triumph, to stick it to Foxtail and Long-Distance and all the other assholes who'd shunned her and gossiped about her and called her crazy? She was brilliant. Brian Parrish saw it, and soon so would the rest of the world. She didn't need school anymore. Maybe she never had.

"Okay," she said.

Things happened quickly from there. Two days later both of them signed contracts with Axiom, and a few days after that, Karina went back to her dorm room and packed up her belongings. Louisa had moved out completely, taken down her posters, stripped the bed. Strange. Didn't she know that you were allowed to leave your stuff in your room over winter break? Then Karina realized that Louisa must have requested—and been granted—a room transfer. The thought pinched at her heart.

Preston helped her pack, even though Wrynn was pressuring police to treat his email as a crime and he was technically no longer allowed on campus. She'd mail the boxes to their new apartment in Bushwick, which Preston had hastily secured through some techie friend of his.

The twenty or so paintings that she'd made at Wrynn over the past year and a half would be shipped directly to Axiom Art, courtesy of Brian.

She'd tasked Preston with packing up her coat hangers, forgetting that her closet was where she'd hidden Wally.

"What's this?" Preston said, holding up her frame.

It made her oddly nervous, seeing Wally in his big hands.

"Did you make it?" he said.

Karina continued emptying her chest of drawers. "I wish. It's an Egon Schiele."

He whistled. "Why's it in your closet?"

She slipped a stack of folded shirts into a suitcase and held out her hand. "Just keeping it safe."

"You know Schiele was a sex offender, right?"

Karina didn't reply. She wrapped Wally in a sweater. She didn't feel like explaining that it wasn't Schiele she treasured but Wally herself, the way she lived on in Schiele's lines. She didn't think Preston would understand.

Karina was walking back from the post office the day before she and Preston were scheduled to leave for New York when her phone vibrated. She answered without looking at the caller ID.

Her father's voice in her ear: "Karina, did you take the Schiele that was in your bedroom?"

She stopped in her tracks. "Yes," she said, the truth slipping out before she could think of a plausible lie.

For a few seconds Harry was quiet. "Okay. I know you've been upset with us, but do you understand that that piece doesn't belong to you? You stole it, do you get that?"

"I don't see it that way."

"You don't, do you?" Harry's voice was clipped with impatience now.

Karina lifted a hand to her mouth, chewed off a hangnail, spat it out onto the salt-caked sidewalk. "It's been in my bedroom since I was born. I've looked at it every day of my life."

Harry laughed. "Do you seriously—I could call the police right now and tell them where you are." There was anger in his voice now, and Karina felt her own rage rise to meet it.

"If you call the police," she said, "I'll tell them all about you and Stella McNamara. How do you think a statutory rape charge will hold up in the divorce?"

There was a long silence. Then Harry said, "Karina, I have a bill for next semester's tuition sitting right here in front of me. I'm not going to pay it until you return that Schiele. Do you understand?"

"I understand," she said, and hung up, smiling.

PART TWO

Chapter Nineteen

Other men—men more adventurous than Robert, or braver, or in possession of more frequent-flyer miles—might've started over someplace else. Berlin, for instance, was the art mecca of Europe, and in Guatemala you could live like a king for next to nothing, and Israel was hungry for disaffected American Jews, and Austin was temperate, still affordable, and despite its location largely devoid of Republicans. But Robert was tired. He was tired and monolingual, and his social skills were drying up with age, and there was an apartment in Crown Heights with his name on the deed—all paid off, thanks to his ex-wife, Diane— and a decent view of Prospect Park from the kitchen window if you craned your neck.

So he gave notice to his tenants—the advertising executive, his wife who'd tired of teaching yoga and had moved on to Pilates, their son, Striker, who didn't yet go by his middle name, though it was only a matter of time—and, in early January, he moved back into his apartment. He found the place unrecognizable. The tenants had slathered the kitchen with chalkboard paint, ombréd the walls in various shades of blue, and hung a mason jar chandelier in the living room. They'd also attempted to create an exposed brick wall in the master bedroom, apparently giving up after chipping off a few square feet of drywall. Robert took refuge in the second bedroom, unchanged save for a grubby area under the windowsill, which he suspected Striker had designated as his booger-wiping spot.

The first thing he did, after wrestling the chandelier off the living room ceiling, was find an art opening to attend. If he was going to worm his way back into the art world, he needed to be seen. He needed to schmooze and make important people laugh and convincingly pretend he'd been somewhat productive in the past decade. Finding an opening whose guests would be happy to see him, however, proved tricky. Two thirds of Robert's mental Rolodex was cordoned off by imaginary yellow police tape reading ON DIANE'S SIDE. Anyone associated with his old dealer, Brian Parrish, or his old gallery, Axiom Art, was similarly off-limits. That left a handful of people he hadn't spoken to since he left the city to teach.

In the end he settled on the opening reception for Claire Kelly's new solo show. Sweet Claire, his old grad school classmate, a kind, fragile girl who'd smeared her canvases with vestiges of her childhood trauma and treated crits like a bizarre form of therapy. And yet, according to the Internet, Claire had hatched and kept alive that most finicky and elusive of creatures: a career—late-blooming and slow-growing, but a career nonetheless.

He'd need a haircut.

Was it his imagination, or were people giving him looks? As soon as he entered the gallery, he swore he saw a young man point him out to his stilettoed companion, who snickered into her wineglass. And the red-haired woman writing in the guest book, her wisp of a body pressed up against the black front desk—had her lips curled disdainfully at the sight of him? Even the gallery itself, so sleek and futuristic, seemed to be staring at him, emitting cool alien hostility. Robert imagined its lines and angles assessing his sags and bulges.

Wrynn's dean, when he dismissed him, had implied that there was art school and then there was the art world, and that what occurred in one had little bearing on the other. In exchange for a quiet, fuss-free resignation and forfeiture of all remaining residency funds, Robert was free to slink back whence he had come.

No one knew, Robert assured the panicked voice in his head. Impossible.

Now the red-haired woman was talking on her cellphone. She had a braying laugh and a long horsey face to match. While she spoke, she doodled on the back of her hand with the guest book pen. Her eyes flickered over Robert—and there it was again, that scornful, *knowing* look.

Robert thought of the dean's office, all leather and mahogany. The chair he'd been sitting in creaked every time he shifted, which was a lot because he fidgeted when he was nervous.

"Preston Utley is *your* advisee, correct?" the dean had said.

"Technically," Robert replied. "Yes."

"The IT people have apprised us that the email came from him. From a device registered in his name."

"I see. Some kind of stunt."

The dean folded his hands. "Were you aware of his plans?"

"No," said Robert. "I had no idea."

"There's also the matter of the contraband in his installation—"

"I had nothing to do with that either."

The dean sighed. "The fact remains that you *did* sign off on his project proposal."

"*None* of that was in the proposal he presented to me."

"So you're saying you didn't properly supervise him?"

"No, I— He must've forged my signature. Look, the student has a documented history of inappropriate behavior."

"As do you." The dean leaned back in his chair, crossing his arms. "You obviously have a vendetta against him. I mean, my god, that piece in *Artforum*—you understand how unprofessional that was."

"I do, of course."

"*You* were the teacher, *you* were supposed to be the responsible one."

"Right, of course."

"And after everything that's happened, I just don't see how you can remain here."

Even weeks later, recalling this exchange made Robert shudder. He

searched the growing crowd for familiar faces. Nearly everyone was decades younger than him. Their voices blurred together, rising and falling as one, butting up against the electro-swing blaring from hidden
speakers. Artist behavior hadn't changed much in the past decade, Robert observed with anthropological interest. The artists—for it was
mostly artists who went to openings, with the occasional critic or collector or hawkish dealer sprinkled in—were visibly alert to one another. As he watched their roving eyes, Robert could almost hear them
sizing each other up, mapping out the invisible networks inside the gallery. Who was talking to whom? Who just got snubbed by someone
important? Who was that leaving early, and why? Who did that person
think they were, wearing an outfit like that?

Who *were* all these people? Surely not all friends of Claire's—she was
the same age as Robert. It occurred to him that Claire was an anomaly
in the art world, one of its rare birds. A female painter who'd achieved
success only in her middle age, whose openings attracted up-and-
coming artists, or young ones at least? Impressive, no denying that.

For lack of someone to talk to, he did what nobody else seemed to be
doing: he looked at the art. That was something else that hadn't changed
either—if you were young and struggling and hopeful, you didn't go to
openings to look at art, you went because you were afraid of missing
out. He was surprised by how good the work was. In grad school,
Claire's paintings had been messy and hysterical, but these were sober,
controlled compositions that conveyed, through simple gesture drawings and judicious use of texture, an indelible depth of feeling. Suddenly
he was flooded with sadness. Claire had struggled in her youth while
Robert's career had soared, but he'd peaked and dropped off the map,
like a burst of flame, hot and fierce but fleeting. And meanwhile, Claire
had plugged away in obscurity for years until her work was ripe and
ready for the world. And what was more—it would last. It would be
remembered, because—oh, he could see it so clearly—it possessed that
rare timeless quality. Claire was an ember burning low and slow. She
was consistent. She could reproduce what worked in her art again and
again. He couldn't.

"Robert, is that you?" He turned and there she was, just as he remembered her—tiny Claire with her fledgling nose and her pale eyes and

those smile lines that bracketed her mouth like a set of parentheses, which she'd had when she was young but were now deeply etched into her face. She wore a long, drapey dress that subsumed her body. They hugged briefly; though it was the sort of aseptic hug that almost precluded touch, Robert felt he might crush her if he wasn't careful.

"Your new work is beautiful," he said. "Absolutely breathtaking."

"Thanks." She ran a hand through her hair. "It's been a journey."

"Slow and steady," said Robert like an idiot.

The corners of Claire's mouth twitched. "You could say that." She licked her lips. "What've you been up to?"

Robert waved his hand in the air, narrowly missing someone's wineglass. "Just a lot of residencies and fellowships. One after the other. If you could date degree-granting entities, I'd be a serial monogamist."

"I heard you were at Wrynn last," she said without expression.

He swallowed. Somebody called Claire's name, and she half turned before remembering to say goodbye: "I'd better get back to it. Enjoy." And Robert understood that this was her version of unfriendliness, that she was unhappy he was here, which meant one of two things: either she *knew,* or his stock had fallen further than he'd thought, had plummeted so much that even a midlister like Claire had the sense to shy away from him.

Robert slogged through the crowd to the bar—which wasn't a bar so much as a long table cluttered with plastic wineglasses and sweating, half-drunk bottles—where he proceeded to sample several varieties of supermarket chardonnay. It was in this condition that he collided with Frank LaCount, another grad school classmate he hadn't seen in years. Frank was a video-artist-turned-sculptor who'd once broken into his uncle's funeral home to film himself dancing to ABBA among the cadavers. The summer between their first and second year at Cooper Union, Robert and Frank had driven an old van to Arcosanti and back, tripping on acid almost the entire way.

"Rob-man!" cried Frank.

"Frankie!" said Robert.

Much hugging and backslapping and reminiscing ensued, during which it emerged that Frank was in more or less the same state as Robert, sobriety- and career-wise. Frank had always had the distinction, in

Robert's mind, of being both a whole lot of fun and pathologically truthful. Over the course of the rest of the night—they soon tired of mediocre wine and moved on to a twenty-four-hour liquor store nearby—Frank told Robert in the bluntest of terms, all while managing to keep him in gales of laughter, that his worst fears had come to pass.

On his phone, Frank showed Robert an email chain ("Subject: didn't you go to school with this guy?") with a link to Preston Utley's review of Robert's retrospective, which had apparently gone semiviral. Frank also showed Robert a screenshot from The Wart, where Preston had posted a detailed account of his expulsion in which he accused Robert of betraying his own artistic and political principles and of throwing Preston under the bus.

Robert had to admit that Preston's stunt had been brilliant. Spoofing, it was called, apparently. Wrynn had immediately gotten inquiries from the press about their plans to increase financial aid. A few students, thinking they were getting free rides, had canceled their loans. Embarrassing thing to walk back. There'd been an uproar from the students, of course, especially the campus Occupy group, which for some time had been lobbying for better financial aid. Wrynn had briefly tried to press charges against Preston, then backed off when it became apparent that this would only further martyr him. *Inside Higher Ed* had done a piece on the fiasco, as had the *Times* (mercifully, neither mentioned Robert).

As Robert lay on his back on a bench in Foley Square, quite drunk, alternately laughing and trying to pretend he wasn't about to cry, Frank unveiled the pièce de résistance: a post on the gossip blog ArtyWag detailing the entire humiliating saga, complete with photos of both Robert and Preston, anonymous quotes from Wrynn students and faculty commenting on Robert's lousy teaching and artistic irrelevance, and a screenshot of Preston's hoax email. The post added that Preston Utley's work had received some attention as a result of "the incident." *Utley recently signed a contract with Axiom Art, the Chelsea gallery owned by dealer Brian Parrish. His debut exhibition is set to open this spring.*

"Now that," said Robert, "is just too much."

"What is?"

"My old dealer signed him! Parrish, that snake."

"Motherfucker," agreed Frank, swigging whiskey from a brown paper bag.

"I feel like a cuckold." He covered his face with his hands.

"This business is *so* polyamorous," said Frank. "Figuratively and literally. My theory is that it has something to do with our incessant lust for the new. Do you know what I'm talking about? Of course you do, you're divorced."

"No wonder Claire was so unhappy to see me."

"Claire's never liked you," said Frank—not unkindly, just matter-of-factly. "It has nothing to do with any of this."

"What?"

"You can't really blame her, Rob. You were always a dick to her in crit."

Robert tugged at his hair, as though the gesture could pull nonexistent memories from his skull. "Was I?"

Frank narrowed his eyes.

"Wasn't I harsh toward everyone, though?" said Robert. "Wasn't that just my art school persona?"

"In Claire's case, as I recall, you specifically went after the emotional content of her work."

Robert cringed. "I did?"

"Well, I kind of thought you implied she was being melodramatic. Not that I'm judging. Lord knows I voiced my share of sexist drivel in my youth. I see it as an essential stage in the normal development of the human male, but I suspect Claire doesn't share that view."

Robert had an uneasy inkling of what Frank was talking about. He took a long pull of whiskey. "This is the end of my career. I'm staring it in the face."

"Okay, but you know that kid wasn't its death knell, right? Nobody cares how you behave or whether you're a shitty teacher. You should've seen the writing on the wall when you stopped selling. That's your only crime. I should know—my career has been in its death throes for years. I play online poker now. I make more than I ever did selling art."

"Yeah?"

"It's great. You never have to leave your house, and you can blame variance when you're crap." A homeless man shuffled by, dragging a plastic garbage bag full of clinking glass. He eyed them for a moment before moving on. "You can have this when we're done," Frank called.

"Do you remember when we were in school," said Robert, "and all the successful artists were making unsellable work?"

"Vaguely."

"Robert Smithson was carving shit into the earth, and that Dutch guy, what was his name, was Krazy-Gluing himself to bridges naked, and there was that European art collective that tried to dye the Venetian lagoon some unnatural color?"

"Right. I forgot about that."

"And the whole point was that it was the End of Art, and nothing they made was supposed to be exhibitable or collectible or auctionable? Do you remember that?"

"Sure. What's your point?"

"Just that that ethos has completely reversed itself now, hasn't it? Your worth is determined by whether or not you're showing, and even if you're showing that's not enough because you have to be selling, but you've only *really* made it if you're selling at auction. But it used to be that you proved your bona fides by making something that *wasn't* for sale, that resisted the market so forcefully nobody could acquire it even if they wanted to."

"Yeah, yeah," said Frank.

Robert shook his head. "I guess what I wonder is, how did all those artists survive? Who was bankrolling them? Maybe I'm just getting old, maybe I've finally succumbed to my natural instinct for greed, but it seems *insane* to me that you would pour blood, sweat, and tears into something and then *not* want to make money off it, even if it's out of some misguided sense of artistic integrity."

"Artistic integrity used to be affordable. Used to be, a strapping young artist could find a squat in the East Village for literally nothing. Now it's all art galleries."

"The irony." Robert rubbed his eyes. "*I* can't afford any kind of integrity, artistic or otherwise. I need an income."

Frank sighed. "That's the trouble with not having a career anymore. When it fizzles out, you scrape your résumé together and the poor chump interviewing you for whatever job it is, which you're probably unqualified for, takes one look and says, 'What the fuck have you been *doing* for the past thirty years?'"

In the three weeks since he'd moved back to the city, Robert had gotten into the habit of checking his spam folder, just in case any job-related emails ended up there by accident. One morning, sandwiched between a Viagra offer and an ad for lonely Russian singles, he found a message from someone named Vanessa Campbell.

Hi Robert,

I hope it's okay for me to reach out—you gave me your card at Zuccotti Park last November. At the time I was organizing for Occupy Museums. I gave you a flyer and we chatted a little bit about our goals. Maybe you recall? Anyway, I'm still involved with OM, but lately I've also been working with a few different groups through the activist collective that I'm a part of, 21 Rector (we're named after our street address haha). We've been doing some work with an organization called Abolish Debt. If you're not familiar with it, what they do is buy delinquent debt—mostly medical, credit card, and student—from banks and other creditors for pennies on the dollar, but instead of collecting it, they abolish it.

We've been operating solely on the goodwill of donors, and we're gearing up for a big fundraiser in early March, and I was wondering if you'd be interested in donating some of the artwork you made for Occupy Wall Street to our auction. Garrett showed me the mockups you sent him—I think the work is great and I'm sorry you didn't get the chance to put it to its original use, but I do think it would be in high demand at auction, both as a collector's item and as a symbol of a historic movement. And of course, we'd be thrilled to have you as a guest of honor at the fundraiser as well.

Thanks for considering!

In solidarity,

Vanessa

Robert wondered if Vanessa had heard about what had happened with Preston. Probably not. She didn't seem like the type to follow art world news. And perhaps in her circle it was a badge of honor to get fired from any institution with a multimillion-dollar endowment.

He marked the email as "Not Spam." His spirits rising, he quickly wrote back saying yes, of course he remembered her and yes, he'd be delighted to donate the artwork and help out in any other way he could. After hitting send, it occurred to him that this would be the first time his work had ever been sold at any kind of auction.

CHAPTER TWENTY

Preston had turned to Slade Carney for help finding a place to live in the city. In addition to investing in cryptocurrency, Slade was also making inroads as a real estate mogul: he'd recently become part owner of an apartment development in Bushwick. He texted Preston a link to the website—*Welcome to Bodega 526 on Brooklyn's New Frontier! Modern residences in an industrial setting—living reimagined through artful eyes*—and offered him a one-bedroom at a reduced rate in exchange for three of Karina's paintings. "Think of it as me buying a futures option for her work's cultural significance."

It made Preston uneasy, but it was a good deal, so he went into Karina's studio the evening before Axiom's shippers were scheduled to pack up her paintings, picked three of the smaller ones, and FedExed them to Slade. Neither Brian nor Karina appeared to notice there was work missing.

Preston hadn't told Karina that, at Winter Exhibition, he'd repeatedly dropped her parents' names in front of Brian. And that Brian had seemed much more interested in representing them once it was established that Karina was one of *those* Pionteks.

He felt bad about it, he did. He was ashamed of what Andrew would think, what his mother would think. But he also knew that she would've wanted him to be happy. And he and Karina—they were happy together. He'd nursed her through that little meltdown she'd had—even if she refused to admit it, he knew that was what it was—and he'd keep taking care of her. He'd helped her find a studio space in East Williamsburg and had put a lid on the "painting is dead" rhetoric. Now he offered her encouragement and praise whenever she showed him a new work-in-progress. He took care of all the housework. He went down on her more often. He'd been bad—he'd stolen from her, and he'd lied to her—but now he was trying so hard to be good, and it was working. Karina seemed happy, and that was what mattered. It had all worked out in the end.

On a frigid morning soon after New Year's, they left their apartment and headed to Axiom for their first official meeting with Brian. As they waited for the M train, Preston said, "You haven't met Brian before, have you?"

"No," said Karina. "But I've heard of him." She looked pale and beautiful in a long black peacoat and blood-red scarf.

As the train roared into the station, she said something else that Preston didn't catch.

"What was that before?" he asked after they'd gotten on.

"I said that we should be careful with him."

"With Brian?"

"Yeah."

"Why?"

Karina folded her gloves in her lap. "He's been known to pump-and-dump."

Preston grinned. "Is that something sexual?"

"He's been known to buy up work by emerging artists and pump up its value. Like, hype it really aggressively, but then dump it if the artist gets too big too fast and the market for their work gets saturated. On Wall Street they'd call that stock fraud, but in the art world it's totally aboveboard. And potentially career-wrecking if it makes your prices crash."

"Is that what your parents do?"

Karina gave him a stern look. "Of course not. They're collectors, not speculators."

"Why didn't you tell me any of this before?"

A pregnant woman got on, and Karina stood to free up her seat. "I didn't think it was that noteworthy. He's not the only one who does it. The art market is like Wall Street in the eighties right now, even with the recession."

"A meat market," said Preston. He took her hand and squeezed it.

Karina looked out the window. They didn't speak as the train carried them the rest of the way to Chelsea. The gallery, when they got there, was the furthest thing from a meat market: huge, airy, and white, thousands of gleaming square feet spread out over the first and second floors of a renovated industrial building on West 21st Street. In the entryway hung an enormous painting of five long earthworms crawling across a pair of oiled buttocks flecked with chopped herbs. Behind the front desk sat two black-clad gallerinas, each typing away on a MacBook Air. Neither acknowledged Preston and Karina's arrival.

"Welcome!"

Preston turned to see Brian descending the staircase, arms outstretched. Instantly, the gallerinas' demeanor changed. Both women looked up, smiling, and one of them, a blonde with a tiny upturned nose, rose from behind the desk and said she'd get them all some coffees, unless they preferred tea or sparkling water.

"I've *so* been looking forward to this," Brian said, shaking Preston's hand. A large man with an abundant midsection, he had a mane of gray hair pulled into a loose ponytail. He wore burgundy trousers and a matching blazer over a crisp pink button-down. "And this," he said, turning to Karina, "must be the famous Miss Piontek."

Karina smiled tolerantly.

"How are your parents?" Brian said.

"Fine."

"I sold them a beautiful Janklett a few years back."

"Right," said Karina. "They put it in one of the guest bedrooms."

"Why don't we go up to my office?" said Brian.

As they traversed the gallery, they passed more paintings in the same vein as the earthworm/buttock piece. One was a close-up of raw egg yolks, wet coffee grinds, and pulpy rotting fruit; another depicted an open wound crawling with maggots, but with the slick style and hyper-saturated color of a fashion ad.

"What do you think?" Brian said. "They're by this wonderful young painter, Julia Alexopoulos."

"I dig the aesthetic," said Preston. He meant it. He could easily see these images getting lots of clicks on The Wart.

"The feminine grotesque is huge right now," said Brian.

Brian's office was all windows and polished wood and black leather upholstery. They sat down, and a moment later the blond gallerina entered with a tray of coffee and pastries.

"Thank you, Audrey," said Brian.

Preston glanced at Karina. She was looking down at her hands, twisting the gold ring on her middle finger round and round.

"So, Karina," said Brian, pouring the coffee. "You'll be glad to know that your work has arrived safely."

She raised her chin. "That's great."

"I had a chance to go look at it in our storage facility yesterday, and I was just blown away."

Karina smiled wanly as she poured cream into her cup. "Thanks."

"The way you manipulate stylistic conventions is wonderful. You're going to have a hell of a show."

Karina kept twisting that ring round and round. "I'm glad to hear it."

"Now, if we set the opening for mid-May, how many more pieces do you think you'd be able to produce by then?"

"At least five or six, I should think," said Karina. "Probably more."

"That's music to my ears. They'll be flying off the walls, so the more the better." He turned to Preston. "Now you, I'm also very excited about."

As much as it weirded out Preston to admit it, it felt kind of nice to have an older guy's approval. Even though Wrynn had ended up dropping the charges, his father had all but disowned him after his expulsion, leaving him an irate voicemail and cutting off his access to the credit card accounts. Preston had turned to Andrew for help, just enough to tide him over while he waited for his Axiom stipend to kick in. Andrew agreed to wire him the money, but he sounded cold on the phone, and after Preston hung up he'd felt momentarily overcome with shame.

Brian bit into a Danish. "Your name has already been floating around," he said, his mouth half-full.

"Yeah, I heard about the article in ArtyWag." Preston had it bookmarked on his computer.

"Such a provocative piece of performance art, the thing at Wrynn. It's always so refreshing when someone exposes the hypocrisies of this world we operate in, isn't it? What did you have in mind for your show? Something similar to what I saw of yours last month? I just *loved* those drug sculptures."

Preston leaned forward. "I was actually thinking of doing something similar to the Whitney, maybe. Their biennial's coming up, right? So what if we set up a mirror website that looks exactly like the Whitney's but claims, for example, that they're cutting ties with their financial sector sponsors because of their role in the crisis? And then, when the Whitney has to walk that statement back, affirming that actually, it *does* have a vested interest in upholding the status quo—"

"Out of the question," said Brian, polite but firm.

"But—"

"You've heard the expression 'don't shit where you eat'?"

"Sure."

Brian spread both hands out in a *there you have it* gesture. "Which isn't to say that I don't love the whole 'bad boy' thing. I think that's very much your brand. It's interesting, isn't it, when a piece of art sets out to be deliberately obnoxious. Because if you're annoyed, you're not indifferent, right?"

Preston liked being perceived as transgressive, but he did *not* like the idea of being a brand. He thought of his work as embodying the most primal impulses of online behavior. It was provocative, but also affectless. It refused meaning. It was no more a brand than Internet trolling was a brand.

Preston had put a lot of thought into his Whitney plans. Caught off-guard, he went red and heard himself begin to ramble: "I was thinking I don't want to display any objects at all. Maybe just images projected onto the walls. Or some kind of interactive sound installation. Or something to do with virtual reality."

There was a moment of awkward silence. Karina made a noise like she was suppressing a sneeze.

"That won't work," said Brian delicately. "You need to have salable work. You can include some difficult pieces in the show, of course, but you also need to have *objects,* as you say, for collectors to buy."

Preston's whole body flushed with heat. He said nothing.

"Preston. Look. I've been in this business for forty years," Brian said. His tone was kind, but his nostrils flared with impatience. "You're gonna be huge, and once you're huge you can do all the virtual reality you want, get conceptual up the wazoo, but in order to reach that echelon you need to be selling. I know that in school they tell you art is all about ideas, but in the real world it's about buzz. High prices—that's what's going to put you on the map. I need you to trust me on this."

Preston glanced at Karina. She briefly met his gaze before looking away.

He supposed he had no choice, not if he wanted to continue living his current life. "Okay," he said. "Objects it is."

All the warmth sprang back into Brian's face. "Wonderful!"

Over the next twenty minutes he and Brian hashed it out: Preston agreed to produce at least ten salable pieces, not including the installation he'd displayed at Wrynn, which would also be part of the show. Brian indicated that Preston shouldn't simply print out images from The Wart and stick them in frames: "These are serious collectors you're courting. The blog is a wonderful side dish, very much an integral part of your brand, but these people are looking for a heftier entrée, so to speak."

As they left the gallery, Karina remarked, "So much for the disruption of the meat market."

Preston stared at her crooked half smile and was suddenly overcome with the urge to fill his hands with her hair and hurl her into the oncoming traffic, watch her body arcing through the air like some pale bird. The intensity of his rage terrified him. He'd always lived in fear of the day some genetic switch deep inside him would flip and he'd turn into his father—his back stiffening, his vision narrowing, his mind snapping shut, closing in on itself like a dark, windowless room.

But then Karina's smile broadened as she jabbed him in the ribs. "Relax. I'm just teasing."

The rage drained away. Preston slung his arm over her shoulders and kissed the top of her head. "Come on. We're gonna be late for lunch with Slade. He's been dying to meet you."

CHAPTER TWENTY-ONE

Early in January, Louisa's mother called. "So your uncle Rick has a new girlfriend. And guess what her name is."

"What?" Louisa was distracted. Because she couldn't afford to ship her paintings, she'd taken the canvases off their stretchers and rolled them up. Now she was trying to fit the rolls into a duffel bag without crushing them.

"Taylor Swift," Mom said. "Like the singer."

Louisa didn't laugh. "That's funny."

For the past week and a half, she'd lived in Bowen with a handful of international students wintering on campus. She'd spent most of that time holed up in her single, sleeping and watching YouTube videos, venturing outside only to pick up to-go boxes from the cafeteria.

"It was Taylor's birthday recently," Mom said. "And Grandma and Pepere wanted to get her a gift, so they were asking Rick what she might like, but there was a misunderstanding because what they ended up getting her was a Taylor Swift CD. Should've seen her face."

"Yeah, I bet."

"And then here's the best part, Taylor had a Christmas party and invited all of us, and guess what she played all night long."

"Taylor Swift."

"Ah, chère, you should've been there."

In a different context, Louisa might have found this amusing, but now all she heard was a veiled rebuke: *Why weren't you with your family on Christmas?*

"I have to go," Louisa said. "My Greyhound leaves tomorrow and I'm not done packing."

The next morning, she somehow made it down the snowy hill with her unwieldy baggage, onto the bus—Neel had been right: Greyhounds *were* gross—through grimy, stinking Port Authority, into the deafening, dungeonlike subway station, and then finally up the five narrow flights of stairs to Ines Fidalgo's apartment in Washington Heights. Ines had flown to Italy the day before, leaving the key with a neighbor.

The apartment was small and tidy, the walls cluttered with photographs and paintings in many different styles—gifts, Louisa imagined, from Ines's artist friends. There was a mantel with potted ferns and succulents (Ines had asked Louisa to water them), and a braided rug, and a sofa heaped with cushions. The bookshelves held exhibition catalogs and heavy art books with glossy pages. Louisa took a picture of the living room and texted it to Alejandro. *I want her life.*

He wrote back: *OMG this is SO u in 10 years.* He added: *R u feeling better??*

Yes, she replied, though she wasn't sure she meant it. She was still a little embarrassed by the meltdown she'd had when she learned that the email from President Fowler had been a hoax, that Preston Utley, the person responsible, had been expelled and that a professor had been fired. To see it celebrated on campus as some brilliant piece of performance art, by people she considered her friends—it had been sickening. She'd disliked Preston to begin with, but now she felt a loathing so intense it verged on a kind of glee. For the most part, though, she'd kept it to herself. There'd been other pockets of anger toward Preston, largely from the impulsive people who'd canceled their loans, but the general feeling among the student body was that he was David to Wrynn's Goliath.

As soon as Louisa had seen the fake email, she'd thought, with a sudden jolt of clarity, *I don't want to go to New York. I don't want to go home. I want to stay here with Karina.* She'd cried a lot in the days that followed, not just because her hopes had been dashed, but because she knew that the choice to strike out on her own was one she'd made with her head, not her heart. Throughout it all, Alejandro had been so good to her. "I promise I'll come visit you," he'd said before flying home to Texas. "Are you going to be okay, though?" And she'd said yes, because what other choice did she have?

On her third day in New York, Louisa took a forty-five-minute train ride to Akito Kobayashi's studio in Long Island City. Her nerves were tempered with excitement. She'd latched on to the idea that working as a studio assistant could prove nearly as fruitful for her career as going to art school. Apprenticeship was an age-old tradition, wasn't it? If she worked hard and proved herself, maybe Akito Kobayashi would take her under his wing—advise her, guide her, introduce her to the right people. She'd learned in Art History that Rodin had spent several years working for Carrier-Belleuse. And hadn't George Condo started out as Andy Warhol's assistant?

When she arrived at Kobayashi's studio, she presented herself to the manager, Craig Nivens, who turned out to be a slouchy, middle-aged guy with a gin blossom nose. He explained that the test given to prospective assistants consisted of copying one of Kobayashi's several hundred psychedelic skull designs. He handed Louisa a binder and a blank canvas on a twelve-inch wooden stretcher. "Never touch the surface of the painting if you can avoid it. Akito doesn't like smudges or fingerprints. And wear these." Craig passed her some latex gloves. "You have two hours for the exam."

Louisa sneaked a glance around. The studio was cavernous: tall white walls, long south-facing windows, chilly concrete floors. It was almost completely silent, though a handful of assistants were scattered around at trestle tables and easels, painting saucer-eyed cartoon monsters and grimacing mushrooms and psychedelic flower tapestries. Kobayashi was nowhere to be seen, though she supposed this made sense: she'd read online that he operated studios in London and Tokyo as well as New York.

"Good luck," said Craig.

Louisa flipped through the binder. Many of the skulls seemed too complex to copy in the allotted time. Would it look bad if she did one of the simpler ones? She settled on a skull with a pointed chin and baby blue teddy bear ears, slipping the page from its plastic sleeve and taking it with her to the supply area on the far side of the studio, where she sorted through shelves of acrylic paint tubes, matching colors to the printout. She grabbed a heat gun and some paintbrushes and found an empty trestle table to work at.

Thankfully, the canvas had already been gessoed and sanded; its surface was flat and glassy. Louisa copied the skull in pencil, then applied paint thinly, blasting the canvas with heat in between layers.

At the end of the two hours, Craig came down from his lofted office and looked at her work. "This is nice." He held the canvas up to the light. "No visible brushstrokes."

"Thanks."

"Akito *abhors* visible brushstrokes. He likes it to look like it's printed on the canvas."

"Oh."

"He'll need to approve this. I'll be in touch."

Good, Louisa told herself as she left the studio. *This is good.*

These days, money was pretty much constantly on her mind. She was down to her last fifty dollars and had somehow managed to max out her credit card. Since arriving in New York, she'd subsisted on rice and beans and the occasional dollar slice of pizza. And though she had a six-month grace period before she'd need to start worrying about her student loans, come June that twenty-thousand-dollar-plus-interest bill would be staring her in the face. Even so, she allowed herself a fifty-cent bag of M&M's from the newsstand in the Jackson Avenue subway station. She ate them on the train back to Washington Heights, letting them melt into her tongue. The subway was no less strange and overwhelming than it had been the first time she took it. Everything here was strange and overwhelming. Every day was an assault on the senses.

She got off at 163rd Street and walked the four blocks to Ines's building. As soon as she opened the apartment door, Syd and Cleo demanded their dinner. Louisa peeled open a can of Friskies and spooned it into their dishes. While they ate, she made a cup of tea, put on her winter coat, and went out onto the fire escape with her sketchbook and a pencil, even though it was freezing. She'd seen an ashtray on the railing, full of cigarette butts and pencil shavings, and she wanted to be like Ines; she wanted to be an artist who drew on her fire escape. As she sat with her sketchbook propped against her knees, trying to draw the view across the street—the dip and rise of the roofline, the crouching water towers, their wooden ribbing stained greenish black—she thought about the details of this view that she had yet to notice, that would reveal themselves to her over time, replicating themselves in her hand, taking their place in her catalog of the world.

Everyone here lived crowded together, on top of one another in a way she'd never seen before. You could glimpse people's whole lives through their windows. In the building across the street, a dark-haired man was stirring something in a pot, a cutting board heaped with chopped onions at his elbow. In the apartment below, a woman with sad eyes was brushing her hair.

Louisa's bird woman paintings were still rolled up in her duffel, untouched, unlooked at. Even so, they occupied the edges of her thoughts, always; she was mindful of them the way a person newly in love is always half thinking of their lover.

She often caught herself half thinking of Karina. Sometimes, on the subway or the street corner, she'd catch a glint of silvery hair and her stomach would do a little flip, but then she'd blink and Karina would be gone, her face replaced by a stranger's. Louisa usually tried to hold her feelings about Karina at arm's length, but whenever this happened it all came rushing back: those nights in studio, Karina's hair slipping between her fingers. She made an effort not to dwell on these memories. Admitting to herself that she'd been in love would mean admitting to a greater loss than she felt capable of handling right now. She kept thinking of that line from *The Picture of Dorian Gray*, which she'd read last year in an English class at SLCC: *The sitter is merely the accident, the occasion. It is not he who is revealed by the painter; it is rather the painter who, on the colored canvas, reveals himself.*

Louisa looked down at her drawing. It wasn't any good. It was impossible to focus, to slip into that special state of mind, when thoughts of money and Karina kept intruding. Never mind. It was too dark to draw now, anyway. She set down her pencil and sipped her cold tea. She knew she ought to unroll and re-stretch her bird woman paintings. She ought to photograph them and put them online. She ought to create a website for her work. She ought to make some new paintings. But it was all too much, everything she had to do to get from where she was to where she wanted to be. Plus, stretchers were expensive, and she didn't have access to a wood shop anymore.

She looked up from her sketchbook. In the apartment above the one where the man was cooking, a light had come on, and Louisa could see directly into a bedroom where two figures were undressing each other with the kind of tender urgency Louisa was intimately familiar with. She knew she ought to look away.

A piteous meow rang out, and Louisa startled. She turned to see Syd's huge green eyes regarding her through the window. She tapped the glass with her fingertip. "Just a minute," she said. "Give me one more minute."

Four days later, an email from Craig:

> On behalf of Akito Kobayashi, I am pleased to offer you a position as an assistant in his New York studio. Base pay is $20/hour, with potential for merit-based raises and year-end bonuses depending on output. Speed and accuracy are of the utmost importance. So is discretion, meaning you'll be asked to sign an NDA along with the standard hiring paperwork. Studio assistants work Monday through Friday, 8 to 6, but you may be asked to come in on nights and weekends if we're up against a deadline. Let me know if you have questions.

Louisa allowed herself a squeal of glee before calling her mother to share the news.

"I know it's common now for people to have studio assistants," said Mom, "so maybe I'm just old-fashioned, but it seems wrong to me that *you* make the paintings, but then the artist gets to sell them under his name."

"Rembrandt had assistants."

"Sure, but he still painted the faces and the hands. Does this man do any of his own work?"

"Wouldn't you call *envisioning* it work?" Louisa's voice rang stiffly in her own ears. Why did her mother have to ruin this one good thing? "It's what Warhol did. It's the vision that determines authorship, not the execution."

Mom sighed. "Let's not fight. Your grandfather's here. He wants to talk to you." There was a rustling as she handed over the phone.

"Lulu?"

"Hi, Pepere."

"Did you hear the loons last night?"

"No, I didn't."

"Lord, they were loud."

"Pepere, I'm in New York."

"New York! You must be important. What's your address? I'll send you a little somethin."

"I already gave it to you, remember? When I replied to your email?" She felt a twinge of anxiety.

"Your mama wants to say somethin to you. Makin that face at me."

"Wait, Pepere—"

More rustling, and then Mom was back on the line. "Louisa?"

"I'm here."

"Has he sent you any checks?"

"No."

Mom lowered her voice. "If he sends you one, could you please let me know? And then just tear it up? He's been a little . . . off."

"Off?"

She sighed. "Yeah, you know, just forgetful. Your grandmother doesn't want him handling any of the finances right now."

"It's not dementia, is it?"

"No." There was an edge to her voice.

But it must be, Louisa thought. Wasn't that how it happened, a stroke followed by the mind's gradual decay?

Cleo nuzzled Louisa's shin. She reached down to scratch the cat's neck. "I'll let you know if I get anything from him."

CHAPTER TWENTY-TWO

On January 27, a Friday, Karina woke just as a lambent pink began to fringe the sky. Beside her, Preston snored softly. She crept out of bed and into the living room. Detritus from Preston's latest brainstorm lay scattered across the floor: crushed energy drink cans, plastic climbing-wall handholds, crumpled notebook paper covered in his cramped handwriting, and a teal Furby, a toy Karina recalled briefly coveting circa 1998. He'd gotten messier since they'd moved to the city. She kept telling him to get a studio, and he kept saying he was opposed to studios on principle.

"Karina?" came Preston's voice, creaky with sleep.

"Yeah?"

"Happy birthday."

She felt a sudden rush of gratitude and warmth. She hadn't really expected him to remember. She was still learning to reconcile the two Prestons: the one who said and did outrageous shit and had gotten Robert Berger fired, and the one who was sweet and generous and remembered her birthday. He held his arms open, inviting her back into bed. She climbed in and pressed herself to his chest.

"Are your parents taking you out tonight?"

She looked at him in confusion before remembering that of course he didn't know about the threats that she and Harry had exchanged last time they'd spoken. He didn't know that for weeks now she'd let her parents' calls go to voicemail. That she deleted their emails without reading them. That Harry and Fiona didn't know where she was.

"Not tonight," she said. "They're out of town."

When she was little, Harry and Fiona had taken her to dinner at Keens or La Grenouille for her birthday. Her parents drank old-fashioneds while she sat, stiff in one of the gauzy pastel dresses Fiona bought her for such occasions, sucking down Shirley Temples till her molars ached. At dessert, they presented her with a gift—a toy or a doll or some electronic gadget. When she became a teenager the birthday dinners stopped, the gifts replaced with infusions to the account that also housed her allowance and bat mitzvah money, along with a card reading *Buy yourself something special*. But she'd never bought herself much other than art supplies and clothes, and now she was glad for that. Before leaving Wrynn, she'd gone to a credit union in downtown Stonewater and transferred all her funds, plus the prize money from Winter Exhibition, into a new account. She hadn't told Preston about it.

"How does it feel to be twenty?" said Preston.

"It feels like nothing. Like just another year."

"You're just saying that because it's January."

"Maybe. January *is* the worst birthday month."

Preston tipped her face up to kiss her and she felt a heat spreading through her. It surprised her how much he'd nourished her lately. He'd been patient and gentle with her during her depression, and once she emerged from it, he'd been so encouraging of her. What had happened with Louisa had shattered her, but now she felt herself slowly regaining strength.

The kiss deepened, and Preston hooked his thumbs inside the waistband of her pajamas, peeling them off. As he swung himself on top of her, she caught a glimpse of his face: stupefied delight, a little boy punch-drunk with pleasure. She felt herself responding to his touch, mirroring his movements. As he hovered above her, working himself into her, his eyes unfocused, lost in ecstasy, it occurred to her that what she loved most about sex was seeing herself through her lover's gaze. It turned her on beyond belief to imagine herself in Preston's body, desiring herself through him.

Afterward, she lay under him, feeling the skitter of his heart. "I have to go."

"Noooo," said Preston, his voice muffled by her hair. "Why?"

"Because I need to paint. And you need to do whatever it is you do all day." She wriggled out from under him and went to the bathroom. Preston followed, stopping outside the half-closed door.

"We should go out tonight. Since you're not doing anything with your parents."

She folded a length of toilet paper in half. "What did you have in mind?"

"Slade invited us to a party."

Karina couldn't decide if she liked Slade. She'd met him once, at a lunch a couple of weeks ago, and saw immediately why Preston gravitated toward him. They both had a reckless way of moving through the world, but whereas Preston was exuberant and impish, Slade just seemed calculating. Which was probably why Slade was a tech millionaire and Preston wasn't.

"I don't know . . ."

"Slade said it's like four blocks away from us. You can check it out and come home if you don't like it."

"Yeah . . ."

Recalling Slade's crisp navy suit and the showy way he'd insisted on picking up the bill at their pricey lunch, Karina had a flashback to her parents' parties: the finance men and their pretty young wives in Hermès cocktail dresses, the artists shoveling down hors d'oeuvres and smiling in quiet desperation.

"Don't you think it'd be fun to meet people?" Preston said. "And supposedly the party's in this abandoned mannequin warehouse, so that could be interesting."

"Why is Slade getting invited to hipster parties in Bushwick?" Karina said. "Shouldn't he be hanging out with finance bros?"

Preston shrugged.

She pushed out her lips. "Okay, fine. I'll go."

The sun had risen, salt-white and blinding, by the time she left the apartment. A man in a puffy red coat rolled up his storefront's grate, then squatted in the doorway and lit a cigarette. This New York was so different from the one Karina had been raised in. Bushwick was gritty and loud, a universe away from the sedate buildings and uniformed doormen of the Upper East Side. Here there were technicolor-bright murals on every other block and industrial warehouses that looked abandoned but housed condos or pop-up restaurants or anarchist bookshops, and the air smelled like garbage and dog shit and grilled meat.

She took the bus to East Williamsburg and let herself into her studio building, an old cannery. On the fifth floor she unlocked her studio, sliding open the heavy metal door. Morning light sluiced over the floorboards. Her workspace was a long, rectangular room with faded brick walls. One end was almost entirely glass, three huge, dingy windows that opened sideways with a metal crank. A big old-fashioned bucket sink stood in one corner. Naked lightbulbs hung from the twelve-foot ceiling—she'd had to borrow a ladder from Allison, a woodworker with a studio downstairs, to switch out the burned ones. Her only furniture was an easel and worktable, a padded rolling stool, a space heater, a mini-fridge, a microwave, and a coffeepot. And a safe, of course. Where she kept Wally.

Karina slid the door shut behind her and knelt by the safe. She twisted the dial, carefully removing Wally. She always looked at her first thing, before she did anything else. The sight of Wally, the perfect tousled lines of her—it galvanized Karina, drove her toward excellence. She hadn't drawn Louisa's face since the last time they'd spoken. Wally was replacement enough.

After a minute she nestled the drawing back in the safe, locked it, and brewed some coffee. She went back to work on her half-finished canvas, a semi-abstract piece with Pop Art colors. Within the past two weeks alone she'd completed three paintings for Brian, all wildly different: one was a surrealist landscape overlaid with hints of text, another an androgynous nude, its lines verging on cartoonish; the third was a mixed-media piece incorporating a broken tricycle wheel she'd found on 3rd Street and mounted to the canvas in a nod to Duchamp. On his last studio visit, Brian had encouraged her to keep experimenting. "Just make interesting work," he'd said. "Don't worry about fitting into a niche. You're so multifaceted and versatile."

After an hour of work, Karina took a cigarette break, opening the window a crack to blow out the smoke, then kept painting. She'd put her phone on the floor when she'd plugged it in to charge; now she heard it vibrating against the floorboards. She crouched, peering at the screen. A text from Fiona: *Happy birthday.*

Karina unplugged the phone and put it on her worktable, but she didn't reply.

A few minutes later: *I'd love to talk to you.*

Karina kept working. A while later she took another cigarette break by the window. When she returned, there was a new message: *I'm your mother and I miss you. Don't you think you should talk to the person who gave birth to you on your birthday?*

Karina tapped the call button. Fiona sounded surprised when she picked up. "Where are you?"

"At school."

Her mother's voice curdled. "No, you're not."

Karina ran her tongue over her teeth.

"I thought you might be dead, did that occur to you?"

"Well, clearly I'm not."

Fiona sighed, relenting. "Happy birthday, love."

"Thanks. How are you?"

"I've been better."

"Oh?"

"Yes, my daughter stole a painting and dropped out of college and now I have no idea where she is."

Karina pushed away the guilt. "I'm fine. I'm safe. And it's a drawing, not a painting, and it's not even that valuable compared to the rest of your collection."

"Your father's livid."

"I know."

"You need to give it back, love."

"No."

"And you need to go back to school."

"I don't want to go back to school."

"You don't mean that."

"I do."

A pause. "I think you'll regret this when you're older," Fiona said at last. "I think you'll want the independence and clout that a degree can give you, and to be hon—"

"Because going to Yale and meeting Dad made you *super* independent."

"That's enough!" said Fiona. "What's gotten into you?"

"I've got to go now, Mom. Thanks for the birthday wishes."

"Are you still in Stonewater? Let me buy you a train ticket."

"I just—I need some space." Then, registering the edge of fear in her mother's voice, she added, "But I'm okay. I promise. Don't worry, all right? I'm fine."

She hung up before Fiona could say anything more. There was a knock at the door. Karina went and answered it, grateful for an excuse to ignore her phone, which was vibrating again. It was Allison, the woodworker from downstairs, her hair powdered with sawdust. "Sorry, just wondering if you have any cigarettes? I'm all out."

"Sure. I'll smoke one with you."

Allison was older than Karina, late twenties maybe, but she carried herself with the loose, sloppy confidence of a teenage boy. She was pretty in a jagged, punky sort of way, and she was the only artist in the building who'd formally introduced herself when Karina moved into her studio. Allison had even shown Karina around her own workspace: she made wooden sculptures, some twisted and slender, evoking tree roots, others geometric and modish, like space-age totem poles. She sold her work out of a small, kooky gallery in Clinton Hill ("It's the kind of place aging hippies go to buy wedding presents for their nieces") and waitressed on the side. When Karina told her she had a debut show opening at Axiom in the spring, Allison had said, "Wait, *how* the fuck old are you? How'd you manage that?" and Karina had mumbled something about dumb, extraordinary luck.

Now Karina led Allison over to the windows, where she'd left her half-empty pack of Dunhills on the sill. She shook out two cigarettes.

"You don't want to open the window a little more?" said Allison.

"It's freezing."

"Your studio will stink, though." Allison lit up, inhaling deeply. "It'll get into the paint. Your paintings will smell like an ashtray. Your collectors will say, 'This piece reeks of the artist that made it!'"

Karina said, "They've found cigarette butts in Pollock's drip paintings."

"Ha! Of course they did. That old drunk." She glanced around the studio. "Damn, girl, you've been busy. Are these all pieces for your show?"

"Yeah."

"I see why Axiom wanted you."

Karina said nothing, which was how she generally responded to praise.

Allison tipped her chin up and blew a plume of smoke at the ceiling. "You up to anything tonight?"

"I might go to a party in my neighborhood."

"Where do you live?"

"Bushwick."

Allison's eyes lit up. "No way! Me, too. Whereabouts?"

"Cedar and Evergreen."

"Oh nice. I'm like way on the opposite side, near the cemetery." She had sawdust in her eyebrows. It glittered where the sunlight caught it. "So," Allison said. "Do you live alone or with like roommates or a boyfriend?" A slight pause. "Or a girlfriend?"

Karina hesitated. "I have a roommate."

"Cool." Allison flicked her cigarette butt out the window. "Well, I'm going to a party in my neighborhood tonight, too, so maybe we'll see each other." She met Karina's eyes and smiled.

"Yeah, maybe."

"Thanks for the smoke."

After Allison left, Karina painted into the early evening, her mood curiously light.

That night, Karina put on black jeans and a low-cut black sweater and her leather jacket and did two lines of coke off the kitchen counter with Preston. As she was rubbing the residue into her gums, enjoying the burst of energy and alertness, he presented her with a small velvet box. She went rigid at the sight of it. But when she opened it, it was just a necklace: a simple silver disc hanging from a thin chain.

"Happy birthday."

"Thanks." She fastened it around her neck, feeling silly. "It's beautiful."

They went downstairs to meet Slade and walk over to the party. On the way there, they passed one of the neighborhood's ubiquitous murals, harshly lit under floodlights.

"Karina, you should take a pic here for your Instagram," said Slade.

She looked at him, unsure if he was teasing. "I don't have an Instagram."

"Or whatever social."

"I don't do that," said Karina.

"Why not? Shouldn't you be building your brand?"

"That's kind of my dealer's job."

Slade looked, for some reason, irritated. "There are people invested in your future, though. Don't you think you should—" He cut himself off as Preston shot him a sharp glance. An odd look passed between them, and Karina had a sudden vision of the two men as naughty middle school boys.

Preston cleared his throat. "Social media's more my bailiwick, man. Karina's the monastic type."

Monastic. It wasn't a word Karina would have used to characterize herself, but it did describe Louisa. She'd never seen anyone work the way Louisa did. When Louisa painted, it was almost as though she were dancing with the canvas. Karina chased the memory from her mind. No use dwelling on the past.

The party, when they arrived, was similar to the artsy hipster parties at Wrynn, except that this one was in a warehouse and the people were slightly older and seemed to be holding their liquor with more success. Also, there were mannequins everywhere, some wearing wigs or scarves or nipple tassels, others denuded of heads and limbs.

Slade disappeared for a few minutes, returning with three cups full of vodka lemonade. It was too loud to talk; they found their way onto the dance floor. Karina closed her eyes, loosing her body to the techno pop.

Slade went away and came back with more drinks, and then Preston went off and returned with a bottle of whiskey. Karina downed the alcohol in quick swallows, relishing the burn in her throat. The music settled in her chest, roaring inside her, and for a few blurred seconds she felt it might lift her off her feet and carry her above the crowd. Then, suddenly dizzy, she came crashing down.

I'm going to the bathroom, she mouthed at Preston. She wove blindly through the crowd till she found the restroom. Inside, the music was muffled, and Karina had the sensation of being inside a stranger's womb. In a graffiti-covered stall she peed luxuriantly, resting her head against the cool metal partition. When she emerged, she heard a familiar voice: "Karina?"

Allison was standing by the sinks, drying her hands. She wore a hunter-green jumpsuit that made her look like a hot aviatrix, and her face was smeared with glitter. "I was hoping I'd see you here."

Karina grinned stupidly. "Me, too."

"Hey, could I bum another cigarette?"

"Sure. I'll join."

They left through the back entrance, stepping out into an alleyway. Allison leaned against the wall as Karina lit up. In the darkness, she could barely make out the contours of Allison's nose and lips.

"It smells like snow," said Allison.

"Yeah." Karina's chest still pulsed with the music's echo.

"How would you survive the zombie apocalypse?" said Allison.

"What?"

"I think I'd zombie-proof my apartment."

Karina laughed. "How?"

"I'd board up the windows and barricade the doors, duh. Also, I'm on the sixth floor, and everyone knows zombies can't climb."

"Oh, *everyone* knows?"

A smile tugged at Allison's lips. "Clearly you don't watch *The Walking Dead.*" She shifted, moving slightly closer to Karina, who caught the lingering smell of sawdust on her clothes.

"I guess I'll be a goner, then," said Karina. "How old are you?"

"Twenty-seven. Are you implying that it's a show for old people?"

"No. And twenty-seven's not old."

Allison threw her head back and laughed. "Jesus, I know it's not old. How old are *you*?"

"Twenty. As of today."

Allison slipped a finger through Karina's belt loop. "Well," she said, tugging her toward her. "Happy birthday." She leaned in and touched her mouth to Karina's. Then they were kissing in earnest, Karina's hands in Allison's hair—bodies bumping loosely against the wall, fumbling hands and wet lips and smoky breath—and Karina thought only briefly of Louisa. She let herself sink into the feeling of being wanted.

"My apartment is like a ten-minute walk," Allison said.

Karina touched her new necklace and imagined how Preston would panic if he couldn't find her. It wasn't so long ago she'd disappeared inside herself. "I can't tonight. But will you be in the studio tomorrow?"

CHAPTER TWENTY-THREE

Frank had been right: there were few jobs Robert was qualified for. And in the decade-plus since he'd last perused want ads, the market had spawned an astonishing number of nonsensical positions. What the hell was a "chief visionary officer"? Robert sent his CV to a handful of arts nonprofits and museums, with no response. Even his old friend Dean Blanchard, who'd published his piece at *Artforum,* had stopped replying to his emails.

"Everyone got the memo that I'm a pariah," Robert told Frank when they met for drinks on a chilly evening in mid-February. The bar was decorated with droopy garlands of paper hearts. "I feel like I'm invisible. I've worked in this industry my entire adult life, and now it's like I never even existed."

Frank was good company, even this attenuated, beaten-down-by-time version of him. In his presence, Robert felt unaccountably desensitized, emotionally bubble-wrapped, cushioned from the full weight of his anger and humiliation.

"See," said Frank, "that's the trouble with job hunting in the age of the Internet."

"What is?"

"Anyone can type in your name and read the entire history of your ignominy."

"That's comforting," said Robert. "Thanks for that."

"The Internet has revealed the ugliness of the human condition more clearly than art or literature. Belly up to the cold light of day." Frank flagged down the bartender and ordered them another round. He was in a good mood. He'd had a profitable day playing online poker, though he wouldn't say how much he'd won.

Frank glanced at Robert. "Is it that dire? You know I can give you a loan."

Robert shook his head. "I mean, I have the apartment—"

"I still can't believe you ended up with that apartment."

"—but I still have to feed myself. Clothe myself."

"Diane must've been *pissed*."

"Drug myself."

"I'm astonished she didn't sue you. She was the *lawyer* in the marriage."

"And I'm burning through my savings."

Frank took a long pull of beer.

"It'd be nice to have a job," said Robert. "It'd be nice to have a purpose."

"Isn't art your purpose?"

"Hasn't felt like it for a while." He had the Abolish Debt auction in a few weeks to look forward to, at least. Not that he'd be making any money off it.

"Have you considered teaching?"

Robert shook his head. "The art schools are all in a cabal together."

"I didn't mean college," said Frank. "Hold on, let me see if I can find it." He pulled out his phone. "Here. Check this out."

The website was sleek, muted color palette and stylish sans serif font. A gauzily lit photo of a child playing the violin.

Need help nurturing your child's creativity? You've come to the experts! Art-sitters Atelier® exclusively employs professional artists to meet the childcare needs of parents of gifted children. Whether your child is a budding actor, painter, writer, dancer, or musician, we help them reach their full potential by matching them with a professionally trained artistic caregiver.

"The *fuck*?"

Frank finished his beer. "You might be good at it. Don't take it as an insult."

Five days passed with no job prospects before Robert decided to apply. He filled out the online form and uploaded his résumé and portfolio. A day later, he received an email inviting him to schedule a phone interview. The call didn't go great. Robert felt like an idiot as he haltingly described his childcare qualifications (zero), so it was something of a surprise when someone named Jessica Coatney emailed him soon after, asking to meet in person.

The Artsitters Atelier offices in Midtown were decorated with potted plants, area rugs in primary colors, and framed photographs of smiling children holding paintbrushes and playing the piano and doing pirouettes in sequined tutus. Jessica Coatney was a trim young woman in a pencil skirt, her hair twisted into a sleek chignon. She seemed a little surprised that he'd even shown up at all. "To be honest," she said, "we were all kind of confused when you applied. We thought at first it might be some kind of performance piece."

Robert laughed. "Are you serious?"

"You're an unusual candidate. The artists who work for us are typically young, just out of school."

Robert's face grew hot.

"I can see from your résumé," said Jessica, apparently oblivious to the discomfort of middle-aged men, "that you have lots of teaching experience, but it's all college-level. And I can tell you right now, just from having googled you, that you're not going to pass our background check. But the reason I asked you to meet with me is that we have a sort of unusual client that we've been struggling to find the right Artsitter for, and I think you might be a good fit for him."

"Unusual how?"

Jessica grabbed a yellow stress ball and gave it a lusty squeeze. "Very precocious, for one. A bit of an oddball. And a genuinely talented painter. A lot of the parents we work with can be a little, ah, deluded about their children's abilities, but this kid's the real deal. His name's

Adrian, and he's twelve, and his parents have very specific criteria for the kind of caretaker they want."

"Such as?"

"Well, they're a lesbian couple, and it's important to them that Adrian have a strong male role model."

"Right."

"So that rules out most of our team. They've also been quite choosy about the *kind* of artist they want for Adrian. They rejected two candidates just based on their portfolios."

They sound awful. "They sound difficult."

"This is a family with high standards, let's put it that way. Now, I took the liberty of forwarding them your portfolio. They're both connoisseurs, so they've heard of you, and they're *very* excited about the possibility of you working with Adrian."

"Great."

Jessica folded her hands on her desk. "So here's what we're proposing. We'd like to hire you on a *provisional* basis. We're going to waive the background check requirement with the understanding that you'll be working exclusively for this one family, who appreciate that you're not the typical Artsitter and that you've had an . . . eclectic life. Are you CPR-certified?"

"No."

"Okay, you'll definitely need to get certified before you start. I'll give you the number for the training center we use."

Robert pictured himself performing flailing chest compressions on the limp body of an unconscious child. "Can I ask what you're charging this family for your services?"

Jessica smiled evenly. "Our fee is $120 an hour, of which you keep half. Now, since you'll technically be a contract worker we can't guarantee your hours week to week, but my understanding is that the family is looking for a consistent after-school caretaker. Does that sound all right?"

"Sure. And, uh, can you tell me what I'll be doing, exactly?"

Jessica's earrings chimed softly. "Your primary job is to nurture Adrian's creativity."

"So . . . art lessons?"

"Intensive and engaging instruction, tailored to Adrian's needs and learning style. Our clients often expect us to mold their children into creative geniuses." She let out a fake little laugh. "For the vast majority of children that's of course an unrealistic expectation, but like I said before, in *this* particular case I think we can expect great things from Adrian."

Robert was genuinely curious to meet this boy Picasso.

"Now," said Jessica, "I do need to tell you that the job will also involve normal babysitting duties. Snacks, school pickups, homework help, and so on."

"No diaper changes, though, right?"

"He's twelve," she said blankly.

It had been Robert's feeble attempt at a joke, but he didn't try to explain. "I think I can handle that."

"Excellent. Shall we get started on the paperwork?"

A day after completing a two-hour-long CPR course from which he emerged feeling unqualified to resuscitate anything other than a mannequin, Robert received a heavily bullet-pointed email from thehallidaygallegos@gmail.com. He was sitting with Frank at a bar in the financial district—Frank had won another poker pot and was, once again, treating Robert to a drink—when his phone buzzed.

"Huh," said Robert. "This kid's parents have a joint email account. I've never seen that before."

"Oh, it's a thing now," said Frank. "Joint emails, joint Facebook profiles—it's like you're not *really* committed unless you're digitally fused with your spouse." He tugged his orange beanie down over his ears. He wore the thing all the time, even indoors. Did his head get cold now that his hair was thinning? When would that fate befall Robert? He turned his attention back to his phone, scrolling through the email. "Geez."

"What?"

"The people had Adrian tested—"

"Who's Adrian?"

"The kid I told you about. They had him tested for creativity."

Frank laughed. "That's not a thing."

"It is, apparently. They said he scored, quote, 'in the ninety-eighth percentile on the Torrance Tests of Creative Thinking.' Also, he's allergic to avocados. They sent me a whole dossier, like I'm being briefed by the CIA."

"That's sad." Frank finished his beer and signaled the bartender for another.

"Yeah . . . Imagine going through life and never tasting guacamole."

"Ha," said Frank. "I mean that the kid's been *labeled* creative. Now he's gonna go through life thinking that that's the only way for him to *be,* and if it turns out he's not—for any number of fucking reasons, like hell, maybe life just gets in the way, or maybe the test was a fluke and he's only in, you know, the sixtieth percentile, or maybe he *is* creative, but it doesn't get him anywhere—then he'll think he's a failure. He'll feel like he wasted his entire life trying to live up to a standardized test he took when he was thirteen."

"He's twelve," said Robert dully. It had just occurred to him that Vince was *his* Torrance Test. Vince was the one—the *only* one, because by then his father was gone and his mother didn't give a shit—who'd insisted that Robert had talent, had potential, the one who'd dragged him to his first art opening when they were both seventeen, talked him into slicking back his hair and crashing a group show. Vince was the one who'd plied him with sour red wine to get him talking to the gallery director, and after Robert managed to get a drawing into the gallery's next group show, Vince was the one who'd told him to keep it up, to get his work in front of as many eyes as possible, to apply to Cooper Union even though Robert doubted he'd ever get in. And later, when Robert's career was off to a slow start, Vince was the one who'd kept reminding him that he was playing a long game, and that his work was just as important as what Vince did with Mobilization for Youth, even though as time went on it seemed more and more like Vince was out there leaving his lucent mark on everything while Robert ricocheted aimlessly, never landing anywhere. And of course, Vince hadn't been a perfect person—he could be quick-tempered and passive-aggressive; he cheated at board games and never showed up to things on time—but he was, fundamentally, a good egg. It had taken Robert decades to realize how lucky he was to have met him at such a young age, and to have kept his friendship for so many years.

Robert had looked to Vince for reassurance that *he* was a good person, that his work mattered, that it wasn't just good but *good* in the ethical sense—and what if Vince had been wrong? What if Preston had been right? What if the truth was that art would always fail because it could only ever be an approximation of something else? That it wasn't the same as activism, just as opinion wasn't the same as politics and a picture wasn't the same as an experience?

"Want another beer?" Frank said.

"What?"

He pointed at Robert's empty glass.

"Oh, sure. Frank? Did you ever have a teacher that was important to you?"

Frank tossed back a handful of bar nuts. "There was one when I was an undergrad at RISD. British guy. Taught my sculpture class."

"What'd he do?"

"Well, so I turned in an assignment—I don't remember what it was, but I'd definitely half-assed it—and he takes one look and says, in this Queen of England accent, 'Throw that piece of shit away, but not in my trash can.'"

"*What?*"

"He was a bastard, don't get me wrong, and I was humiliated, but what I got out of it was the idea that if you're dedicating your life to something, it's an insult to half-ass it, you know? It's like, sit or stand, but whatever you do don't wobble." He shrugged. "Anyway, it's why I quit."

"You're serious?"

Frank pried the shell off a pistachio. "Yeah, I mean, I just spent years *wobbling*, you know? Because I'd bought into the idea that if I didn't at least try, then I was a failure. But I've come to realize that I'm okay with that."

"Okay with what?"

"With not succeeding at something on someone else's terms."

Frank's phone rang. "Hello?" A smile crept over his face. "Oh *really*? Can you meet now? Your place? . . . Okay, see you soon."

"Who was *that*?" said Robert.

"A friend." Frank sank the rest of his beer. Smiling to himself, he slapped a crumpled fifty onto the bar. "Gotta go. See ya, Rob."

Robert sat there a little longer, watching the Knicks lose, sipping his drink. Had Frank met someone? A whirlwind romance, at his age, was the kind of heartwarming *Modern Love*–worthy tale that ought to give Robert hope for his own future.

Shit, he should answer that email, shouldn't he? The Halliday-Gallegos probably belonged to that rabid school of parenting that expected their kid's teacher to be on call 24/7. Robert tapped out a quick response: if it suited them, he could come over tomorrow evening to meet Adrian, discuss goals and logistics, and draw up a weekly care schedule. Ten minutes later, as he staggered out into the sinking light, his phone vibrated with their reply. Already? Jesus, these women must be surgically attached to their devices.

The Halliday-Gallegos lived in an elegant neo-Georgian on East Seventy-fifth, a stone's throw from Central Park. Robert had googled the family the night before. Cristina Gallegos was a software engineer at a hedge fund, and Lily Halliday ran a private psychiatry practice in Lenox Hill and lectured at Columbia Medical School.

Their apartment was on the sixth floor. The elevator doors slid open and Robert made his way down the corridor, the plush carpeting muffling his footsteps. He rapped lightly on 603. After a moment, the door opened a crack. Robert glimpsed a brown eye and a smooth sliver of cheek.

"Hi," he said.

The eye blinked.

"Are you Adrian?"

The door shut with a snap. There was the sound of a chain lock sliding in its track, and then the door swung open. Robert saw the retreating back of a smallish boy in a rugby shirt—beetle-black hair, gray sweatpants, bare feet padding down the hallway. "Lily! Cris!" the boy shouted. "He's here!" His voice was childish, but a hoarse raggedness

crouched behind it, hinting at imminent metamorphosis. Robert recalled, suddenly, how odd it had been when Vince's voice changed—
overnight, it seemed, as though he'd been possessed by some croaky
nocturnal spirit. A few months later, when the same thing happened to
Robert, he'd marveled at the stranger that had taken up residence in his
throat.

Adrian disappeared around the corner. Robert hovered in the doorway. In a spacious foyer, there was a faded Persian runner, a console
table heaped with keys and water bottles, jackets and scarves hanging
on a coat stand, and a metal shoe rack overcrowded with sensible low-
heeled pumps and dirt-crusted sneakers in violent neon hues. An
amoeba-shaped mirror hung opposite a canvas of greens and blues and
oranges apocalyptically colliding, a half-decent Kandinsky ripoff.

"Hello?" said Robert.

A woman came striding into the foyer. She had a long, thin face
framed by a blunt silver bob. She wore neatly pressed slacks, a white
blouse buttoned to the throat, and pearl earrings, but no shoes, as
though she'd only just gotten home from work and hadn't had time to
change into something more comfortable.

"Hi," she said, shaking Robert's hand. "I'm Lily. Sorry about Adrian.
He's in a mood." She looked over her shoulder. "That was very rude,"
she called. "Adrian? When we have a guest, we say hello and invite them
inside."

"Please don't worry about it." Robert bent to unlace his shoes.

"Would you like something to drink?" said Lily, leading him into the
living room. Here were more Persian carpets, more undemanding, aggressively abstract paintings. Recessed lighting and tasteful midcentury
modern furniture. "Water? Coffee? Wine?"

A glass of wine would take the edge off nicely and bring out his latent
charm, but it seemed improper to imbibe in the vicinity of the child he
was supposed to be mentoring. "I'd love some water, thanks."

"I'll let Cris know you're here. And I'll drag Adrian out from wherever he's hiding."

Robert took a seat, admiring the coffered ceiling. The built-in shelves
were lined with leather-bound volumes and glossy coffee table books.

A wicker basket by the sofa held a neat stack of *New Yorkers*. Vanity set pieces alluding to their owners' good taste. The trashy stuff would be in the bedroom. There was no TV.

The sound of ice cubes clinking in a glass announced Lily's return. "They're coming," she said, handing Robert his water.

A moment later, they were joined by a small-boned woman dressed in jeans and a Stanford hoodie. She was holding Adrian's hand, tugging it as he shuffled in behind her. Robert set his glass on the coffee table and stood to greet them.

"Hi, good to meet you," said the woman. "I'm Cris." She jiggled her son's arm. "Can you introduce yourself, please?"

Staring at his feet, the boy mumbled something inaudible and Cris spoke to him in Spanish, her voice edged with impatience. Out of the corner of his eye, Robert saw Lily slide a coaster under his abandoned glass of water.

The boy raised his eyes. "My name is Adrian," he said in a soft, hoarse voice.

"*¿Y qué más?*"

"Nice to meet you."

Robert smiled. "Nice to meet you, too."

Cris draped her arm across her son's thin shoulders. Their resemblance was striking. They had the same rounded features and dark, liquid eyes sunk deep in their sockets. Cris was much younger than Lily, who had to be around Robert's age.

They all sat down; Robert took an armchair and Lily and Cristina sat on the sofa with Adrian, looking bored and unhappy, sandwiched between them.

"We're very excited to have you here," said Lily. "This is going to date me, but I remember what a huge deal it was when *Dying Man* went up at the Whitney. It took my breath away the first time I saw it. I just *sobbed*."

Robert hadn't attended the opening reception—he'd heard through the grapevine that some ACT UP people, friends of Vince's, were planning to show up and confront him. "Thank you."

"I dabbled in art when I was younger," Lily said. "But I was hopeless at it. So I found my way to med school." She reached across Adrian and patted Cris on the knee. "And my wife here works in tech, so we're not exactly sure where Adrian got his talent."

"Adrian," Robert said, "where do you like to paint?"

"My room," he replied sullenly, scowling down at his own hands.

"Can I see what you're working on?"

If he could just get the kid to like him, he wouldn't have failed at his one fucking task for the day. Cris whispered something in Adrian's ear. The boy got up and returned with a sixteen-by-twelve-inch canvas.

"May I?" Robert took the painting, holding it out in front of him. Chains of carmine circles floated on an indigo background. Dark green lines curled dreamily through them, like vines floating in a gentle current. "This is very impressive, Adrian." His enthusiasm was genuine. Adrian's brushwork was confident and exuberant, and his technical skill and eye for composition were evident. The question remained, though: how much had he been coached?

"Robert's a *professional* artist," Lily said to Adrian. "And you know what? His paintings are in *museums*. So he *really* knows what he's talking about."

Annoyance flashed across the boy's face, but Lily didn't seem to notice.

"Adrian," Robert said, "if you don't mind, I'd love to see your studio."

The boy rubbed his chin against his shoulder. "This way." He pulled his sleeves over his hands and led Robert down a long carpeted hallway lined with framed family photos. There was a picture of Adrian as a laughing baby with enormous, gleaming dark eyes, another of him as a toddler holding a pumpkin-shaped bucket, and one of the three of them in front of city hall, the women each clutching a bouquet while Adrian squinted at the camera.

His bedroom was large and unremarkable. There was a bin full of Legos, an Xbox and a small TV, Miyazaki posters and Totoro figurines. There was a messy painting area, an easel and stool on a paint-flecked plastic tarp. Stacks of canvases leaned against the wall. Robert pointed at them. "Mind if I take a look?" The boy gave a slight nod. Robert knelt and thumbed through the paintings. Adrian definitely had a recognizable style: gurgling shapes and eddying lines framed by simmering fields of color, the brushstrokes meandering but sure-handed. The pictures exuded a playful doodles-ness, a palpable *youth*.

"You're a wonderful colorist," Robert said. "I love the rhythm you created in this one." He ran his fingers over the paint. "All these different shades of yellow. Very subtle."

"Thanks."

"Do you ever paint from life?"

Adrian hesitated.

"Do you ever paint things or people just by looking at them and copying what you see?"

Adrian shook his head.

"Okay, so that's something we could try together," said Robert. "Painting from life is a good skill to have, even if you decide you like abstraction better."

"Adrian, abstraction just means shapes and colors," said Lily, appearing in the doorway. Cris hovered close behind her.

"I *know* what abstraction means," said Adrian. The sullenness had crept back into his voice.

Lily's mouth tightened.

"*Adrián*," Cris said sharply.

The boy cut his eyes at her, seeming both much younger and much older than twelve. Cris stared at her son for a long moment, then turned to Robert. "Shall we discuss schedule?"

"Sure." Robert scratched his cheek.

"May I be excused?" said Adrian. His voice dripped with huddled anger.

Cris gave a terse nod. "*Pero te quedas en tu cuarto. Más tarde tú y yo vamos a hablar.*"

As Robert followed the two women back to the living room, he heard Lily whisper to Cris, "What did you just say to him?"

"I told him to stay in his room and that we'd talk later."

Lily took the lead again, briskly going over pickup times and emergency contacts. Robert was to fetch Adrian from Fieldston every day at three-thirty—except Thursdays, when he had chess club till five—and ride the bus home with him. He'd fix the boy a snack, supervise homework, then give him an art lesson.

"And you're comfortable with occasionally making dinner?" said Lily.

"Um, sure."

"Just something simple like pasta or a frozen pizza. We try to make sure one of us is home by dinnertime, but some nights we both have to work late."

"I'm not a great cook, but I can manage pasta."

Lily insisted on paying for a cab back to Brooklyn. An unspoken apology for the awkwardness of the whole evening? Robert thought of calling Frank and asking to meet up for a drink, but then he remembered he still needed to touch up the pieces for the Abolish Debt fundraiser. At least someone still wanted his work.

Chapter Twenty-Four

Preston's plan for the Furby—interrogating and subverting the '90s nostalgia that his generation cultivated on the Internet—had been dead-end, stupid. He shouldn't have indulged himself bidding for it on eBay. Forty bucks down the drain. He dropped the toy's sticky, teal-fuzzed components in the trash can and slammed the lid shut.

Sometimes he felt paralyzed, his whole body contracting with self-doubt. Whenever he sat down to work, he found himself flummoxed in the face of *materials*. The hours he'd wasted taking apart the Furby and attempting to reassemble it in some visually interesting way reminded him how frustrating it had been to work on his Winter Exhibition installation: that lack of undo button, that maddening gap between his imagination and his hands.

Preston shuffled to the fridge for a fresh can of Red Bull. It was nearly noon, but he was still in his pajama pants, shirtless and barefoot. Karina had been gone when he woke up that morning. He'd wasted a good while just lying in bed, blankly staring at a strand of hair on her dented pillow, wondering what to do with the Furby.

If he was honest with himself, his dejection was definitely tied to the current state of their relationship. When he and Karina had first moved to New York, things between them had been great. And then, after Karina's birthday, they suddenly weren't. And it wasn't even that they were fighting a lot—it was that, overnight, Karina had more or less absconded from the relationship. She left for studio before Preston woke up and came home after he'd gone to sleep. It took her hours to answer a text. And on the rare occasions when he did see her, if he dared suggest that they establish a regular date night or at least make the effort to eat a meal together once in a while, she'd blink at him and say something like, "Things will settle down after our show." But it was only February, and their show wasn't till May. Did she really expect him to put up with three more months of this?

He draped himself over the couch and pulled his laptop onto his stomach, the whirring metal warming his skin. These days, Photoshopping was the only thing that soothed him. It wasn't procrastination. Over the past few weeks he'd generated some great content for The Wart: three men in loincloths walking over a bed of Flamin' Hot Cheetos (*Rite of Passage*), a stack of floppy discs on a plate, drizzled in maple syrup and topped with whipped cream (*Nostalgic Eats*), a blow-up sex doll wearing a "The Future Is Female" crop top (*Girl Power*), four frat boys laughing and drinking beer in a hot tub filled with spaghetti (*Male Bonding*), a baguette cut in half to reveal a purple geode interior (*How French Women Stay Thin*), a dildo covered in cactus spines (*Don't Yuck My Yum*), swastika latte art (*Your Barista Is a Nazi*), and Osama bin Laden wearing hot-pink Crocs (*Still Think 9/11 Was an Inside Job?*). The Wart's follower count and page traffic increased every day, and Preston had been able to use the heightened interest to drum up buzz for his upcoming show, so it was a little ironic that while his online audience swelled, his physical work remained stunted, the artistic equivalent of a malformed fetus.

Today, even Photoshopping felt like a boondoggle. Preston emitted a hiss of frustration and closed his laptop. What he needed was a good long run. Just to clear his head. A quick shot of endorphins. He changed into workout clothes and went out. One block, two blocks, three, four, faster and faster, trying to rid himself of his fear, his self-doubt, his jealousy of Karina. Karina, who churned out painting after painting—with his praise and encouragement, no less—while all Preston could do was sit and sulk and Photoshop pictures that Brian didn't want. He'd thought of their future together as a drama where she'd play the supporting role, but now he found himself on the sidelines while she prepared to take the lead.

As Preston neared an intersection he slowed to a walk, then stopped, panting hard as he braced himself against his knees. A piece of cardboard gusted across the street, flapping in the wind. From the church across the way came the faint, breathless whine of an organ. Preston was goosed, suddenly, by a rash of memories: his mother singing hymns at church, her high whispery voice, how one Saturday night his father had grabbed her round the neck as she washed the dishes, how the next morning she hadn't sung at mass, just moved her lips silently to *Here I Am, Lord*. The crosswalk light changed to *Go*. Preston felt dizzy. He straightened, loping across the street. At the bodega, he bought a Gatorade and, on impulse, a pack of cigarettes for Karina.

When he returned to Cedar Street, he found a small knot of people holding signs outside his apartment building. MI CASA NO ES SU CASA, IT'S NOT REVITALIZATION IT'S GENTRIFICATION, BUSHWICK IS NOT 4 SALE, HIPSTERS GTFO, ART + CULTURE = EXCUSE TO RAISE RENTS, GENTRIFICATION IS THE NEW COLONIALISM.

As Preston swiped his access card, they yelled at him: "Bougie scum!" "Fuck you, Wes Anderson!" "Go back to Manhattan!"

Cold guilt washed over him. If Sammy Nakamura could see him now. From an Occupy encampment to this. Preston tried to ignore the protesters, but upstairs he could still hear them, so he put on Netflix to drown them out (and yeah, maybe to procrastinate a little longer). He noodled around, finally settling on a documentary about artificial intelligence. Onscreen, men with square haircuts talked about DeepMind and the Turing test and the uncanny valley. Then the film's focus shifted to a burly, tattooed music producer who designed neural networks that yielded AI-generated songs.

What we're doing is feeding the computer massive amounts of source material—top forty pop hits, disco, classic rock, you name it—and teaching it to analyze the music and identify patterns. The software homes in on things like tempo, chords, melodies, et cetera, and then starts generating its own original material.

Preston thumbed the spacebar, pausing the video, his imagination firing with every cylinder. He had an idea. He had an idea!

The only thing was, he'd need Slade's help again. Being in debt to Slade made him anxious. But Preston texted him anyway: *u free for lunch today? I have a business proposition 4 u.*

Slade's reply came right away: *doing a cleanse rn but could meet for coffee.* He followed up with an address. Preston jotted down a few notes-to-self and hopped into the shower.

At the coffee shop—all froufrou organic fair-trade cold-brewed whatever—Preston ordered a latte and sat down. Slade arrived wearing a navy parka and polarized sunglasses. He greeted Preston and went to the counter, returning with a smoothie the color of wasabi.

"Do you know anything about artificial neural networks?" Preston said.

"I'm somewhat familiar with the technology." Slade unwrapped his straw. "It's machine learning. Why?"

Preston explained what he had in mind. Slade looked skeptical. "I don't know, man, there's a hype bubble surrounding AI right now. Like, even tech people seem to think we can make computers do everything people can, and that's just not true. Machine learning takes a fuckton of time and requires lots of clean data sets. Plus, it involves so, so much trial and error. The software isn't just gonna give you the output you want right away. You'll have to sift through a lot of junk."

"That's okay. I have time."

This was not, strictly speaking, true. Brian was getting impatient. He called at least once a week, nagging about a studio visit, though Preston had explained to him repeatedly that he *didn't have a studio.*

"Another thing," said Slade, "is you'll need a fair amount of computational power. What kind of hardware are you running?"

"I have a 2010 MacBook Pro."

"If you don't want this to take months, you'll need a much better graphics processor."

"So how much are we talking in terms of upgrade? A couple hundred bucks?"

"Nah, you'll need a new computer. Maybe a few thousand?"

Preston winced. "Okay, so if I got the equipment, could you set up the software for me and teach me how to use it?"

At the next table, a baby was fussing in its stroller. Its mother kept going *shhhh shhh.*

"What's in it for me?"

Aha. There it was. Preston tried to conceal his irritation. "Um, do you have like an hourly freelance rate or something?"

"How about a cut of your sales instead? Fifty percent."

"Fifty per—Slade, that's more than my gallery takes."

Slade tipped his head back and took a huge gulp of smoothie. "And I'd love it if you'd convince Karina to promo herself more. I'm not gonna get a good return on my investment if nobody knows who she is."

Preston couldn't help laughing. "I would if I still saw her. She practically lives in her studio these days."

"Shouldn't she be, like, networking, though?"

"Why don't *you* tell her that? You practically did the other day when we were going to that party. Tell her you're hoping on a great return on your investment and could she please grease some elbows and beef up her Instagram for you, please and thank you."

Slade leaned back in his chair, wearing a wry half smile. "I wouldn't do that to you."

Preston was silent. He ran his thumb over the lip of his empty coffee mug. The woman picked up her baby, which was full-on wailing now, and bounced it in her arms.

"She doesn't know you gave me those paintings, does she?"

Preston went cold.

"So," said Slade, his tone businesslike once more, "it's a deal, then? Fifty percent?"

"Thirty percent of my cut."

"Forty."

"Fine," Preston heard himself say.

"Great. I'll email you my recommendations in terms of hardware and stuff." Slade slurped the last of his smoothie and stood to go.

By the time Preston got home, the protesters were gone. He stood at the kitchen counter, drinking a beer and contemplating the prospect of maxing out his credit card on a new computer. He thought of that Schiele drawing of Karina's. A few weeks ago, in a moment of idle curiosity, he'd tried to find out how much it might be worth: based on what he'd seen online, anywhere between six hundred thousand and two million dollars. The knowledge had given him a queasy shot of adrenaline, like running a half marathon after being down with the flu.

On impulse, he went into the bedroom, opened Karina's dresser drawer, sifted through the tangle of clothing. Next he checked her bookshelf, running a hand behind the rows of dusty paperbacks. In the closet, he found a thick pile of sketchbooks but no Schiele. He straightened and dragged a hand over his face. He felt ill. Sick of himself, of inhabiting his own mind and body.

That night, he waited up for Karina. "I need to talk to you," he said when she finally came home a little past midnight.

"Okay." She seemed distracted, kept opening and closing the fridge and fidgeting with her keys.

"Can we sit?"

Karina perched herself on the kitchen counter. Preston sat beside her. "Listen," he said. "I need to borrow some money."

At first she didn't say anything. She hopped off the counter, took a beer from the fridge, then climbed back up and opened the can. "You know my stipend's the same as yours, right?"

"From your parents, then." He felt a terrible smallness, a shame pinching deep in his gut.

"How much do you need?" She took a long drink, cuffing her mouth with the back of her hand.

He swallowed. "Two, maybe three thousand."

"What for?"

"My show. I need a more powerful computer."

She still wouldn't look at him. She kept flicking the pull tab on the beer can. *Ping, ping, ping.* "Couldn't you ask your brother?"

"Andrew already lent me money to help me—to help *us* move."

"How about your dad?" Out darted her pink tongue, lapping a droplet of foam off her lip.

Preston shook his head. "I guess I haven't told you this yet." He felt a sudden tightness in his chest and struggled to continue speaking normally. "He—he cut me off. He's really fucking mad at me." Preston laughed, the kind of laughter that said *none of this is funny.*

Karina swung her legs, banging them against the cabinet. "So apologize. Make nice. Do what you have to do. I do it all the time with my parents."

Preston could feel it coming, the awful building pressure, like a ball expanding in his throat. And now it had grown too big; it was too late to swallow it. He was a child, a freakish overgrown child. It seemed grotesque that he was crying and that Karina wasn't. It seemed a monstrous imbalance. He buried his face his hands. A moment later he felt Karina stroking his back, her thin fingers tracing his spine.

"I can't ask my dad," said Preston, wiping his hands on his pants. "I fucking—I *hate* him." He felt himself shaking as though with silent laughter. "Did I ever tell you how my mom died?"

"No." Her demeanor had changed. Her body straightened, tensing. She threaded her arm through his and gripped his hand. Softly, she said, "Was it suicide?"

Preston thought of the empty garage, the sirens in bright sunlight. He could smell the beer on Karina's breath, a faint whiff of sawdust. "I was the one who found her. My dad treated her like . . . like . . . a punching bag. His personal punching bag. One day I guess she couldn't take it anymore."

Karina looked at him, and he could see in her eyes that she was horrified, that in no way had she expected this. "Jesus Christ. How old were you?"

"Fourteen."

She gripped his hand tighter. "Preston, I'm so sorry."

"I remember afterward, my dad pulled me out of school for a few weeks and Andrew came back from Boston, and at the wake he stood up and called my dad a murderer. We were all standing around eating fucking—fucking spinach and artichoke dip, and he said it in front of everyone. *You murdered my mom, Preston.*" He felt another surge of tears coming. He took a deep breath and managed to make it recede. "I'm a Junior, did I ever tell you that?"

Wordlessly, Karina shook her head, and for a moment it seemed as though she were about to cry, too.

"And then Andrew left, he got a hotel room rather than sleep at my house, and all my parents' friends pretended like nothing had happened. And if anyone ever brought it up again, it was always with this attitude of, like, oh, poor Evelyn had a psychotic break." His voice broke.

"That's awful," Karina said. She stroked his hand. A silence elapsed before she added, "But, so . . . you're not in contact with your dad anymore?"

"No."

She put an arm around his shoulders, though she could hardly reach across them. "That's good, then," she said, gently. "A silver lining, right? That's he's out of your life?"

Preston looked up and found her watching him intently, her eyes full of pity. Another wave of misery passed through him and this time he succumbed to it, dissolving once more into tears. Karina took his face in both her hands and kissed him. When she drew away, he saw that her lips were wet. "I'm sorry I haven't been around," she said. "I'm so sorry, Preston."

He closed his eyes and allowed himself to lean into Karina's body, the solid warmth of her. Her hands roamed his back, making shushing sounds against the fabric of his shirt.

"You can use my Winter Exhibition prize money," she said, speaking quietly into his hair, her breath warming his skull. "You don't need to worry about it anymore."

CHAPTER TWENTY-FIVE

During her first few weeks as Akito Kobayashi's assistant, Louisa painted a three-tailed cartoon bat monster with violet flames erupting from its nostrils, a stylized spaceship orbiting a many-ringed planet, and a four-eyed daisy with rainbow petals. She also spent the better part of two days gluing gold leaf to a larger-than-life fiberglass sculpture of a blue-skinned woman with melon-shaped breasts.

The work was more tedious, and much more stressful, than Louisa had anticipated. Craig maintained a zero-tolerance policy for improvisation or creative license of any kind. Every Sunday, Kobayashi emailed him high-resolution digital mockups of the pieces he wanted made, specifying the materials, paint colors, and fabrication methods to be used. At the Monday morning staff meeting, Craig assigned the assistants their project for the week. You were required to document the fabrication process from start to finish, photographing the piece every step of the way. On Friday afternoon, after you'd handed in the work for inspection, you emailed Craig a fabrication report and a file containing the photos in chronological order.

If the piece passed inspection, you stenciled Akito Kobayashi's signature onto it, then set it aside to be packed and shipped. The gallery that represented Kobayashi was an international behemoth, a sprawling multimillion-dollar business with outposts in major cities across the globe—Louisa overheard one of the assistants snidely comparing it to Walmart—and a stable of over two hundred blue-chip artists both living and dead. The packages on the loading dock were bound for Paris and Sydney, Buenos Aires and Hong Kong. Louisa pictured the art soaring across the ocean, a jet stream of paint and gold leaf.

If the piece didn't pass inspection—maybe there was a smudge visible only to the eagle-eyed Craig, or a platinum particle was misaligned by a fraction of an inch—then it was returned to you, and you either corrected the error or, if Craig deemed the work unsalvageable, started over from scratch. Louisa quickly learned to live in fear of making such a mistake. Craig had seemed so mild-mannered when she'd met him; it shocked her the first time she saw him make an assistant cry. He was loud when he got angry, and his shouts reverberated scattershot across the concrete floor; even if you were working at the opposite end of the studio you were still privy to his displeasure.

Louisa had hoped she'd find community with her co-workers and was disappointed that the other assistants, though polite and helpful, rarely hung out together save for the occasional after-work drink at a nearby bar. During the workday, they plugged in their earbuds and went into their own little worlds, never exchanging more than a handful of words. Most of them were older than Louisa—some were married with small children—and seemed frankly uninterested in befriending her.

In the evenings, Louisa tried to work on her own art, though often she was too tired for anything more than a lazy sketch. She cooked beans or instant ramen in Ines's kitchen and packed herself peanut butter sandwiches for lunch. On weekends, she went to Fort Tryon Park and drew in the Heather Garden for as long as she could stand the cold. On Sundays she called home and spoke briefly to Mom, who put her on speakerphone so she could say hi to her grandparents. Their conversations followed the same script: the weather here, the weather there, Pepere's health, Mom's job, Louisa's job. Often Mom sounded harried, or like she was itching to get off the phone.

Louisa still kept in touch with Alejandro, exchanging texts every few days. He sent her photos of his new Pop Art–inspired paintings (*No more telephone wires!*), told her about summer fellowships he was applying for. When he asked *How are you?* she said *Doing great!* She still hadn't unpacked the bird woman paintings.

After a nerve-racking call from a debt collector, she'd started making the minimum payments on her credit card again. She was trying to save up for the security deposit and first month's rent she'd need when Ines came back at the end of February. She'd drawn up a budget, and she figured she could just manage it as long as she was careful.

When Louisa had been working at the studio for a month, Craig announced that Akito Kobayashi would be visiting on February 15, the day before Louisa's twentieth birthday. The prospect of meeting the artist invigorated Louisa. She resolved to try to make an impression on Akito—maybe, without being too pushy, she could find a way of showing him photos of the bird woman paintings.

Akito, when he arrived, was reedier and more unassuming than Louisa had expected. He was of average height, slim. He wore a long-sleeved T-shirt over toffee-colored cargo pants, and white tennis shoes. His black hair was graying in elegant streaks at the temples.

He inspected the works-in-progress without saying much to the studio assistants, though he conferred often with Craig, who took notes on a legal pad. Louisa felt jittery and overeager, like a dumb puppy. She kept trying and failing to come up with an excuse to approach Akito and strike up a conversation. At noon, the artist ordered lunch for everyone from a gourmet sandwich shop. The assistants sat around awkwardly, eating in near silence while Akito and Craig went up to the office to talk.

Before leaving, Akito stood in the middle of the studio and addressed the assistants. "I am honored," he told them, his voice crisp and softly accented, "that each of you wields a brush in my name. In my London studio, the assistants have a little game. When they are first given a canvas, they write their name or draw a little doodle and paint over it. And then, if anyone asks, they say their work sells for thousands of dollars and it's the truth. Our little joke!"

There was a ripple of uneasy laughter. Louisa felt a jolt of something hot and bitter: indignation. After Akito was gone, Craig took out the legal pad and read off a long list of pieces that Akito wanted redone, among them the one that Louisa had been working on all week.

In the waning afternoon light, she started over on a fresh canvas. Before blocking out the composition, she dipped a brush in red acrylic and scrawled ART IS SHIT across the blank, gessoed surface. She waited for it to dry, then slowly and mechanically painted over it.

They worked until late that night, and afterward a few of the assistants went to a bar on Jackson Avenue, where Louisa passed one of her coworkers three crumpled dollar bills and said, "Could you buy me a PBR? I'm underage."

"We should unionize," said Teddy, an assistant from Queens with a neat black beard. He clinked his glass against Louisa's beer. "Cheers."

"You want to get fired?" said Bianca, a brisk woman who did all the studio's metalworking.

"I want to pay off my MFA before I die."

Bianca laughed darkly.

"Akito seemed nice, at least," said Louisa.

"He's nice 'cause he outsources his assholishness to Craig," said Bianca.

"Yay capitalism," said Teddy.

"Do you think you'd ever do what he does?" said Louisa. "If you got successful enough?"

"Would I pay midlevel management to do my dirty work?" said Bianca. "Sure."

"No, would you hire people to make your work for you?"

Bianca shrugged. "I want to say I wouldn't? But I honestly don't know."

"It just seems like what would be the point, you know?" said Louisa. "Like, where would the joy be? Would it even be yours anymore?"

It was late by the time Louisa left the bar. The trains, she'd discovered, ran less often the later it got, and it was alone at night on a subway platform that she felt most anxious and lonely. Even when there were other people waiting with her, they always had their headphones on, lost in their own little worlds, avoiding even the possibility of eye contact.

It was nearly midnight by the time Louisa returned to Ines's building. As she stood in the hallway fumbling for her keys, she heard noises inside the apartment: garbled voices, bursts of muffled laughter. She froze. Ines wasn't due home for another two weeks.

The door swung open and a middle-aged man in an orange beanie stepped into the hallway. Instinctively, Louisa raised a clenched fist, keys poking out from between her knuckles, the way Mom had taught her to do when she walked alone at night. The man smiled quizzically. "Uh, hi. Can I help you?"

"I'm calling the police," Louisa managed.

To her consternation, the man looked perplexed, then began to laugh. "Ines!" he called over his shoulder. "Did you forget to tell your cat sitter you were coming home early?"

"Oh fuck!"

A small woman with a pixie cut appeared in the doorway. She was younger than Louisa had expected, midthirties maybe, and very beautiful, with tawny skin and big dark eyes.

"Oh no," Ines said. "You're Louisa, aren't you? Those must be your bags in my bedroom?"

Louisa took a deep breath. "Sorry. I thought someone was robbing your apartment."

The man laughed. "I guess I do kinda look the part. I'll take that as a compliment." He shook his head and, still chuckling, headed down the staircase.

"No, *I'm* sorry!" said Ines. "I was gonna go to Venice after my residency ended, but then that trip got canceled and I *had* on my to-do list to email you, but I must've totally spaced, and—Goddammit, Cleo!"

One of the cats had darted out from between Ines's legs and was making a run for it. Louisa dropped her backpack and chased her down the hall, grabbing her round the middle just as she was nearing the staircase. She carried the squirming bundle back and deposited it into Ines's arms.

"Ugh, thank you. Cleo, you're incorrigible."

Louisa smiled. "She did that a couple of times with me, too. She's pretty nimble."

"Come in," Ines said. "Frank just went around the corner to pick up our takeout. You hungry?"

"I don't want to intrude."

"Don't be silly. We ordered enough food for like ten people."

Her initial panic abated, Louisa's worries turned to housing. Would Bianca or Teddy—the two assistants she was on friendliest terms with—let her crash for a couple of days until she found a new place? She had some housing leads, a few rooms in Brooklyn she'd made appointments to see, but not till the weekend. She tapped out a group text: *Hey the person I'm cat sitting for came home 2 weeks early, any chance I can crash with 1 of u?*

"The whole time I was in Italy," Ines was saying, "I had these *intense* cravings for bad American Chinese food. So as soon as I got home I said to Frank, 'We *must* order from King Garden!' Good thing they're open late."

Inside, the shades were drawn, the blinds ticking softly against the sill. Most of the furniture had been shoved up against the backmost wall. In the middle of the room, the blue corduroy couch and its two matching armchairs had been arranged facing each other, a fitted navy sheet draped over all three. A blanket fort. These two adults were building a blanket fort. It was lined with cushions, blankets, and towels, all various shades of blue.

"Frank and I are making a bowerbird nest."

"Oh," said Louisa politely. "I've never heard of that."

"Bowerbirds? They're these birds that are obsessed with the color blue. When the male builds a nest to attract a female, he decorates it with blue objects."

"Blue objects," Louisa echoed.

"You know, bottle caps, pebbles, plastic, little pieces of string, just stuff that he scavenges. One man's trash is a bowerbird's treasure. You'll have to google 'bowerbird nest' and take a look, they're *so* beautiful. They're art, really. You look at them and they strike you as so human."

"Why are you building it?"

"It's all Frank. It's how we met, actually. When I was in grad school he came to campus and built one on the quad—a proper one, with branches and everything—and I was just so enchanted with it. And we've kept in touch ever since. We build one together once or twice a year. Speak of the devil."

Frank had returned bearing an enormous paper bag, its bottom spotted with grease. Ines dragged the coffee table back into the middle of the room, and Frank set the bag down and unpacked the food. Ines went to the kitchen and returned with plates, a bottle of wine, and glasses.

"Sit," she urged Louisa. "Help yourself."

Ines had an intimate, emphatic manner that put Louisa at ease. She heaped her plate with dumplings and orange chicken.

"So," said Ines, pouring the wine. "How's Maureen?"

"Good, I think?" Louisa nudged a clump of rice onto her plate. "I haven't seen her since December, though."

"She spoke very highly of you. Said you were super conscientious."

So that was how Maureen saw Louisa. Conscientious. Dutiful. A girl one could trust to keep cats alive. A girl one could trust to use the right color and paint inside the lines.

"I also went to Wrynn," said Ines. "About a million years ago. That's how Maureen and I know each other. She was my teacher, too. Did you just recently graduate?"

"Actually—" Louisa hesitated. "Not exactly. I had to drop out. For financial reasons." Though she knew, rationally, that none of what had happened had been her fault, she still felt ashamed.

"I'm sorry to hear that," said Ines.

"Degrees are a racket," said Frank. "I wish I'd been an autodidact. I think you're better off. School's an echo chamber. That's why art doesn't reflect the real world anymore; it just reflects the art world. You know who was self-taught? Van Gogh. Frida Kahlo. And you know what they call self-taught artists these days? *Outsider* artists. Can you imagine if van Gogh were alive today, calling him an outsider artist?" Frank blew air out of the side of his mouth and pointed his chopsticks across the table: "Pass the rice?"

"Frank may *sound* like a bitter old bastard," Ines stage-whispered, "but secretly he's full of joie de vivre."

Frank grinned. "Lies. That's what too many crits do to you: they make you bitter."

"And so what are you doing now, in the city?" Ines asked Louisa.

She briefly described her job at Kobayashi's studio.

"Kobayashi's a funny guy," said Frank. "I went to a retrospective of his at the Getty a couple of years ago, and there were these Prada handbags that he'd designed displayed in the gallery, right next to his paintings. And then as you left the exhibit you passed through the gift shop, and the exact same handbag was for sale right there by the postcards."

"Did you buy one?" said Ines.

"Ha! They were three grand."

"Maureen helped me get that Kobayashi job, too," Louisa said. "She's been really kind to me. It's weird . . . she was hard on me all semester—like, she told me to destroy my paintings—but as soon as I asked for help, she did all these nice things for me."

Ines laughed, refilling Louisa's glass. "She doesn't believe in praise. That's what she'd always tell us, that all praise does is make people complacent. I can count on one hand the times Maureen has said something nice to me about my work. And really, I don't think she's wrong. You can't be doing this for validation. My god, you just can't. It's not sustainable. There has to be something else motivating you. Maureen told me that for her it was spite."

Louisa had seen Maureen's paintings at a faculty exhibition once; they had a raw, splintered beauty, and Louisa could tell, though she couldn't quite explain why, that they were very, very good. But what an achingly difficult path to take. To be constantly at war with the world?

"Do you have any advice?" Louisa asked, addressing both Frank and Ines. The shyness in her own voice surprised her. She didn't feel the least bit shy, not at this moment. Did her body default to shyness in the presence of people who might judge her? Was this what Maureen had meant by *conscientious*?

"For what?" Ines said.

"For being an artist." Louisa spoke with quiet precision. "Out here, I mean." She looked at Frank. "In the real world."

"Don't," said Frank. He laughed dryly. "I know that sounds terrible, but if there's anything else you enjoy and you're good at, do that instead. Art will cheese-grater your heart."

Ines shook her head. "No, no, no, I disagree." Her voice was firm. "The secret, I think, is to make sure it's still fun for you, even when it's work. It's always, always going to be work, but it needs to feel like play, too, otherwise you're sunk."

They fell silent. The next-door neighbor's dog began to bark. Ines said, "I want to finish that bowerbird nest. Shall we?"

"Let's *inhabit* the bowerbird mindset," said Frank, "and find every goddamn last blue thing in this apartment."

Louisa checked her phone. Neither Bianca nor Teddy had replied to her text. "Actually, I should probably get going. Do you know of any cheap motels around here?" A few nights in a motel would decimate her savings, but she couldn't think about that right now.

"Don't be ridiculous," said Ines. "You're staying here. This was my fuckup."

Politeness demanded that Louisa demur, that she be all *Are you sure, I don't want to impose,* but she was too tired and poor for that. "Oh my god. Thank you. That would be amazing."

Ines made an *it's nothing* gesture. "My couch is open as long as you need it."

"She can sleep in the bower," said Frank.

Ines clapped her hands. "The bowerbird girl of Washington Heights!"

Louisa couldn't help but catch their enthusiasm, and the three of them spent the next half hour scouring Ines's apartment for blue things. Frank found a willow-patterned teacup, a notebook, a pencil, and a Walmart tote bag. Ines found a galaxy marble, a cat charmer tufted with azure feathers, and an old business card. Louisa found a pair of sunglasses, a frayed mitten, and a Yankees cap. It was two in the morning by the time Frank bade them good night.

"Bedtime for me, too, I think," said Ines. "But first I want to take a picture of you in the nest. Will you indulge me?"

"Sure."

Ines brought out her camera, flicked on a few lamps, and directed Louisa to sit inside the bower. She peered through the viewfinder and adjusted the lens. "And you're even wearing blue. How perfect is that?

Okay, look at me, please." The shutter clicked, an insectile sound, like a mechanical cricket. "Excellent. Okay, let's do a few more. You don't have to look at me anymore." *Click. Click.* "Imagine you're a young bowerbird." *Click.* "You've just built your first bower." *Click. Click. Click. Click.* "You've worked on it for days." *Click. Click.*

Louisa felt wine-fuzzed and exhausted. It was cozy inside the bower; she wanted to curl up and go to sleep. *It's my birthday,* she realized. *I'm twenty years old.*

"You've collected all the blue you can find." *Click.* "You've scoured the earth for every little scrap of blue." *Click.* "And you've arranged it and rearranged it until your bower is perfect."

Click. Click. Click. "You've worked so passionately, so obsessively." *Click. Click. Click.* "And now all that's left is for you to wait for someone to validate your work." *Click. Click.* "It might be that you've done it all for nothing." *Click. Click. Click.* "It might be that your bower seduces no one." *Click.* "But you're too compelled by the blue to care."

CHAPTER TWENTY-SIX

Adrian's forehead knocked softly against the window, smudging the glass as the bus heaved its way across Manhattan. The game on his phone emitted a tinny soundtrack, orchestral violins punctuated by electronic grunts. Adrian's thumbs moved swiftly, steering his muscled avatar over parapets and through torch-lit chambers. Robert had to keep resisting the urge to glance down at the screen; it made him queasy. Tomorrow, Robert told himself, he'd remember to bring a book or a magazine so he wasn't just *sitting* there like some brainless body-guard. For the first twenty minutes of the bus ride, he'd tried talking to the kid, really scraping the bottom of the barrel in terms of conversation topics. Eventually he gave up and settled into thinking ahead to the Abolish Debt fundraiser, which he'd be heading to directly after this—his first babysitting shift—was over.

The bus made a wide turn onto East Seventy-sixth Street. A warm block of early March sunlight drifted across Robert's face and torso. He closed his eyes. Some time later, he felt a hand tugging at his sleeve. "This is where I get off," came Adrian's soft, hoarse voice.

As the bus pulled to a stop, the boy edged past Robert into the aisle. The back doors folded open with a pneumatic wheeze, and Adrian sprang onto the sidewalk, skipping ahead with a sudden burst of energy.

Robert followed Adrian around the block and into his building. He aimed a polite nod at the doorman, and into the elevator they went, avoiding each other's gaze in the mirrored paneling. An afternoon snack, an hour of homework—word problems involving a Sally and a Daniel and a blueberry pie, a sentence-diagramming worksheet, chapter four of *Island of the Blue Dolphins*, Adrian's lips silently shaping the words as he read—and then it was time for the first art lesson.

Robert had decided to start off with the basics. While Adrian was reading, Robert went into his bedroom and dragged the plastic Legos bin into the middle of the floor. On top of it, he arranged a few random objects he'd brought with him in an old tote bag: a plaster skull, a chipped cereal bowl, a copper bracelet, a small clay crucifix, and a chunk of driftwood. Then he circled the toy bin, making small adjustments here and there so that from every angle an interesting composition might be gleaned. Finally, he positioned a lamp beside the bin, angling it for the most dramatic shadows.

"What's that?"

Adrian stood inside the open doorway. He'd taken off his socks; green lint fuzzed the gaps between his toes.

Robert nudged the cereal bowl a little closer to the skull. "It's for us to practice drawing."

Adrian tilted his head. "I know how to draw." His tone wasn't rude, but it was in the neighborhood of surly.

"So do I," said Robert. "But that doesn't mean I don't need to keep practicing. This is called a still life arrangement, and it's just as much for me as it is for you."

Robert produced two brand-new sketchbooks and a tin of drawing pencils. He placed one of the sketchbooks on Adrian's nightstand and set the tin down beside it; the other he kept for himself. He opened it to the first page, sat on the floor, and began drawing. For a moment Adrian watched him work from the doorway. Then he went away. Robert heard him wandering around the apartment, opening and closing the fridge. Some time later he returned, gnawing on a granola bar. Robert continued to sketch, pretending not to notice him. Adrian walked over to the nightstand, picked up the sketchbook, and flipped through its pages. Robert heard a metallic creak as Adrian opened the pencil tin and the *clack-clack-clack* of wood on wood as he ran his fingers over the pencils. Then Adrian sat down across from Robert—the still life arrangement between them, half-blocking their views of each other—and began to draw.

"Sit like I'm sitting," said Robert quietly. "You want your sketch pad tilted toward you at a ninety-degree angle so you get the proportions right."

Adrian shifted his body to mirror Robert's.

"Good. Now hold your pencil lightly, and try to draw with your whole arm, not just your hand."

Time ticked by, the room silent save for scratching pencils and traffic noise drifting up from the street below. When the sun began to set, Robert got up to switch on the overhead light. "Mind if I take a look at what you've got so far?"

Adrian's gaze broke upward. "Not yet," he said. He licked his lips. "I'm new at this."

"Fair enough." Robert watched the boy sink back into his drawing; presently, he followed suit.

This was how Cristina found them when she came home—both too absorbed in their work to hear the key turn in the door. When Adrian saw his mother, his face came alive. He sprang to his feet, sketchbook and pencil clattering to the floor, and wrapped his arms around her waist. Cristina kissed the top of his head.

"Did you have a good day?" she said, running her fingers through his hair.

Adrian said something to her in Spanish. She laughed. Robert looked away. It felt too private to watch them. Cristina's gaze rose over her son's head. Her eyes scanned the still life arrangement before landing on Robert, who was still sitting on the floor. His legs had gone to sleep. "This looks like fun," she said. Adrian disentangled himself from her and wandered off, leaving his sketchbook and pencil abandoned on the floor. Robert rose stiffly to his feet. As he and Cristina made polite chit-chat about the weather and tomorrow's school pickup time, he debated stealing a look at Adrian's drawings, then decided against it. It would be a violation, however small. Before going home, Robert asked Cristina not to disturb the still life. "We'll keep drawing from it tomorrow."

Robert went straight to the Abolish Debt fundraiser at 21 Rector Street, the group's eponymous headquarters. The week prior, Robert had shipped Vanessa his finished canvases, but he'd never actually seen the headquarters in person. In a vast room with dingy windows and round white pillars, mismatched folding tables and chairs were set up in front of a stage with a large screen displaying the words ABOLISH DEBT. On the walls were posters of somber people holding up handwritten signs. FIRED FROM WHOLE FOODS BECAUSE I NEEDED TIME OFF FOR SURGERY, said one. I WORK 2 JOBS AND CAN'T AFFORD TO MOVE OUT OF MY PARENTS' HOUSE EVEN WITH A ROOMMATE. Another read, YOU ARE NOT A LOAN. There was a photo booth where you could have a picture taken mugshot-style with the amount of debt you owed. A bar was set up adjacent to the stage.

When Vanessa spotted Robert from across the room she waved, then ran over and shook his hand. She was wearing a red dress and scuffed black sneakers over fishnet stockings. "I'm so glad you came! The paintings came out great; I'm so excited for people to see them." She showed him to a table near the stage marked *Reserved for Donors,* and a few minutes later a young man in a leather jacket brought him a glass of wine and told him, "Drinks on the house tonight." Soon Robert was joined by several more people: a middle-aged woman who'd donated a sculpture to the auction, a soft-spoken Frenchman whose restaurant had provided the catering free of charge, and a heavily mustached man who cheerfully explained that he was looking for creative ways to give away as much of his inheritance as possible and "get the old man rolling in his grave."

As Robert was starting in on his second glass of wine, a fourth person joined the table: a swarthy, broad-shouldered man about Robert's age. He looked familiar, but it wasn't till he took off his sweater, revealing a tattoo of an anatomical heart peeking out from under his sleeve, that Robert placed him.

"Cal Butler?"

The man turned his head and met Robert's gaze. His smile wasn't entirely friendly.

"Ah," said Cal. "I thought that might be you."

"You know each other?" said the Frenchman.

"Used to," said Robert. "We ran in the same activist circles." Though really it was Vince who ran in the activist circles. Robert just tagged along.

"You should change seats with me," said the Frenchman, and before Robert could protest he found himself sitting next to Cal.

Impossible not to think of the last time they'd spoken. The way Cal's lower lip had trembled as he yelled at Robert, accusing him of martyring Vince, rendering him helpless, hopeless, flattening him into a victim: "He's a dead butterfly pinned to Styrofoam. That's all he is to you. You didn't even say his name." Cal was one of the ACT UP members who'd protested at the Whitney's unveiling of *Dying Man*.

"So," said Cal now. "How are you?"

"Doing okay," said Robert. "You?"

"Can't complain. Thought I'd be dead by now, but—" Cal lifted his hands in a gesture of surrender. "Here I am."

Death was the dividing line back then, whether or not you'd been condemned to it. Robert recalled watching Vince speak at ACT UP meetings—this was after he'd dropped out of law school to go on disability and become a full-time AIDS activist—and being awestruck by the rawness and authenticity of his delivery. You couldn't perform that kind of sincerity. For people like Vince and Cal, the political was beyond personal; it lurked inside their bodies.

"What do you do these days?" Robert asked.

"I head up an AIDS nonprofit. We do a lot of community outreach."

"Is that why you're here?"

"Not specifically. I've been involved with 21 Rector on the side for a few years now. What about you?"

"Me?" said Robert. "Oh, I just donated some paintings to the auction."

"Ah," said Cal, in a tone that Robert couldn't parse. "I see."

"It doesn't feel like art is enough anymore, though," said Robert. "It's become so monied and elite—"

"We weren't making art," Cal interrupted.

"Pardon?"

Cal fixed him with a cold look. "We weren't making art, back then. Art was never enough. We were making propaganda. We were at war. We're still at war."

At that moment, the lights dimmed and the show began, emceed by a man in a torero costume. He opened with "Mama, Just Killed the Bull," sung to the tune of Queen's "Bohemian Rhapsody."

"Four months ago," he said, when the song was over, "we were evicted from Zuccotti Park. Tonight, we evict Wall Street from our lives! The banks got bailed out while we got sold out. Tonight, we bail out the people!"

This was met with deafening cheers, but Robert sat frozen.

Despite the dinginess of the venue, 21 Rector had secured the participation of several high-profile musicians and entertainers. In addition to a couple of well-known bands from the '90s and early aughts, there was a stand-up set by a woman Robert vaguely recognized, a magic act by a duo that headlined in Vegas, a gospel choir, a mariachi band, and a troupe of flamenco dancers. Behind the stage, the screen displayed a livecast of donations pouring in from around the country. By the time the performances ended and the auction began, the fund was nearing half a million dollars. When Robert's paintings came up for auction, he watched, astonished, as each sold for nearly ten thousand dollars apiece. By then he was quite drunk, and he found himself moved almost to tears.

The evening concluded with rapturous applause. As Cal stood to leave, Robert reached out and grabbed his arm. "I just want to say . . ."

Cal looked at him evenly. "Yes?"

"I just . . . I'm sorry I disappeared after Vince died."

Robert hadn't been able to face the anger of Vince's friends. And so it'd been Cal and the others who'd sewn Vince's panel for the quilt, Cal who'd carried his ashes to Washington and scattered them on the White House lawn.

Cal eyed Robert for a second. Then, to Robert's surprise, he sat back down. "I liked your paintings," he said.

"Thanks."

Another beat of awkward silence.

"Are you optimistic about"—Robert waved his arm around—"all of this? Compared to what ACT UP accomplished?"

Cal sighed. "I don't know. I hope it can find a way to move forward. It's hard when a movement doesn't have a clear set of goals. And the imperative here is different than it was with us."

"Death is quite the imperative."

Cal inclined his head. "Yes, it is. And then, of course, we all came out of the revolutionary committee meeting mentality. You remember, we had to plan out every three-second sound bite because it was our one shot at getting the message out there."

"Now everyone's a social critic," said Robert.

"Right. Nobody says, 'Let's have a community meeting about what to tweet today.'"

Both men laughed, and Robert felt some of the tension ease. He thought briefly of Preston, wondered what he and Cal would make of each other.

"Robert! Good, you're still here."

He turned and saw Vanessa coming toward them. "Oh, hi, Cal," she said. "You guys know each other?"

"We do," said Cal simply.

"So hey," Vanessa said, turning to Robert. "We're staging an action at the Guggenheim day after tomorrow if you're interested. You'll be there, right, Cal?"

"Yep."

"What are you protesting?" said Robert.

"You know how the museum's building a branch in Abu Dhabi?" Vanessa said.

"I think I heard about that."

"Well, the labor conditions are abhorrent. Slave labor, practically. Not to mention half their donors are, like, plutocrats who think they can clean their hands with cash. And their board's all rich and white. But mainly it's about the labor conditions."

"Day after tomorrow?" said Robert.

"We're assembling on the fifth floor of the rotunda. One P.M."

The day after tomorrow was Friday. Robert needed to pick up Adrian at school at three-thirty. The timing might be tight depending on how long the protest lasted, but he could probably make it to the Bronx by dismissal as long as he didn't get arrested. God, how long since he'd been to a protest?

"I'll be there."

On Friday, Robert arrived at the Guggenheim at 12:45, bought a ticket, and made his way up the spiraling white nautilus. On the top level he found Vanessa conferring with Cal. When she saw Robert she reached into her purse and pulled out a wad of cash. "Here."

Robert looked at Cal. "Is this like—?"

Cal gave a quick nod. "Yep."

In 1988, a year after Vince died, Cal and some other ACT UP people had put on nice suits and stuffed leather briefcases with replica bank notes xeroxed with $10, $50, and $100 on one side and slogans on the other: FUCK YOUR PROFITEERING. PEOPLE ARE DYING WHILE YOU PLAY BUSINESS. They went into the mezzanine of the New York Stock Exchange, and when the bell clanged, they dumped their briefcases, shutting down trading. Robert had read about it in the newspaper.

With some difficulty, because the wad was very thick, Robert shoved it in his pocket.

"Throw them when you hear the signal," Vanessa said quietly. "Now go be a tourist."

Robert was contemplating an Albers when a choir bell rang out. He walked over to the balcony and looked down. In the middle of the rotunda, a woman was ringing a bell, holding it above her head and tipping it slowly back and forth. As curious onlookers leaned over the railing, the woman stopped, put the bell in her backpack, and disappeared into the crowd. All at once the air was filled with dollar bills. Like fall leaves they spun, fluttering slowly downward. Murmurs turned to exclamations as hands reached out to grab the money. Cameras flashed and clicked. Robert took the wad from his pocket, peeled off a handful of bills, and tossed them into the rotunda. They were printed with YOU CAN'T CURATE JUSTICE and THE GUGGENHEIM EMPLOYS SLAVE LABOR and ART BUILT ON OPPRESSION IS A LIE. The bills

bore images of oil rigs and had 1% in each corner instead of a denomi-
nation.

Someone began to chant, "Who is building the Guggenheim Abu
Dhabi?" and soon others added their voices. Robert joined in with as
much gusto as those around him. He felt—what was it people said in
church?—filled with the spirit. Purposeful, like he was participating in
something greater than himself, but angry, too. Angry at this industry
that had embraced him before summarily rejecting him. At its hypocrisy, its casual cruelty. The way it hid behind a mask of nobility and authenticity. Nowhere else did purity and corruption skirt so close to each
other.

"Guards!" someone warned. Below, museum security was making its
way through the crowd. In the distance, a siren wailed. Robert threw
the last of his bills into the air, stuffing one into his pocket as a keepsake,
and hightailed it to the elevator. When he emerged on the ground floor,
security guards were clearing visitors from the museum. One of them
spoke into a bullhorn: "The museum is closing! Exit this way!" Robert
joined the stream of people pouring from the building.

By the time he arrived at Adrian's school, his phone was filled with
updates from a 21 Rector group chat that Vanessa had added him to.
There'd been a couple of arrests, but the protest was an overwhelming
success. Videos of it were going viral online. *Hyperallergic* and *Gothamist*
had been the first to pick up the story; now the *New York Times* was re-
porting on it.

Robert was skimming one of the articles when Adrian appeared, his
backpack slung over one shoulder. "Hey," Robert said, placing his palm
lightly on the boy's sun-warmed head. "How was your day?"

Adrian shrugged. "Fine."

"What did you do?"

"Nothing."

The bus came. They got on and Adrian settled into a window seat
and took out his phone.

"I went to a protest today," Robert offered.

Adrian glanced up. "What were you protesting?"

Robert explained about the Guggenheim's treatment of construc-
tion workers in Abu Dhabi. "We went to the top floor and threw hun-

dreds of these in the air." He showed the crumpled bill to Adrian, who took it and examined it with interest.

"Hundreds?" he said doubtfully.

"Oh yeah. Thousands maybe. It looked like it was raining money. Here, check it out." On his phone, Robert found a video, filmed from the ground floor, and showed it to Adrian.

Adrian half smiled. "Cool. Did you get in trouble?"

"A few people got arrested, but it was worth it because now it's all over the news."

Adrian held up the fake bill. "Can I have this?"

"Sure."

When they got home, Adrian quickly did his homework at the dining room table, then went straight to his bedroom and picked his sketchbook up. His enthusiasm pleased Robert.

Robert opened his own sketchbook, and it was like being back in Vince's bedroom that summer before sophomore year, drawing the ribbons of sunlight on the floorboards, Vince sitting up in bed reading *Johnny Got His Gun*, smoking his mother's Camels, blowing the smoke out the window, over the rooftops and up into the sky.

But when Robert looked at Adrian, he saw none of the frustration that had stymied him in those early years—his disappointment in himself, in his inability to bridge the distance between what his eyes saw and what his hand could do. There was none of that in Adrian's face. He looked utterly calm.

Late in the afternoon, just as Robert was thinking he ought to put a frozen pizza in the oven, Adrian looked up and said, "Can I see your drawings?"

"Can I see yours?

They exchanged sketchbooks. As Robert flipped through Adrian's, his eyes widened. The proportions in the drawings were off, but the details were beautifully articulated. That alone wasn't what made them remarkable. No, what gave Robert chills was the luxurious, tactile quality of the lines, and the *cognizance* of them—a kind of frankness that seemed to convey that Adrian actually saw the things he looked at, saw them as they were. The drawings didn't look labored-over—there were erasures here and there, yes, starts and restarts, but for the most part he'd drawn with a sure hand. And his natural ability seemed to reveal something deeper about the architecture of his mind. His drawing of the cereal bowl, for instance: the way he'd zoomed in on every little chip and ding, the myriad intonations of light on cracked ceramic, but with a gaze that was somehow forgiving, as though he recognized that age alone didn't render a thing worthless.

"Yours are *really* good," said Adrian. He raised his eyebrows high as though for emphasis.

"Thanks," said Robert. "I've had a lot of practice. Yours are very good, too, but I can help you improve them. So for example, one thing I've noticed you doing is erasing, and I'm going to encourage you to stop for now. Keep the mistakes and just draw over them. Work with them. Show your work."

"Like in math?"

"Exactly. It's not just about the correct answer—it's about communicating how you arrived there."

"Okay," said Adrian. "Is this all your stuff?" He gestured at the still life arrangement.

"Yep."

"Where'd it all come from?"

"Different places."

"Like where?"

"Um, let's see. The driftwood's from Cape Cod. The skull—it's not real, by the way—my ex-wife bought it at Target or something for Halloween. And the crucifix my best friend's mom gave me."

"Are you Christian?"

"Nope, Jewish."

Absently, Robert began sketching the little crucifix.

Adrian yawned and said, "Lily said you used to be kind of famous."

"I wouldn't say famous. Well-known, maybe."

"Well, Lily said you made a painting of a dead guy, and that the painting is famous."

Robert's heart stuttered. "He wasn't dead. He was dying. I was visiting him in the hospital." He bent over his drawing and shaded in the crucifix. How he and Vince had laughed when Mrs. Russo gave it to him. "For your bar mitzvah!" Vince had howled, red-faced. For years

Robert had kept it only because it was an inside joke, a piece of junk attached to a funny story. And then, later, he'd held on to it because it
linked him to Vince. But here, the crucifix was neither a joke nor an
object of tragedy. It was just something to draw.

"What was the dead guy's name?"

"Vince."

"Did he ask you to paint him, or what?"

"He didn't, no."

"At my school they have this really strict rule about how you can't
take pictures of people without permission. Because they might end up
on the Internet, and because everything can be Photoshopped."

"That seems smart," said Robert. His face felt hot.

"Is it the same for paintings?"

Robert looked up and found himself held by the boy's eyes, and all at
once he was struck by the obvious: Adrian had seen *Dying Man*, he'd
googled it, very likely he'd read about it on Wikipedia. He'd been planning this conversation for some time. He'd been working himself up
to it.

"To be honest," said Robert. "I don't know."

CHAPTER TWENTY-SEVEN

All through February, Karina had accomplished very little. Now it was March, and her daily routine remained unchanged: Allison would come upstairs first thing in the morning with a bag of muffins, and Karina would brew a pot of coffee, and then they'd fuck on the futon that Karina had bought for the nights she slept in her studio, of which there were more and more.

Allison had a braying laugh—"I'm basically a donkey with boobs," she told Karina—and long, coltish legs blotched with scabs from playing roller derby on the weekends. She'd lived in Buenos Aires for a semester and Madrid for two years, and she'd spent a summer on Puget Sound farming geoducks ("Have you ever seen one? It's like a clam attached to a pornstar-caliber dick. Proof that God has a sense of humor"). She'd had two threesomes—one with a married couple where the wife was four months pregnant—and had been briefly involved in a polyamorous relationship. She'd worked as a waitress, a cabinet maker, a buyer for a vintage clothing shop, a butcher's assistant, and a Spanish tutor.

"What about you?" Allison asked.

Karina was unused to playing the role of the naïf. Sometimes she allowed herself to imagine what it might have been like to fumble down this path alongside Louisa rather than sprinting to catch up with Allison. It wasn't that she didn't like Allison. She did. She *did*. But Allison could be condescending and petulant, and she had a tendency to launch into rambling monologues. Karina often found herself comparing her unfavorably to Louisa: Louisa was prettier, and she had a way of listening very closely, whereas Allison seemed to view conversations as an exercise in one-upmanship.

Regardless of her ambivalence toward Allison, Karina knew she needed to break up with Preston. But since he'd told her about his mother, she'd felt a debilitating tenderness toward him. When she looked at him, she thought, *I could've been you.* She understood him better now: he was an angry, hurt little boy, deeply afraid of himself, always questioning his own choices. What had first excited her about him— that brash self-assurance—was gone. Karina couldn't bring herself to sleep with him. She contemplated telling him that she needed to be celibate until she finished the paintings for her show—artists had indulged stranger whims—but it was simpler to just go home as little as possible.

In the second week of March, Brian arranged for an interview with Karina to be published in an online art magazine. The interviewer showed up at her studio one afternoon with a photographer in tow. He was a well-known critic in his late thirties or early forties, handsome and lanky. Joshua Van Something. The interview took about an hour, and afterward Joshua asked Karina if she wanted to get a drink. She looked at his expensive haircut, the way his eyes skipped up and down her body—for the photo shoot she'd worn a simple, form-fitting black dress—and she knew she could make him make her famous.

He took her to a bar in Park Slope—oak paneling, velvet banquettes— and made a transparent effort to impress her, dropping names between sips of Negroni. Afterward he invited her back to his apartment on Ninth Street and she fucked him on his vast white ship of a bed.

A few days later, the interview appeared online. Allison rushed into Karina's studio that morning, phone in hand. "Holy shit, K. Did you see this?"

"See what?"

Allison read off her phone: "*Piontek is brilliantly unclassifiable. She promises to push her medium in radical new directions.*"

Karina had expected a swell of happiness or triumph, but she felt nothing. Allison had coffee breath.

"*Piontek's upcoming debut show will be one of the highlights of the spring.*"

"Cool."

Allison looked up questioningly. "What's wrong?"

"Nothing."

"You're not excited?"

"No, I am. Just tired."

"Okay, good." Allison leaned forward and kissed Karina. "Because I'm just saying, if we weren't dating I'd be insanely jealous of you right now."

Were they *dating* now? How could that be, when they hadn't even been to each other's apartments? When the things that Allison didn't know about Karina vastly outnumbered the things she did?

"Hey," Karina said. "I kind of have a lot to do right now."

Allison lifted a palm. "Message received. I'll leave you to bask in your glory."

Brian called about an hour later. When Karina picked up, he greeted her as "my lovely wunderkind."

Karina made a silent gagging face for no one's benefit but her own. "Hi, Brian. How are you?"

"I'm wunderbar."

Karina shook the last cigarette from her pack and wedged it between her lips. With her free hand she rummaged in her bag for a lighter.

"You know what you need to do now, right?" Brian said.

"Nope," she said sweetly. "What do I need to do now?"

"You have to keep up the momentum. Ride that wave."

God, he could be such a schmuck. Men shouldn't be allowed to get old and successful. One or the other, fine—but not both.

"So," Brian said. "Here's what's next."

She sparked the lighter. It hissed but didn't flame.

"I need you to start going to more openings. Show your face, do a little cheek-kissing."

"I don't have time."

Brian made a tongue-clicking sound that set Karina's teeth on edge. "Don't be ridiculous. You're all set, my dear. You've done the prep work. We're not even going to have the space to show all your paintings as it is, unless we use some of the square footage I allocated for Preston. Which, now that I think about it—"

"No," said Karina quickly. "Don't do that." Best not to put any more strain on Preston's brittle ego. Recently he'd been wearing the hunted, scraped-hollow look of a wounded predator. She'd once heard a friend of her father's, a hedge fund manager who went big-game hunting in Tanzania, say that animals were at their most dangerous when they were wounded.

"Here's all I'm asking," Brian said. "One opening a week until *your* show opens. Just show up, have some wine, make some chitchat. It'll take an hour, tops."

Karina tapped the unlit cigarette against the windowsill. "All right."

"What a doll. You free tomorrow night?"

"I think so."

"All righty, so Ines Fidalgo is having a vernissage for her new show at Arcadia Haus."

Karina went very still. Suddenly she was thirteen years old again, reading Tamora Pierce on her bed. A dark-eyed beauty was telling her about Wally Neuzil.

"She's up-and-coming," Brian said. "Not huge yet, but she just came back from a very prestigious residency in Bellagio—and hey, you know what, that's exactly the kind of thing you should be applying for. You should ask her about it tomorrow."

That actually wasn't a terrible idea. Could be an excuse to sever ties with Preston. *I'm sorry, I just can't do a long-distance relationship.*

"I'll be there, too," Brian was saying, "so I can pass you around to some critics, maybe get your name in print a couple more times before the big day. What do you say?"

"Um, sure."

"Terrific. I'll have Jenny put your name on the list because it's invite-only. I'll email you the details."

"Okay, Brian. Sounds good."

"Wonderful. Oh, and Karina? You're welcome to bring a plus-one if you'd like, but—" He hesitated. "I would prefer it if it isn't Preston. Just because . . . you're the one I want to be spotlighting, not him."

So Brian was shrewder than he appeared. "Understood. I'll tell him I'm working late."

The line went quiet for a moment. Then: "Good girl. See you tomorrow. Wear something that photographs well, okay?"

Would Ines remember her? Would she hold her surname against her? Maybe she ought to bring Allison, who was always moaning about how she'd be further along in her career if only she'd networked more. Having Allison on her arm would show Ines that Karina was nothing like her parents.

She went downstairs to invite Allison and to borrow her lighter. When she came back up she had a text from her mother: *My love, I saw the news. I'm so proud of you.*

Karina took a long time deciding how to reply. In the end she wrote, simply: *Please don't come.*

She arranged to meet Allison a block from the gallery, because Allison had insisted on not walking in by herself. Karina wore the same simple black dress she'd donned for her interview. Allison had on a navy jumpsuit and long silver earrings.

"I'm nervous," Allison said, giggling. "This is the most exclusive party I've ever been to."

Her nervousness irritated Karina more than her clinginess. "You'll feel better after you have a drink." She dug inside her purse for some lip balm. It was nice not to feel like the ingenue for once.

Karina gave her name to the door attendant, and they went inside. The show was called *Appearances and Disappearances: Women in the In-Between.* Arcadia Haus looked a lot like Axiom Art, on the outside and on the inside.

"Did I ever tell you about the catering gig I had one summer?" said Allison. "Health code violations like you wouldn't believe. If there's tuna tartare, I suggest you give it a wide berth."

But Karina wasn't listening. The photographs on display had seized all her attention. They were printed large on heavy matte paper. The colors were so vibrant, so snappingly bright, that the prints appeared to be glowing from within—like windows, Karina thought wildly. Windows onto other worlds. Almost all the photos depicted women of various ages, though in many the subjects' faces were blurred or hidden, and their bodies had a ghostly, disintegrating quality that reminded Karina of stereoscopic prints from the Victorian era.

"I'm gonna find the bar," she heard Allison say. "You want anything?"

"Gin and tonic."

Karina moved deeper into the gallery. In one photo, a woman crawled through a copse of spruce trees on her hands and knees, an eerie green light splashed across her bare shoulders, her hair dragging through the dirt. In another, three women stood naked in a room with dusty pink floors and wallpaper peeling off in long strips, holding wooden ping-pong paddles in front of their faces.

In a third, a girl sat cross-legged inside a blanket fort, surrounded by objects—a notebook, a pencil, a teacup, a flattened Yankees cap—arranged in concentric circles. It took a moment for Karina's mind to resolve the image in front of her; when it did, her heart stumbled. It was Louisa. Her hands rested on her knees, fingers splayed. She wore jeans and a ribbed sweater that bagged a little at the waist. She gazed beyond the camera, an expression of contentment—or maybe it was surprise, or amusement—playing over her features. Her lips were parted slightly, and her eyes, fringed by a thicket of lashes, gleamed with an exhausted alertness.

Karina looked at the wall text.

Bowerbird, 2012, Digital print

"Karina!" Brian called.

She turned and saw him walking over with Ines. Ines's hair was shorter, but otherwise she looked the same. She wore a velvet tunic the color of mango flesh. Karina stood mute, motionless, Ines's presence reverberating through her body like a physical jolt.

Brian said, "Karina, I'd like you to meet Ines. Ines, this is Karina, the young artist I was telling you about."

"We've met," Karina said. Her pulse drummed in her throat.

Ines smiled uncertainly as she shook Karina's hand. "Have we? I don't recall."

"It was years ago. I was a kid. You came to my house for a party."

"I did? What'd you say your name was?"

"She's Harry Piontek's daughter," said Brian. He had a piece of spinach caught between his teeth. Karina wished violently that he'd go away. Ines's smile faded. Allison was hovering a couple of feet away, holding a drink in each hand and wearing a tight, tentative smile that said *I'm waiting to be introduced.* Karina felt jumpy with irritation. *If you want to talk to them so bad,* she thought, *just barge in. Take control like you always do, what the fuck is it about right now that's holding you back?*

"Excuse me," Brian said. "I'm just going to pop over there and say hi to someone I know."

Ines rolled the dregs of wine around in her glass. Karina stepped toward her. "I wanted to ask—" But Allison chose that moment to sidle into the empty space Brian had left. Wordlessly, she handed Karina her drink.

"This is my friend Allison," Karina said stiffly.

Allison wasted no time in chatting Ines up. She asked probing yet flattering questions, finding subtle ways to reference her own work. Karina stood there watching them, taking bracing gulps of her gin and tonic. *Go away,* she thought. *Go away and leave us alone.*

"I'd better eat something so I'm not schmoozing on an empty stomach all night," Ines said finally, "but it was really nice to meet you guys."

"Likewise," said Allison. "Do you mind if I give you my card?"

Ines looked briefly taken aback, but then she quickly composed herself. "I'd be delighted."

After Ines had gone, Karina handed her empty glass to one of the circulating waiters and told Allison she was going to the bathroom. She caught up to Ines near the refreshment table.

"Excuse me?"

Ines turned, her expression impassive. "Yes?"

"I'm sorry," Karina blurted. "I know my parents didn't treat you well, and I'm sorry."

Ines eyed her for a second. "I appreciate you saying that, but it wasn't your fault."

"I wanted to ask—" Karina was stammering. "Who's that—who's the young woman in the photo back there?"

Ines lifted her eyebrows. "I shoot a lot of women."

"It's the one of the girl—the woman—inside a blanket fort. *Bower-bird.*"

Ines's face softened. "Oh, I love that one. Last-minute addition. The subject is a young artist who was cat-sitting for me while I was out of the country. Why?"

Karina's throat tightened. "I know her. Does she live in the city?"

Ines picked up a plate and spooned some crab dip onto it. "Yeah. I invited her to come tonight, but she had work."

"I'd like to buy that print," said Karina, surprising herself.

Ines's eyes narrowed. "If you're trying to, like, make up for your parents or something, you really don't have to."

"That's not—my parents and I don't speak."

"Oh." An awkward pause. "I'm sorry to hear that."

"Don't be. I'd still like to buy the print."

Ines placed a slice of baguette on her plate. "Well, thank you. You'll have to check with Jenny. Sometimes pieces are already reserved."

Someone called Ines's name. "Be right there," she said. Turning to Karina, she said, "Hey, listen, I feel like I maybe gave you the wrong impression." She sighed and made a face like she was chewing over her words. "I don't have a problem with your mom. She was always lovely to me." Then, before Karina could summon a response, Ines was gone.

Karina put a cracker in her mouth and chewed without tasting.

"I thought you went to the bathroom."

Karina turned to see Allison glaring at her almost comically, hands on her hips.

"I did."

"I was watching you this whole time," Allison said, her voice dripping with scorn. "The bathrooms are way over there."

Karina lifted her shoulders. "Okay? Why are you being pissy?"

"Why am I being *pissy*?" Allison inhaled sharply. "Why did you introduce me as your friend back there?"

"Did I?"

"And you've been ignoring me all night. Do you not want me here or something?"

Karina felt the blood rush to her cheeks. Any other time she'd have had no trouble lying to Allison, but now her body was betraying her.

Allison threw up her hands. "I can't believe this."

"Keep your voice down."

"I can't fucking *believe* you."

"Allison, for fuck's sake, keep your voice down." Karina grabbed her arm and pulled her out of the gallery and onto the sidewalk. As soon as they were outside, Allison jerked out of Karina's grasp. The door attendant looked up with mild curiosity. Some part of Karina registered that the night was chilly, that her bare shoulders were cold.

"Do you not want me here?" Allison repeated. "All night you've been a bitch to me, so do you not want me here? Answer me."

"No," Karina admitted. "I don't."

Allison lifted her eyes to the sky. "Then why the fuck did you invite me?"

"I don't know," Karina said. Her voice was shaking. What was *wrong* with her tonight? "I don't know why I invited you."

Allison looked at her with contempt. "You're a good artist, but god, you're a shitty person." Clutching her purse, she disappeared into the night.

A few seconds later, Brian poked his head out the door. "What was that?"

Karina fumbled for a cigarette. "What was what?"

"That shouting."

"My friend and I had a fight."

"Next time invite someone less dramatic? It looks really unprofessional."

"Sorry."

"And listen, I love that dress—it looks great on you and it photographs well—but isn't it the same one you wore for the photoshoot? For the Joshua Van Lingen piece?"

"Yeah?"

"I know it's silly," Brian said. "But people notice that kind of thing."

"Can you point Jenny out to me?"

"Excuse me?"

"Jenny," Karina said. "The gallerist. Can you point her out to me? I want to buy a piece."

It was late by the time Karina's cab pulled up to the building on Cedar Street, but Preston was still up. Even if he hadn't been, she would've woken him.

"I don't love you," she told him as gently as she could. "We can still do the show together, but not as a couple. Our work . . . it's just too different at this point, you know? I don't even know what you have planned."

"That's because you're never home," Preston said sharply.

"I don't know that my being home would make your work better."

Preston's face reddened. Abruptly, he grabbed a glass from the coffee table and hurled it at her. She ducked; it exploded against the wall behind her.

"What the fuck," she said. "What the fuck, Preston." She'd gone all rigid, but she heard herself speaking flatly, her voice leached of emotion. How was that possible, when her insides were roiling with fear? She thought of Fiona—how sometimes, when Harry yelled at her, a strange, numb sort of calm would descend over her, as though her mind had temporarily detached itself from her body.

Shards of glass glittered on the floor around Karina. As she took a step backward, she felt them crunching under her shoes.

Preston groaned and flung himself onto the couch, sinking his face in his hands. In an instant he'd gone from charging bull to cowering puppy. "I'm sorry," he mumbled. "I'm sorry, I'm sorry, I'm sorry."

Dimly, Karina realized she was shaking. She went into the bedroom and gathered her things as quickly as she could, haphazardly stuffing clothes and books and sketch pads into a duffel bag. There wasn't much to pack; she'd already migrated most of her belongings to her studio. When she placed her copy of the apartment key on the kitchen counter, Preston raised his head and said, so softly it was almost inaudible. "I know you stole that Schiele."

Karina's stomach flipped. "What?"

"Some guy came poking around here the other day while you were gone," Preston said dully. "Said he worked for your parents. Said you stole a drawing from them."

Her mouth went dry. "What did you tell him?"

"Nothing. I said I didn't know anything about it."

For a long moment, they watched each other without saying anything. Karina was the first to look away. "That's a lie," she said, opening the door and stepping out into the hallway. "I didn't steal anything."

CHAPTER TWENTY-EIGHT

After Karina left in mid-March, Preston felt sick. He hardly ate, subsisting on coffee and energy drinks and beer. Some nights he dreamed of making love to her, other nights of fucking the shit out of her. Sometimes he woke up in the morning and couldn't say for sure whether he'd slept or not. He was able to resist the urge to call or text her, but eventually he succumbed to the temptation to check up on her online. The first item that popped up was an interview:

This 20-Year-Old Art School Dropout Is the Art World's Latest Wunderkind

It's rare for a rising art star to be young enough that she is barred from legally drinking at the opening of her own debut exhibition, but Karina Piontek, a 20-year-old painter who left Wrynn College of Art midway through her sophomore year and now lives and works in Brooklyn, can claim this distinction.

In the photo, Karina stared into the camera, unsmiling, a sylph clad all in black, surrounded by her cornucopic paintings.

JOSHUA VAN LINGEN: Your work seems to reference a very diverse set of influences. As an emerging painter, do you ever feel weighed down by the canon?

KARINA PIONTEK: No. I'll often see some small element in someone else's painting—maybe it's the way a shadow falls across a figure or a certain juxtaposition of color or an interesting texture—and I'll lift that one aspect and use it in my own work. But that happens to me all the time outside the quote-unquote canon, too. I'll see things when I'm out and about and I'll sort of mentally squirrel that little visual tidbit away to use in a painting later on. In a way it's a very collagist approach.

Several photographs of Karina's paintings accompanied the interview. Preston zoomed in on them one by one, blowing up each image until it filled his entire screen. They told him nothing.

It had been a hideous mistake, asking her for money, telling her about his mother and father. He'd lost control of himself, and then he'd done it again when he hurled that glass at her. He couldn't believe he'd tried to hurt her.

He forced himself to close the tab. Out of his chair and into his shorts. He'd been going on a lot of runs lately. When he got back, he discovered that Brian had called and left a voicemail. His voice was calm but icy: *Preston, if I don't have eyes on those pieces soon, you will be in breach of contract and I'll be forced to pull you from the show. Don't make me do that, man. Call me.*

Preston still hadn't caught his breath. He felt his pulse in his fingertips. He texted Brian: *will send you jpgs this week. Don't worry.*

He'd bought a new computer with Karina's Winter Exhibition money. Now he called Slade. Slade, who'd been surprisingly sympathetic when Preston told him about the breakup. "Let me know if you need anything," he'd said. Well, now Preston did.

Slade agreed to come over right away. It took him an hour and a half to install a machine learning program on Preston's new computer, a half hour to teach him how to upload example images and type in commands, and an additional hour to sit at Preston's kitchen table drinking Preston's beer and monologuing about a luxury wine-tasting tour of Napa Valley he was going on in July.

As soon as he'd left, Preston sat down at his workstation and stared into the yawning web of math Slade had spun for him. First, to "train" the neural network, he flooded it with visual data, uploading the thousands of images he'd posted to The Wart, plus a few hundred B-sides that hadn't made the cut, but which he'd saved for a rainy day in a backup folder titled ZITS. Then he typed in the commands Slade had taught him. One at a time, the program began rendering a series of computer-generated images. Theoretically, the algorithm was supposed to identify and mimic the defining characteristics of Preston's style, but the images it spat out were low-res and fuzzy. Also, despite the beefed-up hardware, the process was snail-slow. Preston grunted in frustration. He tweaked the settings, rebooted the system, and went out for another run. When he returned, the network had produced images of only marginally better quality, so he decided to diversify the example data set. He combed through the contents of his photo library, thousands and thousands of pictures, going back years, from the time he'd first learned to use his mother's camera. He zeroed in on some photos he'd taken in high school: topless amateur boudoir pics of an on-again, off-again girlfriend and blurry shots of a scraggly-bearded Slade and other friends shotgunning beers at a ping-pong table in someone's basement.

Preston created a new neural network for each loosely grouped data set—images that were similar to each other—feeding each set into the system separately. Slade had told him that neural networks perceived mirror images of the same photo as two distinct visual data, so Preston doubled the amount of available input by flipping the photos he already had. Running several different neural networks at the same time slowed the computer down, so instead of torturing himself by waiting around to watch the results creep in, he decided to take the rest of the day off.

He went to a bar a few blocks away, ordered a whiskey, and sat in a corner booth. As he sipped his drink, he scrolled through the news on his phone. Unemployment in the eurozone at ten percent; Mitt Romney ahead in the GOP primaries; Guggenheim shut down by a protest over labor disputes in Abu Dhabi. Preston clicked on a video of protesters dropping leaflets and chanting. Off-camera, someone could be heard saying, "Maybe it's a performance piece." Preston skimmed the accompanying article. The protest had been staged by some group called 21 Rector, an activist collective that predated Occupy Wall Street.

Preston shut off his phone and dispatched the rest of his whiskey in one hard swallow. It should've been him shutting down the Guggenheim. Hell, he'd have thrown more than leaflets. But no, here he was, spending his time trying—and so far failing—to make shit for rich people to buy. Briefly, he wondered if Occupy Wrynn was still going. Sammy Nakamura had been transparently impressed with the hoax email, though Preston suspected this had something to do with his resulting deal from Axiom. Still, what would Sammy and the other organizers think of Preston now? He signaled the waiter for another drink.

The next morning, the first thing Preston did was check the algorithm's results and let loose a howl of disappointment. Glitchiness was still an issue, but that paled against the *contrivedness* of the images the system had produced. The photos had been contrived to begin with, in the way that all deliberately composed shots were, but the neural network had somehow emphasized that very human artificiality rather than smoothing it out. The images were worse than bad. They were predictable. They were *boring*.

Preston slammed his fist on the table. Back to the drawing board. Maybe the solution was to go back even further in his photo library, to a time when he hadn't even known how to compose a shot, hadn't been versed in the visual vocabulary that was later shoved down his throat.

Down Preston scrolled, past high school and into the reaches of middle school, and there he found—his heart seized—picture after picture of his mother. He'd forgotten—how had he allowed himself to forget?—just how often he'd used her as a model in those early years, how she'd let him train his lens on her even when she was in her pajamas or not wearing makeup, laughing at the faces he pulled behind the viewfinder. Here was a picture of Evelyn walking their dog, Bowser—long dead, poor little guy—the leash wrapped around her hand, her arm outstretched as he tugged her across the lawn. And here was one of her on that vacation they'd taken in Newport, Rhode Island, one summer, just her and Preston and Andrew because his father had been abroad for some summit: sand crusting her kneecaps, lounging on the beach in a floppy straw hat that bathed her whole face in shadow. And another of her in church, singing, palms raised, chin lifted to the sky.

He heard himself let out a guttural noise. He lowered his face into his hands and pressed his palms into his eyes, hard, and saw sunbursts bloom in the darkness. After a long moment he lifted his head, blinking in the glow of the monitor.

Resolute now, he started over from scratch, retraining a new network, this time feeding it only pictures of his mother. He let it run for three hours before checking the output. The images were eerie and distorted, the figures in them recognizably human, but only barely. Smeared, contorted faces, orbs of flesh rearing up from enlarged torsos, everything shrouded in currents of mottled color. Melting body parts, one limb dissolving into the next. Some of the pictures showed monstrous, doglike shapes, curved yellow teeth caught in whorls of black and white fur, glistening pink tongues. Here and there Preston saw glimmers of Evelyn: a blue-green eye staring out at nothing, the shape of a hairline.

He'd fed the network images of lightness and color, eyes and smiles and hands and light through windows, trees and ducks and water. He'd fed it happy images, but the algorithm had distorted the happiness. It had laid bare a loss, the sense that something real had been flung into the abyss of decaying memory.

Preston took a breath. Maybe these would work. The images were serious enough, vague enough, to suggest high art. He could have them printed on canvas, cook up a suitably cryptic artist statement, and *voilà*.

The computer was still churning out monster-Evelyns and monster-Bowsers. Preston sorted through the images, exporting the most interesting ones. He converted them to jpgs, attached them to an email—*more to come,* he wrote—and sent them off to Brian.

CHAPTER TWENTY-NINE

Eventually, Louisa found a room to rent in a West Harlem three-bedroom shared by a couple of Columbia Law students. It wasn't big, but it had decent light and a large window with a fire escape. And it was hers—she'd paid for it with money that she'd earned, and eventually she'd fill it up with the oddments of her life. Ines helped her move her stuff, and Louisa thought that would be the last she'd see of her, so she was surprised when, not three days later, Ines invited her to an opening.

More surprising: Ines kept inviting her to things. And Louisa kept saying yes, kept putting on heels and lipstick and standing in the corner drinking too much wine, kept looking out at crowds of terrifyingly beautiful people, kept wondering, *What is the difference between me and them, where is the bridge I need to cross to get from here to there?* Kept shriveling up inside when someone looked straight through her as though she weren't there at all.

Ines, for reasons that Louisa didn't understand, had decided to take her under her wing. And Louisa was grateful for the way she tried to include her, the way she put her arm around her and said to people, "Have you met Louisa?" Possibly there'd been someone who'd shown

Ines the ropes when she was young, and now she was paying it forward. But Ines was good at parties—she was pretty and charming and funny—and Louisa wasn't.

It was exhausting. Wrynn all over again, but worse. Here was another language she didn't speak. And so, when Ines texted her to say, *I'm having a show for the work I made during my residency and I just put your name on the guest list for the vernissage FYI!* Louisa didn't even bother looking up what *vernissage* meant. She wrote back saying she was swamped at work, which wasn't untrue. The big summer art fairs were approaching, and the studio had ramped up production to prepare. Increasingly, Louisa worked nights and weekends. Craig hired ten new assistants. Louisa felt as though she were part of an army. A faceless soldier, her hands the only useful part of her.

Most days she was too busy to sit with her feelings and examine them in depth, but anytime she stilled—lying in bed at night, in the shower, waiting for the subway—misery snuck up and overcame her. She had no friends here, unless you counted Ines. Whenever she called home and talked to her family, she lied, said she was doing great.

There was one bright spot, though: Alejandro had kept his promise and was coming to visit her. He'd booked bus tickets for the last weekend in March; in preparation, Louisa borrowed a blow-up mattress and sleeping bag from one of her new roommates.

On the Friday Alejandro was to arrive, Louisa was painting a three-eyed bunny monster with long curving fangs, when her cellphone vibrated. CALLING: INES FIDALGO. Ines had never called before, only texted. Louisa set down her paintbrush, peeled off her gloves, and went to the restroom, locking herself in the corner stall.

"I have good news," Ines said. "But also a confession. You ready?"

Louisa sat down on the toilet seat. "Uh, yeah?"

"Remember those pictures I took of you in the bower?"

"Sure."

"So they came out beautifully, and I decided to put one in my show."

"Oh. Okay. Cool."

A memory, jostled loose: how it had scared Louisa to think of the bird woman paintings as *ours* instead of *mine*. How Karina had seemed to seep into the work, overshadowing Louisa's brushstrokes in a way that felt like a kind of authorship. But here was Ines, an artist who depended on other people to produce successful photographs. Louisa recalled something Mom had told her when she was fifteen and going through an obsessive landscape-painting phase: *You need to put a figure in there. You need a narrative. When you add in a figure, you invite the viewer into a story about what they're looking at.*

"I should've asked for permission," said Ines, a little ruefully. "Normally I have subjects sign a release, but it was a very last-minute decision, I'm sorry."

"It's fine," said Louisa quickly.

Louisa wondered how she appeared in the photograph. Did she look, as she often did in pictures, like a drab, washed-out version of the person she felt herself to be?

"So I sold a print," said Ines. "That's the good news."

"That's great. Congratulations." An image of her face that would adorn a stranger's wall.

"And I'd like you to have half. The gallery keeps forty percent, but I want you to have half of my portion."

"Oh, that's okay! You don't need to do that."

"Louisa, I want you to have it."

Louisa's eyes filled unexpectedly. She heard Craig come out of his office, his footfalls on the staircase. There was a tightness in her chest; she wanted to go home and lie down and be alone. "Thank you. That's—that's incredibly generous. Hey listen, I'm at work—"

"Just real quick, there's one more thing I wanted to tell you."

Louisa began nervously shredding a square of toilet paper. "Yeah?"

"The person who bought the print—she knows you."

"Really? Who is it?"

"Her name's Karina Piontek. Does that ring a bell?"

Louisa couldn't speak. Her heart soared; her throat grew thick.

"Are you there?"

"Yeah," she managed.

"Do you know her?"

"I do."

"Okay, well, I don't know how *well* you know her—"

"She was my roommate at Wrynn."

There was a pause. "Oh," said Ines. She sounded surprised. "Well, I . . . I was just going to warn you—you know what, never mind."

"No, go ahead."

Ines hesitated. "I don't want to talk shit about someone I don't know."

Louisa couldn't help but laugh. "Plenty of people who don't know Karina talk shit about her. Go ahead."

"I guess it's not really about her . . . it's more about her family."

"Hm. Okay?"

"Yeah, just since, you know, they're such big collectors you're likely to end up dealing with them at some point. And her mother's fine. I mean, she enables her husband but she's a fine person."

"Okay . . ."

"It's her dad you should stay away from."

Louisa said nothing. Ines seemed to interpret her silence as a question. "I really don't want to get into it right now. It took me such a long time to process what happened and regain my, my *confidence*, but I had a bad experience with him years ago when I was maybe a little older than you and I just—he's not a good guy."

"Is Karina here?" Louisa asked, unable now to hide the urgency in her voice. "In New York?"

"I mean, yeah." Ines seemed startled.

"She lives here?"

"She has a show opening at Axiom soon, so I assume so?" Ines paused. "It's funny, she asked the same thing about you."

Louisa felt her heartbeat climb. "And she has a show?"

"Yeah, it's like a joint debut with some guy, I forget his name."

Louisa went still. "Preston Utley."

"That sounds right."

Fury flared inside Louisa, as keen and biting as it had been when she'd first learned that Preston had been responsible for the hoax email. *He* had an exhibition going up? And with Karina? The unfairness of it made her mouth go sour.

Louisa heard Craig begin to yell at someone, that slow, simmering anger that would soon ramp up to explosive rage. "Ines," she said, whispering now. "Thank you so much for the money. I really have to go now, I'm sorry."

＋— —＋

That night, Louisa met Alejandro at Port Authority. On the train back to her apartment he filled her in on the goings-on at Wrynn.

"They finally tore down the Occupy encampment," he said. "Honestly, I think the organizers were kind of relieved to have an excuse not to sleep out in the cold anymore. Oh, and Clark Strickland is being investigated for sexual harassment. With old Maureen at the vanguard."

Louisa smiled. "I'd expect no less of her."

"And your friend Karina dropped out. With her loverboy. They got a rep offer from Axiom, lucky dicks."

Louisa's heart quickened. "I know." She explained about Ines and the bowerbird nest and the print that Karina had bought.

Alejandro whistled. "That's a power move. Also—I mean, sorry if this isn't what you want to hear—but it's kind of romantic, isn't it? Like in a creepy way?"

Louisa reddened. "I guess."

"What are you going to do about it?"

She shrugged.

When they got back to Louisa's place, Alejandro seemed taken aback at the spareness of her room. She hadn't bought a bed frame yet, had no furniture except for an old nightstand she'd found on the street corner. She'd wedged the blow-up mattress at the foot of her own mattress. She was still more or less living out of a suitcase. She hadn't painted in weeks.

"Did you just recently move, or . . . ?" said Alejandro.

"It's been like a month maybe?"

On the other side of the wall, one of her roommates was washing dishes in the little galley kitchen. Though her roommates were courteous and clean, they'd made it clear that they had zero interest in befriending her. It was strange, living with people who didn't care about you. It made you feel like you didn't fully exist. Even Karina, who'd at first pretended that she didn't care, had cared very deeply, and Louisa had felt that—subconsciously, maybe, in the beginning, but she'd felt it. It was the feeling of being watched, of being *seen*.

The next day was Saturday, and Louisa slept unusually late, waking to the soft *tap-tap* of Alejandro typing on his laptop. She sat up and blearily looked at him.

"Guess what?" he said. "I got that summer fellowship. Two months in Florence."

She searched inside herself for jealousy or resentment and found none. "Alejandro! That's amazing." It had been a long time since she'd felt genuinely happy for another person. "What do you want to do today?" They had one full day to spend together; Alejandro was going back to Stonewater on Sunday morning.

"There's this show opening in Greenpoint—"

"No. No more openings."

Alejandro looked intrigued. "Okay . . . I'm sensing there's a story there?"

"No story, just—I'm really bored of them."

"Look at you, jaded already. How about a museum?"

Louisa thought for a minute. "Natural History?"

Alejandro agreed, though he seemed a bit surprised.

They both brought their sketchbooks and spent several quiet hours surreptitiously passing Alejandro's flask back and forth, drawing the mammoth skeleton, and the taxidermied brown bears with their curious, humanlike faces, and the swoop of the blue whale. Afterward, they wandered around the Ramble, the treetops humming with warblers. It was finally spring; almost all the snow had melted. The woods were slick and shiny and bright, like something good to eat. You could almost pretend you weren't in a city.

Over dinner at a cheap taco place, Alejandro gave Louisa one of his piercing, candid looks and said, "Dude, you seem pretty miserable."

She was flushed and tired from drinking tiny sips of whiskey all day, too sapped to mount a robust defense. "I'm okay."

"Was moving here the right call, do you think?"

Some of the meat spilled out of Louisa's taco. "I'm still waiting to see, I guess. I wasn't happy at Wrynn at first, but I was starting to get happier, and I think I could've thrived there eventually." She picked up a piece of chicken, considered its charred, craggy surface. "I think I just need to meet people."

"What about Karina?"

"What about her?" Louisa said, mouth half-full.

Alejandro gave her an *I can't believe you're making me say this* look. "Have you thought of tracking her down? Maybe through her gallery?"

"No."

"Liar, you've totally thought about it."

She felt herself betray a tiny smile.

"I think you should," he said. "You deserve to be happy, you know."

"I know," said Louisa, though in that moment she realized that she didn't really believe it. Did someone who'd abandoned her sick grandfather deserve to be happy?

"You guys had a good thing going before it fell apart," Alejandro said.

"She has a boyfriend."

He smirked. "That didn't stop either of you the first time. And anyway, he's a dick."

Louisa didn't correct him. She said, "Do you think this waitress will card me if I order a margarita?"

The next day, after Alejandro had gone back to Stonewater, Louisa lay in bed and pulled up Karina's number on her phone and stared at the digits till her vision blurred. She felt insane for letting Karina have this kind of hold over her. She felt insane for wanting to call her.

Phone in hand, she got up, opened the window, and climbed out onto the fire escape. The air smelled floral and heavy, honey locusts and cooking gas. On the sidewalk below, two teenage girls walked by, sharing a cigarette, passing it back and forth between them, and the sight made Louisa's insides go hollow.

She tapped the call button.

Karina picked up after two rings with a low-pitched "Hello?"

"Hey, it's Louisa." The vowels turned to syrup in her mouth.

There was a half-second pause. "I recognized the area code."

Louisa looked down at her bare feet; the tips of her toes were the pale pink of flower buds.

On Karina's end, a breath of hesitation. "Did Ines tell you?"

Louisa leaned back against the railing, the metal pressing into her back. Her heart was in her throat. "Yes."

"Do you think it's creepy that I bought a photo of you?"

"No," said Louisa truthfully. She thought of how Alejandro had put it: *romantic but creepy.* "Though I can see how it could seem that way." She wondered how much Karina had paid for the print. She'd forgotten to ask Ines.

"I'm relieved to hear you say that."

Louisa laughed, though she couldn't tell if Karina was being serious.

"So we're even now, right?" Karina said, that familiar playfulness creeping into her voice. "You have paintings of me and I have a photo of you."

Her words sent a warm current humming through Louisa's veins. "Those paintings are rolled up in my closet at the moment. So if you really wanted us to be even you'd stick that photo in *your* closet and never look at it again."

"I'm not doing that," Karina said, her tone curt but soft.

In the distance, the ping of a crosswalk light. The teenage girls had perched themselves on a stoop across the street. One of them lit a fresh cigarette.

"So," Karina said. "I hear you're a New Yorker now."

"I guess I am."

"How do you like it?"

"Right now I kind of hate it," Louisa said. "But maybe it just takes getting used to."

"Couldn't tell you; I was born here."

"Then you're used to it. You have to be." On the other end, Louisa heard the *snick* of a lighter. "Is that a cigarette?"

"Mmm-hmm."

"I wish I had a cigarette right now."

This made Karina laugh. "You could go buy some."

"No, I can't."

"Why not?"

"Because," said Louisa, "I have a rule. I'm only allowed to bum cigarettes off other people. If I buy them then I'm a smoker, and I'm not a smoker."

"That's not super sound logic."

"Yeah, maybe not, but it helps to tell yourself enabling stories in life, I've found."

Karina laughed again, and Louisa felt herself spinning toward her, a satellite pulled into her orbit. "I'd like to see you," Louisa said.

On the other end, Karina exhaled. "Because you want to smoke my cigarettes?"

"Well, yes," said Louisa. "But not only that."

Chapter Thirty

It surprised Robert how easily he'd settled into a routine with Adrian. Bus, homework, snack, occasionally a playdate. And lessons, of course. Adrian was turning out to be a good student. He was diligent and enthusiastic, rarely balking when asked to paint color wheels or do master copy drawings, assignments that college students might've dismissed as rote. It took about a month for Robert to realize that maybe he was actually a pretty good teacher.

He hadn't been one before. In their end-of-semester evaluations, his students had found him unobjectionable but tepid. Robert had never had any trouble shrugging off the lackluster reviews. He was always "in residence," always "visiting"—whatever the school chose to call his position, it meant he was a wandering bard, and so what if his temporary audience found him dry? Soon enough he'd be gone; he'd forget them, and they'd do the same. Teaching was a day job. What kind of artist aspired to excel at his day job?

But now, watching Adrian labor over that afternoon's assignment, he marveled at the pride he felt in his student's rapid improvement.

Robert's phone chimed with a text from Lily: *so sry for the late notice, but it's shaping up to be a late night. I should be home around 11ish? I know it's friday, I hate to ask . . .*

Robert: *No problem.*

Lily: *Thank u!!!! Feel free to take A out for dinner. Save ur receipts. If u could make sure A's in bed by 10 that would be great. Try to keep screens to a minimum pls. And help urself 2 anything from the bar. ;)*

"Hey, Adrian?"

"Mm?"

"Your parents have to work late. So I'm gonna hang out for a while, okay?"

"Okay," said Adrian without looking up.

"What do you want to do tonight?"

"Videogames," said Adrian without hesitation.

"Your mom said no screens, I'm afraid."

"A movie?"

"Still a screen, my friend." Robert typed *kids activities in NYC tonight* into his phone. "It's Free Friday at MoMA. Any interest in that? We could go out to dinner after."

MoMA had a Diego Rivera exhibit that Robert was curious about. Rivera was one of the first political artists he'd been drawn to—that myth-making prowess was irresistible to a teenage boy—and he remained one of Robert's favorites.

"Okay," said Adrian.

By the time they got out the door, it was past six and Robert was getting hungry. They'd make it a quick visit, he decided, and then they'd get noodles at Xi'an Famous Foods.

The museum was crowded: couples on cheap dates, families pushing strollers, teenagers with sketchbooks under their arms. In the atrium, Adrian tipped his face up, his mouth hanging slightly open. A gigantic Rivera fresco dominated the space. In it, a man and a woman with a baby at her hip fended off an attack from a uniformed soldier. Behind them, a crowd clashed with more soldiers, some of them wrestling demonstrators to the ground. A clenched fist rose above the fray. It was titled *The Uprising*.

"You heard of Diego Rivera?" Robert said, grabbing a map from the information stand. "He was an activist as well as an artist. His work was all about class struggle."

Adrian's face was still tipped skyward. He sniffed at the air. "Someone farted." He grimaced. "Ew. It's really bad."

The smell had reached Robert, too: rotten eggs. "*God*. Stink bomb."

This cracked Adrian up. "Really?"

Behind them, a trumpet sounded. Robert turned around and saw people unfurling a banner: OCCUPY MOMA—LET WORKERS UNIONIZE. He laughed with surprise when he recognized Vanessa. Then he saw Cal standing behind her, a pair of sunglasses perched on his head.

Somebody whooped, and the protesters crossed the atrium and planted themselves in front of the Rivera fresco. Spotting Robert, Vanessa beckoned him over. Robert hesitated for half a second before grabbing Adrian's hand and hustling him across the floor to join them.

"What's going on?" said Adrian.

"Everything's fine."

"Is this a protest?"

"Yes."

Adrian grinned. "Cool."

They joined the huddle of protesters—Robert counted about thirty people—and Vanessa turned to him and whispered, "Hi." Cal glanced at Adrian before aiming a polite nod at Robert.

"Mic check!" yelled a man.

"MIC CHECK!"

"What would Diego have said?"

"WHAT WOULD DIEGO HAVE SAID?"

"Hang art, not workers!"

"HANG ART, NOT WORKERS!"

Vanessa stepped forward and began reading what Robert recognized as Diego Rivera's Manifesto for an Independent Revolutionary Art: "We can say without exaggeration that never has civilization been menaced so seriously as today."

"WE CAN SAY WITHOUT EXAGGERATION THAT NEVER HAS CIVILIZATION BEEN MENACED SO SERIOUSLY AS TODAY!"

Adrian joined in the chants with wide-eyed enthusiasm. Did he have any idea what he was saying? Some of the onlookers had added their voices to the protesters'; others heckled: "Are you done yet?" Museum guards looked on, but unlike at the Guggenheim, they made no move to break up the demonstration.

"True art is unable not to be revolutionary, not to aspire to a complete and radical reconstruction of society!" Vanessa cried.

"TRUE ART IS UNABLE NOT TO BE REVOLUTIONARY, NOT TO ASPIRE TO A COMPLETE AND RADICAL RECONSTRUCTION OF SOCIETY!"

Flyers fluttered down from above. Robert grabbed one and quickly scanned it: it called for MoMA to cut ties with Sotheby's auction house, whose workers had been picketing for months, demanding better pay and benefits. A banner unfurled from one of the balconies: IF ART IN-SISTS ON BEING A LUXURY, IT WILL ALSO BE A LIE.

The protest went on for about a half hour, ending with a rousing round of "WE ARE THE NINETY-NINE PERCENT!" Robert kept an eye on Adrian, alert for signs of fatigue or distress, but the kid was having a ball, yelling till he was red in the face. When the demonstration was over, the protesters began to disperse, a few of them making a beeline for the reporters that had gathered in the atrium.

Vanessa turned to Robert and playfully punched his arm. "Thanks for coming, dude!"

Cal, who'd been doing something on his phone, looked up and said, "Nice to see you again."

"This is pure serendipity," Robert admitted. "I was just taking Adrian here to see the Rivera show."

"I didn't realize you had a son," Cal said.

"Robert's not my dad," Adrian piped up. "He's my tutor."

Robert silently thanked him for not calling him his babysitter.

"Ah, my mistake," said Cal.

"I don't have a dad," Adrian offered. "I have two moms, actually."

Cal smiled. "A modern boy."

"I'm hungry," Adrian announced.

Robert put a hand on the boy's shoulder. "Chinese noodles sound good?" To Vanessa and Cal, he said, "Good to see you guys. And hey, listen, let me know when you have another one of these planned."

"For sure," said Vanessa. "We're staging an action at Clerestory next month. I'll put you on the listserv."

Robert took Adrian to Xi'an Famous Foods, where, over bowls of spicy cumin lamb noodles, Adrian asked, "What were they protesting?"

In the most kid-friendly terms he could muster, Robert explained the concept of unions.

"Oh," said Adrian. "Why were they shouting 'ninety-nine percent'?"

Robert did his best to explain income inequality.

"Are you in the one percent?" said Adrian.

Robert laughed. "No. I'm definitely a ninety-nine percenter."

"What about me?"

Robert hesitated. "That's a question for your parents."

After they'd gotten back to the apartment and Robert had hustled Adrian off to bed with a book, he poured himself a nip of bourbon from the bar in the living room. He sank into an armchair and perused Lily and Cristina's collection of old *New Yorkers* but found himself unable to concentrate. He was still buzzing from the protest, full of anxious energy.

By the time Lily came home two hours later, he'd indulged in a second, then a third glass of bourbon. Lily looked exhausted. Her eyes were puffy and there was a small yellow stain on her shirt collar.

"I'm so sorry," she said, collapsing on the sofa.

"It's completely fine."

"Have a drink with me before you leave?" she said. "For your trouble?"

Without waiting for his reply, she got up and poured them both bourbons. If she noticed that Robert had already been partaking, she didn't mention it.

"Rough day?" he said as she handed him the glass.

"Very." She sank into the couch and dispatched her drink in two neat gulps.

"Look, Lily, I feel like I should tell you that Adrian and I participated at a protest at MoMA earlier today."

"A protest?"

"Nonviolent, obviously," said Robert. "It was in support of the workers' union. Adrian had a good time, I think."

She got up and refilled her glass. "Oh. Well. Experiential learning, right?"

"Right. He might have some questions for you about income in-equality."

Lily laughed grimly. "The privilege talk will have to wait, I'm afraid. Which reminds me. God, I really fucking hate to ask, but could you take him tomorrow? And maybe Sunday? I'll pay you double."

"Umm," Robert stalled. "Let me look at my calendar." He made a show of pulling out his phone.

Lily looked stricken.

"Everything all right?" he said.

Her eyes shone as she shook her head. "Cristina's mom is really sick. Stage four lymphoma—we just found out."

"Oh my god. I'm so sorry."

"Cris flew to San José this afternoon to be with her."

"They have good doctors there, don't they? Kaiser Permanente and all that?"

"No, not California. San José, Costa Rica." Lily ran a knuckle under her eye. "Adrian doesn't know yet, obviously. We're not sure how long she'll be out of the country, and work is a clusterfuck for me right now, and it's just . . . it's a lot."

"I can take Adrian tomorrow."

"We're having a family Skype call in the morning. If you could come over after the three of us are done talking, that'd be great."

"I can do that."

Lily gulped her bourbon, wiping her mouth with the back of her hand. "He's going to be so unhappy."

"Is he close with his grandmother?"

"Yes, but it's not just that. Cris could be gone for months and months, we just don't know. And you've seen how he is with me—he prefers Cris, he always has."

Robert didn't know what to say to this.

"I've always had this fear," Lily said, "that there's something missing. Because he's not biologically mine. It's such a taboo thing to say, I know."

"I was never very close to my mother, and she definitely gave birth to me."

Lily put her feet up on the coffee table. "I should've learned Spanish. That's what I should've done."

Robert thought of his parents' arguments in German. The language of their crumbling marriage. "He'll be fine. I went through something, well, sort of similar when I was his age."

"Did you?"

"Yeah. My dad left my mom when I was thirteen. I was much closer with him than I was with her."

"Was that difficult for you?" Lily was clearly tipsy, but her voice was soft, caring. Her therapy voice. Of course—she was a shrink. Robert had stopped seeing Dr. Sullivan when he'd left Wrynn, and now he was without health insurance and shrinkless for the first time in nearly a decade.

"It was. It was very difficult, at first."

"What got you through it?"

Robert thought of that long-ago day on the rooftop in Jersey City. *What are you drawing?* "I had a very close friend—he sort of became my lifeline."

"Are you still in touch?"

"No. He's been dead for years." And then, because Robert was drunk and Lily's face was kind, he added, "I've always kind of thought it was my fault he died."

Lily's eyebrows rushed together in concern. "Why?"

The trouble with therapy, the main issue Robert had always had with trying to cram his life into a series of neat one-hour slots, was that even though it was *his* pain, the moment he put it into words and presented the bleeding package of it to someone else, it became secondhand information. It was like playing a very long game of Telephone. So much was bound to get lost in time, in translation. Robert could explain that he'd known Vince was attracted to him, and that instead of doing the decent thing and rejecting him, he'd led him on, kept him close. He could say he'd acted this way because he loved how Vince made him feel—it was the feeling of being chosen, of being *seen*—and that he'd been unwilling to relinquish the adoration of the most passionate, most *alive* person he knew. That, after years of this, Vince had gone looking for love elsewhere, and that, somewhere along the way, he'd been exposed to the virus that killed him. All because Robert had been incapable of loving him the way he deserved to be loved. But these were just words. Anything Robert told Lily would be a shoddy translation of the truth. No, not truth. Memory. And how to convey the dark, densely forested path of memory?

Lily was still gazing at him, benevolent and intent. "No real reason," he said. "Just, you know, congenital guilt." He got up to leave. "See you tomorrow, then?"

The next morning, the air in the apartment had an oppressive quality that made Robert want to open all the windows. Lily, neatly dressed in a gray pantsuit, seemed to be holding it together, though her eyes were red and her mouth had a pinched quality that put Robert in mind of his own mother. "Adrian's in his room," she said. "I need to make a run to campus for an emergency meeting, and then Cristina and I have a call with her mom's medical team. If you could keep him out of the house till the afternoon that'd be great."

"How'd he take the news?"

Lily sighed. "It's so hard to tell with him. He just—he shuts down when he's upset." She glanced at her watch. "Shit, gotta run. Will you make sure he eats something?"

When Lily was gone, Robert knocked on Adrian's bedroom door. "It's me," he said.

"Come in," came Adrian's soft, hoarse voice. He was sitting up in bed, sheets snarled around his feet. Still in his pajamas, a book spread open in his lap. Had Lily woken him up, delivered the news while he was still groggy, still rubbing the sleep from his eyes? *A family meeting.* There'd been no such meeting at the Bergers'; Wolf had simply left—Robert woke one morning to find him gone. His mother had refused to explain; Robert had only gotten the full story months later, through one of her friends. It had taken him a long time to forgive her, and to understand that what had prevented her from speaking of it was a deep, abiding shame from which she'd never recovered.

Robert opened the window to let in some fresh air. The skin around Adrian's eyes was puffy, pink, and rawly translucent. Robert felt a rush of tenderness toward him. "How about breakfast?"

"I'm not hungry," said Adrian tonelessly.

"Not even for donuts?"

"No."

"Okay, well, you don't have to eat, but you do need to get dressed."

Adrian looked down at his book.

"Look," Robert said. "I can't promise you'll feel better if you go outside, but I can guarantee you're gonna feel worse if you spend all day in bed."

On the street below, a motorcycle screamed by.

"I'm going to go make myself a cup of coffee, and when I come back I want to see you ready to rumble." Robert cringed at his own forced cheer, but it seemed to have an effect: Adrian closed the book and climbed out of bed. When Robert returned, he'd gotten dressed and was sitting on the floor lacing up his sneakers.

"Let's take our sketchbooks to the park, yeah?" Robert said. "It's a perfect day to draw some nature." It was finally April, and the dogwoods were in bloom, flowerbeds everywhere lurid with color.

As they walked down East Seventy-fifth, Robert tried to keep up a steady banter, but Adrian remained silent and withdrawn. Robert recalled how, after his father left, he hadn't wanted to talk to anyone, and how adults kept foisting themselves on him, battering rams at the floodgates of his grief. How only Vince had left him alone, Vince with his towel and his sunglasses and his Vonnegut novels. Robert lapsed into silence, allowing the city's noise to fill the space between them. When they got to Central Park, Robert said, "Where should we go? Conservatory Water?"

Adrian hummed in assent. The pond was dotted with toy sailboats this time of year. They found a bench near the Hans Christian Andersen statue. Two children attempted to climb onto its bronze shoulders as their parents looked on, snapping photos.

"The tricky thing about drawing nature," Robert said, "is that nothing stays put. The light changes, the shadows shift, the birds fly away."

"So how do you do it?"

"I like to capture the gist of a scene first—starting with the things that don't change, then choose a moment to capture. Like, say, the shape of that man on that bench over there. Or keep drawing how he moves. You can show transformation if you want. That can give a drawing more life." Robert began roughing out the view: the glassy surface of the water, the buildings rising over the treetops like rows of broken teeth. Adrian sat drawing beside him, swinging his legs, his gaze roving over the joggers and dog walkers.

"The water's hard," said Adrian after a while.

Robert glanced over at his drawing. "You're doing great. The waves and ripples, you see them as roughly perpendicular to the horizon, right? You might want to try active, loose pencil strokes that get smaller and thinner as they recede into the distance, like this." He demonstrated on his own pad. "You can't draw every ripple. It's impossible, and it won't look natural if you try."

They fell silent again, Adrian's hand flitting like a dragonfly across the page. After some time, Robert reached into his knapsack and pulled out a bottle of water and a bag of trail mix. Wordlessly, he held out the food, but Adrian shook his head. His face was half in shadow, his bangs falling into his eyes. Robert left the water and trail mix on the bench and went back to his drawing. Having sketched out the view more or less faithfully, he decided to embellish it. He paused, looking out over the water, and smiled to himself. He added a giant crocodile erupting from the middle of the pond, a shrieking figure clamped in its jaws. A giant spider crouched on a rooftop and flexed its hairy legs, eyes glinting with cunning. An asteroid plummeted toward the earth, a trail of fire in its wake. One by one, the treetops burst into flame. The pond boiled over.

"What are you doing?"

Adrian had scooted closer to him and was peering at his sketchpad.

"I'm drawing. What are *you* doing?"

Adrian laughed. He gestured at the pond. "None of that is *there*."

"This is what I used to do when I was your age. I used to— After my dad left my mom, when I was right about your age, I used to go up to the roof of my building and draw the skyline—I lived across the Hudson in Jersey City, but I could see New York from my rooftop—and then I'd add to the drawing like I'm doing here with this one. I would take what I saw and make it into a hellscape."

"Why?"

Robert exhaled. "I was very angry, for one, and for two I've always been a literal person. I kind of felt like my life had split into a Before and an After, and I could picture both very clearly but I didn't know how to—how to make them fit together. So I drew the Before and layered the After on top of it. I don't know, does that make sense?"

Adrian nodded. A gust of wind swept over the pond, crinkling the surface like a sheet of aluminum foil.

"There are very few moments in your life like that," Robert said. "But they do happen to everyone, eventually." He closed his sketchbook and tucked his pencil into his breast pocket. "What do you think about going to a museum again? Maybe we can actually look at the art this time."

Adrian scratched his chin, watching a toy sailboat zoom across the water. "What museum is your painting in? The one of your dead friend?"

Robert's heart turned over. "The Whitney."

"Let's go there. I want to see it."

Adrian's cheeks were sun-flushed, his expression muted.

"I'll make you a deal," Robert said. "I'll take you to see it, but only if you eat something first."

"Deal."

Robert bought them slices of pizza from a place on East Seventy-ninth and Lexington. They ate quickly, then walked over to the Whitney. Adrian was silent as they stood in line for tickets. Robert approached a docent. "Excuse me, where might I find the painting *Dying Man*? It's by Robert Berger?"

The docent pursed her lips. "Try the third floor." She handed him a map. "Unless the piece is currently in storage, which is possible."

Robert herded Adrian toward the elevator. "Did you hear that? The painting might be in storage. We might not be able to see it."

God, he hoped it was in storage.

Adrian looked at him curiously. "Why don't you know where it is? Haven't you ever come here to look at it?"

He hadn't. He'd had neither the heart nor the balls to visit. The last time Robert had seen the painting was over three decades ago, in the storage room at Axiom Art, a week or so before the Whitney's acquisition went through.

"Museums move their art around a lot," he said. Adrian seemed to accept this explanation, though his gaze lingered on Robert for an extra second.

The elevator doors slid open with a terse *ping*. Blood thundered in Robert's ears. It didn't take them long to find the painting. It hung at the end of a short hallway, between a David Wojnarowicz collage and a Robert Therrien sculpture that resembled a butt plug.

Christ, he'd forgotten how enormous it was, how much of your field of vision it gobbled up. The canvas had filled up the whole back wall of his East Village apartment—he'd been too poor, at the time, to afford a proper studio. The smell of the oils had seeped into everything he owned.

Vince's long, pale, bony face. His cheeks hollowed out, as though someone had taken a knife and carved the flesh off the bone. His skin all yellow and papery, the cracked, crumbling mosaic of his lips. Mouth hanging open, tongue like something forgotten in the back of the fridge and left to rot. Eyes milky, turbid pools, blind gaze locked on something beyond this world. The brushstrokes loose, almost frantic, the colors a shade beyond naturalistic, edging toward phantasmagorical, the paint scumbled in some places and blended smooth in others.

Robert tried to remember what he'd felt during the months he'd worked on the painting. Grief, yes, and anger and fear and self-doubt and dread, but also a deep, unsettling thrill that told him he was on to something extraordinary. When he finished, he knew it was a great work of art. He showed the piece to Brian Parrish, who'd only just taken him on, and the dealer confirmed it. "This painting will be the making of you," Brian said, and gave him a solo show.

Later, when Mrs. Russo came to his apartment and begged him not to display it, not to let the world see Vince like that, Robert wavered, but only for a moment. He held Mrs. Russo in his arms, both of them shaking, and after she left in tears, unable to extract from him a promise that he wouldn't show the painting, he convinced himself that what he was doing was courageous, even groundbreaking. That Vince would have wanted this. As soon as he received his portion of the sale, he mailed Mrs. Russo a check. She never cashed it.

I took something I shouldn't have, Robert thought. *I stole this. That's what made it great.*

Adrian made a noise then, a breathless little "oh," and Robert remembered himself, remembered where he was and who he was with. "You okay? I should've warned you this might be upsetting to look at."

Adrian nodded, his eyes still glued to the painting. "I saw it on the Internet," he said. "But I didn't realize it was so big."

CHAPTER THIRTY-ONE

Karina arranged to meet Louisa after work on Thursday, April 5 at a diner in Greenpoint. When Karina walked in and saw her sitting in a booth, chin cupped in one hand as she perused the menu, she felt something rise up inside her and catch in her throat.

"Hi," she said, sliding in across from Louisa.

Louisa lifted her head. "Hey." She wore a white T-shirt speckled with green paint. Her hair, slightly greasy, fell around her shoulders in a confusion of split ends. She was thin and pale and tired-looking, but still lovely.

"Good to see you," said Karina.

"You, too." Louisa picked up the saltshaker and set it back down. "Weird, though."

"Is it?"

"When you walked in just now it was almost like seeing this—not a ghost, but . . . Wrynn feels so long ago."

"I know what you mean."

The waitress came to take their orders. Louisa asked for a chocolate milkshake, and Karina said she'd have the same.

"I think the last time I had a milkshake was, like, elementary school,"

Louisa said, and at the same time Karina said, "Why did you leave Wrynn?"

"Money," said Louisa flatly. "You?"

Karina shrugged. "I got offered representation, so it was, like, what's the point of school?"

Louisa pressed her lips together and looked away. Karina's stomach sank. Her flippancy had been a mistake. She couldn't act this way around Louisa: flippancy didn't impress her.

"Good for you," Louisa said. The corners of her mouth were turned down.

Tongue-tied, Karina stared at her hands. She was doing it again. She was doing the thing that pushed everyone away. She leaned across the table and said, "That guy I was dating for a while? He helped me get the gallery deal. And to be honest, I—I guess I wasn't entirely sure about him. We're not together anymore, by the way. But I needed an escape. From Wrynn."

"I could tell."

"That I was unhappy?"

"Yeah."

Karina fidgeted, her back sticking to the booth's upholstery. "I didn't have anyone there. I didn't have friends or anyone who cared about me or—"

"That's not true," said Louisa quietly.

The milkshakes arrived then, and it came as a relief for Karina to busy herself with the simple task of consuming nourishment, the unwrapping and bending of the straw, the thick sweetness coating her tongue. A song came on the radio, the one about being young and setting the world on fire.

"So what are you doing now?" Karina said.

Louisa told her about her job at Akito Kobayashi's studio.

"Do you like it?"

"No," Louisa said. Her mouth was still turned down. "It's kind of wretched."

The bitterness in her voice caught Karina off-guard. "Do you wish you could go back to school?"

Louisa looked away. "I miss working on art."

"Do you not do that anymore?"

"Not really."

"Why not?"

"I don't have the time. Or the energy. Or the space. Or the money." Louisa gave a wry smile. "Take your pick."

Karina thought of the check she'd written out to Preston, weeks ago. She folded her arms against her stomach. "I'm really sorry, Louisa."

"Don't be."

"I'm sorry I was a bitch to you." Karina recalled that first crit: Louisa's dark head bent over her sketchbook, white-knuckling her pencil.

Louisa gave a feeble smile. "It's fine."

"No, it's not. I guess I just—I don't know. I felt threatened."

"By me?"

"Yeah."

"You're kidding, right?"

Karina stirred her milkshake. "Is it so hard to believe I'd find you threatening?"

"Kind of, yeah." Louisa shook her head in amusement, or maybe disbelief. "Do you know how *jealous* I am of you? What a mind-fuck it is to feel that way after . . . after everything?" She rubbed her face with her hands, and for a moment Karina thought she was crying, but when she lifted her head her eyes were dry.

They sat there in silence, each avoiding the other's gaze, and Karina felt the moment slipping away from her. "I think—" she began. "I think that the people we become infatuated with are the ones who have the qualities we want."

Louisa seemed to consider this. "You might be right."

Karina pushed her milkshake aside. "Do you want to go get a drink?"

"Do I want to get a drink?"

"Yes," Karina said. "A real drink. With alcohol in it."

"Where? I don't have a fake ID."

"I have a bottle of gin in my studio. It's not far from here."

Louisa laughed, for some reason.

"What?" said Karina.

"No, I'm just relieved. I thought you were gonna suggest we go to a gallery opening or something. Yeah, I'm down to drink your gin."

Karina paid for both milkshakes—Louisa didn't object, but she didn't say thank you—and hailed them a cab to East Williamsburg. As they stepped inside the studio, Louisa looked around and let out a soft "Holy shit."

Karina tried to see the space through Louisa's eyes: the high ceilings and broad windows, the paint-spattered floors and canvases stacked five or six deep along the walls.

"This is where you work?" said Louisa.

"And live. I'm not supposed to, technically, but I do. The bathroom is two floors down, so when I have to pee at night I just do it in the sink."

"Where do you shower?"

Karina grimaced. "I take sponge baths. And use a lot of dry shampoo."

"Wow. I'm so jealous," Louisa said, laughing, but her voice was sad.

"You haven't gotten close enough to smell me yet," said Karina weakly.

Louisa wandered over to the open windows and leaned out, resting her elbows on the sill. Karina found two mugs and poured them both an inch of gin.

"Here you go," she said. "Sorry I don' t have any ice."

Louisa raised her cup. "Cheers."

"What are we cheersing to?"

"I don't know. Does it matter?" Louisa tossed back the drink. Karina watched her, mute with want. She held out the bottle and Louisa took it, splashing more gin into both their cups.

"You should come work here, too," Karina blurted. "This studio is too big for me."

Louisa turned her head, her gaze drilling into Karina.

"I'll give you a key," Karina offered.

Still Louisa said nothing.

"It'd be nice," Karina said, a note of desperation creeping into her voice, "to work together again."

They were standing close enough that Karina could see Louisa's pulse in her throat, the dry skin scabbing the corners of her mouth. She stared at her, this beautiful girl with uncombed hair, and even though the evening was warm and the gin blazed in her belly, Karina began to tremble. She placed her empty cup on the windowsill and, taking a small step forward, grabbed Louisa's hand and ran her thumb across the small hot palm.

"Hi," Louisa said in a low voice. She closed her hand around Karina's.

"Hi," Karina echoed.

Karina wasn't sure who closed the distance between them, but a moment later they were kissing. When they broke apart, Louisa said, "You do smell kind of ripe."

Karina grinned. "Sorry."

"I'm still jealous."

"Sorry."

Then they were kissing again and Karina was nudging Louisa toward the futon, or maybe Louisa was pulling Karina. And now they were lying down, wriggling out of their clothes. Louisa's legs were rough with stubble. She straddled Karina, a strangely determined look on her face, and Karina reached down and slid two fingers inside her. Louisa closed her eyes, lifting her hips toward Karina. With her other hand, Karina cupped the smallness of Louisa's breast, running her thumb lightly over her nipple. Louisa let out a low moan and whispered something inaudible.

"What did you say?" Karina said.

Louisa opened her eyes. "I missed this."

"Me, too," Karina said. She moved her fingers inside Louisa, whose eyes slid shut again. "I really, really missed this."

In the morning, Louisa was gone, though she'd left a note on a scrap of sketchbook paper. She had the neatest cursive Karina had ever seen.

Went to work. Will take you up on that offer of studio space. See you soon?
XO L

Karina liked that Louisa hadn't just sent her a text message, that she'd left something tangible, something Karina could put in her pocket and look at throughout the day. She was making a grilled cheese sandwich for dinner when Louisa returned, arms laden with rolled-up canvases.

"What are those?" Karina said.

"My bird woman paintings."

"Oh." Karina both did and didn't want to see them again. She slid the grilled cheese onto a plate and sliced it in half.

After they'd eaten, Louisa said, "Do you have any two-by-fours lying around? I need to re-stretch these."

"No, but I have those." Karina pointed at a stack of blank, pre-primed canvases. "We can just take the canvas off and use the frames. Some of them are the right size."

"Are you sure?"

"Yeah, I can always buy more."

They worked in silence, using pliers to remove the staples, peeling the blank canvases off their frames like bedsheets. Then Karina watched as Louisa unrolled one of her bird woman paintings, spread it facedown on the floor, and placed a frame on top of it. She pulled the center of each side of the canvas to the back of the frame and stapled it, making a taut cross. Then she began stretching the canvas from the center to the corners, standing and crouching by turns, eliminating creases and sags, stapling every three inches. Karina helped as best she could. Though she knew how to stretch a canvas, she didn't do it very often; it was easier and faster to buy them pre-stretched.

When they were done, they lined the canvases up against the wall.

"They look good," said Karina. She'd forgotten how much she loved them and how they made her feel, at the same time, denuded. Scooped hollow.

"Do they?" said Louisa doubtfully.

Karina came up behind her and put her arms around her shoulders. She was taller than Louisa, tall enough that she could comfortably rest her chin on the crown of her head. Louisa twisted into Karina's embrace, hands slipping under her shirt. Like the night before, they had sex on the futon. Karina buried her face between Louisa's legs, took in the ocean taste of her. Afterward, Louisa rolled over onto her side, pink-faced, and Karina pressed her cheek to her back. Louisa's breathing deepened and slowed. Just as Karina was drifting off, Louisa said, "I'm scared I've lost it."

Karina lifted her head. "What?"

"I've lost the joy in my work. Like, the sense of play. It's gone. I don't love what I'm doing. Even when I'm just doing it for myself, like it's after work and I'm just messing around in my sketchbook, I have to treat myself like a taskmaster, like I'm only doing it out of duty and guilt." Louisa turned to face Karina. "Sometimes I wonder what I'm doing. Like, seriously, what's the point?"

Karina laid a hand on Louisa's belly, ran her thumb over the dip and rise of her navel.

"Painting doesn't bring me joy, either," she said.

Louisa looked at her in surprise. "But your work is so good."

"What brings me joy is the idea of existing among the greats." Karina rolled onto her back and looked up at the ceiling. "The idea of my work having incalculable value. Of that value affecting the way people feel about it. About me."

"Are you serious?"

"Money changes how people perceive things, how they react to them." She paused. "When I behold something really valuable . . . I can feel it in my body. It's almost erotic."

Louisa didn't say anything. Karina got up and turned on the box fan, angling it so it was blowing at the futon. She lay back down next to Louisa.

"But what do you *feel* when you're painting, then?" Louisa said.

"I feel like I'm someone else."

Louisa looked at Karina with an odd expression that she realized, with a jolt, was pity.

They quickly settled into a routine together. In the daytime while Louisa was at work, Karina tried to paint, though increasingly her time was swallowed up preparing for her show, now only three weeks away. Getting ready for a professional exhibition, it turned out, involved much more than just making the paintings for it. There were gallery layouts and price lists and wall labels to approve, an artist statement to write, Certificate of Authenticity forms to have notarized, pictures to take and inventory, art handlers to coordinate with, phone calls to make and emails to answer.

But Karina put the work down as soon as Louisa walked through the door. Louisa had begun keeping a toothbrush and a change of clothes in the studio, only occasionally returning to her Harlem apartment, which Karina had yet to visit. Together they prepared dinner on the hotplate, or else, if they were feeling lazy, they went around the corner for Thai takeout (Karina always paid; Louisa never thanked her). After they'd eaten—or sometimes, if they were impatient, before—they had sex on the futon, beneath the *Bowerbird* photo, the only décor Karina had hung on the wall. In the middle of it, Karina often felt like a different person. New nerve endings came alive under her skin. Noises she'd never heard before flew from her throat.

Afterward they'd lounge around naked, talking and drinking and smoking by the open windows.

"I'm not intimidated by you anymore," Louisa declared one evening.

Karina laughed, trailing her fingers through Louisa's hair. "Why not?"

"You seem realer to me now."

"Realer?"

"I can see the shape of you."

Karina cleared her throat. "The shape of me." Did Louisa see her brokenness, then? Her freakishness?

"At school I'd sometimes hear rumors about you. I'd never know what was real and what wasn't."

Karina looked away and lit a fresh cigarette. She didn't want to hear about how she existed for other people. She wanted to exist for Louisa. For the past few weeks she'd felt ferociously, dementedly happy. Now she wondered how long it could last.

"Did I say something wrong?" said Louisa in a small voice.

"No. Let's make a painting."

Louisa brightened. Since their reunion, Karina had begun posing for her again, and Louisa had made two new bird woman paintings. Karina thought they were even better than the ones from the original series— larger, lusher, more daring and erotic.

Louisa set up the room, dragging a stool into the middle of the floor and switching on a floor lamp. Karina was already naked; all she had to do was run a brush through her hair. She sat, holding herself still. For a while, the only sound was of Louisa sketching out the composition. How mesmeric it was, to watch her work.

"What are you worrying about?" Louisa said after some time.

"What?"

"You bite your lip when you're worried. What are you worried about?"

It emerged from Karina without forethought: "That we don't understand each other."

Louisa put her pencil down. She tipped her head, smiling slightly. "What do you think it is I'm trying to do here?"

The next day, Karina stopped by Axiom to sign some paperwork. "Brian's in his office," said Audrey the gallerina. "Just go on up."

Karina found him sitting at his desk, a tumbler full of amber liquid at his elbow.

"My dear," he said, rising from his seat. "I was so sorry to hear about you and Preston."

"It was a long time coming," she said.

"Can I offer you a drink?"

Karina glanced at the clock. It was only a little past noon, but Brian was already pouring and it seemed rude to stop him now.

"Thanks." She hadn't eaten breakfast. It was probably unwise to drink on an empty stomach. She took a small sip.

"I hope the opening won't be too awkward," Brian said, eyeing her.

Karina thought of how Preston had looked in the split second before he hurled the glass at her, his flattened lips, his small, flinty eyes. "It'll be fine." She took another, larger sip and set the tumbler down. "We're both adults. I'm sure he'll keep his distance and I'll keep mine."

Brian took her hands in his and squeezed them. "I want you to know," he said. "That I'm here for you. Anything you need."

"Thanks, Brian." He was too close. She could smell the whiskey on his breath, stale coffee underneath.

"If you ever want to talk." He gripped her hands tighter.

"I appreciate that."

Brian pulled her toward him, into him, and pressed his lips, cold and rubbery, against hers, and she was too shocked to do anything but stand there. He pushed her up against his desk—the edge cut into the backs of her thighs, and a sudden coldness shot up her spine as she felt his erection nudging at her hip bone—and he shoved his hands up inside her shirt. She grabbed at them, trying to push them back down, but Brian seemed to take this as encouragement and instead cupped her ass, squeezing it hard.

"Stop," she managed, but he didn't seem to hear. She felt her heartbeat thundering in every part of her body. She put her palms up against his chest and pushed, but it was like pushing away a brick wall. Panic seized her and she froze, her mind rising to float somewhere above her. Now Brian was unzipping himself as he lapped and sucked at her neck, groaning nonsense into her ear, and she felt her stomach convulse with revulsion, bile rising in her throat, and she turned her head and vomited bitter, whiskey-tinged liquid onto the glass surface of his desk.

Abruptly, Brian stopped and took a step back, his nose wrinkling at the smell. His open belt buckle jangled as he moved, and Karina knew at once that that sound would always remind her of this moment.

"Sorry," she gasped. "I think I'm coming down with something."

"Can I get you something? Water?" He was flushed and panting.

Karina moved toward the door. She could hardly breathe. "I just need to go lie down."

She hurried down the staircase before he could reply, straightening her clothes as she went.

"See you soon!" chirped Audrey. She was watching something on her laptop; cheerful music rose from the speakers. For a half second their eyes met and Karina thought, *Has he done the same to you?* But then Audrey looked back at her screen.

Karina pushed through the doors and wandered around in a daze; she wasn't sure for how long. Eventually she ended up at Chelsea Park. She sat on a bench and watched the soccer players in the distance. Her thoughts were fuzzy, moving at half speed. She could still taste vomit in the back of her throat. Her mind kept replaying the scene on a loop. Hands shaking, she lit a cigarette and smoked half of it in quick, sharp drags. She knew that she needed to speak with someone who'd understand. She reached for her phone and dialed.

"Karina?"

"Mom?" She began to cry. The rest of her cigarette fell to the ground.

"Where are you?" said Fiona calmly. "Wherever you are, I'll come find you."

As she waited for her mother, Karina lit another cigarette—her hands still shook as she sparked the lighter—and lifted her shirt and looked down at her smooth pale belly. Some part of her had expected to see bruises or oily streaks. She could still feel Brian's hands, his fingers digging into her flesh. She wanted to take off her skin, unzip it and douse it in bleach.

Fiona arrived twenty minutes later, explaining that she lived close by, had just moved to a new place right off the Christopher Street Pier. When they embraced, Karina felt herself melting into her mother's body.

"You're shivering," said Fiona. "Let's get you indoors."

At her new apartment, Fiona sat Karina on the couch, wrapped a blanket around her shoulders, and made her chamomile tea with honey and lemon. Karina blew on it and took a mincing sip. She'd stopped crying, but her throat was still raw. She felt strangely detached from herself, as though some indifferent stranger were jerking her body around like a marionette.

Her mother sat down beside her. "What happened?" she said softly.

Karina swallowed. "Someone . . . took advantage of me."

Fiona's eyes widened. "Do you need me to take you to the hospital?"

"No no no. Nothing . . . *happened*."

Fiona scooted closer, and almost by instinct Karina threaded herself around her, resting her head in the crook of her mother's neck, something she hadn't done since she was very small.

"Who was it?"

Fiona *knew* Brian. Not well, perhaps, but she'd bought from him before. Maybe he'd even attended one of her parties.

"Was it your boyfriend?" said Fiona. "Did he hurt you?"

"No. We broke up."

"Does this person . . . ? Do you want to press charges?"

Karina's chest felt tight. She squeezed her eyes shut. She pictured what would happen if she said yes: police, lawyers, her show canceled, her name forever tied to Brian's, to those horrible five minutes in his office. "I don't want to talk about it."

For a while they sat together in silence, leaning into each other, lulled by the distant thrum of traffic. Then Karina sat up and ran her palm over the fabric of the saffron-yellow sofa.

"It's different, I know," said Fiona. At their townhouse, all the furniture had been black or white or gray.

"No, I like it. But where's your art?" The walls were mostly bare.

"I'm starting from scratch, as you know," her mother said. "Haven't had a chance to shop for anything new."

"Was it you who sent someone sniffing around my old place in Bushwick?"

Fiona grimaced. "No, that was your father. I told him not to."

"But the auction's going forward?"

Fiona betrayed the faintest of smirks. "Your dad and I communicate through our lawyers now, so I can't say for sure, but I assume he's made peace with it."

"Oh."

"I did always love that Schiele. I bought it when I found out I was pregnant with you."

Karina looked at her in surprise. "You never told me that."

"Why do you think I put it in your bedroom?"

Karina hesitated. "Did you know, when you were pregnant with me, that Dad . . . was the way he is?"

Fiona looked at her carefully. "Yes."

"Why did you stay with him?"

She sighed. "Too many reasons. We'd been together since we were kids. I thought I could fix him. I believed I deserved it. I was ashamed. I was attached to our house, our way of life. Should I go on?"

"You don't have to."

"I think that—" Fiona interrupted herself, then started over. "I think it's easy, when . . . when you're neglecting your own happiness, to inadvertently neglect the happiness of the people you love. It's sort of like you think you're being selfless or self-sacrificial or something, but really you're just sowing misery everywhere you go. So I'm sorry for that."

Karina had always pictured her parents as a pair of synchronized skaters. But that wasn't what they were at all. All her life, she'd thought of herself as the broken one in the family, the one who'd been ruined by her parents' tumultuous marriage. But it had been Harry, not Fiona, who'd ruined things. And Fiona was broken, too. Karina thought of Preston. How close she'd been to following her mother's path. And Brian? She couldn't think about Brian right now. Her opening was in three weeks. She'd have to do what her mother had always done: grit her teeth and soldier through it.

CHAPTER THIRTY-TWO

The day of Karina's opening dawned crisp and blue, a perfect mid-May morning. Louisa woke up filled with dread. The last few weeks had been like a dream: she'd begun painting again, really and truly painting. Karina had offered to share her studio, her supplies, and, most crucially, her body. But Louisa's proximity to success felt asymptotic. And she didn't want to watch her own fantasy play out in front of her, not with someone else in the starring role.

She'd started having strange dreams again. But instead of the bird woman, now Louisa dreamed, simply, of birds. In these dreams, she floated in the middle of Lake Martin—not on a kayak or a pirogue, but in the water itself, her body light and buoyant. Birds—usually ibises and herons, sometimes roseate spoonbills—circled her, paddling around her, thrusting their beaks at her. Then, one by one, they spread their wings and flew away. The dreams always ended the same way: Louisa would look down at herself and realize she wasn't a person at all—she was herself a bird. Then she'd fly up into the sky and look down again and see that familiar landscape spread out beneath her, wet and green and teeming with life. She'd wake up filled with a craving to paint home.

Louisa rolled over in bed and looked at Karina, who was still asleep, hair plastered to her forehead, dark with sweat. She'd had a nightmare last night, had woken Louisa up with her thrashing and mumbling. Louisa dressed as quietly as she could and went to work. She spent the day filling a canvas with tiny Technicolor psychedelic mushrooms; it would be displayed at the Clerestory Art Fair next month. The studio staff were routinely working till eight or nine these days, but Louisa had received permission from Craig to leave early. By the time she got off, her neck was stiff and a headache was gathering in her temples. She wanted to order takeout and watch something dumb on Netflix and go to bed early.

Instead, she took the train to her apartment in West Harlem—she hadn't been back in over a week—and dug a dress and heels out of her closet. She made her way to Axiom alone—Karina had been onsite since midday, busy with press photos and last-minute prep—and arrived just as the crowd was beginning to swell.

In the front half of the gallery hung Karina's paintings: twenty-five canvases of various sizes, some familiar to Louisa, others new. There were maplike grids, frenzied swabs of puckish color, and wide, rolling, empty landscapes that might've been desert or ocean or both. There were couples kissing, silk-screened scraps of handwriting, and bicycle wheels affixed to canvas that tempted you to spin them with your finger. A few pieces, cartoonish renderings of animals that wouldn't have looked out of place in a child's bedroom if not for their ghoulish undertones, seemed to deliberately push against the bounds of good taste. The show was consciously self-referential, with some paintings making cameo appearances in others as though guest-starring in each other's imaginary TV shows. A sinuous energy coiled between the images. Karina had created an alternate dimension, a web of painterly wormholes. It was a world entirely unto itself, with its own language and secret back passageways.

"She's got to be the most protean artist of her generation," Louisa heard someone say. "That seems a little premature, don't you think?" came the reply. "She's what, twenty?"

Louisa weaved, unnoticed, through the crowd. On the far end of the gallery hung Preston's work. But it was as though someone had drawn an invisible line down the middle of the floor, inviting the audience to side, gym class–style, with their preferred artist, and three quarters of the gallery-goers had unhesitatingly declared their allegiance to Karina. *Good,* Louisa thought. *Serves you right, asshole.*

Preston's work consisted of photographs printed on canvas, but what they depicted wasn't immediately clear. The images were blurred, glitchy, and distorted. Louisa skimmed the wall text, which explained that the works had been created via artificial intelligence.

"There you are! I've been looking for you." Karina came toward her, arms outstretched. Her hair glowed against the dark field of her emerald dress, and she was smiling.

"How's it going?" said Louisa.

"Brian just told me that almost everything has sold. He wants me to be his lead artist at Clerestory next month." Lowering her voice, she added, "Preston isn't taking it well. He's in the back room throwing a fit. Brian's trying to calm him down." Louisa felt a frisson of schadenfreude. She suppressed a smile.

Karina glanced over her shoulder. "This journalist has been following me around trying to interview me, so I'm gonna go get it over with, okay? I'll come find you when I'm done."

Though she wasn't hungry, Louisa wandered over to the food table in search of something to occupy her hands. There, piling her plate with grapes, she found Ines.

"What are you doing here?

Ines gave a slight smile. "Hello to you, too."

"No, I mean, it's just— Last time we talked it seemed like you weren't a fan of Karina's."

"She came to my opening. Rude of me not to come to hers."

"Oh."

"But actually, I'm glad I ran into you. I was going to mail this on my way home, but this is better." Ines dipped her hand into her purse and pulled out an envelope. Inside was a check, made out to Louisa, for two thousand dollars. "Sorry it took so long."

"Wow. Thank you." It was the most money Louisa had ever held in her hands.

A passing waiter offered flutes of champagne. They both took one.

"To be honest," Ines said. "I also came to see if the hype was warranted."

"And?"

Ines shrugged. "I'm on the fence. I don't think art should constantly talk at you, which is kind of what I see happening here. I feel like it's almost making up for something. Like there's no real vision behind it."

"I hadn't thought of it that way."

Ines spread some Brie on a cracker. "On the other hand, a decade ago I would've been mad with jealousy. I couldn't understand why a few bright young things got anointed and everyone else got ignored."

Champagne bubbles traveled up Louisa's nose. She suppressed a sneeze. "Do you understand better now?"

Ines swallowed a bite of cracker before replying. "It's an uphill battle if you're a woman or you're not white, that's for sure. But to be honest, I don't think anyone understands. It's a mystery."

It comforted Louisa to hear that Ines had dealt with her envy, that she hadn't allowed it to eat her alive, that she'd gone on to make art and thrive. She told Ines so.

But Ines laughed with uncharacteristic bitterness. "I wouldn't call what I do thriving."

"You wouldn't?"

"No. I've made sacrifices. I've given up a lot to do what I do."

"Like what?"

"The usual," she said briskly. "Money, security, kids. I don't know if I'll regret it. Maybe I will."

Louisa thought of her mother, who'd made the opposite choice, forgoing the possibility of an art career to raise a daughter in relative stability. "But it was worth it, right? You're successful."

Ines smiled sadly. "I'm *moderately* successful. I'm not famous and I'm not rich, not by a long shot. Which, don't get me wrong, isn't what I want. But none of what I do is building toward long-term stability. I'm liable to drop off the face of the earth if I ever stop hustling."

"Oh."

"Did Maureen ever tell you about the ten-year rule?"

"No."

"How'd she put it? Basically, 'If you want to be an artist, you have to be okay with making art for ten years and not have anyone look at it or talk about it.' When I was your age I thought, yeah, for sure, I can do that. But you don't really understand till you're in the thick of it how lonely it is." Ines set her empty plate on the table. "I should be heading out. I'm supposed to meet Frank soon."

"Are you building another nest?"

Ines laughed. "No, just getting a drink." She gave Louisa a fond look before stepping forward and hugging her. "Take care of yourself, okay?"

After Ines left, Louisa found herself consumed with thoughts of her mother. Would she have been better off without Louisa? In Louisa's absence, would Mom have become a Karina? Or would she have been an Ines, achieving middling but not outstanding success? And if she'd been an Ines, would she have felt that she'd cast off another kind of life in service to the one she now had? Was this what life, real life, actually was, just a maze of forking paths and missed opportunities?

Louisa was beginning to feel like an idiot hovering there by the food, not eating, lost in thought. Where was Karina? Shouldn't she be done with her interview by now? Louisa scanned the room for the bright beacon of her hair and spotted her twenty feet away, deep in conversation with a middle-aged man in a floral-patterned sports coat.

She procured a fresh champagne flute and found a relatively empty corner in which to drink it.

"Hey, how's it going? What's your name?"

Louisa turned to see a tall, generically good-looking young man holding a glass of white wine. He wore skinny jeans paired with an untucked button-down and a thin black tie, and he had the breezy, confident air of a high school athlete.

"Louisa," she said.

"I'm Slade." He smiled at her, his eyes sliding down the length of her body. "Are you a collector?"

She laughed at the absurdity of this question. "No, I'm just browsing."

"The Pionteks are incredible, aren't they?"

"They are."

"I actually own three of them."

Louisa considered the best way to extricate herself from this conversation. She'd been raised to be polite to a fault and had never really learned how to deflect unwanted male attention.

"Yeah? Did you just buy them tonight?"

"Oh, they're not in this show." He gave a sly grin. "I acquired them months ago. Actually, I think I might be her very first collector."

"Really?" said Louisa, confused.

"Well, I have a personal connection to the artist."

"What do you mean?"

Slade, who seemed to mistake Louisa's sudden attentiveness for flirtation, leaned in closer. "The other artist showing here tonight, Preston Utley? He's a childhood friend of mine. He and Piontek used to date, you know. I don't know if that's common knowledge. Between you and me, apparently they had a really nasty breakup."

"Wait, back up," Louisa said. "Karina sold you some paintings?"

"Well, Preston did. So I guess I technically got them on the secondary market. That's what they call it in the art world, right?"

Louisa looked at him in disgust. She was so sick of this. Out of the blue, a terrible longing overcame her. She wanted to go home—not home to Karina's studio, or even to her own apartment, but *home* home. She wanted to be alone, the kind of alone you could only be out in the middle of Lake Martin.

"Excuse me," she said, turning to leave.

Slade's face fell. "Hold on, could I get your number?"

"No." Louisa began moving toward the exit. She was almost out the door when she felt a hand on her back.

"Are you leaving?" Karina said. She took Louisa's hand and pulled her back inside. "Please stay? I'm sorry, I didn't mean to ignore you, I—"

"You cunt!"

They both jumped, springing apart. Preston Utley stood in the middle of the room, swaying drunkenly, a glass of red wine in his hand, an empty circle widening around him as people backed away, some of them filming him on their phones. Karina stared at him, her face pale and frozen with terror.

"Karina Piontek, you're a cunt and a liar and a thief!" Preston shouted. "You're a fucking fraud!"

Louisa felt a surge of rage bubble up inside her, fierce and seething. She stepped in front of Karina, shielding her from Preston. "You're the thief," she said.

"Who the fuck are you?" Preston said.

Preston ignored Louisa. To Karina, he said, "You're just a rich bitch." He raised the glass of wine and threw it at one of her paintings. A gasp rose from the crowd. Some people, the ones who had their phones out and had been filming, looked openly delighted.

"You're the thief," Louisa repeated, her voice trembling with anger. She drew herself to her full height. "You're the fraud. You're the liar and the thief. You stole from her. You took her paintings, and you gave them to your slimy friend over there." She pointed at Slade, who caught her eye and shrank into the crowd.

"You hurt people, but none of your little schemes ever cost *you* a thing. And you call yourself anti-establishment? You're just as much a vulture as the people you attack. And either you're too stupid to see it or you're a shameless hypocrite. I don't know which is worse. Either way, you're not much of an artist." She turned to Karina, who looked dazed. "Come on," she said. "Let's go."

Quietly, Karina said, "You can't stand a woman being better than you, can you?" She paused. "Just like Daddy."

At this, Preston's face seemed to collapse in on itself. He lunged at Karina, but the gallery's security guard was on the scene by then and restrained him, along with the man in the floral sports coat that Louisa had seen talking to Karina.

Louisa grabbed Karina's arm and pulled her out the door. At the street corner, she hailed a cab. Only once they were safely in the back seat did Karina's composure crumble. She began to sob, choking as she tried to pull air into her lungs.

"She okay?" said the driver.

"Yes," said Louisa tersely, cradling Karina's head against her chest.

The taxi dropped them off at the studio building, and Louisa helped Karina up the stairs. She'd stopped crying, but she was breathing raggedly. On the fourth-floor landing, a young woman Louisa hadn't seen before, small and pretty with short hair, was locking up her studio. "Oh my god," said the woman. "Karina?" Her tan shoulders were salted with sawdust. "What happened?"

Karina began to answer, but then her eyes grew bright with tears again and she buried her face in her hands.

"Rough night at her opening," Louisa explained. "But she'll be all right."

Inexplicably, the woman's face hardened. "Good luck with her. You'll need it."

CHAPTER THIRTY-THREE

Preston woke to someone poking him in the ribs. He was in a cell with concrete walls, draped in a blanket that smelled faintly of piss. His head throbbed. Everything throbbed. And sometime during the night, a tiny malodorous creature had for sure taken a shit on his tongue before curling up and dying somewhere in the vicinity of his uvula.

"Rise and shine," said a ruddy man wielding a black baton, which explained being poked in the ribs.

Preston put his hands over his face to block out the light. His eyeballs felt like squashed grapes. Summoning what remained of his mental faculties, he attempted to piece together last night's events. He shouldn't have started drinking so early in the day, but the prospect of seeing Karina again, for the first time since the breakup, was wrecking him. He'd soothed himself with a little vodka at lunch, then a little more in the afternoon. In the evening, he'd brought a flask to Axiom as a security blanket, taking liberal comfort from it when Brian nastily informed him, "You'll be pleased to know that no one has inquired about buying your work," when a photographer from the *Times*'s Style section snubbed him in favor of a pair of socialites in black jumpsuits and wide-brimmed hats, and again upon overhearing someone exclaim, "What is

this nonsense!" regarding his artist statement. He'd also partaken liber-
ally of the gallery's champagne. Halfway through the night, his memory
got patchy. He had a vague recollection of sitting in Axiom's back room
with Brian, who kept plying him with bromides and glasses of water.
Then he was hitting on one of the socialites, tracing the brim of her hat
with his fingertip. Then he was watching Karina holding hands with
some doe-eyed chick·who the next minute was accusing him of stealing
Karina's paintings (how had she known?) and all the pent-up rage and
resentment inside him was overflowing and spilling out and—*oh*.

"Your friend's here," the cop was saying.

Preston belched softly, his eyes watering when he caught a whiff of
his own breath. "What?"

"Your friend's here to bail you out."

Slade was waiting for him out in the lobby. "You look like shit," he
said.

"I feel like shit."

"Come on, I've got some Gatorades back at my apartment."

Once Slade had gotten Preston settled on his couch with a cold drink,
he said, "Are you a celebrity bad boy that gets thrown out of clubs now?
Are you gonna be on Page Six?"

"Shut up," Preston muttered. He sank into the cushions and closed
his eyes.

"I'm googling you right now," Slade said.

Preston groaned. "Don't."

"Wait—holy shit. That was fast."

Preston's eyes flew open. "What'd you find?"

Slade read from his phone: "*A hotly anticipated debut exhibition at Axiom
Art, featuring art world newcomers Karina Piontek and Preston Utley, ended with
Mr. Utley's arrest and Ms. Piontek's early departure after the two artists exchanged
angry words during the opening reception. A spokesperson for Axiom said police
were called to the scene after Mr. Utley, creator of the art blog The Wart, 'became
intoxicated and belligerent.'*"

"Is that the news?"

"Sort of. It's from *Slate*. 'Hyped Young Artist Duo Explodes At Take-
off.'" Slade read on: "*Though Mr. Utley and Ms. Piontek were once romanti-*

cally linked, a source reports that Ms. Piontek recently ended their relationship. The reason for their argument was unclear, though an attendee at the opening, who has not been identified, accused Mr. Utley of stealing Ms. Piontek's work. Some insiders speculate that the altercation might have to do with the sharply differing receptions of the two artists' work. While Ms. Piontek's paintings have been near-universally lauded as groundbreaking—with one critic hailing her as 'a prodigy . . . the most protean artist of her generation'—Mr. Utley's work has received decidedly more mixed reviews. His use of neural networks, a type of machine learning, in creating eerie computer-generated images of his late mother has been dismissed as 'muddled' and 'half-baked,' with one critic pronouncing Mr. Utley's work 'conceptually intriguing but lost in a digital fog.' Ms. Piontek, meanwhile, will be Axiom's lead artist at Clerestory, New York's second-largest art fair, which takes place in mid-June on Randall's Island. This is not the first time Mr. Utley's behavior has drawn controversy. Last year, when he was a senior at Wrynn College of Art, he orchestrated a hoax email falsely claiming that the school had decided to liquidate a large portion of its art collection in order to expand financial aid. Wrynn denied this and expelled Mr. Utley, drawing widespread condemnation from its student-led Occupy group."

Preston groaned again, and Slade looked up from his phone. "Don't worry, Karina comes off badly, too. *Ms. Piontek is no stranger to controversy herself. Several art world insiders, who asked to remain anonymous in order to speak freely, have complained about her erratic behavior. One person noted, 'She has a reputation as a drama queen. Every opening she goes to she gets into a screaming match with someone.'"*

Wordlessly, Preston sat up and took out his own phone, typed his name into the search bar. Besides the *Slate* article, there were a couple more news items, as well as posts from art and gossip blogs. One outlet had published a grainy cellphone snapshot of Preston screaming at Brian. He had no memory of this, none at all. The caption read: *Preston Utley telling art world magnate Brian Parrish to "go fuck [himself] in the ass with a sharpened broomstick."*

"I'm screwed," Preston said.

"Drink up," said Slade. "You'll feel better after you've hydrated."

Too tired to protest, Preston chugged his Gatorade. Slade was right—as soon as he'd emptied the bottle, the pounding in his temples eased. Fatigue sluiced over him. He wanted to sink into the couch and never wake up. "Okay if I take a nap?" he said. "My head feels like someone went at it with a hacksaw."

"Go ahead."

It was early evening when Preston woke, the sky a soft plum color, and for a moment he lay there awash in drowsy bliss before the screaming white horse of memory crashed over him. He checked his phone. His father had left two voicemails. The first: *Preston, a colleague has forwarded me a very disturbing news article. I need to speak to you as soon as possible. Call me immediately.* His voice was slow, deep, and measured, but with that simmering rage just beneath the surface that only Preston and Andrew—and once, their mother—could hear. The second, recorded an hour later: *You worthless piece of shit. How dare you disrespect her like that.* His voice hot and loose, that rage come to a boil. Hearing it, Preston broke out in a cold sweat.

He deleted both voicemails and checked his email. His inbox brimmed with unread messages. There was a perfunctory note from Brian Parrish's lawyer, informing him that his contract with Axiom had been terminated effective immediately, and giving him one week to collect his artworks before the gallery disposed of them. There were requests for comment from reporters. An automated message from his bank warning him his balance was low.

To soothe himself, he pulled up his blog. For a moment he thought there must be a glitch in the website, because overnight, The Wart had gained twenty thousand new followers. And his latest post, an image of a hammer and sickle carved into an apple (*Apples Are Red & Delicious!*) had gotten thousands of likes, reblogs, and comments.

> *Preston utley is a BAMF*
> *Yaaasss bitch fuck his ASS w dat broomstick*
> *PU u a hero man*
> *THIS is good art*
> *All kinds of yes ha!*
> *#AestheticGoals*
> *#UtleyAesthetics*
> *#UtleyASSthetics*

A quick glance at Facebook and Twitter told him that thousands of people were sharing images from the blog across the Internet. Slowly, the dread churning in Preston's stomach morphed into excitement.

"You awake?" Slade wandered into the living room, eating out of a takeout container.

Preston glanced up from his phone. "The most insane thing is happening."

"What?" Slade flopped down across from him, shoving a tangle of noodles into his mouth.

"I'm going viral. The art world hates me, but the Internet fucking loves me."

They loved him *because* the art world hated him.

"Nice," said Slade. "Every millennial's dream."

Preston's mind was whirring, his thoughts tripping over one another. The incident at Axiom might have ruined his reputation in the art world, but online, it had only boosted his credibility. And the art world was, relatively speaking, tiny. Whereas the Internet—well, the Internet was practically infinite.

"I wanted to ask you something," said Slade, interrupting Preston's thoughts.

He looked up. "Hmm?"

Slade set down his chopsticks. "What's the best way to go about selling Karina's paintings? Should I go through an auction house or take them to a private dealer or what? ArtRanker just listed her in their Top Ten Up-and-Coming Artists and I want to be ready to flip them when she peaks."

"What ranker?"

"ArtRanker."

"What's that?"

Slade showed him on his phone. It was some kind of consultancy service claiming to rank artists based on a system of "qualitatively weighted metrics including web presence, studio capacity and output, market maker contracts and acquisitions, major collector and museum support, gallery representation, and auction results." Artists were sorted into categories including "Buy Now," "Sell Now," and the ominous-sounding "Liquidate."

"Is this a joke?" said Preston.

Slade looked annoyed. "No, a friend turned me on to it. The founder wanted to apply investment banking algorithmic trading methods to art assets. Apparently, he got the idea right after the 2008 crash because he noticed that during a recession, investors tend to park their money in SWAG."

"SWAG? What the fuck?"

"Silver, wine, art, and gold. Karina's prices are spiking, see? She'll probably peak soon, so I want to be ready to flip when she does."

Preston recalled Karina's warning about pumping-and-dumping. This was the kind of speculation she'd been talking about, the kind that could tank her career. They were broken up, but still—she was a person, not a stock pick.

Preston cleared his throat. "So, listen, actually, I'm going to need you to return those paintings."

Slade laughed. "What are you talking about?"

"Dude, a whole crowd of people heard me accused of theft last night. I don't know who you've been talking to or what you said, but you saw that article, that's what people think now."

"That sounds like a you problem." Slade twisted his mouth. "And it wasn't exactly a false accusation."

Preston groaned. "Come on, man. You got the paintings for free. It's not like you'll be losing money if you don't sell them."

Slade darkened. "Yes, Preston, I'm glad you brought that up."

"What's that supposed to mean?"

"Why don't we talk about the money I've lost betting on *you*?"

"Excuse me?"

"Let's talk about that investment I'm not gonna recoup because your gallery dumped you. Or the rent money I'm losing out on by subsidizing your apartment. Or the bail I just paid. As far as those paintings are concerned, I feel entirely justified holding on to them as long as you're in debt to me."

"Jesus!" said Preston. "You know I don't have any money right now."

"Then *make* some."

Preston's mouth opened in shock. But really, a little voice reminded him, none of this should come as a surprise. He'd always known about

Slade's mercenary streak; he'd seen him deploy it against other people—just never against *him*.

Preston licked his lips. He was in dangerous territory here; he needed to tread carefully. Getting evicted would be disastrous right now. There was no way he was going back to his father's, and he couldn't ask Andrew to bail him out again. "There's always The Wart."

"What the *fuck* are you talking about?"

"I can monetize The Wart."

Slade blew his lips out in contempt. "Not that again."

"No, no, hear me out. I have an idea."

It took shape in his mind even as he explained it, as though his imagination were sprinting just steps ahead of him. But Slade seemed unconvinced.

"Look, give me three weeks," Preston pleaded. "In three weeks, I'll make my first repayment."

Slade looked dubious. "How much?"

Preston rubbed his face. "I dunno, a thousand? A thousand a month."

"Two."

"Fine," Preston said, relenting. "I'll pay you back two thousand in three weeks."

"Deal, I guess," said Slade coldly. "You should probably leave now, don't you think? I know where to find you."

As soon as Preston got back to his apartment, he made a new blog post. No images this time, just text. He added a link where participants could submit a Bitcoin payment. Two clicks and the post went live. Then he found the contact info for that activist collective he'd seen protesting at the Guggenheim on YouTube and emailed them a link. Finally, as an afterthought, he also posted the link on 4chan. Then he changed into shorts and went out on a run. When he returned forty-five minutes later, the post had been shared more than three thousand times and he had a new email from someone named Vanessa Campbell.

Chapter Thirty-Four

Robert didn't hear about the auction until a week after it happened. Hammer price: just under half a million. A former colleague forwarded him the *ArtNews* article. *Congrats!* the colleague wrote. Of course, Robert wasn't entitled to a penny of the profits. The sale enriched only the painting's original buyer, some punk singer who'd purchased it back in the late eighties for approximately a fiftieth of the auction price before descending down the drain of cultural memory, taking the painting with him.

Robert chalked the whole thing up to sheer dumb luck. A scathing documentary about the Reagans had just come out in which *Fly High, America* briefly appeared—some rich liberal must've seen it and coveted it. It wasn't exactly the kind of thing you'd hang in your living room, though: Nancy faced the viewer head-on, naked, breasts sagging, gaze boring through the canvas. In one hand she held a golden snuff spoon piled with cocaine; the other clutched a veiny red, white, and blue dildo. Robert had had fun painting it, but come on. Even he could admit it was a little heavy-handed.

When he didn't hear from anyone but his old colleague, Robert figured it wasn't such a big deal after all. This wasn't his big comeback. Just a blip in the market. For the super-rich, half a million was a drop in the bucket.

But then one night in late May, just after he'd sent Adrian off to bed—Lily had asked if he'd mind staying late so she could have drinks with an old friend—he received a call from Brian Parrish.

"Hell of a time getting ahold of you!" said Brian. His voice was gravelly, jocular, and as familiar to Robert as a police siren.

"Uh, hi," said Robert.

"Great to hear your voice. It's been, what, ten years?"

More like fifteen. Robert hadn't spoken to his old dealer since before he'd started farming himself out to colleges in earnest, as a career move rather than the occasional semester-long jaunt when he needed a change of scenery and a break from his marriage. This shift was necessitated by the fact that Brian had more or less fired him. He'd been a coward about it, had done it via email: he was "trimming his program" and Robert hadn't made the cut, "unfortunately." A sensible move on Brian's part. Robert's prices had been declining for years; financially speaking, he was a deadweight.

"I heard your good news," Brian said, "and it turns out that I actually have some empty space in my program at the moment. The confluence of events—it just seemed like . . . a sign."

Wow, Robert thought, *you don't beat around the bush, do you?*

"A sign," he echoed. "You sound like a man trying to win back his jilted lover."

There was a startled pause, and then Brian burst out laughing. "It's a relief to hear you joking," he said. "I figured you'd never forgiven me."

"Oh, I haven't," said Robert, but Brian, who seemed to think that too was a joke, laughed again. "You still in the city?"

"Brooklyn."

"So you've probably been hearing from dealers left and right."

"Not really."

Robert wondered what Brian looked like now, if he'd gained weight, if he'd dyed his hair. He'd been a bit of a dandy back in the day, bespoke suits and high-end wristwatches. Great fun to hang out with—he loved to party with his artists, especially in those early years—but as Axiom grew in stature, he'd become increasingly petty and status-obsessed.

Robert had seen him throw a tantrum over the location of his gallery's booth at an art fair, and, at the height of Robert's career, he'd created a waitlist for collectors in line to buy Robert's work. The collectors were ranked not by affluence but by reputation. Some would-be buyers, not deemed elite enough to be "offered" a work, were left off the list entirely.

Brian cleared his throat. "I'm thinking we take advantage of this—throw a show together ASAP. Get some old work on loan and showcase maybe four or five new pieces. Advertise really aggressively in the lead-up. I just had to cut loose an artist kind of in your mold. Hoping to round out Axiom's program again."

"Which artist, out of curiosity?" He already knew who; he just wanted to hear Brian say it.

"Preston Utley. Total nightmare. So . . . what do you think?"

And Robert, to his own surprise, found himself seriously considering the offer. He'd felt so good about the work he was doing with Adrian that he thought he'd made peace with ending his career. But Adrian would outgrow him before long, and then what? And the thought of making money again, well . . . Money was easy enough to reject when it was out of reach, but once it was dangled in front of you it took on a luster that was hard to ignore.

"My style is different these days," Robert warned. Was he making a mistake? Would he come to regret his pragmatism? (Had it been pragmatism that moved him to paint Vince as he lay dying? Or had it been love?)

"Of course I'd expect your style to have changed," Brian was saying. "You've matured."

"Right . . . So I'm going to want some leeway in terms of subject matter."

What would this mean for his relationship with Adrian's family? Robert supposed it wouldn't be too difficult to continue working with Adrian while also preparing a show. Most of what he and Adrian did together was make art, anyway.

"Subject matter is your prerogative," said Brian.

"And I want you to cover the cost of materials," Robert added on impulse. "Considering the short notice."

Brian hesitated for half a second before agreeing. Emboldened, Robert asked for a 30/70 commission split, and Brian, to his surprise, again said yes. Robert hung up feeling like a different person. Since when did he possess negotiating skills? He lifted a day-old newspaper off the coffee table and stared at the headlines without reading them. Then he put it down and picked up his phone again, typed *preston utley* into the search bar.

He clicked the first news result, skimmed the text, stopping when he came to a familiar name. *Karina Piontek.* Wasn't that Fiona Piontek's daughter? Yes, her name *was* Karina; he was almost certain. She'd been ten or eleven at the time, so that meant she'd be nineteen or twenty now. Robert kept reading, the story taking shape in his mind: a love affair, a falling-out. Fiona's daughter had been at Wrynn, too. Unsurprising, given her parents. What was surprising was that any daughter of Fiona's would be involved with someone like Preston.

Robert experienced a strange urge to reach out to him. He still had his email address. But after a moment, the urge passed. Young men never wanted to hear what older men had to say. Boys, in their reckless confidence, were all the same.

Presently, Robert drank some of Lily's Scotch and fell asleep on the couch.

It was light when he woke, a blanket tucked around him.

"Morning."

Lily stood in the doorway, a steaming mug in each hand. She set one on the coffee table next to Robert's head. "There's half-and-half in the fridge."

Robert heaved himself upright.

"You have sleep lines here," Lily said, pointing to her cheek. Robert pressed his palm over his face.

"I didn't want to wake you last night," she said. "It was just so late and you were conked out."

Robert sipped his coffee, scalding his tongue. "What time is it?"

"A little after eight. Adrian's not up yet. I'm taking the rest of the week off work, so you should feel free to go home. You look like you need a vacation."

"You sure?" It was only Tuesday.

"Yes. Go home. Shoo." She sat down and began writing out his check. Since last month, when she'd found out about Artsitters Atelier's fifty percent commission, she'd been paying him directly. "Hey," she added. "Have you heard of that art fair on Randall's Island?"

"Clerestory? Oh sure, it's been around for a decade now."

"Do you think that's something Adrian would enjoy?"

"Probably, yeah. Art fairs are basically amusement parks these days." He supposed if he was going to sell out, he might as well begin by introducing his charge to the wonders of luxury shopping.

"Great! I'll buy you both tickets." As Robert stood to go, Lily said, "I don't know what we'd do without you."

For the rest of the week, Robert slept in and took long walks. He smoked a joint and went to a matinee, sat alone in the dark empty theater and ate popcorn and felt content. Twice he met Frank for drinks. They talked about the Kentucky Derby and books they'd loved as children and whether Frank should adopt a dog, but something kept Robert from telling him about the Nancy Reagan painting or his deal with Brian.

Robert even painted a little, put down plastic sheeting on the floor in the second bedroom and set up an easel by the window. He painted without a plan or an agenda—abstract pieces, splashes of color and texture, more like Adrian's work than anything he'd ever made for Brian, albeit with more subdued color sensibilities. And for the first time in a while, he liked what he'd made—or didn't *like* it, exactly, but saw its potential.

On Sunday night, he was checking his email when he saw a new message from the 21 Rector discussion list.

Subject: *Action planned for opening day of Clerestory—Volunteers needed!*

Robert deleted the message without reading it. It would be disingenuous of him to continue his involvement with 21 Rector now that he was back in bed with Axiom. He could face Vanessa and Cal from across a picket line, but not as a hypocrite among their ranks. Whatever they had planned, he supposed he'd find out soon enough.

CHAPTER THIRTY-FIVE

Karina knew she ought to be happy. Her show had been a success, the incident with Preston generating more publicity than anyone had expected. "Everyone loves a scandal," Brian said. But in the three weeks since that night, Karina had felt mired in anxiety and sadness. The revelation of Preston's theft had knocked the legs out from under her. She felt violated. But more than that, she felt stupid. How could she not have noticed him taking advantage of her?

There were other matters to worry about, too. A few enterprising buyers had already flipped some of her paintings, potentially inflating her prices beyond what the market could sustain this early in her career. And there was Brian—the fact that being in his presence always left her feeling light-headed and vaguely nauseated.

She couldn't seem to stop herself from pulling away from Louisa. Kind, earnest Louisa, who'd stepped up to protect her. Karina had never seen her like that: ferocious, determined, incandescent with rage. As she'd watched Louisa defend her, hurling accusations that Karina herself had never voiced, though she knew them to be true, she'd thought, *Where have you been all my life?* And the truth was that it scared her. It scared her to feel so loved.

She spent more and more time at the parties, dinners, and openings she'd begun getting invited to. Most nights she found herself alone in crowded galleries and strangers' living rooms, her mouth a rictus of anxiety, heart racing, wanting to crawl out of her skin. She began having dissociative spells again. She'd open the window to smoke, and she'd forget herself. When she came to, the light would be different, the windowsill littered with cigarette butts. It worried her, how her mind and body were revolting against her.

Because Karina went out nearly every evening, she didn't pose for Louisa as much anymore. And what hurt the most was that Louisa didn't seem to mind. Often, Karina would come home to find that Louisa had spent the evening painting swampy landscapes or fantastical birds or great, greedy, oceanic swaths of sky, the kind of sky that didn't exist in New York and never would. The canvases were almost always exquisite—more impressionistic and far more sophisticated than the Southern Gothic images Louisa had initially made at Wrynn, and perhaps even better than the bird woman paintings. And though she knew it shouldn't, this bothered Karina. It bothered her that Louisa was improving without her help. Louisa, for her part, insisted that the new paintings weren't as good as they might've been if she'd painted them en plein air, and this, too, made Karina uneasy. She sensed that Louisa was beginning to pull away from her life in New York, that she was hearing the siren song of home.

Karina didn't know what to do about the impulses warring inside her. She wanted to keep Louisa close and to push her away. She needed her and she couldn't stand the thought of needing anyone. She was, she understood, deeply in love. It was wonderful and it was miserable.

One evening, a week before Clerestory's opening, Karina decided to blow off her plans—a cocktail party hosted by a MoMA board member—and pose for Louisa. She undressed while Louisa set up the easel. She was unclasping her bra when someone knocked at the door.

"Who's that?" Louisa said.

"No idea," Karina said, though she knew right away that it had to be her mother. She'd relented and given Fiona her address last time they'd seen each other. Karina put on her bathrobe and opened the door.

"Hi, love." Fiona swept into the studio, pale and anxious. "I'm so sorry, I hadn't heard about what happened. A friend sent me the article—are you all right?"

Louisa looked up in surprise, setting down her brush and coming out from behind the easel. She was wearing shorts and a thin tank top through which her nipples were visible. Fiona threw up her hand in a wave, which Louisa tentatively returned.

"Hi," Fiona said, "I'm—"

"Karina's mother. You look a lot alike."

Fiona turned to Karina and pulled her into a hug. "Are you okay?"

"I'm fine."

"He didn't hurt you, did he?"

For a moment Karina thought she meant Brian. *How did you know?* Then she realized Fiona was referring to Preston.

"No, he just yelled at me."

Fiona smoothed Karina's hair and looked around the studio, taking in the futon, the hotplate, the tangle of clothes on the floor, the conspicuous lack of a bathroom. "*This* is where you live?"

"Yes," said Karina defiantly.

"Karina."

"What?"

Fiona smiled slightly and put up her hands. "Fine, I won't comment. Just know you're always welcome to come stay with me if you'd like." Her gaze landed on three of Louisa's bird woman paintings lined up under the window. She drew closer and examined them. "I didn't know you did self-portraits."

"They're not mine," said Karina. "They're hers," and at the same time Louisa said, "They're mine."

Fiona looked at Louisa and then back at Karina, who held her gaze. At last Fiona said, "Well, no wonder they're so wonderful. You can always tell when an artist loves her subject." But there was a new note of melancholy in her voice, and Karina felt a pang at the thought of her mother all alone with no one to love and no one to love her, not even a picture on the wall to look at.

She knew then that she'd return Wally to Fiona. Maybe not today, maybe not next week, but someday. She'd make her mother promise not to sell her. "Hang her on your bedroom wall," she'd say, and Fiona, she knew, would agree.

After her mother's visit, Karina began to feel a little better. The day before Clerestory opened, she and Louisa made pasta together, then split a bottle of merlot on the floor by the window and watched the sunset slowly bleed into night. In the calm of their studio, with wine warming her veins and the hum of a balmy June evening drifting in from the street below, Karina felt closer to Louisa than she had in weeks. She took Louisa's hand, their fingers curled tightly together, and said, "There's something I need to tell you."

Louisa gave her an uncertain smile. Her mouth was stained purple from the wine. "Uh-oh. This doesn't bode well for me, does it?"

"Oh god, no," said Karina. "I'm not breaking up with you." She swallowed her guilt—she knew she'd given Louisa good reason to doubt the solidity of their relationship—and haltingly described what Brian had done to her in his office.

As Karina spoke, Louisa's expression shifted from apprehensive to horrified. "I am so, so deeply sorry that happened to you. That motherfucker. Are you going to report him?"

Karina looked at the floor and slowly shook her head.

"Are you at least going to try to find a new gallery?"

"I don't know," Karina mumbled.

"You're serious?" Louisa was incredulous. "He tried to rape you, but you're just going to go ahead and make him a whole bunch of money anyway?"

Karina's stomach churned, her heart seizing at the word *rape*. It must have shown on her face, because Louisa seemed to soften. Sliding closer to Karina, she embraced her, resting her head on her shoulder. "There need to be consequences," she said gently. "He shouldn't just be allowed to get away with what he did to you."

"Don't you understand that this is all I have?" Karina said. Her voice had gone high and tight and quavering, like her father when he was angry.

"That's not true," said Louisa in a small voice. "You *know* that's not true." She was quiet for a moment. "I can't believe you'd say that." She pulled her arm off Karina's shoulders and sat back, hugging her knees to her chest. She looked very young all of a sudden, like a child mourning the loss of something beloved.

There was a lengthy silence. The night had soured, the street noises turning discordant and ominous. Desperate for something to do with her hands, Karina reached for her pack of cigarettes and lit one. Louisa turned her face away from the smoke. She looked ill. "I'm going to bed," she said. Karina nodded but didn't reply.

For a long time, she sat there in front of the window, chain-smoking until the pack was empty and her mouth tasted like death. Finally, she stood on stiff legs, stumbled through the dark room, and crawled onto the futon, curling herself around Louisa.

"Are you awake?" Karina whispered.

But there was no answer save for Louisa's soft, steady breathing.

The next morning, Karina and Louisa took the train to Manhattan, then boarded a ferry to Randall's Island. They leaned their elbows up against the railing, squinting into the sunlight, the wind raking the hair over their faces. The skyline drifted by, buildings like smooth cliffs of glass and granite. The ferry's grinding engine and the gusting wind made it too loud for conversation, which came to Karina as a relief. They'd hardly spoken over breakfast or on the train, treating each other with tense, deliberate politeness.

On the island, a vast white tent greeted them. Inside, acres of light blue carpeting and a maze of white booths, each as large as Karina's old Bushwick apartment. Karina felt quivery, twitchy with nerves. Today was important. While the fair's big-ticket items—the Basquiats and the De Koonings—would sell almost immediately, an emerging artist's work was a riskier proposition. Axiom was spending a fortune on shipping and the booth rental, and if any of Karina's work didn't sell, its value would go down because it would have been seen and known not to have sold.

At the Axiom booth, Brian and Audrey were conferring over an iPad.

Brian greeted Karina with a kiss on the cheek and nodded in Louisa's direction, after which he ignored her, addressing himself only to Karina. She tried not to meet his eyes. "So there are a couple of folks I know for sure are stopping by that I want you to meet," Brian said. "Feel free to explore, but keep your phone on. And don't leave without telling me."

"Does he think he owns you?" Louisa said once they were out of earshot.

"He doesn't own me," said Karina sharply. They wandered around, a strange uneasiness coiling between them. The fair was crowded: financiers and their wives buying earthenware sculptures of shoes; the occasional celebrity; young women in peasant skirts snapping selfies in front of a neon sign that read EMPOWERED WOMEN, the ED blinking on and off. Intermittent announcements rang out: *The wine tasting will begin in ten minutes in the Dasani Lounge; Tonight's curatorial summit on culture and censorship takes place at seven in the Citibank Pavilion; A variety of children's activities are available at the Junior Art Hub, sponsored by Artsitters Atelier.*

This was the world of Harry and Fiona, a cosmopolitan club for the super-cool and super-rich. When Karina was small, she used to go to fairs with them. She'd walk behind them as they strolled hand in hand through the booths, paying close attention whenever they paused in front of a piece and put their heads together, conferring in soft, secret voices. She turned to Louisa, who was inspecting a screen displaying abstract forms that warped and reacted to her movements. "What do you think?"

Louisa gave a small, wry laugh. "It's a little depressing, isn't it?"

"How so?"

"I guess it just reminds me how . . . how *unspecial* we are. How unspecial *I* am." She gestured around her. "All these talented, driven people, trying to get to the top. And on their own everyone's extraordinary. But when you shove them all in a tent together, they just drown each other out."

Louisa turned suddenly, striding toward a booth across the way. Karina followed her. As she drew close, she realized the booth was Kobayashi's.

Louisa pointed at a Technicolor mushroom tapestry. "See that? I painted that."

"Wow," said Karina. She hesitated. "How does it feel to see it here?"

"Weird." Louisa peered at the wall label. "Look, it's priced at sixty thousand dollars. I think it took me maybe fifteen hours? So my cut was ..." She stopped to think. "Something like half a percent." She dropped her shoulders, then hitched them up again. She turned to Karina and seemed to hesitate. "Listen, I know you don't want to, but I think we need to talk about last night."

Karina went rigid. "You really think this is an appropriate place for that conversation?"

Undeterred, Louisa said, "You shouldn't ever be alone with Brian again, not even in public. I don't like the way he talks to you. Or the way he looks at you."

"Where did you get the impression that I'm a damsel in distress?"

"Oh, I don't know." Louisa's voice had an edge now, and her mouth was tight with anger. "Maybe from the fact that you can't seem to stop yourself from getting involved with sick men who want to hurt you?"

They held each other's gazes, neither willing to be the first to look away, but when Louisa's phone began to ring, she glanced down at the screen and sighed. "It's my mom. Hold on—Hello? Hello, Mom? I can't hear you, just a second." She lowered the phone. "I'm going to take this outside, okay?"

Alone now, Karina wove through the maze of booths, barely registering her surroundings. After some time, her phone buzzed in her hand, jolting her from her unhappy trance. A text from Brian: *come NOW.*

At the Axiom booth, Brian was waiting to introduce her to a middle-aged couple and their art consultant, a silver-haired man in a linen suit. The husband wanted to know where Karina got her ideas. The wife asked about tools and techniques. After the consultant called Karina "a sound investment," the couple bought two paintings. Fifteen minutes later, an older woman in an emerald cape and her adult son bought three more. Brian was ecstatic. "Do you know who that was? That woman is married to Yuri Fedorov."

"Who?"

"A Russian oligarch."

Karina knew she ought to be pleased and relieved, but all she felt was a bone-deep exhaustion.

At noon, Brian and Audrey went off for a business lunch in the ExxonMobil VIP Lounge. Karina wondered if Audrey got to eat or if she just sat in a corner taking notes. She wondered if Audrey hated her job. Karina had a headache. She sat down at the desk. The swivel chair was still warm from Audrey's butt. Louisa hadn't returned yet. Karina texted her: *where are u?*

For ten minutes there was no answer. Finally, Louisa texted back: *by the dock.*

Karina got up and went to find her. As soon as she was outside the tent, away from the crowds and noise, she felt her limbs loosen up. She filled her lungs with fresh air and scanned the horizon. Across the river, the city glittered in the midday sun. She walked toward the ferry dock and spotted Louisa in the grass by the water. From a distance, she looked like a figure in an Edward Hopper painting: knees pulled up to her chest, arms resting on her legs, lost in thought. Karina was reminded of how she'd seemed when they'd first met, how elusive she'd been, how maddeningly and irresistibly self-contained. But as Karina got closer, she realized something was wrong. Louisa's face was pink and swollen, streaked with fresh tears. Her phone lay in the grass beside her.

"Are you okay?" Karina said. "What happened?"

Louisa turned to look at her, and the sight of Karina seemed to break loose something inside her. She erupted into sobs and slumped over, burying her face in her arms. Karina sat down beside her in the grass. She kissed Louisa's shoulder and rubbed her heaving back. Louisa cried and cried, and Karina felt afraid. She'd never seen her so distraught.

But after a while, Louisa seemed to calm down. Her breathing slowed and she lifted her head, squinting in the sunlight. She was still crying, but quietly now.

"Is this about last night?" Karina said.

Louisa shook her head. "My grandfather died. That was what my mom was calling to tell me." She spoke in a monotone, and her face was slack, her eyes big and wet and dull.

"Oh god. Oh fuck, Louisa. I'm so sorry."

"I didn't get to say goodbye." Her voice was scraped with grief.

Karina wound herself around her, holding her tightly. Her body felt frail and insubstantial. "It's not your fault," Karina said.

Louisa spoke into her shoulder. "Yes, it is. You don't understand. I left him. I abandoned my family. I rejected them." She was talking faster and faster. "I decided they weren't enough for me and I made them feel like I was too good for them and I left a part of myself behind and I'll never get it back and now I'll never get *him* back either."

Karina pulled away and took Louisa's face in both of her hands. "Listen to me," she said, surprising herself with her own vehemence. "It's not a crime to go after what you want."

But Louisa turned her head away and picked at the grass, tearing the blades into tiny pieces and scattering them in the breeze.

"It's not a crime to have ambition," Karina insisted. "You're allowed to want things. You're allowed to want things that other people don't think you should want."

Louisa let her head fall against Karina's shoulder, and for a while they sat there in silence, watching the boats glide up and down the river.

"I've been thinking . . ." Louisa began.

"What?"

"I've been thinking for a while that I need to go home. And now I can't put it off any longer."

Karina nodded. A calm had descended over her. She dug inside her purse and handed Louisa her credit card. "Take a cab back to the studio and pack a bag. Then go straight to the airport, okay?"

Louisa stared at her. "Now?"

"Do you want to go home today?"

She nodded, wiping her face with the back of her hand.

"It's what, a two-, three-hour flight? You can be home tonight if you leave right now. Whatever it costs, just charge it to the card. And call me if anyone gives you trouble."

Louisa still looked disbelieving, so Karina stood up and held out her hand. She pulled Louisa to her feet and led her around to the far side of the tent. It would have been faster to cut through the fair, but Karina couldn't bring herself to go back in just yet. At the taxi stand, a row of yellow cabs sat idling.

"Here we are," said Karina.

Louisa's face briefly crumpled. Then she composed herself. Rising on tiptoes, she put her arms around Karina and kissed her full on the mouth. Her face was still damp and hot from crying. A great gladness flooded Karina. She couldn't have broken the embrace even if she'd wanted to, and it was Louisa who finally moved away. "Thank you," she said. She opened the taxi door and slid into the back seat.

The driver was eyeing them, but Karina didn't care. "Be safe. Text me when you land."

The cab drove off. Karina watched it, feeling at once an extraordinary clarity and a terrible fear that she'd never see Louisa again. Only once it had disappeared from sight did she turn around and gaze up at the white tent. She wanted to be at home, alone with Louisa's canvases, or maybe on the saffron couch in her mother's apartment. But her phone was about to die, and she'd left her charger at the Axiom booth. And she supposed, too, that she ought to tell Brian what she had decided as she'd sat in the grass with Louisa, watching the river shimmer under the bright sun.

The booth was as empty as she'd left it. She found a pad of sticky notes and a ballpoint and sat at the desk. She wasn't quite sure how to say what needed to be said. At last she lifted the pen and began to write. When she was done, she stuck the Post-it in the middle of the desk where Brian couldn't miss it.

Just as she was standing to leave, a man and a boy walked into the booth. She met the man's eyes; he gave her a distant smile. It was Robert Berger. He still didn't recognize her. This time she wasn't angry.

The kid pointed at Karina's biggest painting, a kaleidoscopic mandala. "That's my favorite."

"Why?" said Robert. His tone was warm and affectionate, familiar in a way it hadn't been when Karina heard him speak at Wrynn.

"It's like music," the kid said, "but with paint." Which was, Karina thought, the perfect description.

"Robert?" she said.

He turned and looked at her blankly. "Yes?"

"I don't know if you remember me. My name's Karina Piontek? I'm Fiona Piontek's daughter."

His eyes flicked to the wall label next to her painting, then back to her. "Oh my god. I didn't recognize you."

"It's been a long time."

He shook his head in disbelief, but he was still smiling. "Of course I remember you." He gestured at the mandala. "And this work, my god. It's stunning. You've really come into your own."

Had she? The kid—skinny with dark, floppy hair—seemed to share her doubts. He eyed her with suspicion.

"Is this your son?" she said.

The kid replied, "I'm his tutee."

"Adrian's an artist, too," said Robert. "A terrific one."

Adrian rolled his eyes a little, as though to convey how boring he found this adult conversation, and peeled off to look at the rest of the booth.

"So I take it you're not at Wrynn anymore?" Karina said. It seemed best to pretend she didn't know about Robert's firing. Let him have his pride.

"No."

"Neither am I," she offered. He didn't seem surprised. "I actually tried to say hi to you once. But you didn't recognize me. It was at the beginning of the year, after that Q&A you gave?"

Robert winced. "Oh god, you were there? What a shitshow."

"It wasn't so bad." And, really, it hadn't been. Preston had come off worse than Robert; she saw that now. "So you're still teaching, then?"

"Different age bracket, but yeah," he said, chuckling ruefully.

"No, I think it's great that you're working with kids. When I was little and you were . . . going out with my mom, I used to love hanging out with you because whenever we went to a restaurant together you'd always help me convince her to let me order dessert. And you'd doodle cartoons on napkins for me." She paused. "Do you remember?"

"Vaguely, yeah. Can't really picture the doodles, though."

"You'd do these little portraits of people at other tables. But you'd give them, like, horns and pig noses and face tattoos."

Robert laughed. "That sounds like me."

"It used to crack me up. I wish I'd kept them."

"Maybe I should start doing that for Adrian."

"Definitely, but make sure he hangs on to them. Don't let him repeat my mistakes."

Robert seemed to hesitate, chewing over his words. "How *is* your mom?"

"Doing okay, I think. Going through a divorce."

"I'm sorry to hear that."

"Don't be. I think she's better off."

"From what I remember of your father," Robert said, "I'd have to agree. No offense," he added quickly.

Karina snorted. "Oh, none taken."

They looked at each other, both smiling slightly, and Karina felt an echo of the warm, conspiratorial rapport they'd shared, all those years ago. They understood each other, she and Robert. Or at least they once had.

"I'm *so* hungry," Adrian announced, having returned from looking around the booth. He bounced impatiently on his heels, emphasizing each word.

"Hold on a sec," Robert said. To Karina: "So where does she live these days, your mom?" His tone was studiously casual.

Karina tried and failed to suppress the grin that rose in her then. "She's here still. Just moved to the West Village. I visited her the other day; she has a nice place near the water."

"I found the food court, look," Adrian said, shoving a map at Robert. "There's burgers, and also sushi. But if we get sushi, I'm ordering tempura, okay? Shrimp, not veggie."

Robert obligingly looked at the map, one hand resting on Adrian's shoulder. Watching them together, Karina felt an odd twist in her heart. She grabbed another sticky note and jotted down Fiona's new landline.

"My mother always really liked you."

Robert glanced up and met her eye. "I always really liked her, too."

Karina heard herself speaking very quickly. "She might like to reconnect." She held out the sticky note.

Robert took his hand off Adrian's shoulder and accepted it, folding it in half and slipping it into his pocket. "That'd be nice," he said.

Chapter Thirty-Six

The post read:

The rich are cockroaches! Help me troll them! For each donation of one (1) Bitcoin, I will release one (1) cockroach at a MAJOR gathering of the 1%. Donors will receive more information via encrypted message, plus vids and pics!

Upon completing the Bitcoin transaction, each donor was sent an encrypted email written by Vanessa Campbell, the 21 Rector organizer who'd offered to help Preston orchestrate his plan:

> *Clerestory Art fair is a symbol of modern decadence. Inside this lily-white tent, you will find a grotesque display of privilege and wealth-hoarding, a cabal of galleries hawking objects out of reach to all but the elitist of the elite. Here, a single painting may cost more than a working-class family earns in a year. Who are Clerestory's clientele? The same people responsible for the current economic crisis. While you worry about the bank foreclosing on your home, Wall Street criminals are shopping for art. What are you going to do about it?*

As soon as Vanessa distributed the link to her network of activist discussion lists and message boards, traffic to The Wart ballooned and Bitcoin donations started pouring in. Even after the 21 Rector people insisted on appropriating the first week's worth of funds for something called Abolish Debt, there was still enough left over for Preston to repay a chunk of what he owed to Slade—who seemed unpleasantly surprised that Preston had actually come through with the money—and to live on for at least a few months. And for the purchase and delivery of thousands of "feeder" cockroaches, along with the requisite cockroach care supplies. A handful of 21 Rector members volunteered to help smuggle the roaches into the fair, so Preston found himself caring for only five hundred insects. They arrived in perforated cardboard boxes that, when stacked in the corner of the apartment, emitted disconcerting rustles, especially at night.

All the planning kept Preston busy, but as soon as there was nothing left to do, the little voice returned, its terrible drumbeat: *You tried to hurt her. Not once but twice.* The night before the action, Preston couldn't get it out of his head, couldn't sleep. Around three in the morning, he impulsively called Andrew. It had been over a month since they'd last spoken, longer than they usually went between calls.

"Hello? What *time* is it there?" Andrew sounded mildly annoyed.

"I didn't wake you, did I?"

"No, no, it's morning here. We're just trying to get the boys fed and out the door."

Preston could hear commotion in the background; one of Andrew's kids was crying. "Should I call back, or . . . ?"

"Do you need money?" said Andrew bluntly.

Preston's mouth went dry. "No! No, I— That's not it at all. I just wanted to ask you something.

"What?"

"I'll call back later."

"No, hold on, let me find a quieter place." Andrew said something to his wife in German; the sound of the crying child faded away.

"Do you think I'm like him?" Preston said.

"Like who?"

Preston cleared his throat. "Like my father."

"Do I think you're like your father?" Andrew sounded confused. "Where's this coming from?"

"I—I had a nasty breakup." Preston swallowed before quietly adding, "Andrew, I tried to hurt her."

There was a pause. "*Did* you hurt her?"

"No. I was . . . incompetent."

"Here's the thing about your dad," said Andrew in a cold, hard voice. "In that area, he's highly competent." He drew in his breath. "You don't still want to hurt her, do you?"

"No."

"Good," Andrew said, though he sounded unconvinced.

"Do I remind you of him?" Preston lowered his voice. "Tell me the truth."

There was another pause, this one so long that for a moment Preston worried the call had dropped. Finally Andrew said, "I'm not going to deny that you and he share certain attributes. But Preston, look, no—you don't have to be like him. You have a choice, don't you? You have just as much of Mom in you as you do of him."

The next morning, Preston funneled the roaches from their boxes into opaque Tupperware containers, sides and lids discreetly pinpricked, which he carefully stacked inside a backpack before leaving his apartment. At the fair's entrance, a security guard waved a metal detector over him before asking to check inside his bag.

Heart racing, Preston unzipped the backpack. The guard stuck a flashlight inside and poked around.

"What's in the containers?"

"Lunch," Preston said. "Have you seen what a sandwich costs in there?"

The guard smirked and let him through. Inside, the tent was echoey and blindingly white, a high-end shopping mall. Some of the booths were furnished with chic midcentury modern living room sets—*Your house could look like this!* No wall text anywhere. Most of the work wasn't even titled, just labeled with the price and the artist's name. There was no pretense of this even attempting to resemble a museum-going experience. This was about commerce. This was a bazaar for the ultra-rich. Here was the abundance, the variety, the *choice* that American capitalism prided itself on. Here was every type of art you could ever want, as long as what you wanted was something that could be bought and sold: inoffensive abstract canvases by Flavor of the Month for the timid-hearted to hang over their dining tables, Yayoi Kusama infinity rooms for all your Instagram needs, Akito Kobayashi cartoons to show off your quirkiness. Preston supposed that none of this should surprise him. Hadn't he been saying it for years? And here it was, all out in the open: proof that he was right. Still, what he hadn't expected was that there was something about the quality of the visual overload inside the tent that reminded him of the Internet. He might've admired it, if it hadn't been for its essential emptiness.

Preston found a spot on a bench and unfolded the fair map, giving it a shake to snap out the wrinkles. In the month since that disastrous night at Axiom, he and the other 21 Rector activists had painstakingly planned the operation. Preston had gone to meet them once, at their headquarters, but the rest of the organizing had happened over email and text message. According to a 21 Rector member who used to work in event management, the only places inside Clerestory lacking security cameras were the bathrooms. A detailed blueprint of the fair had been easy enough to obtain ahead of time. Each 21 Rector volunteer had been assigned a bathroom, and one person would attempt to penetrate the VIP area. Preston was supposed to release his roaches in the men's room on the northeast side of the tent.

He checked his phone's charge. The plan was for donors to be able to view live footage of the event on The Wart starting at two P.M. It was now 1:45. He stood, fingertips tingling, and made his way through the crowd, dodging the Bluetooth-jawed businessmen and the boho-chic women wearing way too many rings.

By some miracle, the bathroom, a high-end porta-potty setup that smelled of potpourri with a hint of sewage, was empty. Four stalls faced a row of sinks, the door sandwiched between them. Preston propped the main door open, locked himself in the handicap stall, and unzipped his backpack. He held the first container up to the light. Through the plastic, the roaches' scuttling shapes were faintly visible. He lowered the toilet lid and climbed up on the seat. The time was 1:58. He pried off the container's lid. Immediately, the roaches swarmed upward, spilling out and crawling over his hands. Preston yelped and dropped the Tupperware. The insects scattered. He opened the next container and hastily upended it. Then the next. Only one more to go.

Just as he'd dug his nails under the lid, someone walked into the bathroom.

"What the fuck!"

Preston held his breath. As soon as he heard the door slam shut, he emptied the last container and burst out of the stall, cringing as roaches crunched under his sneakers. He shoulder-barged through the door and propped it open, and the roaches streamed out into the main fair area like a herd of tiny, horrible sheep. Preston hit record on his phone. The roaches were impossible to miss against the light blue carpeting—shiny, darting black splotches that showed up beautifully on camera. Some crawled up the walls, swarming over the artwork. From other parts of the fair, three other live feeds had already begun streaming. There'd be fifteen in total.

It didn't take long for chaos to ensue. A few people screamed, many swore. There were camera flashes and indistinct exclamations. "Do you think it's a performance piece?" Preston heard someone say, and he couldn't help but laugh. Some gallerists abandoned their posts, while others tried to swat the insects off the artwork. One woman accidentally squashed a roach into the middle of a canvas and burst into tears. As the commotion swelled, a child began wailing, then another and another. Three security guards came running and stared at the scene, arms hanging uselessly at their sides. Some people scrambled up onto benches and tables. Others made a beeline toward the exits. One or two seemed frozen in place, their mouths opening and closing like fish. Preston walked around, filming it all. Less than five minutes into the stream, his phone began emitting a cascade of pings—

EPIC
ur a Legend
lolololololololol

genius
XD
holy shit there everywhere
Haha

He checked Twitter and saw that #artroaches and #clerestoryroach-fair were trending, with users posting photos and shaky footage of what was happening inside the tent. A B-list movie actor and a prominent critic were both live-tweeting from inside the VIP area, which had apparently been successfully breached. An entomologist from the Discovery Channel chimed in with that particular species' scientific name. Someone had made a gif of a woman jumping out of her chair and screaming as a roach crawled across her club sandwich, and another one of a dog licking roaches off the floor while its owner tried unsuccessfully to make it stop.

Preston felt buoyant. He felt invincible. He was in a perfect state of flow. This feeling—it was better than a runner's high, better even than sex. He was en route to the food court, hoping to get some close-ups of roaches swarming over people's abandoned plates of food, when he rounded the corner and saw her: Karina, standing by one of the coffee carts. She was watching the chaos unfold, holding her purse against her chest like a shield. As he turned toward her, her face swung into the camera frame. She stared at him, lips slightly parted. The fear in her eyes twisted his stomach. He paused the livestream and took two steps toward her. She shrank back against the wall.

"I'm not here for you," Preston said. He put his hands up. "I'm not going to hurt you."

Her expression shifted; he thought, for a moment, that she was about to laugh at him. He had a flash of how they used to be together, Karina wavering between amusement and admiration and reproach. The fizz and force of their dynamic. She pursed her lips, considering him. "This"—she gestured around her—"is all very you."

He couldn't tell if she was being sarcastic, but regardless, she was right. This *was* very him. He wondered, then, what she'd think if she knew how much money he was making off this. His phone was still blowing up with comments and likes and follows, and the new shape of him was emerging online, the Internet conferring him a persona.

"Thanks," he said. "And sorry."

Karina nodded curtly, then muttered something that might've been *goodbye* or *whatever* or *fuck you*. She slung her purse over her shoulder and turned away, heading toward the exit.

Preston restarted the livestream and filmed the scene for a while longer, but his encounter with Karina had unsettled him, and he found his prior elation dimmed. He no longer felt himself to be at the helm of this thing he'd unleashed. Another security guard appeared, armed with a can of Raid. He sprayed a cloud of it into the air—rather ineffectually, as most of the roaches were at ground level—causing people near him to cough and cover their faces. A mass exodus was under way, the crowd thinning as roaches continued to swarm from every direction. The people remaining inside the tent huddled in small groups, telling one another the story with obvious relish—"So then I look over and they're *everywhere*." "Yes, exactly, out of *nowhere*." "Like a biblical plague."

Preston registered the faint wail of police sirens in the distance. The plan was to rendezvous with Vanessa and the others in front of the Randall's Island wastewater treatment plant in about fifteen minutes, but all he wanted to do was go home, have a beer, and sit at his computer tracking online traffic to The Wart.

Outside, it was a perfect summer afternoon, hardly a cloud in the sky. The air smelled of new-mown grass. A crowd had gathered at the taxi stand. Yellow cabs inched forward, loading up passengers before speeding off. Preston turned around to catch one last glimpse of the tent, and that was when he saw him: Robert Berger. He was standing by the taxi stand, and there was a kid with him. Preston's understanding of his former professor shifted seismically: he hadn't known Berger was a father. He had one hand in his pocket, the other placed protectively on the kid's shoulder. The kid was pointing something out on his phone, and Berger was listening closely, nodding his head. A police car pulled up then, lights flashing, and as it did Berger's gaze rose and met Preston's. A look of shock passed over his face. He took his hand off the kid's shoulder. Then something strange happened. Berger *smiled*. And as he did, he raised his hand and waved at Preston. And before Preston could stop to think, he was waving back. And then a taxi pulled up and Berger opened the door and slid into the back seat behind the kid, and then the cab was driving away and Preston's hand was still in the air, waving at nothing.

CHAPTER THIRTY-SEVEN

The trip home was a blur. Somehow, Louisa got to the airport, charged a ticket to Karina's card, texted Mom, boarded a plane. She sat between two strangers, exhausted and emptied of tears. She thought of how Alejandro had described her ibis painting, almost a year ago now. *The moment before something terrible happens. The loneliness of being alone in that moment.* She closed her eyes against the dry, canned air and slipped into a fitful half sleep; when she came to, the flight attendant was asking passengers to put their tray tables up and Baton Rouge was coming into view under the clouds.

Her mother was waiting for her at baggage claim, though once again she hadn't checked any luggage. As they left the airport, the evening heat settled over them like a soggy blanket. The road was bright and black as it unspooled beneath them, a tarry ribbon snaking over the bayou. When they arrived at home, Louisa was stunned to find the bungalow nearly empty—walls stripped, floors bare, corners swept clean. Even the clutter in Mom's studio sunroom was mostly gone. Only Louisa's bedroom remained as she'd left it.

"Are you *moving?*"

Mom made a face. "Sort of. I'm moving into the big house with Grandma."

"Because of Pepere?"

"No, we've been planning this for a while, since before he passed."

"Why?"

"Neither of them was doing well, and now with him gone, well, all the more reason for me to be closer by."

Louisa lowered herself onto the scrubbed-clean floor. "Not doing well mentally? Or physically?"

Mom rubbed her forehead. "Both. It's hard, getting old."

Louisa pictured her mother tending to a grieving, worn-out woman, both of them growing old in tandem. It seemed so unfair. "Is Rick helping?"

In the distance came the sound of thunder. A moment later, the sky opened up. Mom raised her voice to make herself heard above the rain. "I mean, I'm sure he will, but . . ." She thinned her lips and looked away.

"He's a dipshit," Louisa finished for her.

"He's a man of a certain time and place."

"And you're a woman of a certain time and place."

She didn't dispute this. Her hair was gathering little threads of gray at the roots and temples. Were those new or had Louisa simply never noticed them before? "Anyway," Mom said, her manner suddenly brisk. "I'd love for you to go through the stuff in your room before you leave. Anything you don't want I'll give to Goodwill."

"Okay." Louisa looked out the window. Rainwater swamped the lawn. "What'll you do with our house?"

"Rent it out, I guess. Don't know who's going to want to live way out here in the country, but if we keep the rent low someone'll bite."

Louisa thought of how much she'd loved growing up here, loved watching the river from her bedroom window, how she'd marked the seasons with its rise and fall. How she'd lain awake at night listening to the cicadas, how in the early mornings the egrets slunk across the lawn like ghosts. How the wind on certain stormy afternoons had a moaning, plangent quality that was almost musical.

"Unless . . ." Mom said, giving Louisa a meaningful look.

"What?"

"Well, *you* could live here, if you wanted. You'd get the family rate, I'm sure."

"What's the family rate?"

She grinned. "Oh, like free-ninety-nine."

Louisa allowed herself a brief fantasy. A part-time job, just a few hours a week, enough for groceries and art supplies and minimum payments on her student loans. She could swing it, especially with that check from Ines. Her days stretching out before her, wide open. Painting in the sunroom. She could make an Instagram account and post photos of her paintings, try to find community online. Drive to Lafayette or New Orleans or Baton Rouge and visit the galleries there, see if any were interested in her work.

The rain began to slow. Then, as abruptly as it had begun, it stopped. The ceiling fan hummed softly overhead. Louisa thought of Karina. "I can't," she said. "I'm sorry."

Mom nodded as though she understood.

The next morning, Louisa rose very early, just as the sky was beginning to lighten. She got up and went into the sunroom. Three blank canvases were stacked in the corner, along with a box of brushes and half-used paint tubes. Tucking the canvas under her arm, Louisa picked up the box and walked with it to the river. She sat on the neighbor's dock and painted the water beaded with light under the flat, hazy sky. Eventually, the sun rose bright and hot. A great blue heron cried, *roh roh roh*. She felt safe.

She'd misunderstood her mother's instructions to *draw what you see*. It didn't mean to depict things exactly as they were, but rather as you felt them, as they moved through you. Karina had taught her that, had taught her to make the motion of her brush into the motion of the river.

When she was done, she walked back to the bungalow and set the canvas in the sunroom to dry.

⁌— —⁌

At the funeral a week later, everyone cried. Even Rick was misty-eyed, holding hands with his girlfriend, Taylor Swift, who looked nothing like Taylor Swift.

After the service, there was food in the church basement and a zydeco band headed by Pepere's best friend, Ed LeBlanc, played songs from Pepere's youth, and everyone danced, even the old people and the children. Louisa felt curiously light. Mom flitted among the mourners, shaking hands and kissing cheeks, radiant even in all black. *She is loved here,* Louisa thought. Maybe that was why she'd stayed all these years. Why leave a place when you love it and—miracle of miracles—it loves you back?

The wake wound down around eight. Louisa and her mother, together with some of the church ladies, cleaned up the basement. Then they took Grandma home and Mom helped her up to bed. When she came back downstairs, she uncorked a bottle of white wine and took two glasses from the cabinet. "Let's go sit on the porch," she said.

It had rained earlier in the day, so the night was cool, or what passed for cool in Louisiana in late June.

"Is it strange," Louisa asked her mother, "to move back into the house you grew up in?"

"Yes and no."

Louisa rolled the wine around inside her mouth, its fizz prickling her tongue.

"Don't get me wrong," Mom said. "If you'd told me when I was a teenager that someday I'd be middle-aged and single and moving back in with my mother, I'd have been fucking *horrified*. I'd have told you to go jump in a lake. Or I might've thrown myself in a lake, come to think of it."

Louisa laughed. Mom drained her glass and splashed more wine into it. Her cheeks were flushed, her dark eyes shining in the porch light.

"You know how I know when you're drunk?" Louisa said.

"How?"

"It's the only time you ever swear. I think I've heard you say the F-word, like, three times in my entire life."

Mockingly, Mom patted herself on the back. "I did such a good job raising you."

Louisa laughed, rolling her eyes.

"I did, though." She reached out and touched Louisa's cheek before pulling her close. "Look at you. You're my great accomplishment."

Louisa thought of Karina. She thought of Maureen's ten-year rule. She thought of what Alejandro had told her the last time she'd seen him: *You deserve to be happy.* She was beginning to believe him. She hugged her mother tightly and told her she loved her.

Mom kissed the side of her head. "There's a poem I read recently that made me think of you." She took her phone out of her pocket. "It's by this Greek poet Constantine P. Cavafy. Have you heard of him?"

"I don't think so."

"Odd guy. He only became known after his death, kind of like van Gogh. When he was alive he wrote all these great poems—he was really obsessive about it, every line had to be absolutely perfect—but then after all that effort he never wanted to formally publish anything."

"Weird."

"Yeah, he'd send his poems to newspapers instead, or else he'd print them himself and just give them away for free. I kind of love it. Sometimes that's exactly what I feel like doing with my art. Anyway, let me see if I can find the one I'm thinking of . . ." Mom typed into her phone. "Okay, here it is. It's called 'The First Step.'"

> *The young poet Eumenis*
> *complained one day to Theocritos:*
> *"I have been writing for two years now*
> *and I have composed just one idyll.*
> *It's my only completed work.*
> *I see, sadly, that the ladder of Poetry*
> *is tall, extremely tall;*
> *and from this first step I now stand on*
> *I will never climb any higher."*
> *Theocritos replied: "Words like that*
> *are improper, blasphemous.*
> *Just to be on the first step*
> *should make you happy and proud.*
> *To have come this far is no small achievement:*

what you have done is a glorious thing.
Even this first step
is a long way above the ordinary world.
To stand on this step
you must be in your own right
a member of the city of ideas.
And it is a hard, unusual thing
to be enrolled as a citizen of that city.
Its councils are full of Legislators
no charlatan can fool.
To have come this far is no small achievement:
what you have done already is a glorious thing."

The next day, Louisa woke up alone in her bungalow. She felt her next step. It was as though she'd made up her mind while she slept, as though she'd weighed the possibility in dream form. In her dream, there'd been two of her, her present self and her younger self, and her present self had said, *Listen, you'll be half asleep in your own life, but then you'll wake up.*

She got out of bed and poured a glass of water, drank it out on the porch. It was barely dawn. Snow-white egrets moved through the grass, shining in the darkness. Napoleon prowled under the oaks, his eyes gleaming where they caught the porch light.

In the past week she'd been so busy helping her mother with the move and funeral arrangements that she hadn't had time to talk to Karina, though they'd texted every day. Now Louisa picked up the phone and called her. It was early still, even in New York, and she'd intended to simply leave a voicemail, but Karina answered after three rings: "Hey there, early bird." When she was sleepy, she sounded so much younger.

"Did I wake you?"

"Mmmm yeah, but I'm glad you called."

Louisa sat on the porch steps and picked at a callus on her heel. "Tell me about your week," she said.

Karina recounted meeting her mother for lunch, and the movie they'd gone to see, and their walk afterward in Hudson River Park. She didn't mention Brian or Clerestory or art at all, except to say that

Louisa's paintings had been keeping her company in their studio. She sounded centered and calm, and Louisa felt a pang.

"I have something to tell you," she said at last. And then, before she could lose her nerve, she told Karina that she was staying here, in Louisiana, for a little while at least. She explained that if she was going to be ignored for ten years, she couldn't do it in New York. That she couldn't keep waiting for her life to begin. "This is a place where I can live a life in service to my art," she said. "Maybe you can, too?"

"Maybe I can what?"

Louisa spoke quickly, the words emerging from her in an ecstatic rush: "You can come live here with me. We'd have our own house, our own studio. It's so beautiful, Karina. You wouldn't believe how beautiful it is."

Karina was silent.

"Are you still there?"

"I'm here."

"You don't have to decide right away," Louisa said. "I know it's a lot to take in."

Karina drew in a long breath. "Let me think about it."

It wasn't a yes, but it wasn't a no, either, and for now that felt like enough. Uncertainty could be a kind of hope.

After they'd said goodbye, Louisa sat on the porch steps, stroking Napoleon and considering how she would fill her day.

In a little while, she'd go clean out Pepere's wood shop. It was her wood shop now, where she'd build the stretchers for her paintings.

In a little while. Now she walked once more to the riverbank. The sun was rising; in the distance the fields were lush and brilliant green. She picked up a stick and drew in the silt, each mark quickly resorbing into the mud. She heard her mother's voice inside her head, the way she always had and always would: *Draw slowly. Touch the surfaces of the objects with your eyes. Feel them. Focus on the feeling of touching and drawing being the same action. You don't even have to think about it.*

AUTHOR'S NOTE

Though the characters in this novel are wholly fictional, some of their art is inspired by the work of real artists. I owe a debt of the imagination to Jamal Awadallah, Maisie Cousins, Noah Fischer, Son Kit, Dave Lowenstein, Micki McGee, Takashi Murakami, Brad Troemel, Laura Owens, and Francesca Woodman. I'd also like to single out Cayla Zeek, whose work inspired Louisa's bird woman paintings, and Hannah Lutz Winkler, whose 2013 installation *Bower* was the model for Ines and Frank's bowerbird nests and the source for some of the ideas I explore in this novel.

The following works influenced me and the writing of this book: *Seven Days in the Art World* by Sarah Thornton, *True Colors: The Real Life of the Art World* by Anthony Haden-Guest, *Old in Art School* by Nell Irvin Painter, *The $12 Million Stuffed Shark: The Curious Economics of Contemporary Art* by Don Thompson, *Dark Side of the Boom: The Excesses of the Art Market in the 21st Century* by Georgina Adam, *How to Be an Artist* by Jerry Saltz, *Why Art Cannot Be Taught* by James Elkins, *Ways of Seeing* by John Berger, *Interaction of Color* by Josef Albers, *101 Things to Learn in Art School* by Kit White, *Strike Art: Contemporary Art and the Post-Occupy Condition* by Yates McKee, *The Price of Everything* directed by Nathaniel Kahn, and the podcast *A Piece of Work* hosted by Abbi Jacobson.

ACKNOWLEDGMENTS

'd be nowhere without my agent, Marya Spence, who appeared in my life like a fairy godmother and made my most cherished dream come true. Enormous thanks to everyone at Janklow & Nesbit, particularly Natalie Edwards.

Thank you to my brilliant editors: Andra Miller for championing my work and for her loving, keen-eyed gaze, and Anne Speyer for her gifted insight and unwavering support in seeing this novel to completion. Thank you to everyone at Ballantine Books and Random House for their passion and enthusiasm: Jesse Shuman, Lindsey Kennedy, Morgan Hoit, Corina Diez, Cindy Berman, Caroline Cunningham, and Amy J. Schneider.

Thank you to my teachers, whose wisdom and generosity helped me become a writer. At Brown: Ottessa Moshfegh, Meredith Steinbach, and Stephanie Merrim. At the University of Minnesota: Julie Schumacher, Sugi Ganeshananthan, Charles Baxter, Douglas Kearney, and Kim Todd.

I'm indebted to my grad school cohort and to the friends and classmates who read early drafts and excerpts of this novel, often multiple times: Hannah Suchor, Tess Fahlgren, Clare Boerigter, Ron Edwards, Zining Mok, Purvai Aranya, Liana Roux, Brooke White, Noel Haines, Maria Bowler, Sruthi Narayanan, Julian Robles, Asha Thanki, Tim Reynolds, Sandesh Ghimire, Curtis Fincher, Chelli Riddiough, Gregory Smith, Amanda Minoff, May Lee-Yang, Damian Johansson, Dylan Reynolds, Jasmine Araujo, Tom Andes, Katy Foda, and Jake Bartman.

The MFA program at the University of Minnesota gave me the time and the creative and financial support I needed to finish this book. Thank you to Holly Vanderhaar, who steers that ship. Thank you, also, to the literary organizations that have supported my work, and to the friends and readers I found there: the Community of Writers, Tin House, and the Mendocino Coast Writers' Conference.

I'm grateful to Danielle Evans, Margaret Wilkerson Sexton, Kristen Arnett, Julie Buntin, and Curtis Sittenfeld for their kindness and encouragement, and to Michelle Lyn King, who published an early excerpt of this novel in *Joyland*.

A heartfelt thanks to Carrie Napolitano, OG roommate and sister in all things literary; to George Silvertooth, Cajun consultant and honorary brother-in-law; to Kshitij Lauria for random FaceTime calls and excellent reading recommendations; to Lorraine Fei for conversations on queerness, desire, and identity; and to Anne Blenker for sharing her experiences at art school. For their love and support, thank you to Mimi Methvin, Michael McManus, and Jim McManus.

I'm profoundly grateful to my parents, Percy Angress and Livia Linden, who raised me in a house full of love and art and good books and bad jokes. A special thanks to my dad for letting me steal the real letter he wrote at thirteen in defense of Muhammad Ali and put it in my novel. Thanks to my sibling, Rapha, who gave me a crucial piece of advice that changed this book for the better. And thank you to my grandmother, Ruth Klüger (1931–2020), who nurtured the writer in me from early on. I'm sorry you didn't get to see me publish my first novel. I hope you would've been pleased.

Finally, I'd like to thank my husband, Connor, who is my favorite artist and my first reader, and who fills my life with color and joy.

ABOUT THE AUTHOR

ANTONIA ANGRESS was born in Los Angeles and raised in San José, Costa Rica. She is a graduate of Brown University and the University of Minnesota MFA program, where she was a Winifred Fiction Fellow and a College of Liberal Arts Fellow. She lives in Minneapolis with her husband, the artist Connor McManus. *Sirens & Muses* is her first novel.